Praise for Catherine

'Alliott is quick, observant and on top form'
Daily Mail

'Sensitive, funny and wonderfully well-written'
Wendy Holden, *Daily Express*

'Witty and compulsive' *Heat*

'Charming, clever, well-written, laugh-out-loud funny
with a great plot' *Irish Times*

'A rollicking rollercoaster of fun and wild romance'
Sunderland Echo

'A tongue-in-cheek romance intelligently
laced with humour' *Radio Times*

'Wickedly funny romance' *Bookcase*

'Alliott's got a light, humorous touch' *Options*

'A compulsive page-turner' *Today*

'Beautiful and forever memorable' *Bangor Chronicle*

Olivia's Luck

Catherine Alliott

headline
review

First published in 2000
by HEADLINE BOOK PUBLISHING

First published in paperback in 2001
by HEADLINE BOOK PUBLISHING

This edition published in paperback in 2006
by HEADLINE REVIEW

An imprint of Headline Book Publishing

1

ISBN 0 7472 5787 6 (A format)
ISBN 0 7553 3470 1 (B format)

Typeset by Letterpart Limited, Reigate, Surrey

Printed and bound in Great Britain by
Mackays of Chatham Ltd, Chatham Kent

Headline's policy is to use papers that are natural, renewable and
recyclable products and made from wood grown in sustainable
forests. The logging and manufacturing processes are expected to
conform to the environmental regulations of the country of origin.

HEADLINE BOOK PUBLISHING
A division of Hodder Headline
338 Euston Road
London NW1 3BH

www.reviewbooks.co.uk
www.hodderheadline.com

For my brother, Stephen

Chapter One

Alf regarded me with his one good eye. It was brown and troubled and beginning to look as glassy as the other one. He frowned as he tried to make sense of it all.

'What – you mean he's left you, like?'

'That's it, Alf.'

'For good? Scarpered?'

'So it appears.'

He struggled with this conundrum. 'And – and so what, ain't he never coming back then?'

I caught my breath at the brutality of my husband's plan laid bare, swallowed hard. 'No, Alf, apparently not. Total desertion does indeed seem to be his overall game plan.' I raised my chin and somehow cranked up a smile.

Alf continued to look mystified. He scratched his grizzled old head, and then the penny – slow to drop at the best of times – began its gradual descent. It finally fell with a deafening clunk.

'Well, bugger me,' he gaped, stunned.

I licked my lips. 'Quite.'

Leaving him to his open-mouthed astonishment, I turned briskly to my other two builders, who, thus far, had been silent throughout this gnomic exchange, though more, I suspected, from pity and embarrassment than lack of comprehension.

Alf's brother, Mac, the foreman, the boss-man, and the brains of the team, was watching me closely, his blue eyes assessing this dramatic shift in situation, whilst Spiro, the emotional young Greek in my incongruous masonry trio, was having trouble keeping his jaw from wobbling. His black, mournful moustache drooped low and his dark eyes were filling ominously, but then, if you told Spiro it looked like rain he tended to reach for his hanky.

'He *leave* you?' he spluttered incredulously. 'Your husband *leave* you? Alone, here, with a young child and a dreadful falling-down house and bad drains and rats and peeling walls and –' his eyes grew wide as he regarded me with horror – 'looking so *terrible*?'

'The house, I hope, not me, Spiro,' I quipped nervously. He frowned. '*Ti?*'

'Um, no, never mind. Yes, well, of course, you're right, the house *is* in a terrible state but then we're bang in the middle of rewiring and replumbing, aren't we?' I said brightly. 'We're stripping it all back, Spiro, laying it bare, getting back to the bones. It's bound to look worse before it looks better, but once it's gutted—'

'*You're* gutted!' he roared. '*I'm* gutted! I cannot believe what sort of a man *do* this to you! What sort of – of an *animal*!' With that he snatched his tea-cosy hat from his head and, with a great wail, buried his face in it. I had a sudden urge to snatch it from him and do exactly the same. Instead I patted his shoulder.

'Come on now, Spiro,' I muttered. 'You're sweet but, well, it's not as bad as all that. It's going to be fine, honestly.' I waited while he composed himself, blowing his nose violently into his hat and then plonking it back on his head at an unusual angle. His dark eyes blazed.

'All men are bastards,' he informed me unequivocally,

shaking his finger furiously. '*All* men.'

Well, I wasn't going to argue with that. In fact I rather approved of his fixed-bayonet relish. Perhaps we could both pull on our snotty hats and go and kill the bastards together. Spiro's blood was certainly fiery, and when it was up, it was hot.

Mac, meanwhile, was clearing his throat ostentatiously. He spat dexterously on to the concrete beside him.

'So you'll be giving all this up then, will you, luv?'

I straightened up to my working foreman, ever the pragmatist, ever the one to get straight to the point, and met his bright blue eyes defiantly. He wasn't much bigger than me, fiftyish, tiny, spry and, unlike his bear-like brother, Alf, very switched on, very sharp.

'How d'you mean, Mac?'

'Well, now that it's all gone pear-shaped you're not gonna want to carry on, are you? You're not gonna want to cope wiv all this malarkey just for yourself and Claudes, are you?'

He jerked his head dismissively at the building site around us: the excuse for the kitchen where we were standing, with its open rafters covered by a flapping blue tarpaulin; the soggy concrete at our feet; the rotten sash windows with their broken cords; the sixties-style Formica units – half of which had been ripped from the walls, the rest still clinging on tenaciously – and finally, the huge gaping hole in the back wall, to which Spiro, on hearing that Greece had been knocked out of the World Cup, had accidentally taken a sledgehammer, and then been so mortified none of us had had the heart to berate him. Yes, this 'malarkey' that was my home.

I cleared my throat. 'Actually, Mac, that's exactly why I've asked you all to take a break and down tools for a minute. You see, the thing is, I fully intend to go on.' I drew myself up to my full five foot three and tucked my short dark hair meticulously behind my ears, struggling to look braver than I felt. 'Fully intend. The mere fact that my husband has seen fit to abscond is neither here nor there, because as far as I'm concerned, we're going on as planned. We're going to finish the kitchen, get all these units out, replaster the walls, put the new cupboards in, get the wooden floor laid, replace all the rotten windows and then, when we've finished that, we're going to start on the upstairs, OK?'

'She so brave,' whispered Spiro in a choked voice, woolly hat back to mouth. I couldn't look at him. I raised my chin, suddenly feeling a bit Churchillian.

'Give up?' I warbled. 'Good heavens, no. I took on this tip of a house with the sole intention of restoring it to its former glory, and that's still very much the plan, very much my dream.' Crikey, I was Martin Luther King now, but there was no stopping me. 'And I'm not going to skimp either,' I warned, swelling my oratory to a preacherly roundness. 'I don't want you to rush things and cut corners just to get it finished any old how so I can flog it, because I'm not going to flog it! I'm going to live in it, and I'm going to live in it for a very long time, and – and if I feel like having Rococo in the bathroom or . . . or – I don't know . . .' I cast about wildly, 'gilding in the guest room, or gazebos in the garden, I'll jolly well have it. As far as I'm concerned this is still a for ever house and I want it done properly. I want to match up the old panelling, do the picture rails, the dados, and doodahs, and whatnots, the whole blinking shooting match. The master bedroom needs a complete makeover, a total rethink—' I broke off as, to my horror, my voice wobbled at the mention of this.

Around me, there was a bit of embarrassed scuffing of toes in the dirt and faces turned to the floor. A moment later I'd regained my composure. I swallowed hard.

'Listen, boys, I'll level with you,' I said quietly. 'I wanted to put you in the picture because I know there's been talk,' I eyed Mac beadily here, 'and I know you've all been wondering where the hell "the guv'nor" is. Well, frankly, I'm fresh out of ideas. I'm right out of management buy-out courses he might be on, or corporate finance lectures he might be attending, or – or weekend golf tournaments that seem to go on all week, and squash matches and – oh God, I'm just sick to the back teeth of having to lie. Constantly. To you, to my friends, to everyone at Claudia's school. In fact if you must know, I feel like renting a ruddy great billboard and pitching it outside the front gate with – "MY HUSBAND'S LEFT ME, OK?" plastered all over it.'

There was a short and sympathetic silence. Then Mac spat in his dirty hand and, ever the gentleman, wiped it on his trousers. I had a nasty feeling that hand was coming my way for a warm, supportive shake so I braced myself, had mine at the ready. He stuffed it in his pocket.

'What about the moolah then, luv?'

I blinked. 'Sorry?'

'The dough, the money.'

'I'm not with you, Mac.'

'Well, I hate to seem heartless, but this place is costing you an arm and a leg, and if he's done a runner and we're gonna go on wiv the work as planned, we need to be clear that at the end of the day, we're gonna get paid. That everyfing's sorted.' He raised his eyebrows and gave me a wry, quizzical smile. 'Know what I mean?'

'I know exactly what you mean, Mac,' I said smoothly, 'and I understand your concerns, but believe me, you've got no worries on that score. My husband might have seen fit to remove himself physically, but financially, I'm OK. Huge and guilty contributions are still being paid regularly into the Privy Purse – which no doubt assuages his conscience – so money is not a problem. You will be paid.'

'At the end of ev—'

'At the end of every working week.'

'In the usual—'

'In the usual, mutually acceptable manner of folding readies in a big brown envelope – yes, Mac, business as usual.'

Mac pursed his lips thoughtfully. Then he smiled. It was a slow illumination. He turned to his workforce.

'I suppose we'll have to say that that's all right then, won't we, boys?' He raised his eyes to his towering older brother, who, whilst higher up in the vertical scale, was lower down the evolutionary one, where thought processes were slow.

'You mean,' he said at last, glass eye flashing in bewilderment, 'you mean we're *not* gonna get paid, like?'

'No, you dozy prat, we *are* gonna get paid, that's what she's just bin saying!'

'Has she? Oh. Oh well, yeah. Yeah, that's all right then.' He scratched his head, still mystified.

Mac nodded. 'Zorba?'

'I would work for you for nothing,' hissed the young Greek passionately. 'I consider it an insult to be asked. On my honour I would feenish the job with my dying breath. I curse the Meester McFarllen who has done this to you. I speet on his mother's grave and his grandmother's grave and then I speet –' he demonstrated with a flash of saliva to concrete – 'on his crotch. May it be sore and blistered, may his piles hang like grapes, may his backside gush like a donkey's, may—'

'Oh, thank you, Spiro,' I broke in breathlessly. 'That's so – so supportive of you! So spirited!' Heavens, if I didn't cut him off in mid curse he'd be impaling himself on his plumbing rods next, kamikaze style.

He seized my arm and brought his face very close to mine. 'I want you to know that I will toil sweat and blood for you, Meesis McFarllen. But him—' he curled his lip scornfully and I tried not to flinch as I felt his whiskers, 'pericolor testatosis!' he finished emphatically.

'Well quite,' I murmured, backing away. 'Um, thank you, Spiro.'

As I surreptitiously wiped some spittle from my face I wondered what the devil that was all about. I was pretty sure the 'testatosis' bit wasn't particularly polite, though. Young Spiro had his fair share of earthy directness and only the other day he offered to show me his little stiffy. I hadn't liked the sound of it at all but, being too polite to say no, was just preparing to faint nonchalantly, when I realised he was reaching into his jeans pocket for a crumpled photograph. Stiffy, it transpired, short for Stiffano, was his baby son; six months old, almond-eyed and adorable – or at least I thought so, so relieved was I to see him. I sighed. Actually, I couldn't help thinking a bit more honour and crotch speeting wouldn't go amiss amongst the jobs-worthy Englishmen.

'We'll get on wiv it then, shall we, luv?' said Mac kindly, as if reading my mind. 'Get back to work, like?'

'Please, Mac.' I smiled gratefully, but I also knew that this was my cue to leave. Now that the delicate little matter of the money had been 'sorted', the interview was over as far as Mac was concerned. No worries, just so long as they all got paid.

As I left them to it and moved on through to the hall, I

couldn't resist turning back for a moment, watching them unobserved. 'Getting on wiv it' in Mac's book merely meant that the morning's work was over and that the lunch ritual was about to begin. At five past twelve it wasn't worth picking up tools again, and anyway, the table had to be laid. To this end, Alf was lumbering across the concrete floor in search of a milk crate for them to gather round, and various boxes to sit on. He carried this furniture back heavily, seeming always to veer slightly to the left pursued by the rest of his body, then set it all decoratively in the middle of the room, his mouth taut with concentration.

Mac, meanwhile, pale, sinewy, and dressed for this sweltering weather in a vest and navy-blue shorts, his marble-white legs hairless, and looking nothing like the powerhouse he really was, was attending to the more domestic side of things. Bending down to gather filthy mugs from the floor, he reached also for the broken Pils can that served as the sugar bowl and plonked in a couple of sugar-encrusted spoons. Then he swilled the milk around in its cheesy carton, before plugging in the kettle and preparing to be 'Mum'.

Only Spiro, I observed gratefully – who was only in this country in order to earn himself enough money to return to his remote Ionian island, build himself a house, install his young family and set himself up as the local master builder – was still bristling with righteous indignation. Standing alone and ramrod straight, he flicked out a Rothmans, lit up, and puffed away furiously, too distracted to eat or drink.

Alf and Mac, of course, had no such qualms. They lowered their backsides slowly to their wooden boxes, Alf gave a great ceremonial belch in lieu of grace, and then they were off, tucking into their usual fishpaste sandwiches and PG Tips with relish. To be fair, in between mouthfuls, there was a degree of deliberation on the downfall of my marriage, and even some pondering on man's inhumanity to woman.

'Bastard.'

'Yeah.'

''S not on.'

''S right.'

'Not wiv a kiddie.'

'Nah.'

'Pot Noodle?'

'Yeah, go on then.'

Oh no, they weren't completely heartless.

I took one last look at the happy domestic scene unfolding under the flapping blue tarpaulin, which, crackling in the sunshine, cast a light like some subterranean swimming pool, then turned and went on through to the hall.

'Mind you,' Alf's muffled tones stopped me again, ''s not gonna be easy for her, is it? I mean – how old d'you reckon she is?'

I didn't hear the entirety of Mac's response, but enough to suggest that had I been a chicken, it certainly wouldn't be springtime. Clenching my fists and swallowing hard I passed by the front door, stopped at the loo, opened the door, and pausing only to take the briefest of glances at my bloodless reflection in the mirror, turned to the lavatory pan and threw up.

Chapter Two

I'd been testing some Crown Matchpots in the front hall when Johnny had announced his intentions.

There I was, behind the front door, painting away merrily above the skirting boards, when I heard the garden gate go, heard his familiar footsteps up the gravel path. Knowing instinctively that hot foot from his evening commute, from the human lasagne of the City trains, he'd be tired, bad-tempered and in need of a drink, I knew better than to smile brightly and enquire, 'Good day, darling?' to which he'd probably snap irritably, 'Tedious, thank you,' and instead, sat back on my heels and arranged my expression into one of amused contemplation. As his head came round the door, I looked up with a wry smile.

'You know, anyone would think they aim these paints at the dirty-mac brigade,' I said, holding up my two little pots. 'You have a choice here, my darling,' I waggled them at him, 'Beaver or Muff!'

I grinned, enjoying my little joke and waiting for him to laugh, but as he stared back I noticed his face was very pale, his lips tight.

'I don't care what colour you paint the sodding hall,' he muttered. 'I'm leaving.'

And so saying, he pushed past me and on up the stairs, at

which point I do recall that I at least managed to say – in a voice fully intended to travel – 'Beaver it is then!' Knowing full well he'd prefer Muff.

Yes, that was how my husband left me. Those were the very special words with which he chose to end our marriage. I remember sitting there with my paintbrush in my hand thinking – in a shocked and stunned sort of way – that you had to hand it to Johnny. Not for him the usual garbage departing husbands give about needing to find themselves and having room to breathe, blah, blah, blah. No, his was very much in the Rhett Butler school of departure, because frankly, my dear – I paused. Except that, no, that wasn't true either. Up until recently he *had* given a damn. Up until five months ago to be precise, and for the last five months I'd certainly seen this coming but, in the same way as one sees the articulated lorry hurtling round the corner, it's still quite a shock when it hits you.

Functioning on automatic I dipped my brush conscientiously into the turps to stop it drying out, then rested my head back against the wall and shut my eyes tight. Squeezed the life out of them, in fact. For a while there I couldn't move, but I knew I had to, because, after all, he was only upstairs packing a suitcase, and in a few minutes' time he'd be pounding downstairs again before exiting through the front door, and I surely didn't want to be the stepped-over wife, as well as the passed-over one, did I?

Somehow I eased myself up and stumbled blindly towards our tiny makeshift kitchen. Originally I think it had been the old scullery, but now it just housed an ancient Baby Belling stove, a small sink I'd found in a junk yard and a mini fridge, a temporary arrangement all cobbled together any old how because, after all, we were only using it until our splendid new kitchen was finished. In the middle was a small pine table. I sat down shakily, resting my elbows and clasping my hands together, almost in an attitude of prayer. I listened. Upstairs, drawers were shooting in and out with a vengeance, coat hangers were clanking and the wardrobe slammed shut – wham bang – all sounds of a speedy exit. As I reached for a cigarette I noticed my hand was shaking. I shut my eyes again, and his pale, tight-lipped face swam to mind. Chin jutting out, that hard, impenetrable look in his eye – now where had I seen that look recently . . .?

Well, it was just a few Sundays ago, actually, at a tense, silent, lunch in this very room, the majority of which Johnny had spent behind a propped-up newspaper, the only evidence of his continued existence on the planet being the disappearance of French bread and Stilton behind the broadsheet. Claudia and I had sat in silence too, gazing bleakly at the back of *The Times*, until Claudia could bear it no longer and, pausing only to shoot me a swift what-the-hell's-up-with-Daddy look, had slipped from the room and gone upstairs to play on her computer. I'd done quite a bit of ostentatious sighing, and then in my usual, martyred fashion, got up to clear the plates. There I'd been, elbow-deep in suds at the sink, when I'd turned for a moment to scrape some rubbish in the bin, and as I'd done so, I'd seen his face. He'd left the table and was standing at the window, staring out at the rain-soaked lawn, in the middle of which sat a huge pile of rubble from our gutted house. As I'd watched, he'd raised his eyes to heaven and mouthed 'Jesus Christ'.

I'd turned back quickly so he didn't know I'd seen, but I went very cold. You see, I'd known what he was thinking: Jesus Christ, in this all there is? After a few moments I dropped the greasy plate back in the water and turned, smiling, wet hands on hips.

'Oh, by the way,' I said brightly, 'I saw something in the back of *The Times* last week, in the classified ads section. There was this thing about a hot-air ballooning weekend in Normandy and I thought – well, why not? You've always wanted to do it and it sounds quite fun, so why don't we go for your birthday? What d'you think?'

Johnny had turned slowly from the splattered window-pane, raised one partially interested eyebrow and said, 'Where?'

'Here.'

Quickly wiping my hands on a tea towel I'd scurried to get the paper from a drawer, spreading it out hastily, knowing exactly which page it was on and which column to find, because I'd saved it for just such an occasion. I'd pointed, then stood back to let him read the ad, hardly daring to breathe as I'd watched his face get gradually brighter. It was a slow transformation, but by the time he'd got to the end, he'd been almost excited.

'D'you know, this isn't such a bad idea, Livvy. We could get the ferry across and maybe ask Marcus and Jane if they want to join us.'

'Exactly. That's what I thought.' I'd stepped forward tentatively.

'And we could all go in one car – pointless taking two – and take the Michelin too, do a sort of gastronomic tour of the local hostelries. It's all cream and Calvados country round there – we'd be spoilt for choice!'

'Precisely. All those cheeky cheeses—'

'Plenty of *vin rouge*—'

'Hoovering up the *escargot*—'

'And we could leave Claudia behind with your mother.'

I paused. 'Yup.' We could. We always left Claudia behind with my mother.

'In fact the weekend after next is a bank holiday so, hang on . . .' he'd gone to the calendar on the door, 'if I took the Friday off . . .'

I'd joined him as he'd flipped the pages over. 'And we came back on the Monday night . . .'

'We'd still be back in time for the Palmers' drinks party on the Tuesday! Good idea, Livvy.' He always called me Livvy rather than Olivia. 'I'll go and ring Marcus, see if he's up for it. Bound to be, mad bastard!'

Oh, bound to be. And off he'd scurried to the phone, full of beans, full of plans, equilibrium restored. And I'd shut the paper slowly, put it back in the drawer, pushed it in softly. Right. So. Suddenly, we were off to France for four days. We couldn't afford it; I'd miss Claudia; Mac and the builders needed constant supervision in this wreck of a house; and I wouldn't get the runner beans in either, but no matter – the crisis had been averted. I remember turning to watch him through the kitchen door as he'd spoken on the phone to Marcus, his face a picture now, all animation and smiles, like a small boy cajoled out of a sulk by a trip to the zoo.

In case you think I'm the kind of girl who'd rather get the runner beans in than embark on a gastronomic tour of Normandy, I'd like to make it clear that I'm not. It was simply that Normandy was the latest in a long line of exotic treats designed to take Johnny's mind off life. Oh, I conjured them up almost weekly. I'd only have to turn from the television to make a remark and find that he was watching me, staring at me intently – and not in a way that suggested he was mesmerised by my beauty – and I was nervously reaching for the phone. Somehow, in a matter of minutes, I'd have the last few Eric Clapton tickets to be had at the Albert Hall, some front row seats at Brands Hatch, a few impossible-to-come-by Twickenham tickets – heavens, at this rate we'd be holidaying at Sandringham soon. I felt like a door-to-door salesman unpacking my sample bag – here, how about this, or this? – but whilst Johnny smiled and nodded and accepted my wares, I knew that one day I'd empty it all out on the doorstep and he wouldn't want anything. No, I don't want that, or that, or that – not today, thank you.

Well, I thought wryly, dragging my cigarette down to my Docksides as I sat at the tiny kitchen table, that day had come.

I stubbed the butt out in an old saucer and cocked an ear above. It was quieter upstairs now, but I could tell he'd moved to the bathroom and was rummaging around in the cabinet, getting his shaving things together, his toothbrush. I fumbled for my cigarette packet and immediately lit another, blowing the smoke out in a long straight line to the fridge. I stared. On it was an ancient photograph of me and Johnny. It was one Claudia had found at the bottom of a drawer, pounced on in delight, and screaming with laughter at our impossible eighties clothes and hairstyles, had stuck up with a magnet. I narrowed my eyes at it now. I was about, ooh, seventeen, I suppose, and in someone's garden, Johnny's perhaps. There I was, small, skinny, awkward-looking, with wide-apart grey eyes and a slightly too large nose – gamine, my mother would say, or even Audrey Hepburn, at which I'd guffaw. And there was Johnny beside me, who to my mind hadn't changed. Tall, broad-shouldered, laughing merrily, those bright blue eyes staring frankly and challengingly at the camera, and a flop of blond hair falling permanently in his eyes, as it still did. In the background I could see Imogen and Molly, and maybe even Peter too so – yes . . . it must have been about seventeen years ago. Half my life, when I'd first met Johnny.

I'd been with the witches at the time, of course. Everything I did in those days was with the witches and, to a large extent, still is. 'The witches' was Johnny's name for the three of us, Molly, Imogen and me. 'Full of bubble, but an *awful* lot of toil and trouble!' he'd hiss, stirring an imaginary cauldron, and we'd giggle like mad over that, secretly delighted that three such hard-working, sheltered, inseparable convent girls, who'd never been in a scrape in their lives, could be regarded as 'trouble'. Mad, bad and dangerous we certainly weren't, but it was a nice idea.

It was Molly who saw him first, at the fair on the village green that Saturday night, believe it or not, the first Saturday night I was ever allowed out on my own.

'You get nasty rough types at a fair,' my mother had sniffed, scrubbing away at our tiny Formica kitchen. 'Gippoes and all sorts, but then again, that's probably why you want to go.'

'No,' I said patiently, 'I just want to have some fun with the girls.'

'Well, you wouldn't catch Lady Diana going to a fair at your age,' she snapped. 'She'd still be locked up at school!'

'Yes, and look where that's got her; nineteen years old and about to become a virgin bride. Talk about a recipe for disaster. And for the last time, Mum, I am not Lady Diana!'

'No, you're not, and you're a long way from coming anywhere close to her, my girl.' She whipped a dishcloth around an immaculate stainless-steel sink. 'Go on then, off you go. Go and flaunt yourself.'

I stared at her in amazement for a moment, but then I was out of that back door like a shot. When you got a green light from Mum, you didn't hang around for it to turn.

And so there I was that night at the fair, trying to keep the huge excitement of being out at night to myself, trying to pretend it was nothing new. Of course, for Imogen and Molly it wasn't. Going to discos and cinemas had been part and parcel of their lives for a couple of years now, but not mine, and I hugged the experience excitedly, loving it all: the flashing lights against the dark sky, the bustle and noise, the smell of candyfloss and toffee apples, the thumping disco music, the lithe boys jumping on and off speeding carts, that heady sense of danger and excitement which stirred my teenage soul. Shrieking with laughter we made our way round every single ride, and were all piling out of a Dodgem car, ready to go round again – when Molly spotted him. She stopped dead; seized my arm.

'Holy *Moley*!' (As I said, we were quite sheltered.)

He was standing with a couple of friends in the queue for the big wheel; tall, tousled, blond, with wicked blue eyes, his hands in his pockets, head thrown back and roaring with laughter at something one of them had said. He oozed glamour but also, at a glance, that automatic social ease that comes from an expensive education, a mother who'd never had to do her own ironing and a father who was quite possibly in the Shadow Cabinet. Our plan had been to head back to the ghost train, but without a word of discussion, the three of us turned as one, and made our way to the big wheel. Molly, vivacious, curly-haired, with dark, dancing eyes, pranced up, and deliberately queue-barged her way in front of him, with Imogen and me giggling in her wake.

'Hey, what's your game?' he rounded on her.

'Sorry, we didn't realise you were queuing,' she smiled sweetly.

'Oh right, so what did you think we were doing then – standing in a line behind total strangers just for the hell of it?'

Molly's dark eyes widened. 'Well, it's a possibility. You look sad enough to try and make friends that way, but to tell you the truth, I really hadn't considered you at all.'

Nudging and giggling we then piled into the next empty cart as it conveniently came to a standstill in front of us, and Johnny and his friends had to make do indignantly with the one behind. As we soared up into the night sky they hooted and catcalled after us, pelting us with peanuts, and we dutifully squeaked and ducked, pretending to be outraged, but loving every minute of it. I remember swinging round right at the top and catching Johnny's eye, shrieking as he took aim, wondering – as his peanut hit the mark, like a perfect Cupid's arrow, right between the eyes – if he knew the effect he had on people. I believe he did.

Of course, we lurked around after the boys for the rest of the evening then, trailing them mercilessly and popping up giggling behind every shooting range and coconut shy they went on, as they, in turn, went through the adolescent ritual of groaning and trying to lose us. Inevitably, though, all six of us ended up together outside the only pub on the green, equipped with far too many goldfish, candyfloss in our hair, cigarettes glowing competitively, and all eyes bright with possibility. Johnny, aged eighteen, went in for the drinks and we sat on the grass outside. We gleaned from the other two boys that they were all at Harrow, but that such was the enlightened attitude of boarding schools these days, they'd been allowed out for the evening. 'So long as we're back by – ooh –' one of them coolly flashed his Rolex – 'about midnight, I suppose.' Suitably impressed by their bravado but just about managing not to show it, we'd sipped our lager-and-limes; Molly, flirting like billyo, Imogen, blonde and beautiful and not needing to, and me, certainly needing to but not having the confidence. As ever, I wished I wasn't so tongue-tied, but Molly made sure every silence was filled, which gave me a chance to observe.

'Posh-gob Scot' was how Johnny described himself, with generations of Scottish ancestors behind him, but brought up in England and sent to Harrow like the rest of his family.

'Only child, I'll bet,' said Molly, her dark eyes flashing with amusement, 'of totally indulgent parents. Ponies for Christmas, a convertible for your birthday, the apple of Mummy and Daddy's eye. They probably peel you grapes for breakfast.'

He grinned. 'Wrong, actually. Three sisters.'

'Ah, only boy. Yes well, that explains it.'

'Explains what?'

'Your Godlike demeanour. Clearly the world revolves around you at home and you're waited on hand and foot. Loo seats are probably warmed for you and you've been mistakenly led to believe in the superiority of the male species. They obviously think the sun shines out of your wotsit.'

He laughed. 'God, I wish! Those wretched sirens torment me, gang up on me, they probably stick pins in little effigies of me.'

'Ah, shame. So you're put upon?'

'You bet.'

'Misunderstood?'

'Totally.'

'In need of a little analysis?'

'No fear. Those shrinks would have a field day with me!'

'Even so, worth a try. Here – lie down on my couch.' She patted her lap and Johnny, grinning, obligingly put his head in it. Oh, to have Molly's nerve. She frowned with mock concentration. 'So . . . a tortured soul, eh, teased mercilessly by your sisters, and I imagine Mummy's no help because – let me see now – Mummy's always in the beauty parlour having her nails done?'

'Christ – in her dreams!' he chortled.

'And Daddy, well, Daddy's no help either because he's – let's think, what would Daddy be? Certainly something in the City; something fairly enormous. Pr-o-bably the Governor of the Bank of England, and pr-ob-ably called – Peregrine?'

'Wrong again. His name's Oliver and he's a trainer.'

'What, fitness?' I said without thinking.

Johnny sat up, startled. Then he and the other boys hooted with laughter.

'No, racehorses!' he cried. 'God, fitness. I'd like to see Dad in a leotard!'

We all laughed, but I felt foolish and could feel myself reddening as I joined in. It didn't escape Johnny and he shot me a kind look. I don't believe he meant to embarrass me.

'So back to your mother then,' persisted Molly, yanking his shoulders down into her lap again. 'Shut your eyes, please. I must have total concentration in my counselling rooms. If she's not in the beauty parlour, she's . . .?'

'Oh Mum, well, she's a bit dizzy. "Creative" is how I'm sure she'd like to be described.'

'Ah, a bit off-the-wall.'

He opened one eye. 'Well, only in the sense that loo paper is.'

We giggled, and then for some reason we couldn't stop laughing, and we all fell about on the grass in a heap.

We roared at Johnny's jokes for most of that summer. After that first meeting, it somehow seemed only natural for the six of us to hang around together. The schools were breaking up for the holidays, we all lived relatively close to each other in the stretch of green belt that wrapped itself around the foothills of the Chilterns – it was fun, it was convenient, it was easy. Secretly I think the boys felt they were too old to be hanging about at home and should have been spending their final holiday from school backpacking in Istanbul, or smoking ganja on some remote Caribbean beach, but since they weren't, they deigned to swagger along beside us, to the events on offer locally. Keen to be equally cool, we girls sneeringly dismissed the discos and parties as 'so-o-o incredibly tame' – quick flick of the hair, quick drag on the cigarette – as they no doubt were, but there was no convincing my mother. She saw drug pushers and rapists at every Pony Club dance and tennis club party, and I had practically to shin down the drainpipe to join my friends.

On one occasion when she forbade me to go to a concert in London, I rather daringly ignored her and went anyway. Halfway through some throbbing Supertramp keyboard number, a man came on stage, interrupted the music, and asked if an Olivia Faber could please leave now because her mother was waiting for her in the car park. I remember going literally rigid with shock in my seat, then blushing to my roots. I didn't move. Molly and Imogen on either side of me both reached out and squeezed my hands. A few minutes later the music resumed, but then ten minutes after that, the man was back. Could Olivia Faber *please* leave now, because otherwise the police would be called and the concert could not continue. I got to my feet, puce with shame, and passed down along the rows. I remember going past Johnny, who caught my eye sympathetically, and then, to titters of 'home to Mummy', left the stadium.

Sure enough, Mum was waiting. I got in the car without a word and maintained a tight-lipped silence all the way home, as did my mother. To this day we've never spoken of it. I think we both knew that she'd overstepped the mark, but then again, so had I, and there was a delicious symmetry to it which resulted in a stalemate. Looking back, I wonder we didn't hurl more insults and recriminations at each other, but we never did, we were more careful. Once those things are said, they're out there for ever, hanging in the air and, at the end of the day, we loved each other. She was all I had, and vice versa. Thereafter, though, I did detect a perceptible loosening of the reins, and certainly towards the end of the summer, there wasn't a party I didn't go to or a dance I didn't make.

It's incredible to me now that I can only just remember the names of the other two boys. Peter, I think, and Ben. All eyes were firmly on Johnny, you see, and there was no question of second best. As the summer wore on, though, it became clear that one of our number was forging ahead in the popularity stakes, and two of us would have to resign ourselves to back seats. It was Molly, after all, who'd spotted him first, Molly, who'd wooed him, Molly who'd put in all the hard, flirtatious work, and now Molly who was firmly staking her claim. Every slow dance was hers, every joke addressed to her, every look came winging her way, whilst Imogen and I sat dumbly by, enviously awaiting the first kiss.

During this time we more or less lived at Johnny's parents' house, which, like son and heir, was something of an eye-opener. I'd never seen anything quite like the McFarllens' estate, and probably never will. It was huge, it was Jacobean, it was turreted – it was even *moated*, for God's sake – in short, it was the sort of place where you suppressed a 'bloody hell' as you went up the drive. Here they talked of land rather than garden, watered the orangery rather than the conservatory, and had a clock tower instead of a weather vane. The lifeblood of the place was, of course, the stables, or 'the yard', as I came to call it, which was adjacent to the house, and run like a slick, well-oiled machine – just like the thoroughbred racing machines it housed, who nodded their elegant, arched necks over every green stable door.

Inside, the house was full of colour and drama. There was a blood-red dining room, a pale blue morning room, vibrant chintz in the sitting room, murals in the bathrooms and, at every window, curtains as thick as duvets hung from fabulous, coroneted pelmets. Every bedroom was painted a deep jewel colour – sapphire, ruby or emerald – and as I crept around upstairs one day on a rather spurious search for a loo, I was also startled to note that each bed had a huge crucifix hanging over it. This, it transpired, was down to Oliver, Johnny's father, who, born a Protestant, had apparently seen the light in later life and made a sweeping and dramatic conversion to Catholicism. Like most born-agains he was messianic in his belief and, insisting that the rest of his family should join him on his road to Damascus, had filled the place with the trappings of his new-found religion. Huge church candles and prayer books loitered in the most unlikely places – next to a pile of *Horse and Hound* in the loo, or in the case of the candles, chewed to bits by the latest puppy in its basket, because for all Oliver's religious fervour, one didn't have to look far to find signs of a hedonistic lifestyle. A velvet curtain, ripped accidentally during a raucous party a few years ago, still hung forlornly by threads from its pelmet, there were shot gun cartridges in the bath, empty whisky bottles behind the loo, and betting slips in every overflowing ashtray, all of which, I thought, gave the place a thrilling air of debauchery.

Oliver McFarllen, tall, handsome and urbane as he

strutted about the place in his breeches in an impossibly Mr Darcy-like manner, was altogether a glamorous, if formidable figure. We were all rather in awe of him and kept out of his way, but he wasn't unfriendly and always shot us a cheery 'Hello there!' and a flashing smile if he strode by us in the yard. His moods were mercurial, though, and having once been shocked to a standstill as we heard him bawl out an unfortunate stable girl for not mucking out a filthy stable, we knew better than to hang about in the yard for too long, particularly if clients were viewing their horses. Johnny also told us that the barns at the back of the house, which held Oliver's prized collection of classic vintage cars, were quite simply out of bounds.

The sisters, all younger than us, were terrifyingly good-looking in a pale, consumptive sort of way, and I distinctly remember being introduced to them in the icy splendour of the morning room as they lolled around reading *Tatler* and *Harpers*, glossy blonde hair spilling on to the equally glossy pages. The three of us, Molly, Imogen and I, had stood in the doorway awkwardly, fully prepared to be coolly appraised, then whispered about as we left the room, but to our surprise the McFarllen girls jumped up, pounced on us and dragged us off to the stables, insisting we see their ponies. Once in the privacy of the stables they'd grilled us rigid, bitterly disappointed that none of us had had our tummy buttons pierced, tattooed our bottoms, or at the very least, had sex with their brother. They pretty much ran wild about the place, and rode bareback like demons, and I remember once watching them race their ponies around the gallops for a laugh, waving and shrieking to their father, who was standing up in his ancient, convertible Bristol, binoculars to eyes, playing 'the trainer' for them. As he laughed and roared them on, I remember thinking how alien their world was to mine.

And of course I drank it all in thirstily, parched as I was of this sybaritic lifestyle. It spoke to me, released something pent up and suburban in my soul, as indeed did Angie, Johnny's mother. Bright-eyed, copper-haired and beautiful, with Johnny's brilliant, languid smile, it was she who held the whole chaotic shooting match together, she who was the pivot around whom the household revolved. The kitchen was her domain – although I don't believe she ever cooked in it – but she treated it as her salon and welcomed everyone to it. I can see her now, sweeping saddles from the vast oak table and calling for everyone to sit down together around a steaming pot of soup, placing a trainer next to an old soak, next to a schoolgirl, next to an elderly widow. Once her table was full she'd sit at the head, satisfied that everyone was about her, and then entrance us all, telling stories – but listening too, leaving no one out – and inviting our confidences, until I think I'd told her more about myself than I'd told any adult. I believe Peter and Ben were secretly in love with her, and her husband certainly was, liking nothing more than to show her off.

After a typically liquid lunch with fourteen or so of us around the kitchen table, Oliver, plastered, his pale blue eyes swimming rheumily, would stagger round to her end and try to persuade her to sing.

'She's got a bloody good voice, you know; trained as an opera singer before she met me. God, she should be captivating the front row of Covent Garden instead of a crowd of reprobates like you! Come on, Ange, the girls would love it, wouldn't you, girls? Ask her to sing, Molly; she'll do it for you.'

'Bugger off, Olly,' Angie would laugh, swatting him good-naturedly with her napkin and not moving from her chair. 'Why is it that when you're in your cups you have to have everyone on their feet hollering "Flower of Scot-land"?'

'Don't tempt me!' he'd shout, 'Oh God, it's too late – help me Johnny – "Oh fl-o-wer of Sco-tland . . ."' and off he'd go, standing up on his chair, belting it out, head back, roaring at the ceiling, with the rest of the table – son, daughters, family, friends – joining in the bits they knew.

My mother had raised delicately plucked eyebrows when I'd foolishly let this slip back home.

'Singsongs,' she'd murmured. 'How delightfully rustic. Do they light a campfire too, I wonder?'

But she could sneer all she liked, I'd fallen in love with the entire family, the whole, compulsive package. Never in my life had I come across such warmth, such unbridled fun for the sheer hell of it, such a house that rocked, almost literally, with laughter, and in the middle of it all, of course, the golden boy, Johnny.

But the summer didn't last for ever, and that October, after a final, wild goodbye party at the McFarllens', Johnny and the boys went off to university. Molly and I still had another year together at school, but Imogen, being bright as well as beautiful, went up to Oxford a year early to read Fine Art. Coincidentally, Johnny also went up to Oxford, to read Classics, and funnily enough, within a week or two of term beginning, he'd asked Imogen out.

Looking back, I wonder why on earth it hadn't occurred to us before, why it came as such a huge shock. He'd waited for her, you see, waited all summer to make a move, to claim his prize, but being too much of a gent to pluck her right from under Molly's nose in full view of everyone, had hung on until the right moment. And that moment had to be away from the rest of us, out of the spotlight, far from the madding crowd, where Johnny could swing into full, wooing mode, and let the romantic, thirteenth-century hallowed cloisters of Balliol do their damnedest.

Naturally it came as a severe blow to me, losing, as I suddenly had, my partner in rejection, but it was a colossal blow for Molly. She was distraught, understandably, and spitting blood for a while too. She wouldn't speak to Imogen or Johnny when they first came back at Christmas, wouldn't even acknowledge Imogen's letters. Gradually, though, after a couple of months, it all calmed down. It had to. Molly, Imogen and I had known each other since we were seven. We'd played in each other's bedrooms, been in the same netball teams, copied each other's homework, listened to each other's records, borrowed each other's clothes, and Molly was neither stupid nor vindictive. It was easy to forgive Imogen because she loved her, and she wrestled with her pride to forgive Johnny too, which was harder, because she loved him more.

Imogen and Johnny went out for three years, all their time together at Oxford, whilst Molly and I kept watch from less traditional, more redbrick, seats of learning. And they were surely the golden couple: Imogen, tall, slim, with her sheet of blonde hair slipping silkily down her back, slanting blue eyes and high forehead – cruising for a First with an icy cool nerve – whilst Johnny held up the more extrovert, exuberant side of the partnership. A raucous rugby blue, a man's man, partying and drinking till all hours, playing sport until he dropped, scraping a Two-two – 'A gentleman's degree,' he told us with a broad grin, 'means I've had a good time' – and always with the serene, unflappable Imogen on his arm. Deliriously happy, yes, but when they came out of university together, still very young. Still only twenty-one. And, of course, no one had even given a thought to marriage.

★ ★ ★

As I sat in my tiny, makeshift scullery kitchen, I blew a stream of smoke at the faded old photo on the fridge. Yes, it was funny really, I reflected. Molly had claimed him, Imogen had loved him, but at the end of the day, it had been me who'd married him.

Chapter Three

There wasn't a great deal of joy in the house I grew up in.
My father had left home when I was four, but before he'd
flown off to Canberra with Mum's best friend, Yvonne, he'd
thoughtfully provided for my education by leaving the
wherewithal for me to stay at The Sacred Heart Convent
School until I was eighteen. I wasn't too sure if he was even
a Catholic – in fact I wasn't too sure of any of the details
about my father, aside from a blurred old photo I'd found in
Mum's dressing-table drawer of a man in RAF uniform –
but the convent was no doubt a last-minute, guilty sop to
Mum, who was as devout as they come.

Whether her religious fervour was as strong before Dad's
departure as it was after, I'm not sure, but I do know that
once deserted, alone and grief-stricken, she'd transferred
any passion she had left in her soul to God, the Royal
Family and Jean Muir, and not necessarily in that order.

The bizarre Jean Muir fixation had come about because
in her previous, normal working life – before she took up
tormenting teenagers – she'd worked as a fitter in the
fashion world. During this period she'd spent some time in
Miss Muir's couture house, and such was the impression it
had made, that from that day on, she dressed solely in
navy-blue shift dresses, with only a single string of pearls

and earrings as adornment, her hair styled neatly in a dark, black bob, all very chic, all very à la Jean.

She was also half French, as she never failed to remind me, picking me up from school and greeting me with a cool '*Ça va?*' – to which I was supposed to respond accordingly. Mostly I did – every day in fact – but one day it got on my nerves and I snapped, 'Oui, ça va bloody bien, OK?' She never said it again and that memory fills me with remorse.

Mum's standards were high, and, frankly, I found it hard to live up to the Almighty, the Royals and Jean, and privately staged my own mini rebellion, deliberately skipping my Hail Marys, wearing a 'Sod the Royal Wedding' T-shirt under my jumper, and dressing as sloppily, and as unlike her mentor as possible. All very adolescent and futile, but I think because I looked very like Mum – small-boned, dark and petite – I was rather afraid of ending up like her, and made a supreme effort to be different. Genes will out, though – Parisian ones particularly – and however baggy my clothes I still had an unhappy knack of whipping a scarf around my neck and tying it just so, adding a good, chunky leather belt, some unusual earrings, some witty little shoes, so that according to Imogen and Molly I always looked 'together'.

Looks were everything to Mum, and she hoodwinked the world quite successfully, so that it always came as a surprise to people to realise we were poor. After all, I went to an expensive private school and Mum looked like she'd fallen out of *Vogue*, so it was only when people came to the house – a tiny, Victorian terraced villa with threadbare carpets and cheap furniture – that the dawn came up. On the flip side, though, Mum equally loathed ostentation. I remember one occasion, just after I'd left university, when, as usual I was off to a party at the McFarllens' and hastily bolting a cheese sandwich at the kitchen table, waiting for Johnny and Imogen to pick me up. She'd stood over me, fingering her pearls more nervously than usual.

'You're off to those McFarllens again then, are you?' she sniffed.

I didn't bother to look up. 'You know I am, Mum,' I muttered, stuffing in the sandwich, knowing she was rotating the earrings now, radiating disapproval.

'Well, you know my views.'

I chewed on in the silence, and at length she tried again, walking around the table so she was facing me on the other side. She rested her palms on the Formica.

'You haven't met many nouveau riche people, have you, Olivia?'

I cleared my throat. 'Quite a lot of the girls at school had money, if that's what you mean,' I said smoothly.

'Yes, but they didn't flash it about, did they?' she retorted quickly. 'Imogen's parents, for instance – they're wealthy, but you'd never know. They've got far too much breeding.' She shuddered. 'Unlike these, dreadful people.' I munched on in silence. New money was quite a theme of Mum's, as if we had any old. She sat down opposite me, flicking an imaginary speck of dust off her immaculate skirt.

'I saw him in the paper the other day,' she said tartly, 'splattered all over the back page. Tie askew, hair standing on end, holding a bottle of champagne and grinning from ear to ear like an idiot. Now if *Dick* had won the handicap stakes—'

'Hang on.' I looked up. '*Who* did you see in the paper the other day?'

'Whom, actually. Oliver McFarllen, of course.'

'Oh, right, and *whom*, exactly, is Dick?'

'Major Dick Hern,' she said patiently. 'The Queen's trainer.'

Ah yes, of course. Just plain Dick to Mum.

'Now when *Dick* wins,' she went on, 'he just smiles politely, tips his hat everso decorously, and bows out of the ring to let the owner take all the glory. None of this posing around to get his face in all the papers lark.'

I nodded. 'Quite right. Thanks, Mum. Remind me to give Oliver that little tip.' He'll be *everso* grateful, I thought privately, then hated myself for it.

Johnny hooted his horn from outside. I jumped up. 'They're here,' I said quickly, grabbing my bag and giving her a guilty peck on the cheek. 'See you later, Mum,' and I flew off down the passage and out of the front door, leaving her to shut it behind me.

As I ran down the path to his bright red Morgan, Johnny looked past me in amazement to the vision standing in the doorway.

'Blimey,' he said as I squeezed in behind Imogen to the tiny space in the back, 'is that your mother? She looks like one of those Dior fashion plates.'

'Oh, she'd love that,' I said, hugging my knees up in the obligatory garden gnome position. 'I'll tell her when I get home. She might change her opinion of you.' As soon as I'd said it, I wished I hadn't. He turned round, startled.

'Really? Why, what does she think of me then?'

'Oh well, she hasn't really met you, of course,' I said quickly, 'but she's – well, she's always had a bit of a thing about . . .' I hesitated.

'She thinks you're a flash git,' put in Imogen helpfully.

He roared with laughter. 'Does she? Christ!' He blinked. 'Well, she's probably right!'

'Probably?' murmured Imogen, raising her eyebrows as he overrevved the car.

He laughed. 'All right, Miss Ice Maiden, I haven't heard you complaining much.'

She lit a cigarette and gave him a secret smile, and he reached across and squeezed her knee in return, territorial gestures that Molly and I were still getting used to.

'Still,' he mused, glancing admiringly at me in the rear-view mirror, 'I can see where you get "the look" from, Liv.'

'Oh, Livvy was born chic,' commented Imogen. 'I wouldn't be surprised if she was doused in Saint-Laurent talc as a baby and snapped into Chanel nappies.'

I'd laughed, but I couldn't help feeling pleased, too. I'd spent my entire youth wishing Mum wouldn't stand at the school gates in navy-blue couture, complete with gloves, hat, and pigskin handbag, and be like the other mums in a tracksuit, trainers, a Sainsbury's carrier in one hand and a buggy with a toddler in the other, but for the first time in my life, I felt a rush of pride for her. And of course, I liked Johnny all the more for admiring her.

The venue that particular night was the McFarllens' barn, and the occasion, the youngest sister, Tara's, seventeenth birthday. Johnny had rigged the place up in a parody of a seventies disco, with flashing strobe lights and a juke box belting out Abba in the corner, and Tara and her friends were giggling in flares and headbands. Entering into the spirit of the thing, Molly, Imogen and I pranced about around our handbags, whilst the boys played imaginary guitars, shutting their eyes and banging their heads together in mock ecstasy. While we danced, I remember looking out through the open barn doors to the house beyond, which as usual was lit up like a vast beacon in the night sky. Through the dining-room window a dinner party was in full swing, with twelve or so people around a table awash with silver and crystal, and Angie and Oliver at either end. As I watched, I saw Oliver get up, take the decanter around the table, and pause to kiss his wife on the back of her neck before refilling her glass, laughing in the candlelight.

Later, after we'd all piled out of the barn and into the swimming pool, hot and exhausted from dancing, they'd joined us; Angie, ostensibly leading her guests out through the French windows for a drink by the pool, but secretly anxious lest one of Tara's friends had had too much to drink and sank to the bottom, and Oliver, puffing on a cigar, following soon after. I recognised a few racehorse owners from the yard: complacent, florid, mostly overweight men, pleased with themselves and laughing too loudly, with younger, trophy wives on their arms. They were all pretty tanked up too, and as they watched us swim relay races, one particularly loud, portly individual peeled off his dinner jacket and prepared to join us, making a fool of himself in his Union Jack boxer shorts. As he jumped in, suddenly a shout went up from Johnny, and he and his sisters rushed to ambush him, intent on debagging. Amid the inevitable splashing and shrieking, I crawled out of the other end, laughing and enjoying it all but, as ever, not wanting to get too involved. Oliver was beside me. He handed me a towel, and as I wrapped it around me, shivering – giggling as fat man got his comeuppance – I wondered where on earth my own clothes were. I knew it was pretty late and I had to get a move on. I turned to go.

'Perfect, aren't they?' he murmured.

I glanced back and followed Oliver's gaze to where Johnny and his three sisters were still streaking through the pool, their tanned, lithe bodies glistening in the moonlight.

I smiled. 'Perfect.'

Then I turned and scurried off, picking up a skirt here, a

shoe there, a bra – where was my bra? – oh God, *there*, on the rose bush, then climbing back into them all before dashing back and badgering Molly for a lift home, living in fear of the navy-blue avenging angel arriving to collect her daughter, breathing fire over the hedonists in the pool, a rolling pin in one hand, pigskin bag swinging wildly in the other.

I mention this partly because I remember it well. It was the last one, you see. Because a couple of weeks later, something happened that was to change all our lives. On an equally balmy, hot August evening, Oliver McFarllen left his stifling bedroom, wandered downstairs, and pausing only to get a drink of water, went out of the back door into the night. He walked quite a long way, apparently, right across his paddocks to the edge of his land, where, on reaching a far corner of a distant field, he put a gun to his head and shot himself.

The party line was that it had been an accident. That he'd been climbing over a fence and had fallen on top of his gun which he'd propped up carefully on the other side, and that it had simply gone off. But Oliver McFarllen had been handling a shotgun since he was twelve; he shot regularly on the Scottish and Irish grousemoors, he hosted a corporate shoot on his own land, and apart from anything else, he'd been found alone, in the middle of the night, in his dressing gown. Accidental death didn't hold much water, so suppositions abounded. Some suggested that Angie had taken a lover; others, that it was Oliver who had, and some scandalmongers even claimed that he was gay. Another rumour went that he'd lost all his money, that he was bankrupt, a broken man, living on credit, but like most tall stories, they all turned out to be unsubstantiated and baseless, because the fact of the matter was that no one knew why on earth he'd done it, least of all, Angie.

The grief almost swallowed her whole. She clung to her family, but their world had gone black too, and they fumbled around in the dark together, reaching for each other, not believing, not understanding. The house, which I eventually timidly visited – knocking on the front door, getting no answer, finding it open and tentatively tiptoeing down the familiar long corridor to the kitchen – was silent. Where once it had throbbed with vitality, it now seemed full of Oliver's shimmering absence. Grief had washed over it and I found the McFarllens clinging to the wreckage. Tara had locked herself in her bedroom whilst the other two girls were down at the stables, weeping into their horses' necks.

Angie, meanwhile, was in the kitchen, sitting at her huge oak table, her beautiful face pale but composed, as she said goodbye to a neighbouring farmer who'd called to offer his sympathies. As he left, pink-faced, his hat twisting nervously in his hands, she reached out and caught my hand.

'Livvy, so sweet of you to come,' she whispered, '*so* sweet.'

I mumbled how sorry I was, not knowing whether to hug her or run away, not wanting to intrude on her grief, but as she motioned with a trembling hand for me to sit down, I sat beside her, dumbly. At that moment Johnny appeared silently in the doorway. As he stood there, his face white and drawn, jeans and T-shirt creased where he'd clearly slept in them, I realised with a jolt that actually it was Johnny for whom the world had really stopped turning. His beloved father, whom he believed himself to be so like, only not so magnificent – to have ended it all in this terrible way. As he stumbled towards us, his blue eyes helpless and staring, wide with misery, I held out my hand and he clutched on to it. For a while there he stood motionless, gazing straight ahead, and then he sank down into a chair, put his head in his hands, and wept. Angie stroked his blond head absently, staring abstractedly out of the window to the paddocks beyond, her face full of longing, full of other days.

Imogen came back immediately, of course. She'd just started a post-grad fine arts course in Florence – had beaten countless hopefuls to get the place – but she put down her paintbrush and was by Johnny's side for the funeral. Elegant in a long black suit, weeping quietly into her hanky, she was right beside Johnny in his grief, and for a couple of days after, too. But then, of course, she had to go back. Life goes on, and all the other usual clichés, and she couldn't just abandon her course.

Johnny understood. Weeks went by, and he too had to struggle on as normal, making his daily trudge to the City where he'd started in the corporate finance department of a large investment bank. But more than six weeks later, with plenty of weekends in between, still Imogen didn't return. Johnny, too proud to ask, sent a cryptic postcard, which read: 'They paved paradise and put up a parking lot', to which Imogen – perhaps not knowing that the previous line of the Joni Mitchell song went: 'Don't it always seem to go, that you don't know what you've got till it's gone?' – had written back: 'Well, they've got to park somewhere.'

Johnny, baffled, flew out to Florence, and took a taxi straight round to her flat. Hot and dishevelled from his journey, and having climbed a million steps to get to her tiny, top-floor apartment, he was greeted at the door by a swarthy young Latin called Paolo, who, wearing nothing but a towel and a cynical smile, had informed him that Imogen was busy. Johnny, furious, didn't stop to find out more and flew straight home, whereupon Imogen,

distraught, phoned every hour, begging him to believe that
Paolo was just a friend – a neighbour, actually – whose
hot-water tank had broken down, and who was just using
her shower until it was fixed. But Johnny was like prosecut-
ing council, questioning and cross-examining, pushing her
to admit that the Italian wasn't a neighbour at all, or even a
friend, that he was a lover, and that she was having an affair.
Finally, she broke down and admitted she was.

Johnny was not a man to take infidelity lying down, as it
were, and against a backdrop of his father's death, there was
no mitigation, no room for forgiveness. A wall of silence
went up between them, made worse by the fact that Imogen
continued to see Paolo. Molly and I were appalled, but she
was adamant that she was the victim.

'He cast me aside, don't you see? If he'd loved me he'd
have forgiven me one small indiscretion.'

'Yes, but you're still seeing Paolo! You're making it a
huge indiscretion now – what's he supposed to think?'

'Well, what am I supposed to do, live out here like a nun
while he's on the other side of Europe? He can think what
he bloody well likes!'

And Johnny did, indeed, think a great deal. When I met
him for our customary lunchtime drink in the City, where I
was doing a poxy secretarial course and he was shinning up
the greasy banking pole, he was erudite on the subject.

'She's a tart,' he said simply. 'She's not getting it from
me and she can't go without it. She's always been highly
sexed.'

'Oh, Johnny, that's unfair,' I murmured loyally, uncomfortably aware of her nun reference.

'It's true, Livvy. She doesn't love him, does she? Has she
told you she loves him?'

'Well, no but—'

'So what's she doing with him then?'

I sighed. This was typical of Johnny. If you weren't wholehearted, what was the point? Wholeheartedness had been part of his father's make-up, and therefore part of Johnny's. Oliver had raced horses to win, not to come second; he lived in the most spectacular house, was married to the most beautiful woman, and had the most sought-after, glamorous children – what was the point of being a runner-up in life? But then, I thought, picking at some candlewax on the checked tablecloth in front of me, if one's standards were so high, surely one was destined to be disappointed?

'How's Angie?' I asked, changing the subject.

Johnny reached for the bottle of Chardonnay and refilled our glasses.

'Sad,' he said simply. 'Sad and quiet. Come and dig with her this weekend, Livvy. You know how she loves that. Come and stay.'

I smiled. It had been a long-standing joke from way back, this eccentric – at my age apparently – love of gardening. Like his mother, I liked nothing more than to be down amongst the slugs and the earthworms, sowing and separating and potting on, and this secretarial course was really only to mark time until I got up the nerve to tell Mum that that was what I really wanted to do – to take a course in garden design that I'd applied for at Cirencester. She'd be horrified, of course.

'I don't know where you get this strange, earthy streak,' she used to say, wrapping her cardigan tightly around her as she watched me trowelling away in our two square foot of back garden. 'Must be your father's side. There's nothing remotely agricultural about the Du Brays.'

Yes, well, there was nothing remotely human about the

frigging Du Brays either. My maternal grandmother had fallen out with my mother years ago, and although she lived only a matter of miles from us, in the centre of St Albans, as a child I was forbidden to see her. I did try to make contact once, when I was about sixteen, but had been told very sternly by the elderly woman on the other end of the phone in a heavy French accent that 'your grandmother ees not at home', although it was quite clear it was she I was talking to. As I'd put the phone down I'd had a sneaking sense of regret for Mum. With a mother like that, was it any surprise she'd ended up as she had?

Yes, so Mum was sniffy about my gardening, but Angie McFarllen, on the other hand, had treated it as a wonderful surprise. She'd found me, early on in my days at her house, crouched down in her herbaceous border, pulling a few weeds from around the tender young shoots of her aspidistras, and had recognised that same, avid light in my eyes. She'd pounced.

'Good God, Livvy, are you one of us? Are you a secret horticulturist?'

'Well, not exactly,' I'd blushed, sitting back on my heels. 'Mum and I haven't exactly got much of a garden. I'm just an enthusiast really.'

'Then for heaven's sake come and enthuse with me! No one else in this wretched family does. They're all too busy playing tennis or fiddling with their stupid vintage cars. I've got acres here, and no one to attack the weeds but poor old Ron, who's on his last legs, and I certainly haven't the heart to tell him, poor devil. Come on, let's get cracking. Help me separate these flaming day lilies before they take over the garden like triffids!'

And so had begun our horticultural relationship. In the days before Oliver's death, we'd dug away furiously together, breaking forks in her hard, uncompromising chalky soil and roaring with laughter at yet another broken prong, but more recently, as Angie went quiet and withdrawn, just on our knees, weeding around the scented pelargoniums and the lavender, silently and companionably.

On one of these latter, quieter days, I'd looked up from the greenhouse where we were pricking out and potting on more peonies, to see Johnny, charging around the paddock in an open-topped Land Rover with two squealing sisters in the back. I'd straightened up from the bench where we were working, and shaded my eyes to watch. He'd always loved speed, whether it was careering round on a quad bike or performing wheelies on a clapped-out old motorbike he'd found in the back of the barn. In the old days, we'd all ridden in turn on the bike behind him, tearing down the drive, eyes shut, numb with terror, and I remember flushing with pride one day as he'd careered to a stop in front of the others and said: 'You know, Livvy's the only one who's got the guts to lean into the curves. The rest of you are dead weights, like carrying a sack of potatoes. Just watch and learn!'

Well, this was the first time I'd seen him back in the driving seat, as it were. Just for fun, for a laugh. I'd caught Angie's eye as she set aside a seed tray.

'Almost like old times,' I'd murmured.

'Almost.' She'd paused. 'Except his heart's not in it. He's still very vulnerable, Livvy.'

Perhaps she hadn't meant it as such, but I'd taken this as a warning shot across my predatory bows. I buried my face in the baby peonies and took up my trowel again.

Later on, though, as I looked at him across that half-drunk bottle of Chardonnay in that dark City wine bar, I realised that actually she was right. Death had changed him.

I hadn't thought that I could be any more attracted to Johnny than I already was, but vulnerability could be awfully attractive, especially in such a confident man.

'OK,' I said, putting down my glass, 'I'll come this weekend. I need to sort out your herb garden, anyway. The ground elder's practically taken over there. It's a disgrace.'

He laughed. 'Sometimes I think we ought to pay you for this.'

'Of course you should.'

He looked startled. 'Oh! Oh well, Livvy, why didn't you say? I mean, I'm sure Mum—'

'Oh, don't be ridiculous. Belt up, Johnny and pour me another drink. If anyone owes anyone anything, it's me.'

'What d'you mean?'

'Oh, I don't know.' I slid away from his blue gaze. 'For offering me a glimpse of another life, I suppose. A different sort of life.'

He didn't say anything, but as he dropped his eyes to the table, I spotted recognition in them. He'd seen my mother, of course. And he'd seen Hastoe Villas.

To tell you the truth, I'm not entirely sure how it happened – how one weekend's gardening turned into another, and then another, which in turn led to pub suppers alone with Johnny, then trips home on his motorbike under the stars, with me really leaning into those curves, and finally, of course, trips to bed. To me it seemed entirely natural – after all, I'd been dreaming about it for years, so it didn't exactly take me by surprise – and it was utter, utter bliss, but I suppose if it took anyone by surprise, it was Johnny. He sat up in bed one summer afternoon as I lay back on the pillows in his bedroom overlooking the fields, and raked a bewildered hand through his hair. He blinked out of the window.

'D'you know, Livvy, you're an absolute tonic. I swear to God I feel like a new man, I reckon I could jump out of that window, clear that apple tree and race right around those gallops! And I mean – Christ, who would have thought?'

'Who would have thought what?'

'Well, you and me!'

He turned, and I narrowed my eyes at him from my nest on the pillows. 'What, you mean Johnny the *grand fromage* from the big house and little old Livvy?'

He threw a pillow at me. 'Bugger off, I didn't mean that at all. But you must admit, you've crept up on me, Liv. You're a dark old horse.'

'Ah yes, that's me,' I smiled. 'The rank outsider. Long odds, not much to look at in the paddock, pretty dodgy pedigree, but coming up hard on the rails at fifty to one.'

He frowned. 'Why d'you always do that?'

'Do what?'

'Put yourself down?'

I shrugged. 'I suppose I like to get in there before anyone else does.'

He grinned and lay down on top of me. 'Oh, so do I.'

I giggled and wriggled away. 'Hang on, I thought you were about to hurdle some apple trees, race around the gallops like Champion the Wonder Horse!'

'Still might,' he muttered, grabbing me back, 'but I forgot something.'

'Please don't say it's your oats.'

'You've talked me into it, you smooth-talking seductress you!'

After an inevitable scuffle, the rest of the afternoon passed predictably enough, but later on, I thought about what he'd said. Actually, I knew I'd crept up on him. I knew because it had happened before. It wasn't a deliberate ploy on my part, but I'd noticed, over the years, that guys I'd been quite friendly with at university and who I'd knocked around with in a matey sort of way, had suddenly had a habit of going into frenzied stares over their cooling fish and chips in the canteen, or popping up beside me in the library, shooting me hot looks over their Jean-Paul Sartres. I was never the obvious choice, I didn't have the stop-the-traffic looks of Imogen, or the fizz and crackle of Molly, but mine, apparently, was more of a slow burn.

Imogen had to be told, of course, and Johnny certainly wasn't going to do it, so I wrote a long and guilty letter about how it had just sort of happened and how – since she was still with Paolo – I hoped she didn't mind.

'Go for it!' came back her instant missive on the back of Michelangelo's *David*.

I couldn't be more pleased for you, Livvy. You're far more suited to him than I am and, apart from anything else, you won't be bringing an enormous ego into the equation to compete with his!

I allowed this veiled slur on Johnny, tucked the card discreetly into a drawer, and heaved a huge sigh of relief.

Meanwhile, the motorbike rides, the pub suppers, the swimming, the larks, and the bedroom romps continued apace, until, that is, one Saturday, when I received a letter. I didn't say anything, but later on that day, as Johnny was helping me scythe down some nettles in Angie's wild flower meadow behind the barn, he stopped suddenly, put down his scythe.

'What's up?'

I rested on my scythe for a moment, panting. 'What?' I squinted towards him, into the sun.

'I said, what's up?'

'Nothing's up, why?'

'Well, you've been totally silent all morning. In fact you've hardly said a word since you got here. What's occurring?'

'Oh. Have I? Oh, well, nothing really.' I shrugged and gave a half-hearted attempt at the nettles again. Then I stopped. 'It's just . . . well, it's just, I got a letter this morning. I've got into Cirencester. I'll start there in September.'

He gazed at me for a long moment. 'But that's great,' he said slowly.

I swallowed. 'Yes. Isn't it?'

We picked up our scythes again and worked away in silence for a bit. Then he put his down.

'Marry me, Livvy.'

I straightened up, gawped. 'Oh, don't be ridiculous!'

'What's ridiculous?'

'You don't mean that!'

'Yes I do. Don't go to Cirencester, marry me. Let's stay together.'

'Johnny,' I said gently, 'you don't have to marry me for us to stay together.'

'Oh, but I do. I don't want to lose you, Livvy, and I know that if you go up to Cirencester, the chances are some beefy farmer will snap you up and take you off to his ghastly piggery in Shropshire or – or even worse, some stately pile in Scotland, and I just couldn't bear that. You and I were made for each other, you must see that. We want the same things!'

'We do? Like what?'

'Like – all this!' He swung his arm around and I knew instantly what he meant. Not the house exactly, but more the metaphorical hearth: the family, the unit, something I'd never had, and something he'd lost and desperately wanted to recapture. It was true, already we knew each other too well. Knew each other's dreams.

'And?' I challenged, meeting his eye.

'And I love you.'

'You've never said.'

'I'm saying it now.' He walked forward and took my filthy hands in his. 'I love you, Olivia Faber, with all my heart. Don't give up on me, Livvy, don't go away, please. Stay, stay with me, and do me the honour of becoming my wife.'

Well, what could I say? It was an undeniable truth that I loved him completely and uncritically and always had done, so I was on a hiding to nothing. I didn't even pause for breath, didn't let my heart skip a beat, didn't waver for one moment. I just looked into his bright blue gaze and said – yes. Yes, Johnny, yes, of course. Marriage was not something I'd envisaged being even remotely on the cards, but now you came to mention it . . . Mrs Olivia McFarllen? Oh sure. Oh yes, I wanted that more than anything in the world.

Johnny told Angie privately, in the kitchen, with me shaking with nerves in the greenhouse. Eventually she came out to find me and declared herself delighted.

'Really?' I gasped, looked anxiously into her hazel eyes.

'Really,' she assured me, smiling. 'I know you'll make him very happy.'

My face split in two with relief. 'Oh, I will, I will,' I beamed back, not pausing for a moment to wonder if he'd make me happy, or even, whether that mattered.

My own mother, of course, was another matter. Her back was to me as she scrubbed the life out of a pan at the kitchen sink, her dark bob shaking with the effort, not even deigning to look at me.

'So you got him,' she sniffed. 'You "bagged" him, as

they say. It all paid off in the end, all that hard work. Jolly well done, Olivia.'

'Mum, listen—'

'No,' she swung round, 'no, *you* listen. You make your bed in the McFarllens' household, young lady, and you'll live to regret it. No one takes a shotgun to a field, puts it into his mouth, stares down the barrel and pulls hard without very good reason, my girl!'

'What's that got to do with my marrying Johnny!' I screamed.

'It's got *everything* to do with your marrying Johnny!'

'But you hated them *before* any of this happened! You've *always* hated them!'

'And with damn good reason, so it turned out!'

'What's that supposed to mean?'

But she wouldn't say. In fact, tight-lipped and pale, she said very little, right up to the day of my wedding.

In my heart I think I knew Angie wasn't entirely happy, and I certainly knew Mum wasn't. As she helped me get ready on the morning of my wedding, I turned in delight at the reflection of my ivory gown in her bedroom mirror, and suddenly thought how small and fragile she looked beside me, standing watching me in her dark blue coat. I swooped to hug her but, to my dismay, tears poured down her cheeks.

Johnny and I were ecstatic, though, and not even Mum's distress could dampen our spirits. Nothing could detract from our delight. We couldn't take our eyes off each other, and as I swept out of that little Catholic church on the village green with Molly, Imogen and Johnny's three sisters in shocking pink behind me, I thought I must be the happiest girl alive. We'll prove them all wrong, I thought as I smiled confidently into the camera, tossing the confetti from my hair. They'll see, we'll show them!

And so we did. We moved into a tiny basement flat in Hammersmith, which was all we could afford, and were blissfully, ridiculously happy. Johnny continued to trudge to the City, but he began to enjoy it more. He was in Futures now, and he enjoyed watching the millions roll back and forth, riding on the waves of adrenalin, hardly bobbing when it rolled the wrong way, unlike some of the nervier, less sharp boys. As for me, Cirencester forgotten, I got a job at a very smart nursery in Chelsea, which amused my mother no end.

'A garden centre! You've got an English degree and you end up as a shop girl!'

'Not for long,' I assured her sweetly, and it wasn't. Within a year or so I was managing the place, which to my fury, amused her even more.

'Ah, so now you're the manager*ess*!' she hissed happily.

I gritted my teeth and swore to God I'd own the bloody place before long, set up a flipping chain of them just to show her, but before I could embark on my grand, horticultural Empire, a spanner was chucked smartly in my works. All of a sudden I was throwing up in the staff loo, feeling faint at the smell of egg sandwiches, and having trouble with the zip of my jeans. Johnny was delighted.

'But this is what we wanted!' he declared, leaping up on to our terrible old sofa and bouncing about like a child. 'This is marvellous!'

'You don't think it's a bit soon?' I said doubtfully, peering at the wholly conclusive Predictor blue line.

'Of course not!' He jumped off and hugged me delightedly. 'The sooner the better! A family, Livvy!'

Imogen and Molly were not so enthusiastic.

'A baby!' shrieked Molly. 'Bloody hell, what's the matter with you two? You're only twenty-three! God, if you carry on taking life at such an alarming rate you'll be taking P&O cruises when you're thirty!'

Perhaps she had a point, but there was no going back now, and Claudia was born that Christmas. Six weeks premature; tiny, delicate, sickly, unable to sleep, unable to feed from me, and perhaps, not quite what Johnny had in mind.

'Why won't she sleep?' he said as we lay in bed together, exhausted, listening to her scream.

'Because she can't, I suppose.'

'Is she always going to scream like that? I mean, all night?'

'Of course not,' I said, hauling myself out of bed, numb with tiredness. 'She'll settle down. It's just these first few weeks.'

But it wasn't the first few weeks, it was eighteen months before Claudia settled into anything like a routine, and even then, she was always fragile; an asthmatic, sickly child, susceptible to any bug going, allergic to milk, totally distraught if left with anyone other than me – an exhausting child. We adored her unreservedly, of course, but longed for a bright, bouncy boy to pep her up a little, spark her off, put a bit of colour in her pale cheeks with his boisterous games, save her from being quite so precious, and more like Johnny's little sisters had been, exuberant tomboys, full of life.

Nine years later we were still longing. Strangely, while Claudia had been an accident, suddenly, there was not a sausage, not even a glimmer of a Predictor blue line upon the horizon. I suppose it's fair to say we were disappointed, but we weren't obsessive about it, perhaps because Claudia had been such hard work. And equally, whilst I wouldn't say our marriage floundered during this time, it's also true to say it went into remission.

We'd moved to a little house in Fulham and I no longer worked at the nursery but looked after Claudia full time, too nervous of her disposition to leave her with a nanny. Johnny was working harder and harder in the City and now earned a deal of money, but I felt his heart was no longer in it. It was as if he was going through the motions, and if, at times, he became more distant at home, I learnt to cast around to provide some distraction to take his mind off the present, and possibly even the past.

Strangely enough, it was my mother who provided the necessary diversion. She rang one Sunday afternoon as the three of us were slumped in front of an old black and white movie, steadily working our way through a tin of Quality Street.

'Good news, darling! Your grandmother's dead!'

'Mum!' I was deeply shocked.

'Oh, you won't be so pi when I tell you the really good news. She left you the house.'

'What – her house? To me? But why?'

'Well, she wasn't going to leave it to me; she hated me.'

'But she didn't even know me.'

'Which is precisely why she didn't hate you too!'

'Thanks, Mum.'

There was something disarming about her lack of hypocrisy, though, and I have to say, Johnny and I were secretly thrilled. We'd sell it, of course – some ghastly terraced house just north of Watford with a bypass whizzing by its nose, no doubt, and then we'd sell our own poky house, and with the proceeds, move to somewhere central and spacious and light and, oh golly – Holland Park maybe, or even Notting Hill! It was just the boost we needed; it would be a turning point in our lives.

Full of plans we leapt into Johnny's old Bristol – and in fact Oliver's old Bristol – and went off to see it. Amazed that it took us only half an hour to get to this old Roman City of St Albans, we then spent another half-hour trying to find the wretched house. Finally, when we'd walked every cobbled backstreet, grudgingly admired the pretty period buildings, peered in antique shops, climbed the steep hills and marvelled at the ancient, towering Abbey, we found a lane, tucked away behind some cloisters, which led to a crescent of beautiful Georgian town houses. Just as the crescent ended, almost tacked on as an afterthought, was a high old brick wall, with green, double barn doors, slap bang in the middle.

'This must be it,' I said doubtfully, consulting my instructions and map. 'Orchard House, The Crescent.'

'Aptly named for a house in the middle of a city,' said Johnny sardonically.

'Oh, I don't know,' I said, lifting the latch on one of the doors and pushing on through. 'It might be— Oh crikey, look at this!'

We both stopped still and caught our breaths.

'Bloody hell,' muttered Johnny.

There, before us, was the most exquisite little Queen Anne house; white, perfectly proportioned, pretty and low, and surrounded by about an acre of tangled, unkempt garden. On one side was the remains of what had most certainly once been an orchard, and to the other, an over-grown rose garden, which fought with ancient clematis, honeysuckle and the inevitable elder. Even from here, one could see that down at the back, the lawn – which was dominated by a huge old cedar tree – swept down to a stream fringed with bull rushes, which in turn flowed across and along the back of The Crescent. All was walled, all was totally private, and all was a million miles from what either of us had been expecting.

'Oh, Johnny, it's heaven!' I breathed.

'Hardly. It's completely dilapidated and that's just the outside. Don't get excited, Livvy.'

'I won't,' I promised, but I already was. That garden – oh that garden!

Obediently I followed him inside. It was, of course, just as an old lady had left it, with a general air of death and decay, lots of heavy oak furniture, antimacassars on every chair, a frayed rug in front of a gas fire, and chipped Formica and sliding glass doors on the cupboards in the kitchen. But I saw none of that. I saw, like a dolls' house, four, perfectly square and symmetrical rooms downstairs and four above, all with working fireplaces, floor-to-ceiling sash windows, cornices and picture rails, and all, what's more, with views of the garden.

'There's no central heating,' warned Johnny, gazing around upstairs, but I could tell he was impressed. He was jangling his change in his pocket, which was always a good sign.

'OK, so we'll put some in.'

'Oh, it'll need more than that. It'll need gutting, rewiring, replumbing, a new bathroom and a totally new kitchen. We're talking big-time building works here, Liv.'

'So we'll sell the house in London and use the money to renovate it.'

'Lots of money. Lots of time too.' But the jangling continued.

'Fine!' I laughed. 'We've got plenty of both now! Oh gosh, you can see the cathedral from here! Look, Johnny, there, across the rooftops and – oh! Look!'

I had my head well out of the window now, marvelling at

the view, but suddenly I popped it back in. I grabbed his hand and ran downstairs, pulling him out through the French windows, across the terrace to the lawn. As we slid down the bank on the other side together, we came to a halt at the bottom, panting. Johnny stared. There, tucked away behind a tall holly hedge and beneath a riot of ivy, was a small, brick-and-timbered barn. It was ancient, its roof was clearly rotten, but it was still standing, albeit by the skin of its teeth.

'I could keep the Bristol in here, maybe get Dad's old Lagonda in too!' he said excitedly. He walked in and peered up at the beams.

'Quite!' I squeaked. 'And you'd never get a double garage in London, no matter where we lived!'

He bit his lip thoughtfully, patted the thick old walls. Then he turned to me. 'We'll see, Livvy. Let's go home and think about it; do our sums, and see, OK?'

'OK!'

We did, but I knew then he was as smitten as I was. The idea of being half an hour from Central London – which let's face it, one could still be in Camberwell or Clapham – and living in a pretty period house with an acre of garden for me, and plenty of garaging for classic cars for him, was not to be sniffed at. We dutifully did our sums, consulted a few intelligent people who told us we were barking mad – and jumped in with both feet.

That autumn, Orchard House became our home and we were blissfully, ridiculously happy. So what if the eccentric East End builders we'd employed, together with their Greek sidekick, had practically moved in with us? So what if they watched our television, monopolised and stank out our lavatory, smoked my cigarettes and fundamentally ruled our lives? So what if the fires smoked and we were freezing to death, huddled in front of smelly blow heaters? So what if there were rats in the cellar and bats in the attic – all these problems were minor, could be sorted by Mac and the boys, and jolly well would be. Johnny surprised me by being very enthusiastic in the DIY department, I was ecstatic in the garden, squealing with pleasure as I uncovered more and more neglected plants, and Claudia was positively flourishing, happy at her new school, not needing her inhaler nearly as much, loving the garden, delighted to have trees to climb, a stream to fish, and plenty of friends to bicycle with in The Crescent. So all was fine. All was peachy. For a while, anyway.

Until . . . something happened, something . . . that I couldn't quite put my finger on, but as I say, I reckon it happened about five months ago. Something went wrong. And despite my frantic attempts at Twickenham tickets and ballooning weekends in France, my husband continued to stare out of rain-soaked windows. I'd lost him. And now as I sat here, at our kitchen table, in my paint-spattered checked shirt, staring at a photograph on the fridge that was taken seventeen years ago, I realised I was about to find out why.

I glanced up at the clock: seven forty-five. It seemed to me he'd been upstairs for ever, but it must only have been a few minutes. He'd come back on his usual train, after all. Suddenly I jumped. Yes, now I could hear movement on the landing. He was coming down. I quickly lit another cigarette and was just exhaling the smoke as he came past the kitchen door, jacket on, a case in each hand. He saw me sitting there, stopped, and then stepped backwards so he was framed in the doorway. As he gazed at me, his blue eyes were full of remorse. Blue eyes I loved.

'Sorry, Livvy.'

I nodded. Swallowed hard. 'Johnn—' I tried again; my voice wouldn't work. 'Johnny,' I managed, 'is there someone else?'

He held my eyes for a moment, then slid them down to his shoes. 'If you mean am I having an affair, then yes, I am.'

I squeezed my legs together hard. 'And do you –' Couldn't say it. Couldn't say the love word. 'Is it serious?'

He took a deep breath. 'It wasn't . . . was never meant to be . . . but now . . . yes. Yes, it's serious.' His eyes came back to me. 'I'm so sorry, Livvy.'

I nodded. Raised my chin high. And then against my better judgement, out came, 'So where does that leave me?'

He stared. I looked away quickly from the silence.

He hesitated a moment longer, picked up his cases, opened the front door, closed it softly behind him, and set off down the path.

Chapter Four

'I don't believe you.'

'Please try to.'

'Livvy, you are *kidding*?'

'I'm not bloody kidding. Would I kid about something like that? Molly, do me a favour, don't quiz me on the phone. I'm really not up to it. Just get over here, OK?'

There was a stunned silence. 'But I'm shocked. Honest to God, I am so unbelievably shocked! *Johnny!* Of all people!'

'*Molly!*'

'Yes! Right. Right, I'm coming. And Imogen?'

I swallowed. 'Please. But, listen, could you tell her?'

She paused then: 'Course I will, darling. I'll see you soon.'

Half an hour later Molly was ringing my bell. I opened the door to find her clinging to the doorframe, hugely pregnant, panting hard, one arm holding her bump and the other, just about holding Henry, who at eleven months was puce in the face with fury, screaming and kicking to be set free. Molly's dark curls were damp with sweat, her eyes wild.

'Jesus Christ,' she gasped, 'don't let anyone talk you into unprotected sex in October. I tell you, lugging three extra

59

stone around in a heat wave as well as this little bugger is no joke.'

'I think sex, protected or otherwise, is rather off the agenda for me at the moment.'

'Oh, Livvy!' She dropped Henry, put her arm round my neck and hugged hard. 'Livvy, my love!' I gulped gratefully into her damp curls, feeling her bump against me.

'Fine, I'm fine,' I muttered finally. 'Come on in.'

She followed me into the chaos of my tiny kitchen, neatly sidestepping a clothes horse laden with wet washing, noting, I'm sure, the tottering pagodas of washing-up in the sink, the newspapers on the floor soaking up the rush matting which had got drenched when the washing machine overflowed, but happily releasing Henry into it all, like a ferret down a burrow.

'So when did he go?' she gasped, collapsing into an old Lloyd Loom chair and lighting a cigarette.

'About two weeks ago.'

'Two weeks ago!' She sat up. 'My God, why didn't you tell me?'

'Couldn't.' I plucked a cigarette from her pack. 'Couldn't speak to anyone for about a week, Molly; couldn't even get out of bed. I finally broke it to Claudia, who I'd been fobbing off with a Daddy's-got-a-conference-in-New-York-again line, and then when she'd gone off to school, collapsed in a heap again.'

'How did she take it?'

'She said she knew. Suspected, anyway – had done for a while. She's not stupid, Mol.' I bit the skin round my thumb.

'And is she OK?'

I sighed. 'Seems to be, but you know how Claudes is. Never lets much show and takes everything in her stride, but you can never really tell with children, can you? All the books say the emotional scars and all that sort of scary baggage come later.' I gulped and dragged on my cigarette.

'Books?' scoffed Molly. 'What do they know, a bunch of half-baked psychologists spouting out their university theses? Listen, she'll be fine. God, it's *you* I'm worried about. Has he spoken to you?'

'Oh yes. He rang last week to speak to Claudia, and when I picked up the phone he very sweetly gave me his telephone number in case I should care to call him. Or Her? I asked. Sorry? he said. Well, I explained, surely it was Her telephone too? Oh, he said hurriedly, he'd just meant in case of an emergency. I felt like saying the only bloody emergency would be getting the gore off my hands when I'd finished disembowelling the cow.'

'Ah. So there is a cow?'

'Oh yes, didn't I mention that? Most definitely there is. That's why he's gone.'

'But you don't know who she is?'

'No idea.' I gazed beyond Molly, out of the window. 'No idea at all.'

She dragged hard on her cigarette. 'Jesus,' she muttered, flicking ash on to the newspaper on the floor beside her and shaking her head in disbelief. '*Jesus*. And you didn't see any of this coming, Liv? I mean – is this a complete and utter bolt from the blue?'

'Total. Well, the girl and the moving out bit is. He certainly didn't leave any clues – no lipstick on shirts, no condoms in pockets or anything – but . . .' I hesitated, 'if I'm honest, Mol, I knew something was up. *Have* known something was up for ages really. I just stupidly never thought it would be this.' I gave a hollow laugh. 'An affair! Never thought it would be an affair, for heaven's sake, the most obvious thing in the world!' I reached up to a shelf for

61

a wine glass, but as I tried to find a space amongst the debris to set it down and pour Molly a drink, I realised my hand was shaking violently.

She got up, took the glass and reached into the fridge for the bottle.

'He'll be back,' she said firmly, pouring out a large one and handing it to me.

'Of course he will,' I said quickly, grateful for that, wanting her to say that, wanting more.

'After all, this is what men do, isn't it?' she said warming to her theme, knowing she'd hit the right note. 'I mean, this is the seven-year itch, isn't it?'

'Twelve.'

'The flighty forties—'

'Thirties.'

'The classic mid-life crisis, the "oh my God, where did my youth go, am I going bald and does my willy still work?" '

'Precisely.'

'And then before you know where you are, he'll be crawling back here with his tail between his legs, and you'll be force-feeding him humble pie for weeks! Actually, it'll probably be the making of your marriage, especially if you sort of worry him for a bit.'

'What – you mean dither about having him back?'

'Exactly, do a bit of, "Ooh, Johnny, I'm not so sure. You see, I'm making my own way now. I don't know whether you'll fit into my amateur dramatics group, my gym classes, my—" '

' "Tennis lessons with the wolfish young pro"?'

'Much better! And then all of a sudden he'll see his whole life slipping away into a grotty little flat with yet another Fray Bentos meal put in front of him by a floozie who can't iron shirts, and in that split second – which is all it takes – he suddenly won't be able to remember what on earth he saw in her, and he'll be positively *begging* you to have him back!'

'Well, quite.' I took a huge gulp of wine. I'd been doing quite well there, but the mention of the floozie who might not wield an iron spectacularly but who might have other, more exotic talents, made me feel slightly less gung-ho. 'Bastard,' I muttered.

'Oh yes, that goes without saying,' Molly agreed, 'but— *Henry, no*!'

She lunged as Henry, left to his own devices, was quietly helping himself to the delights of a tool box left open by the builders and about to insert a six-inch nail down his oesophagus. Molly grabbed it, but then a frantic struggle ensued with Henry intent on keeping that nail, and prepared to sink his brand-new teeth into his mother's hand to secure it.

'Ouch! You little—' She bared her teeth viciously at him and snarled back. Miraculously, he dropped the nail.

'Well, that certainly worked.'

'Oh yes,' she panted, pinning him to the ground in a half-nelson. 'He bit me the other day, you see, and I bit him back – in Tesco's, actually. Caused quite a stir in the checkout queue. Someone even ventured to ask if I was fit to have another baby, to which I replied no, I'm not, so give me your address and I'll let you have it. And there'll be plenty more where that one came from, I assured the rest of the queue. At the rate I'm breeding, no one need go empty-handed.'

I smiled. Within weeks of giving birth, Molly had fallen for that fatal old wives' tale which tells you you can't get pregnant while you're breast-feeding. Now, on the point of having two children under thirteen months, she was living proof that you can. Married to a lovely, penniless actor called Hugh, who was always *just* on the brink of making that big Hollywood break but meanwhile doing Bonio adverts to tide them over, she lived from hand to mouth in a tiny rented cottage not far from here that was possibly even more squalid than mine. But Molly didn't see the damp marching up the walls, or the confetti of final demands on the breakfast-room table; she had Hugh, she had Henry, she had her bump, and she was bright enough to know that was more than most. Molly had always been effortlessly, unashamedly herself. She wore anything that came to hand – jodhpurs, felt hats, crochet waistcoats – making fashion decisions faster than a speeding bullet, and I'd often felt that if I were more like Molly, it might give me more confidence, more vigour, make being myself less of a labour. She'd never felt she had a thing to prove, you see – which reminded me.

'Did you get hold of Imogen?'

'Yes. She said she was working late, just locking up the gallery, but she said she'd come straight down, be here about nine. Actually, the way she throws that Mercedes about I'm surprised she didn't get here before me.'

'How did she sound?'

'About what?'

'Well – when you told her about me.'

'Oh. Oh well, to be honest, I could hardly hear her – her mobile was cracking up – but, well, shocked, I suppose.' She frowned, trying to remember.

I reached across and grabbed another one of her cigarettes, then paced the little room nervously. I gazed out of the window. The light from the caravan just across the stream at the bottom of the garden shone out like a beacon in the fading evening light. Mac and the boys, sick of trawling in from Billericay every day and getting stuck on the M25, had asked if they could stay during the week, and since it was in my interests to have them start at eight o'clock rather than ten, I'd said yes, fine, as long as you accommodate yourselves and don't expect me to put you up. Bed and breakfast, I'd presumed, down the road somewhere, but the next thing I knew their truck had arrived dragging a socking great caravan. Later that afternoon, after they'd put in a hard day's work, Claudia and I had stood and watched, fascinated, as they'd bustled around it like three little housewives; pulling down beds from the walls, making hospital corners with the sheets, getting crockery out of dinky little cupboards and even plumping up cushions on the banquette seating, before settling down in front of the telly, a six-pack between them, a vindaloo apiece, with no nagging wives, no bloomin' kids – feet up and all ready to watch the footy. Magic.

Claudia was fascinated by this little menage, and one afternoon, when she'd been feeling rather brave, had knocked on their door. I'd found her there later watching the racing – Pils and vindaloo happily substituted by 7-Up and crisps – looking very important and clearly feeling very grown up. My mother had been horrified when I'd mentioned it, but frankly I could see nothing wrong with her watching the 5.40 from Kempton with my workforce before I called her back to do her homework. Right now, of course, she was tucked up in bed, and they were no doubt in there watching something far more risqué.

I turned back to Molly. 'I haven't seen her for ages.'

Molly was on her knees, changing a nappy.

'Who?'

'Imogen.'

'Oh, right. No, neither have I, really. Not since she split up with Dominic anyway.'

I swung around. 'She split up with Dominic?'

'Yes, didn't you know?'

'No! When?'

'Oh God, I don't know, four or five months ago?'

'Four or fi— but she didn't tell me!'

'Oh, well, Heavens,' she looked up, awkward suddenly, privy to information I wasn't, 'you've been so busy with this house, Livvy, and she's been frantic at the gallery – she's had a rush of private views on recently – it's hardly surprising. Anyway, she was never really serious about him.'

'She's never been really serious about anyone except—' I shook my head. 'And I've spoken to her loads of times, Molly. She never even mentioned it!'

'Oh well,' she shrugged and snapped the new nappy on, 'perhaps she wanted to see you to tell you. You know what Imo's like. Listen, are you going to open those Pringles I've just spotted lurking in that cupboard down there, or are me and my appendage here going to have to starve to death?'

I ignored her, knowing full well she was changing the subject, and seized her hand as it went for the crisps.

'Four or five months, Molly. Don't you see? That's exactly when it started, four or five months ago!'

'Stop it!' Molly shook me off, horrified. 'Livvy, how could you? Of *course* it's not Imo!'

'Why not?'

'Because she's your best friend!'

'Doesn't count, Mol.' I shook my head violently. 'Love cancels out everything like that. Friendship, loyalty – it all goes out of the window and, God, they were *so* in love all those years ago and—'

'Livvy, you have got to stop being so insecure about that! Just because he went out with her, for God's sake!'

'It was more than that and you know it. She broke his heart with Paolo, and then through her own stupid pride broke her own heart too. Imo's never found anyone else, Mol, and look at her now, chucking in the towel with one guy after another!'

I was ranting now, pacing the floor, all the pent-up, horrid, suspicious thoughts I'd had over the last few weeks spilling out like serpents from my mouth.

'Don't you see, Molly, it would *have* to be someone as serious as Imo! Johnny would never leave me just for a fling with a floozie. It's not his style. He despises philanderers! He'd rather slit his wrists than join that sordid little band of—'

I froze as I heard tyres on the gravel drive.

'Don't you dare,' breathed Molly, staring at me.

I held her gaze for a moment, then went to the door. I stood for a moment, regarding the paintwork. The doorbell went, I waited a moment longer, then finally opened it.

She was standing on the doorstep, looking as beautiful as ever in a grey, sleeveless Ghost dress, her blonde hair slipping silkily over her shoulders, her pale blue eyes wide, like a baby's. They filled up with tears when they saw me.

'Oh, Livvy! You poor darling!'

I was so glad she hugged me. So glad I could hide my shame in her hair. I was wrong. So wrong. I knew that instantly. But this was what he'd done to me, you see. This was what the love of my life, the ache in my gut, had done. Made me see treachery in childhood friends.

'How are you?' She held me at arm's length and scanned my face anxiously.

'Terrible,' I grinned. 'Despicable too, and nasty with it,

but all the better for seeing you. Come on, come in before Molly and I finish all the wine.'

'Molly's drinking?' she enquired doubtfully.

'Er, well, just a thimble or two.'

'And smoking!' she said, catching Molly hurriedly stubbing out a cigarette.

'My doctor says it's fine,' she said defiantly. 'He says the shock to my heavily addicted, twenty-a-day system would be far greater if I stopped and that one or two is not going to hurt, *plus* a little glass of wine and *plus*, Imo, if *you* were seven months pregnant, flatulent, exhausted, incontinent, and with a one-year-old with a charming habit of projectile vomiting, *you'd* have the odd ciggy too!' Molly got up to kiss her friend. 'How are you anyway, you old bag?' She plonked Henry's bottle in the microwave.

'Well, sorry I spoke, since you ask. But – blimey, it can't be all that bad, surely? I mean, let's face it, millions of women do it every day, don't they? Have babies?' She gave a bright smile, perfectly designed to wind Molly up.

Molly ground her teeth. She and I longed for Imogen to get pregnant. We longed for that perfect size ten figure to swell up to monolithic proportions; for her to scratch and sweat, for her feet to swell, for her tummy button to pop out, and more importantly, for her to suffer the indignities of childbirth. Sadly though, we secretly knew that if Imogen were to get pregnant, she'd just look as though she'd swallowed a doughnut, and that when the time came for the doughnut/baby to be delivered, she'd effortlessly slip the perfect specimen into a gorgeous gynaey's hands, who'd gaze at her with lust and admiration as, pausing only to deposit the babe into the arms of a waiting, uniformed nanny, she shimmied out of his private delivery suite in her size ten jeans, and headed back to the art gallery she ran in

Walton Street for a refreshing spritzer with a client.

She sat down now on the only available seat – which, to her credit, was an upturned milk crate – and somehow managed to make it look like a Conran original. After crossing her elegant legs and flicking back her long, blonde hair, she cleared her throat.

'Livvy darling, I'm afraid I've got something to tell you.'

My heart stopped. I lunged for my glass; spun round to face her like a machine gun. Ah, so this was it, then; my hunch had been right. The serpents slithered back up my throat and I met her eyes challengingly. But Imo's slid away. Imo's eyes never slid like that.

'What?' I whispered.

'He's seeing someone else.'

I nodded. 'I know.'

'You know?' She glanced back at me.

'Yes, he told me.'

'Ah.' She paused for what felt like an eternity. 'And did he tell you who?'

I shook my head. Couldn't speak.

She gave a brief confirmatory nod. 'Her name's Nina Harrison.'

My jaw dropped. 'Nina . . . what? Who? Who the hell's Nina Harrison?'

She shrugged. 'Search me, but I saw them in a restaurant about a month ago. It was round here actually. I came home for Mum's birthday and we took her to that new Italian place on Hollywell Hill. They were in there having supper together.'

'No!' I gaped. 'Why didn't you tell me?'

'Oh sure, come on, Livvy. What – tell your best friend that you've just seen her husband with another woman? And how was I to know it wasn't a colleague from work or something, or even just a brief fling that would be much better you didn't know about?'

'Better I didn't . . .' I was speechless for a moment. 'Well, God,' I blustered finally, 'I think I might have told *you*!'

'Oh, me, maybe, but I'm single with no kids. But think about it, Livvy. Would you have told Molly? Pregnant? With a small baby?'

'Oh, I'd have been highly delighted,' said Molly as she took the bottle from the microwave and handed it to a grabbing Henry. 'I dream of Hugh having a concubine. I'd be very happy with light scullery duties, just so long as she took over in the bedroom and breeding department. Really.' She gave a bright smile and I knew she was trying to lighten the atmosphere.

'So how come you know her name?' I persisted, stunned.

'Looked at her credit card. She paid the bill – which was why I thought it could have been a client or something – and then when the waiter took the saucer away to the counter, I crept to the loo with my pashmina over my face. Saw it as I went past.'

'Did you see her?'

'Not clearly.'

'But?'

She shrugged. 'Small, fairish – not blonde – and pretty, I suppose, but in a very mousy, nondescript sort of way. Nothing special at all, Livvy, and certainly no competition for you.'

She was being kind. Being protective. Dear, sweet Imo, who twice in the space of five minutes I'd cast as a she-devil in my husband's bed, a temptress, a Jezebel. But lovers on the skids have no redress. No dignity either.

'And did Johnny . . .?'

70

'Oh God, no, he didn't see me. I made sure of that. And anyway, they left more or less as soon as we arrived, thank goodness. I was terrified Mum would spot him.'

'Off for a night of spine-shattering sex, no doubt,' I said bitterly.

'She didn't look the spine-shattering type, Liv.'

'They never do,' I said sadly.

I got up and cleared away some glasses. I knew my eyes were filling up, so I ran the taps at the sink and dithered ineffectually with a dishcloth to hide my face.

'Very odd,' murmured Molly to Imogen behind me as she sat Henry on her lap, rubbing his back to wind him. 'I mean, Livvy's right, a tacky affair with a mousy blonde, it's not exactly his style, is it?'

'Hardly,' said Imogen drily, 'and he's always been erudite on the subject of extramarital sex; always been very happy up there on the high moral ground. Well, how the mighty have fallen.'

Down in the sink a plate almost came to pieces in my hands as I wished, not for the first time, that they didn't know quite so much about my husband, about my marriage. I wouldn't dream of making disparaging remarks about their partners, but Johnny, it seemed, was fair game. He was public property, you see, belonged to all of us, always had done, and whilst—

'*Christ!*' Imo shrieked suddenly. I spun round to see her clutching her head, as a stream of yellow liquid splattered on the wall behind her.

'What was that!' she yelled, frozen to her milk crate.

'Projectile vomiting,' muttered Molly, grabbing a dishcloth and hastening past her to mop it up. 'I believe I mentioned it earlier. So sorry, Livvy, your wall. I'll— Oh, Imo, did it get in your hair? Here, I'll—'

'*Not with that!*' screeched Imo, leaping to her feet as Molly brandished a vomit-soaked rag. 'No, really, Mol, he missed,' she breathed. 'I'm fine, truly.' She sat down again shakily, smoothing her hair. 'Jesus, does he always do that?'

'Periodically,' admitted Molly, scrubbing away, 'although he's supposed to have grown out of it. Most babies do at about three months, but not my Henry. He doesn't know when the joke's over. I wouldn't mind betting that in years to come he'll be offering you a gin and tonic and still be taking aim at your highlights.'

Imo shuddered. 'That'll charm the pants off the girls. Let's hope his incontinence clears up by then. Although I have to say,' she smiled smugly, 'whilst I don't know much about children, I don't think you can claim the monopoly on that, Mol. I'm pretty sure all babies are incontinent.'

'Oh, Imo, I'm afraid you misheard,' smiled Molly. 'That's my affliction, not his.'

Imogen looked appalled. 'Molly! God, how *awful*, poor *you*!'

'Yes, poor me. Still lactating with number one, sick as a parrot with number two, and now, thrillingly unpredictable in the waterworks department too, but don't worry, Imo, it only happens when I laugh, and believe me, there's precious little to laugh about in my life at the moment.'

'Evidently,' said Imogen weakly. 'God, remind me to avoid this child-bearing lark. I'll have one in a test tube, or adopt. Yes, that's it, I'll send out for one, like a pizza – except, hang on, now here's one I *would* take home with me. Hello, darling, how's tricks?'

Claudia appeared in the doorway in her nightie.

'Claudes!' I jumped up. 'It's ten o'clock! What's the matter?'

'Couldn't sleep,' she said, fumbling across to the dresser

for her glasses. She put them on. 'But tricks is fine thanks Imo. I like your dress.'

She kissed her godmother, fingering the grey silky material covetously – very much a Du Bray in the clothes department was our Claudia – before going to kiss her other godmother and pick up the baby.

'How come Henry isn't in bed and I am?' she said, crouching down.

'Henry doesn't sleep, darling,' said Molly, ruffling her hair fondly. 'He's a changeling. He doesn't behave like other, normal babies. He's only been put on this earth to vex his mother. He's from the planet Thwart.'

Claudia giggled, then suddenly looked serious. She straightened up, folded her arms. 'She's told you then, has she? About Daddy?'

There was a silence. I hastened across to her anxiously. 'I did actually, darling. Do you mind?'

'Course not,' she said, pushing her dark fringe back impatiently. 'I said you should share it more, not bottle it up.'

'Well, quite,' I agreed nervously. My daughter was ten, going on twenty-four.

'And how do *you* feel about it, my love?' asked Molly gently.

'Oh, I'm OK. Daddy says he'll see me on Sundays and I know from books that he'll feel really guilty about making me a product of a broken home, so I'll probably get loads of treats and things, and trips to Thorpe Park, which'll be cool. I won't get spoilt, though. Susan, in *The Chalet School* adventures hasn't got a father, but she's not spoilt 'cos her mother's strict but fair, so I expect I'll be the same.' She nodded firmly.

'Good, good,' said Molly faintly.

'And, anyway, it'll all come right in the end. Something good will come out of it, I'll be bound.'

'I'll be—' Molly turned wide eyes on me.

'Angela Brazil,' I muttered. 'She found all my old books.'

'Ah.'

'And Mummy should get out more,' Claudia said firmly. 'Don't you think?' She rounded on her godmothers.

'Oh yes, absolutely,' they chorused quickly.

'Mrs Parker, Clarissa's mother in *The Faraway Island*, was devastated when Mr Parker went off to America, but she busied herself, and lo and behold, he came back!'

'So – how do you suggest I busy myself, my darling? Bustling round the kitchen baking scones? A bit of embroidery, perhaps? Then lo and behold—'

'Oh no,' she interrupted scathingly, 'those are just meaningless chores invented for the enslavement of women. No, I thought you could go to the pub with the builders.'

I gulped at this child of mine.

'Why not?' she insisted. 'They go out every single night to the Fox and Ferret before picking up their curries. Well, you could go with them, Mum, get a curry too. You like curries.'

'And some tinnies too, perhaps?' murmured Imo.

'Good idea. And then when Dad comes over to pick me up, you could be down in the caravan, watching telly with them. It's tactics, Mum. I saw it on *EastEnders*. Bianca did it to Ricky. You've got to get Dad to wake up a bit, make him jealous!'

'Right, darling.' I nodded. Tactics. From a ten-year-old girl, drawing on an eclectic mixture of fifties boarding school books and contemporary soaps.

'And you've got to find yourself, too,' she declared importantly.

I sighed. 'Even if did, my love, I'm not sure I'd recognise her.'

'Oh, don't be so wet,' she retorted. 'It's just a case of getting out and about. I mean, Nanette's *always* asking you over.'

'Oh God, not Nanette, Claudes.'

'Who's Nanette?' pounced Molly.

'She lives in The Crescent,' said Claudia, turning to her. 'She's always having things called fork suppers with men in blazers called Clive, and Mum never goes.'

'I think you get the picture,' I muttered drily, clearing the glasses.

'Sounds rather fun,' grinned Molly maliciously. 'Where exactly does this Nanette hail from?' She got up and peered out of the window, knowing that, such was the nature of The Crescent, most houses could be clearly seen.

'There, over there on the end.' Claudia joined her, pointing eagerly at a lighted window with frilly Austrian blinds. As I joined them, to my horror we saw a hand wave back.

'Oh God, she's *seen* you, Claudes. She thinks you're *waving*!'

'Well, that's OK.'

'And now she's disappeared! She's probably coming over!'

'Well, fine, that's fine. She can have a drink. I like her, Mum.'

'And I do too, darling. She's very kind, but—' I spotted her garden gate opening. 'Oh no, she *is* coming over – hide!' I dived down under the table. 'Tell her I'm out,' I muttered, face pressed down into the rush matting.

'Mummy, that's silly. She'll *know* you're here; your friends are here, for heaven's sake. Of *course* you can't hide.'

'I think Claudia has a point, Livvy,' said Imogen. 'And anyway,' she paused, lifting the curtain again and peering out of the window, 'if Nanette looks anything like Cruella de Vil I'm afraid it's too late.'

There was a familiar crunch of gravel, then 'Coo-ee!' – and a rap of jewelled knuckles at the door. Claudia flew to open it, and two seconds later in came Nanette, just as I was crawling out.

'Olivia! Goodness, you're always crawling around under that table! Every time I pop by you seem to be down there looking for something!'

'Dropped my lipstick this time,' I muttered, since make-up was the first thing that came to mind as I looked at her face. Blimey, she always wore the works, but tonight it looked as if she'd applied it with an industrial high-pressure hose. Mid-fortyish and resplendent in a tight cerise sweater which had a sequinned bird of prey lurking ominously over one shoulder, skin-tight white pedal pushers and high pink mules, she also had lipstick all over her teeth when she grinned.

'Nanette, it's lovely to see you,' I lied as I scrambled up. 'Um, come in and sit down. We were just having a drink. This is Molly Piper, by the way, and Imogen Mitchell, my best friends.'

'Oh, *really*?' Nanette looked enchanted, especially by Imogen, and extended a bony, suntanned hand. 'Gosh, and what a shame, I'd *love* a little drinky but I can't stop, I'm afraid. I'm just on my way out to my evening class. It's my sexual awareness and crochet group tonight, you see, but I've heard *so* much about you both,' she lied, 'and I'm thrilled to meet you at last!'

'You too,' murmured Molly and Imogen, looking totally fascinated and agog at this vision.

'But what I *have* brought,' Nanette went on, brandishing a leather-bound book, 'is my diary, and I intend to pin you down once and for all, Olivia! *So* sad about all this ghastly business,' she murmured *sotto voce*, turning to Imogen and Molly, for all the world as if I wasn't there. 'Of course she's told you . . .? Well, of course she has and, actually, I'm afraid everyone knows. Half the county's talking about it – but don't you think she should get out more? Show that randy old so-and-so— Oops,' her hand went to her mouth, ''scuse my French, Claudia. You know how I adore Daddy really – show him just who's boss around here?'

'I'll get Mummy's diary!' chirruped Claudia happily, as my friends nodded mutely at her. 'Here!' She grabbed it off the dresser and handed it to Nanette.

Two heads then bent low together, as my daughter and my neighbour compared, conspired and pencilled in, with Molly and Imogen – less wide-eyed now, and more highly amused – exchanging mouth-twitching, eyebrow-raised glances.

As I scrubbed a plate savagely in the sink, I found myself turning, and looking with new-found hatred at Nanette's jet-black hair. So. She adored 'randy Daddy', eh? So perhaps it was her? Yes, why not? She was local, they'd been seen together in a local restaurant, she was probably a sex maniac, so yes, perhaps it was Nanette that Imogen had seen, in a blonde wig? Nanette – Nina – of course. My eyes flew to the breadknife on the side. I could plunge it into her back right now, just as she bent over the diary, watch the blood spurt out, see the horror on my friends' and my daughter's faces. I frowned. Would they instantly call the police? Where exactly would their loyalties lie? As I gazed at her, wondering what the devil I'd do with the corpse – freezer perhaps? Compost heap? – I suddenly came to. I shuddered and turned back to the sink. God, I was a low form of life, wasn't I? Capable of anything at the moment. And, of course, this was a form of madness, I thought miserably. I suspected anyone and everyone, including my kind neighbour, who wasn't my type – or Johnny's either come to that – but who was only trying to help, and had simply come over to invite me to supper. Nanette snapped her diary shut, satisfied.

'Friday next week then. Nothing too formal, more of a smart but casual affair, six or maybe eight of us in all, and I'll make sure you're suitably paired off, Olivia.' She tapped her pencil on her diary and narrowed her eyes thoughtfully. 'Ye-s, I'll probably do something fairly simple, a salmon en croute perhaps, with a choice of desserts – tirimasu, banoffi pie, that sort of thing – oh, and I'll probably be wearing my beige suede suit, Olivia – you know, my Gucci.' She shot Imogen a quick look to tell her she knew her labels. 'So maybe something like your silk palazzo pants? With a new sweater? I gather Romano's in Radlett have got a sale on at the moment, maybe we could—'

'Thank you, Nanette,' I interrupted weakly, 'that would be lovely, and don't worry, I'll sort myself out, sartorially speaking.'

'Super,' she beamed, 'and I'll make sure the guest list is suitably yummy, particularly *à l'autre côté à toi*!' Nanette had somehow discovered our French ancestry and had a disconcerting habit of breaking into Franglais at a moment's notice. Imogen and Molly were looking more and more enchanted.

'So! *A bientôt, mes chéries*, and don't forget, Olivia, Friday the ninth, eight for eight fifteen, canapés on the patio, Kir Royales in the conservatory, be there or be square! Toodle-oo!' And with that she bustled out backwards with a dinky little wave.

'Toodle-*oo*!' chorused my friends and daughter joyfully.

The moment the front door closed behind Nanette I chucked a plate in the water, strode to the counter, seized the breadknife, raised it high above my head, and with a blood curdling screech of 'HYAA-AACK!' plunged it straight into the heart of a granary loaf.

'Traitors!' I bellowed. 'The lot of you!'

'Oh, Mum, it'll be fun!' insisted Claudia, giggling.

'Of course it will,' gasped Imogen, wiping her eyes. 'It'll be brimming over with gorgeous Clives, and possibly a few Nigels too. You'll love it!'

I thought back to when we were at school, scanned the rows of desks, searching for the girl I wanted: frizzy-haired, cunning-eyed, mean-spirited, never sharing her sweets, let alone her homework, very smelly feet. 'I would rather,' I said carefully, 'spend an entire weekend in Brenda Archdale's company, massaging her toes with my teeth, than endure the evening that is about to befall me.'

'Oh God, really?' Molly looked suitably shocked for a moment. Then she caught Imogen's eye and they both dissolved into giggles. They clutched each other for a moment, until abruptly Molly froze. Her eyes bulged.

'Oh *God*!' She squeaked, snapping her legs together. 'Help!'

'Serves you bloody well right,' I said callously as I reached into Henry's changing bag and chucked her a nappy. 'Here, try this on for size.'

Chapter Five

A few days later I was lying in bed mulling it over. Nina. *Nina*, for God's sake. Who on earth was called Nina these days? It sounded so pre-war, like she wore a cardy and slippers, or sold smellies in Boots, or even – yes, that's it – maybe she was foreign? Nina Mouskouri – no, no that was Nana – or, OK, Nina Simone? Oh God, I couldn't compete with that, I thought hastily, some dark, exotic, dusky maiden. No, far better she was the cardy type. Or could it be an aristocratic name perhaps? I wondered, with a jolt. Wasn't one of the Mitford sisters called something like— No. No, that was Nancy. I sighed and turned over, bunching up the pillow – then stared. Claudia was beside me, feigning sleep, eyelids flickering. I groaned.

'Oh darling, you said you'd try not to *do* this any more.'

'I know, but I couldn't sleep. And anyway, Daddy's not here, so there's plenty of room.'

Well, there was no arguing with that. The sun was also streaming persistently through the curtains now, so I turned back and seized the clock, peering myopically at it. Twenty to eight.

'Claudia! It's twenty to eight!' I shot up like a rocket.

'I know.'

'Well, don't say I know, flaming well get a move on!

You'll be late for school – again!'

She rolled out of bed, pulling the duvet with her, and dragged herself to her bedroom. 'That, Mother dear, was precisely the idea,' she muttered sardonically.

I flew around the room looking for clothes, desperate for a shower but knowing there wasn't time, listening to Claudia slowly opening drawers and dragging her feet. Hardly the sounds of frenzied activity.

'Claudia, come *on*!'

'I *am*!'

I sat down abruptly on the bed feeling a bit of head rush. I held my fingers to my temples. Oh God, I shouldn't have yelled like that so early in the morning. It always made me feel nauseous. And anyway, so what if we were late, just for once? Sometimes Claudia had a point. I flopped back on the bed. She was so like me in so many ways, and so unlike me in others. Aesthetically speaking, it was plain to see we were a mother-and-daughter act: skinny-framed, beaky-nosed and wide-eyed – which, together with pebble glasses and an unusual dental arrangement, was not a combination Claudia enjoyed at ten years old – but, as I kept assuring her, she'd grow into her looks, as I had done.

'What, and end up looking like you?'

'Is that so terrible?'

'No, but it's just a bit boring to already know what I'm going to look like in twenty years' time.'

This was classic Claudia. Not exactly bored with life, but resigned to it, slightly world-weary. She excelled at school academically, but didn't find it particularly stimulating, so almost as if to compensate, in a minor way, she'd recently become something of a troublemaker. She avoided all games and sports citing her asthma – although these days that was rare – she cheeked the younger teachers – taking care not to tangle with the battle-axes – and wore her skirt hiked up at a ridiculous angle, socks well down, tie in her pocket along with her chewing gum. On one ghastly occasion recently, she'd even been caught stealing a comic from Smiths, whilst ostensibly on a school trip.

'I can't believe she did that!' I'd shrieked down the phone to Molly.

'Why not? We've all done it.'

'We have?' I'd gasped.

'Of course. Remember the make-up counter in Boots? Max Factor lipsticks? Those quiet afternoons of jiggery-pokery on the way home from school?'

'No! Not me. That was always you and Imo.'

'Ah, perhaps.'

'And you were at least fourteen!'

'So she's precocious. Relax, Livvy, it's nothing outrageous. She's just showing a healthy lack of respect for authority. Just ground her for a few days.'

'How can I ground her when she's not allowed out yet!' I'd shrieked.

Nothing outrageous, I'd thought, putting down the phone, but all the same, all acts of rebellion that I, at ten, would have been horrified by. Mine had always been a timorous spirit, eager to please, careful not to offend, yet Claudia seemed unable to pledge allegiance to any values that conflicted with her own. I grudgingly admired her for this, knowing full well from whence it came. She got her looks from me and her balls from Johnny.

The one time Johnny and I had really seen her shine, and revelled in the reflected glory, was when she took the lead as Alice in Wonderland in the school play. She'd left the rest of the cast standing, and when we'd congratulated her afterwards – full of pride as so many parents patted her on the back, then whisking her away to the hamburger joint of her choice by way of celebration – she'd confided that the reason she'd loved it so much was because she could pretend to be someone else. This had filled me with dread.

'But what's so wrong with being Claudia McFarllen?'

'Oh, nothing,' she'd said coolly, sipping her milk shake. 'But it's just nice to get away from her once in a while.'

Being a normal, angst-ridden, middle-class mother, of course I'd been sent into a flat spin by this, and for one mad moment I'd almost felt compelled to whisk her off to a child psychologist, such was the contemporary vogue for these people, but Johnny had been appalled.

'Christ Almighty, the one time she gets a buzz out of something and you want her psychoanalysed! Relax, Livvy.'

Relax, Livvy, relax, I thought, heaving myself off the bed and dragging myself, like some rough beast, over to my dressing table. I sat down heavily. That was a word I'd come to hear a lot of over the years. I peered blearily at my reflection in the mirror and sighed. The hair badly needed a cut so I tucked some of it behind my ears, then peered again, hoping perhaps for a miraculous transformation, blinking out through the fringe. On a good day, adjectives like 'elfin' or 'principle boy' came to mind, and on a bad day, 'Oxfam' or 'hermaphrodite'. Today was a bad one. I reached for my nail scissors and had a go at the fringe. Lop-sided, of course. I switched hands and attacked from the other side, ending up looking like Julius Caesar. God, just give me a laurel wreath. I sighed and went to the window.

At the far end of the garden I could see movement in the caravan. The door opened and Alf came out. I watched his listing movement across the grass, large and lumbering in his blue overalls, bound, no doubt, for the Portaloo and a few quiet moments with the *Sun*. The Portaloo had arrived with the caravan, and was sent from heaven, as far as I was concerned. So outrageous had been the pong in mine on one occasion that I'd been forced to race, clenched buttocked, round to Nanette's, banging on the door to use hers.

Alf was soon followed by Mac, coming down the caravan steps and looking critically up at the sky. Far too blue for his liking – what they needed was some rain to curdle the cement, to make bricklaying out of the question, to ensure that they could huddle under the blue tarpaulin and smoke and drink tea for a bit. Finally, came Spiro, woolly-hatted even in a heat wave, dark eyes peering into the sun, and naturally, clutching his Wotsits. Despite a monumental fry up in the caravan every morning, Wotsits were essential to get these boys through the next half-hour, together, of course, with their mobile phones. These wonders of modern technology were never out of their hands, and they could quite easily plaster a chimney breast with one hand and talk to her indoors with the other: Spiro to her in Greece, Mac to his third wife, and Alf to his first, with whom he'd notched up twenty years' hard labour. Her name was Vi and she was a legend in her own front room, according to Mac; a shrew of the first order, who nagged Alf 'something rotten' and bent his ear at the slightest opportunity.

As Alf came out of the loo now, his phone went. Vi, of course. My bedroom window was open and I could hear him as he approached the kitchen.

'Orright, luv, the lean-to, yeah, I'll sort it . . . Yeah, I know, it's a mess . . . OK, it's a buggerin' mess . . . Yeah, I will, I'll do it on Sunday . . . Orright, Saturday, yeah . . . As soon as I get home, yeah. Love you. Bye.'

Harangued but devoted, you see. Perhaps that's where

I'd gone wrong? I'd noticed recently, as I analysed marriages, that women who harangued and nagged on a permanent basis generally had very well-behaved husbands. I looked at mine as he grinned out at me now from our wedding photo on my dressing table. Bloody photos were everywhere, I thought, glaring at it. Every flaming room I went into, there he was, leering at me again. I should have smashed the lot of them, of course, especially after yesterday. I leant my elbows on the table, put my head in my hands and groaned.

Oh God, yesterday had been awful. The first Sunday Johnny had been over to pick Claudia up, and the first of many, no doubt. I, of course, in a frenzy of anticipation, had spent the two hours before his estimated time of arrival prowling the house, disastrously picking a spot on my chin, checking my hair repeatedly in the mirror, and wondering how the hell I was going to play this. What exactly was the estranged wife form? Should I ask him in? Should I give him a cup of tea, or should I simply open the front door and punch his lights out? And I'm ashamed to say I considered my wardrobe very carefully, too. Casual, of course, so shorts, since it was ninety degrees in the shade and my legs were brown, but teamed with a skinny white T-shirt and a rather snazzy little denim jacket I'd found in River Island, which was probably a bit young for me but looked terrific. My freshly washed hair was blown casually just so, I added a hint of lipstick, a slick of mascara – how the hell was he going to resist me? Unfortunately, though, when the big moment came and as I heard his car arrive in the front drive, I was having a nervous evacuation in the downstairs loo, and as I charged out, zipping up my shorts, I realised I'd left the crucial denim jacket in the garden. Claudia began to clump downstairs.

'Don't go without saying goodbye!' I shrieked. 'I'm just getting my jacket!'

Out into the garden I raced, down to the deckchair under the spreading cedar, seized the jacket, wriggled into it when – damn.

'Hulloa, Mrs McFarllen!' Mr Jones, my next-door neighbour, very Welsh, a highly competitive gardener – very into his leeks and radishes – and always with a roguish twinkle in his eye, stuck his head over the garden wall.

'Oh – morning, Mr Jones. I'm sorry I can't stop now, I'm—'

'Ooa, I woan't take up much of yewer time, like, but I just wanted to say how sorry I am, reely reely sorry. Only Gwyneth told me, see, told me last night about yewer terrible predicament!' He twiddled his moustache nervously, gazed abstractedly at my bosom.

'Ah.' I hovered. 'Right. Thank you, Mr Jones.'

'Wha' a thing to happen, eh? Wha' a shock! Terrible. Terrible! You must be devastated, like!'

'Well, yes, quite upset, but bearing up, thank you, under the circumstances.' I glanced nervously through the French windows to see that Claudia was already opening the front door. I tried to inch away.

'Ooa, yes, I dare say yewer are, like, an' I was sayin' to Gwyneth oanly last night, yewer a bewetiful young girl, feisty too, and yew'll bounce right back like nobody's business, but even soa, 's not easy, is it? Soa I was wondering, like,' he reached down behind the wall and picked something up, twinkling at me the while, 'could yew use one of these?' With a sudden flourish he produced a cucumber.

I gaped at it. Blinked. Finally found my voice. '*Sorry*, Mr Jones?'

'Only I've got soa many, I don't know what to do with them, see!'

'Well, I'm not sure *I'd* know what to do with it!' I spluttered.

'And when Gwyneth told me about that rat getting into yewer greenhouse and destroying all of yewers, and all those luverly tomato plants with it, I thought oo *noa* – and I went straight out into the garden to pick yew the biggest one I could find!'

'Oh!' I breathed. 'Oh, yes!'

'And here it is!' He beamed. 'Must be about two foot long, see, and thick with it! Feel that, girl!'

'Yes, yes, I do see. Gosh, how marvellous!'

Out of the corner of my eye I noticed that Claudia was grabbing a jacket from the banisters, picking up her duffel bag. She turned and spotted me in the garden. 'Bye, Mum!' She waved.

'So I said to Gwyneth, I said I'll give her this one, Gwyn, and—'

Suddenly I lunged across the wall and seized it from his arms. Short of decapitating him, it was the only way to shut him up. 'Yes, thank you, Mr Jones,' I gasped, 'thank you so much!' And with that I beetled back to the house, running as fast as my legs would carry me.

'Are you off?' I managed to gasp, racing through the French doors and into the hall – just as the front door was closing. To my relief it opened again.

'Yes, well, Dad's here so I—' She stopped. They both stared at me in astonishment, Johnny looking blond and tanned and lovely in old shorts, deck shoes, and a blue sailing shirt that matched his eyes.

'What's that?' Claudia gaped.

I glanced down, panting. 'This? Oh, this! A cucumber, of course.'

'Yes, but it's huge. And so fat!'

'Yes, isn't it?' I grinned maniacally.

Bloody thing, what could I do with it? I cast around desperately. The last thing I'd envisaged when greeting my estranged husband at the door was to be found panting hard and clutching an outsized cucumber. Finally I flung it on the floor behind me. They both looked startled as it rolled about.

'And whose jacket is that?' persisted Claudia.

'Hmm? Oh, it's mine.'

'I've never seen you in that before. Is it new?'

'What – this old thing?' I laughed. 'No, darling, I've had it for ages!'

'Blimey, you must have done. Either that or you had a complete rush of blood to the head in the high street! That's real teen gear, Mum. Looks like something out of River Island!'

Sometimes I just wanted to kill my daughter. I ignored her and turned to Johnny. 'So. Where are you off to then?' Smoothly, I hoped, with a hint of a cynical smile.

'Oh, London.'

'Ah.' Narrows it down. Was it rude to ask where, exactly? I hesitated. 'Well. Have a good time then!'

'Will do.'

'Bye, my darling – Claudia!' I added quickly, just in case Johnny thought I meant him.

'Bye, Mum.'

I went to shut the door behind them, my head spinning. God – two hours of bathing and hairwashing and make-up and wondering what to say – just for that? For that

two-second interview with my husband at the front door? I
hesitated. Should I walk them to the car, perhaps? Or
maybe, yes, maybe just down to the gate? Hell, I'd see any
other visitor off the premises, wouldn't I. Why not?

I tossed back my head, smiled broadly, and strolled out
after them into the sunshine. Whistling. Which I never do.
They turned round in surprise.

'Have fun!'

'We will,' said Claudia, cautiously.

On I strolled, shoving my hands into my tiny, waist-high
denim pockets, which was a mistake, because when I
tripped over a protruding paving stone, I couldn't get my
hands out in time.

'Ooomph!'

They turned to see me sprawled on the ground, nose in
the gravel.

'Mum! Are you all right?' Claudia started back.

'Fine!' I gasped. 'Fine, darling. On you go!' Bugger.
Also shitsville.

As I got up, gasping, winded, picking gravel out of my
nostrils, I was in time to see them get in the car and to hear
Johnny mutter *sotto voce*, 'Is your mother all right?' I'm
quite sure he wasn't referring to my fall.

Claudia shrugged noncommittally, and off they went. I,
meanwhile, gave a bright, cheery wave, a demonic little
smile, and went sailing back into the house. Once inside I
slammed the front door, seized the cucumber and slammed
it viciously against the wall, smashing the living daylights
out of it until I'd reduced it to a green pulp. Finally I
dropped the shattered remains.

'I'm your wife, damn you!' I screamed at it.

As I raised my head from my hands at the dressing table

now, my eyes went back to the photo. I could swear he was laughing at me. Then they caught the clock.

'*Claudia!*'

I jumped up and raced across the landing to her bedroom. 'Claudia, will you hurry up and get downstairs! We're going to be— Oh, for God's sake!'

Claudia was tucked up in bed again, open-mouthed, thumb just adrift, and sleeping like a baby.

We finally swung into the school gates three-quarters of an hour late, with Claudia insisting she was going to claim a doctor's appointment and that I should write a note to that effect.

'But that's a bare-faced lie, Claudia. I'm not doing that!'

'Oh Mummy, you're such a goody-goody. Everyone else does.'

'I don't care what everyone else does, we are not "everyone else".' My God, did I sound like my mother or what? 'And I will not have you being mendacious. No, we will simply say that we got held up by the builders.'

'But that's a lie.'

I screeched to a halt in the car park.

'Claudia,' I snarled, 'would you kindly stop splitting hairs and remember that I am the mother and you are the ten-year-old girl!'

I got out and slammed the door behind me, then raced round the back to the boot where, puffing and blowing, I lugged out her games bag, her lacrosse stick, her flute, her gym kit, her swimming bag, and all the other energetic paraphernalia that she regarded with such cynical detachment and refused to use. As Claudia yawned and leant against the car, I threw it all on to my back and, like a trusty old packhorse, made off, puffing away across the playing field, with my daughter, shuffling along behind me, hands deep in her pockets. Through a chink in the hall curtains I could see that assembly was still in full swing and, yes, 'Lord of the Dance' was wafting towards us on the air waves. With any luck she could sneak in at the back.

'Go on,' I whispered, giving her a little push. 'I'll put your stuff in your locker and you creep in. If anyone asks, say you've been here for ages, went to the loo or something.'

Claudia opened her eyes wide. 'Mum – *another* bare-faced lie!'

I ground my teeth. 'Claudia McFarllen, one of these days—'

'OK, OK, I'm going!' She reached up, gave me a quick, disarming peck on the cheek then, grinning widely, saun-tered off, no doubt pushing her socks down and hiking her skirt up en route to the hall, if indeed she was even *going* to the hall. I sighed and watched her go. Smart kid that.

As I trudged off to the locker room to dump her stuff, I went past the nursery school. Outside the window I saw a mother I knew, Sarah, struggling with a screaming baby. She had him hoisted up on her hip and was trying to quieten him as she peered through the nursery window at her four-year-old. She had a daughter in Claudia's class too, and I'd often watched her with her brood and thought – by rights, that should be me. Ten, four, and nine months, three children and a busy home to run. I'd watched with envy, as I'd watched other mothers too, unloading young children out of Discoveries and into buggies, tucking a little one under an arm. And I always counted.

'Is he OK?' I asked, coming up beside her and peering through the window.

'Oh, hi, Olivia. No he's not – look.' She jabbed her finger at a screaming four-year-old, his fists clenched, red in the face from sobbing, on the other side of the glass.

'They've got a new teacher this term. Miss Pinter's retired, and the new one's really sweet, but it takes Ned ages to settle with anyone new.'

'Plus he knows you're out here,' I pointed out.

'Yes, but if I just leave him I'll feel terrible.'

Ned was opening his lungs and giving the performance of his life now.

'I'll tell you what. I've still got to dump Claudia's stuff. Why don't you sit in the car and when I come back past, I'll tell you if he's OK? I bet you anything he's calmed down.'

'Oh, would you? Only this one's dying for a feed so I could give him a bottle in the car.'

'I'll see you there in a minute.'

She scurried off gratefully to her car and I wandered off to find Claudia's locker in the changing rooms. A smelly cacophony of gym shoes, sweaty socks and verrucas met my nostrils, and memories of Imo, Molly and me came flooding back. Imogen, of course, had been captain of everything, I'd tried hard but had been terminally useless, and Molly had just skived as much as possible. We'd learnt to smoke in changing rooms like these too, and I wondered how many years it would be until Claudia was hugging a radiator and executing perfect smoke rings with her Ten Number Six or – excuse me – Silk Cut Extra. Probably only about six months, the rate she was going.

As I came back out, I went down the internal corridor to get a better look at young Ned Parker through the double glass doors. Sure enough, there he was, dry-eyed, not a care in the world, busy revving up a tractor and going 'Vrrooooom!' as he ran it up and down a small girl's leg. I smiled, remembering Claudia's nursery days in London.

My God, she'd had to be dragged screaming and kicking, had clung like a sobbing barnacle, had had to be prised off with no anaesthetic, but the moment my back was turned, had apparently cut the crap and slipped off to single-handedly commandeer the pedal car from the big boys. I gave Ned one last glance and was about to move on, when the sign on the classroom door caught my eye. I stared. Miss Harrison. I stared some more. I went hot, and then very cold.

My eyes came up from the sign. I gazed through the glass. An elderly woman looked up from the pasting table where she was helping a child do something seasonal with dandelion clocks and a Pritt Stick. She smiled at me. I knew her; she was one of the assistants, Mrs Hooper – she'd been there for ever.

'Can I help?' she mouthed.

My eyes flashed around the room like a Colditz search-light. The new teacher wasn't visible. She could be in the plastic house, of course, or maybe helping a child go to the loo. Mrs Hooper came bustling towards me, but just before she reached me, I turned and shot off before she could open the door. I ran, panting, gasping, all the way down to the car park. Sarah, sitting in her car, saw me through her wind-screen. She saw my face and clutching her baby, shot out of the front seat, hand to mouth.

'Oh my God – what's happened! Is he all right?'

'He's fine, Ned's fine,' I gasped, clutching the top of her open door. 'Sarah – the new teacher in there, Miss Harrison, is it?'

'Yes, why?'

'Have you met her?'

'Yes, of course.'

'Have you any idea what her first name is?'

'Her first name?' She screwed up her face and thought for a moment. 'Oh God, yes I do know, because one of the other mothers told me . . . something funny. Something very old-fashioned and . . . let me see now . . . Nina! That's it, Nina Harrison.'

Chapter Six

'She's a bloody teacher at her bloody *school*!'

'Terrible, terrible. Here, have an aspirin.'

'I mean, what am I supposed to do, walk past her classroom every morning and say, good morning, Miss Harrison, and how was my husband's performance last night? It's out*rageous*!' I bellowed.

'Course it is. Here, a nice cup of tea.'

Mac handed me the cup while Alf stirred some sugar in. Spiro was bustling around my feet with a stool. 'Up, up,' he muttered, lifting my legs, 'then the blood go straight to the brain.'

'Spiro, there's enough blood storming round my brain at the moment to float an Armada,' I hissed. 'If I have any more I'll bloody haemorrhage!'

Nevertheless, I succumbed to having a stool positioned just so under my feet, then leant my head back and gazed around in a dazed fashion. I appeared to have collapsed in the sitting room and I stared bleakly at it now with its half-stripped walls, ripped-up floorboards, broken windows and, in the foreground, a slightly blurred vision of my workforce, my three burly men, standing over me clutching aspirins and mugs of tea, faces full of concern. I groaned.

'She look pale,' murmured Spiro, peering in.

I stared blankly at him. 'She'll have to be sacked!' I snapped.

He jumped back.

'Of course she will,' soothed Mac.

'The head won't stand for that. What, having an affair with one of the pupil's fathers? *Hah!* No, no, she'll have to go!'

'Hang her!' spat Spiro. 'Or dip her,' he added brightly, 'like they used to do to witches on the island where I come from.'

'You're right, Spiro,' I sat up. 'She *is* a witch. A conniving, insidious, poisonous—' I clutched my mouth. 'Oh, my poor Claudia! My little girl! Imagine the shame, the humiliation – ooooh . . . my poor baby!'

'I go,' said Spiro, turning. 'I go now and keel the beetch!' He shook his fist.

'No, no, Spiro.' I put a restraining hand on his arm. 'You're sweet but, actually, we can't kill her. We can just render her unemployed.'

Mac sucked his teeth dubiously. 'Yeah, well, if you *can*, like, luv. Only it ain't so easy to shift workforce these days, and I should know. They've got written conditions, see, employment rights.'

'*Rights!*' I screeched. 'How can she talk about rights? What right does she have to be shagging my husband? And then, goddamit, to go and teach innocent children! God in heaven – one minute she's pirouetting naked around a bedroom, licking honey off my husband's buttocks, and the next thing we know she's singing "Incy Wincy Spider" to four-year-olds! It's scandalous! No one in their right *mind* would allow it!'

'Of course not, of course not. Head back,' soothed Mac. I obediently crashed my head back on to the chair in fury and

Mac began to massage my shoulders in a very businesslike manner. 'You're very tense, you see, very tense indeed. This is what you need, now relax.'

'He very good,' confided Spiro in my ear. 'I had one. I went bye-byes.'

'I wouldn't mind going bye-byes for bleeding ever,' I muttered grimly as Mac attacked my shoulders.

'Give her the tea now, Spiro,' Mac ordered, pummelling away like billyo.

Spiro obediently put it to my lips like a baby, not letting me hold the handle. 'I do it,' he muttered fiercely. 'I do it for you. Now, more aspirin.' He took one from Alf's hand and popped it in my mouth like a Smartie.

This is surreal, I thought as I crunched away maniacally. Here I am, in this chaos of a building site, collapsing in a pathetic heap, whilst one of my builders pats my feet, another massages my shoulders and another administers the drugs. Jesus! I've lost it, I've totally lost it. I shut my eyes tight. But a teacher. A bloody *teacher*! My eyes snapped open suddenly, like searchlights. So how the hell had he met her then? At a parents' evening or something? Sidled up to her after the school concert and given her the eye? But Sarah had said she was new . . . yes, of course, and I'd never seen her before either. My brain went scurrying into over-drive. Right – so he must have met her just after we moved here – about six months ago – that way the timing made sense. But, good grief, a nursery school teacher? That didn't make sense at all! Because despite the terrible name, I'd secretly had her down as a glamorous investment banker, shooting him hot looks across the dealing-room floor, flicking her ash-blonde hair back over her Armani suit, brushing behind him as he sat at his screen, wafting Chanel up his nostrils. In my worst nightmares I'd even seen her driving him back to her Chelsea pad in her Porsche, peeling off her silk underwear to reveal a seamless tan, slipping seductively between her designer sheets, an aristocratic filly who probably wore her tiara in bed and whinnied at the moment critique, and all the time – all the time she really *was* just a bit of a Nina! I shut my eyes and groaned.

Simultaneously, in my left ear I heard, 'What d'you fink then?' in an anxious undertone. 'Only I got money on it.'

I opened one eye. 'Money on what, Alf?'

Mac, still at my shoulders, cleared his throat. 'Well, Alf was just wondering, like, since we're here an' that, if we could just turn the telly on for a minute an' have a butchers at the 11.40 from Newmarket. Only we've had a little flutter.'

'What?' I peered around as three, expectant faces gazed down at me. I sighed. 'Oh, fine, fine, yes, go on,' I said weakly. 'God, I may as well lose total control here.'

Mac gave Alf an economic nod and Alf instantly flicked the switch. Alf then settled at my feet, Spiro crouched down close beside me – clearly not wanting to leave my side – and then kindly slipped me a bag of Wotsits. I gazed at them blankly in my lap. He sighed, opened the packet, took one out and popped it in my mouth. I munched listlessly, watching blankly as the horses raced out of their starter gates.

'Come on, my darling,' Mac breathed ecstatically in my ear, still massaging furiously, which was a bit disconcerting. I shifted uncomfortably in my seat. 'Come on, my gorgeous . . . my gorgeous . . . little . . . beauty!'

'Who are we on?' I muttered.

'Creamy Carmel,' he said, 'and she goes like a tiger.'

'Bully for her.'

At length there was a collective groan. 'Well, she did last

week, anyway,' said Mac, matter-of-factly. 'Put the kettle on, Alf.'

I was vaguely aware that not a lot of work was being done around here, but Mac's fingers had gone into overdrive and I appeared to be glued to my seat, paralysed, eyes shutting and head nodding, totally unable to take command. After a bit Mac spoke.

'I bin meaning to talk to you about that kitchen.'

'Oh yes,' I mumbled. Kitchen. Good. We could call this a site meeting.

'Yeah, it's about them cupboards.'

'Mmm, yes,' I muttered. 'There does seem to be a curious lack of cupboards, Mac, and you did say—'

'I know, I said I'd make them for you, nice and farm-housey, like, stressed pine.'

'Distressed, I believe, but give them ten minutes in this house and they'll be stressed too.'

'Whatever. Anyway, the fing is there's a lot of them buggers to make, more than I originally fought, and I reckon I'm gonna need more labour.'

'Oh?'

'Yeah,' he sighed. 'I mean what wiv Spiro on bricklayin' and Alf on concrete, I can't do all the joinery meself, so I was thinking of bringing in my Lance.'

'Your lance?' I frowned. Jousting came to mind. Wimples and knights. 'Would that help?' I muttered help-lessly as visions of Mac, galloping round the kitchen spearing cupboards into place, sprang to mind.

'Yeah, my boy Lance – he's my eldest, like. He's a chippy by trade, like me.'

'Ah.' Yes, well that cleared something up. I'd been wondering what Mac was.

'He'll be down here by the end of the week and then

we'll get cracking on them cabinets straight away, orright?'

I gulped nervously. 'Yes but, heavens Mac – four labourers!'

'Now don't you go worrying your head about the money, luv,' he soothed, kneading away furiously now. 'I'm doin' you a nice little package deal here, bein' as how you're in straitened circumstances an' that. Never let it be said that Mac Turner would squeeze money out of an abandoned woman!'

'Ah, so Lance is free?' I asked hopefully.

'Nooo,' he said cautiously, 'not exactly, but he'll be doin' it for half whack, orright? An' he'll be staying in the caravan too, so there's no need to worry 'bout accommodation.'

'Well, I hardly thought he was staying with me!'

'And that way we'll have that kitchen of yours sorted in no time. There.' He gave my shoulders a final slap. 'You're done, luv. Ready for anything now, and if you don't mind my sayin', what I suggest you do – now that you're nice and relaxed – is get down to that school double quick and give them merry hell. If you look sharp and get your skates on you could bend that headmaster's ear in his lunch hour.'

I sat up and glanced at the clock. Gosh. Yes. He was right. If I went now I might just catch old Michael Harty before lessons started. And, how peculiar – I shook my head – I really did feel better – I got unsteadily to my feet – if a bit woozy. I wondered if that really was aspirin Spiro had been slipping me, or valium perhaps. I staggered a bit and then lunged for my handbag. Blimey, anyone would think I was drunk. My audience watched my performance politely and I noticed that nobody seemed to be getting up to do any work, but then again, they had been very sweet, hadn't they? Very considerate.

It seemed churlish to mention it.

'See you later then, boys.' I tottered unsteadily to the door.

'Ta-ta, luv.' Alf settled back comfortably and surreptitiously turned up the volume a bit with the remote control. Spiro's eyes seemed to be slowly shutting.

'Bye, luv,' smiled Mac, who, as the foreman, at least had the grace to get up and see me to the door. 'Now don't forget, give them hell,' he said as he followed me out to the hall. 'Oh, and by the way . . .' He plucked at my sleeve, glancing round to make sure no one was listening.

'What?' I whispered, hand on the doorknob.

He found my ear. 'You'll like my Lance.'

I flushed. Pulled away. 'Well, I'm sure I will, Mac.'

'No, but, you know,' he nudged me. Winked. 'They all like Lance.'

'Excellent,' I muttered faintly, deliberately misunderstanding him. 'Lovely to have popular children. Can't wait to meet him,' and with that I bustled out to the car.

God, that was all I needed, I thought as I slammed the door and crunched the gears into first, roaring out of the drive. Some gum-chewing, heavily biceped beefcake, plastered with tattoos and making goo-goo eyes at me over the cement mixer. Terrific. I shuddered and put my foot down, roaring off down the high street and simultaneously reaching for my mobile phone as I went, careering through an amber light and breaking the speed limit. Molly was out, but I managed to track Imogen down, similarly on her mobile, but in the dealing room of Sotheby's pursuing some fine art. I'm not sure it was entirely convenient, but she loyally listened to my tirade and was suitably outraged, albeit in hushed tones.

'They'll have to sack her,' she hissed firmly. 'She's

completely compromised you – be with you in a minute, Damien – put you in a totally invidious position. We'll get a lawyer on to this, Liv. I know the most marvellous chap in the City who'll stitch her up in no time, but the school will have to let her go, anyway. Quite frankly, they've got no other option.'

Sadly, Mr Harty seemed to think they had quite a few. After much corridor marching I finally ran him to ground in the upper school dining room as he sat at a table that was brimming over with upper fourth and testosterone, his eyes glazing over and looking defeated as he toyed listlessly with his treacle sponge.

'A word please, Mr Harty,' I muttered sweetly in his ear.

He looked up, startled, then recognising a wild-eyed mother, and knowing the breed of old, paused only to wipe the treacle from his moustache before getting up and following me wearily from the dining hall. Hundreds of fascinated pre-teen eyes followed his exit, and somewhere amongst those eyes, I spotted my daughter's. I have an idea they were horrified.

Safely ensconced in his office, Mr Harty scuttled hastily behind his large desk and sat down relieved, presumably hoping that two square metres of reproduction oak gave him the edge. He was a moon-faced man with a totally bald head, who apparently had grown the bushy moustache to compensate. His shiny pate reputedly shone more when he was anxious and, I have to say, by the time I'd finished with him, it was glowing like a beacon.

'Well, this is, of course, a very delicate situation, Mrs McFarllen,' he faltered, fiddling nervously with a pencil on his desk. 'We must tread very carefully here, as I'm sure you'll agree.'

'There's nothing delicate about it at all, Mr Harty. She's

having a totally *in*delicate affair with my husband, Claudia's father!'

'Well, quite, and I can see how difficult that must be for you, but the problem is, she's an awfully good teacher and that's so important in the nursery, you see – so crucial in the formative years. The parents will be up in arms if I let her go.'

'And I'll be up in arms if you let her stay!' I hissed, getting to my feet and resting my palms on his desk. 'What am I supposed to do, say, "Good morning, Miss Harrison, and how was pillow talk with my husband this morning?" Compare notes or something?'

He laughed nervously. 'Ha ha, no, no, but then in all honesty, that situation is not likely to arise, is it? I mean you don't exactly come across her on a daily basis. Claudia's not in the infant school and—'

'That's not the point!' My voice was shrill. 'It's the indignity of the whole thing the – the – God – it's everyone *know*ing! And apart from *my* pain, apart from my abject humiliation, what about the message it sends to the children? Hmm? Answer me that one, Mr –' I nearly said Farty, the children's nickname for him, 'Harty. What sort of moral guidance are you giving these children in your care – what sort of direction? Because, believe me, they'll all know about it, you can bank on that. You can't keep it from them. Oh, mark my words, within minutes it'll be all round the school – Claudia's dad's having an affair with Miss Harrison – and how d'you think Claudia will feel about that? Oh no, Mr Harty, Miss Harrison's position here is totally untenable. You must see that. She has to go!'

I was shaking with rage now, glaring at him over his oak desk. I wanted her head on a plate and I wanted it now. Mr Harty looked like he'd just run in from an icefield, he was glowing so much. He squirmed some more in his swivel chair, fiddled with his wedding ring, his *second* wedding ring, if I remembered rightly, because . . . oh God, it was all coming back to me now. He'd left his first wife, hadn't he? For the biology teacher. Dumped the first Mrs Harty for a certain Miss Quigly, she of the wiggling hips and the burgeoning bosom, all of which had seen quite a bit of action in the photocopying room. There'd been a hell of a furore about it at the time, but Mr Harty, being *such* a good headmaster, and being *so* well thought of, had stayed on and married Miss Quigly in double-quick time, who in turn had produced twins precisely nine months later. I groaned; held my head. If Miss Harrison produced twins in nine months' time I'd bloody top myself. And her. I picked up my bag from the floor.

'Well, Mr Harty, I can quite see how this is a tricky one for you, bearing in mind your own personal domestic history. Miss Harrison is hardly a trail blazer, is she?' I eyed him beadily. 'It's a well-worn path, isn't it, and of course, one wouldn't want to appear hypocritical, would one? Wouldn't want to reek of humbug?' I ground my teeth as he failed to answer. 'OK,' I spat, 'fine. Do nothing. But, believe me, you haven't heard the last of this. I shall fight my corner despite your inertia. I shall be writing to the governors, voicing my concerns. I shall be lobbying other parents for their support. I shall even chain myself to the school railings, if needs be, and rest assured, Mr Harty, I shall have Miss Harrison out of this school within the week. Good day.'

With that I swept out of his office, head high, cheeks burning. I strode to the car park, roared home at top speed – narrowly missing a group of cyclists on a blind bend, who careered nervously into the back of each other in confusion

– before screeching dramatically to a halt outside my house. I sat for a moment, feeling the anger thickening inside my head – clotting actually. Finally I got out and slammed the door. Hard. I set my teeth. And if they're not working in my bloody kitchen, I seethed to myself as I strode up the path, if they're still in *my* sitting room, watching *my* television, swigging *my* PG Tips . . . I flounced in, all guns blazing, ready for action, and slammed the front door behind me so it rattled on its hinges.

'MAC!' I yelled at the top of my voice as I stood on the doormat, fists clenched. Nothing. I strode off down the hall. 'MAC! Oh!' I stopped; stepped back as I went bellowing and stomping past the kitchen. 'Hello, Mum.'

My mother raised herself delicately from the dusty Lloyd Loom chair she'd perched herself on in the little scullery and daintily brushed the back of her skirt.

'Mr Turner is working at the other side of the house in your new kitchen,' she informed me. 'I presume that's what you employ these people to do?'

'Oh, yes. Yes, it is. Um,' I held my head for a minute. It was throbbing madly. 'Right. How are you, Mum?'

'I'm well, which is more than I hear can be said of you.'

I took my hands from my head and met her eyes. Cold and grey. I sighed and brushed past her. Damn. All I needed right now. Really, all I needed.

'Yes, well, things aren't too great around here at the moment,' I admitted, dumping my bag and reaching for the kettle.

'And I have to be the last to know?'

I spun round. 'I'm sorry, Mum. I would have rung only—'

'Mrs Hinton, the greengrocer, told me when I went in for some Granny Smiths. Said she was so sorry to hear about my little Olivia, being left on her own with a kiddie like that. Said it had happened to "her Kylie" too, who'd been left on her own without any "social" either.' She shuddered. 'Yes, that's how I heard that my daughter had separated.'

'Yes, well I'm sorry, Mum, but I was a bit distraught, OK?' I slammed the kettle down angrily on the counter. 'And I didn't want to break down in front of you because I knew I wouldn't get any sympathy either, just a lot of I-told-you-sos. I thought I'd wait until I was a bit stronger before I tackled you, all right? Look, I'm the one that's been left, Mum; I'm the injured party here, not you. Don't make me apologise, OK?'

She regarded me for a moment, then sniffed and sat down again, folding her hands in her lap and crossing her ankles.

'There's a cup of tea in the pot. It'll still be hot.'

'Oh. Right.' I turned and found the pot with its tea cosy on which she'd given me and I never used. I filled up the cup she passed me and one for me too. Cups and saucers. Never mugs. I turned and leant against the counter, sipping it, watching her.

'This place is a disgrace,' she said, looking round. I followed her gaze around the room, taking in the cracked sink, the piles of washing-up, newspapers everywhere . . . God, she had to see it like this, didn't she? Today of all days.

'I know,' I said flatly.

There was a silence.

'When did he go?'

'Three weeks ago.'

'Is there someone else?'

'Oh yes,' I laughed hollowly. 'And I don't know what's worse. To be left for someone else, or to be left because he simply couldn't stand me any longer.'

'The former, I think,' she said quietly.

I looked up quickly. God, how stupid of me to miss the parallel. Of course. This had happened before.

'It was . . . the comparison that I couldn't bear,' she said softly.

I nodded, and a chill went down my spine. Never, never, had I thought I'd be in the same boat as my mother. Sitting here comparing notes. I cast around desperately. I couldn't talk about this to her, couldn't do this. I wasn't her, never would be.

'Do you know who she is?'

'Yes, she's a teacher at Claudia's school.' I didn't recognise my own voice. Flat, toneless. 'I'm going to get her sacked.'

'I see.' There was a silence. 'Do you think that's wise?'

I paused, my cup midway to my lips. My eyes darted to hers. 'What?'

'I said, d'you think that's wise?'

'Yes, I heard you, I just couldn't quite believe it. She's at Claudia's *school*, Mum.'

'Do you want him back?'

'Yes, of course I want him back.'

'You do? Really?'

'*Yes*, dammit, really!'

'And so d'you think that getting his popsy sacked is going to further your cause? Do you think that he's going to look favourably on you, think: dear little Livvy, how well she's behaving, how controlled, how dignified? Or d'you think he'll think: poor, sad, vindictive little bitch?'

I opened my mouth dumbly. She put down her cup, leant across and, for the first time in years, held my hand.

'I've been here, Olivia,' she said softly. 'And I did it so

wrong. I did all the things you're about to do. I ranted, I raved, I went berserk, I threw plates, I slashed clothes, poured paint on cars, wrote terrible letters. I did all the things you can't possibly imagine me doing. And do you know what? I found out later, from another friend, that it had only been a whim, him and Yvonne. A drunken non-sense after a party, a quick roll in the sack, as you might put it. He would have come back, apparently, and she would have gone back to Derek, but I drove them relentlessly together, Olivia. And I not only drove them together, I drove them away. Drove them from the country. They emigrated to Australia, I made their lives such a misery. I did it all so terribly, terribly wrong. Don't follow my example.'

I gazed at her. 'I never knew that.'

'I never told you. Too much pride. Have some now, Olivia. Walk tall and hold your head high as you go to that school. Do nothing, say nothing. If you see her, smile, say good morning, be polite, but most of all, have pride. He'll be back. Men are intrinsically stupid and vain, but give him six months and he'll wonder what he ever saw in her. But you get her sacked and you'll never see him again.'

I stared, my teacup cold in my hand. So rarely did I ever hear anything from her lips that rang true. But this had bells pealing all over it. I gulped.

'Thanks, Mum. I think you might be right.'

'I know I'm right,' she said, getting to her feet. She reached for her handbag. 'I've got to get back now. I've got a man coming to service the boiler. And if you're going back to get Claudia soon, I'll have a lift. I had to get the bus over.'

'I'll take you home.'

'I can walk from Claudia's school.'

'I'd *like* to take you home.'

We didn't talk as I drove, but when we got to her house, my old home, I stopped the car and just sat, staring at the place. Up there was my bedroom window, the glass I'd pressed my nose against countless times, dreaming of being somewhere else. I couldn't wait to get away from that dismal pile of bricks, with its tiny front room, back kitchen, downstairs bathroom, two bedrooms upstairs and its patch of dry lawn at the back. No fun, no laughter – how I'd longed for that – just a mother who'd set her nose to the grindstone and concentrated on the grim task of bringing up her only child, suffering in silence. And she thought she'd never burdened me with her pain. Oh, but she had. If only she'd told me, confided in me, talked it over with me in a chatty, mother-to-daughter sort of way, but her silence had just deepened the suffering. It had dragged her down, and made me desperate not to sink into the quicksand with her. How different it might all have been.

As she got out, I leant across and kissed her cheek.

'Thanks, Mum.'

She gave her usual tight little smile. 'Give my love to Claudia. Oh, and I collected these for her.' She handed me some coffee jar labels. I'd forgotten that Claudia was collecting the tokens for something, but Mum always remembered, sent them in the post. I smiled.

'Thanks.'

As I drove back to the school, glancing at the little bundle of labels on the seat beside me, I felt ashamed. I knew in my heart I'd always mentally dismissed my mother, wanting to stand alone, not beside her, not wanting to be associated with her, but one never could. And rightly so. Flesh and blood was what made one tick, ultimately.

Before I swung into St Luke's gates for the third time that day, I popped home quickly, collected something from the hall table, then crawled back into the half-empty car park. I was early, and Claudia wouldn't be out for another ten minutes, but some of the really tiny children were already straggling on to the blistered playground, hats falling over their eyes, drowning in outsized blazers. I loitered by the nursery, watching, as each toddler with its bundle of wet paintings and egg-box alligators fell into the arms of an adoring parent. When I was sure every one of them had been collected, I sailed into the empty classroom.

Mrs Hooper I'd already seen, trussed up in her headscarf even in this sweltering weather, and heading for home, and the other assistant had gone too. Nina was bending over the story mat, picking up bricks, cars and other toys that had been fiddled with during the tale of 'The Enormous Caterpillar', but discarded the moment their mothers had arrived. Her back was to me, and she was bent at the waist, straight-legged as she picked up things from the floor, which showed an element of elasticity. She was wearing a calf-length, Laura Ashley-style spriggy cotton skirt, a white T-shirt through which I could see her bra strap, and her hair was short and fair. The back of her neck looked curiously vulnerable. Suddenly she heard me, turned with a smile.

'Can I hel— Oh!' She started, hand to mouth.

Ah. So she recognised me. I smiled warmly, taking it all in quickly, noting that she was quite pretty in a pink-cheeked, healthy sort of way, and also quite pneumatic, but heavens, Imo was right, nothing special. She had that sort of skin that blushed easily, and the colour rose up.

'Hello,' I smiled. 'Look, I just thought I'd pop in because I realise this situation could potentially be very embarrassing for both of us, so I wanted to break the ice and say hi. We're obviously going to be seeing each other around a bit and I thought – well, far better to be grown up about it and not let everyone think we're at each other's throats, don't you think?'

'Oh! Yes, well—' she faltered, flushing to her roots.

'I also wondered,' I went on, 'if you'd be kind enough to deliver these to Johnny.' I handed over a package of his letters. 'Only I've been sending them to his office every day, which costs a fortune, and it seems crazy when I could quite easily give them to you.'

Her mouth went slack with shock. 'Oh! Well – yes, I—'

'Is that OK then? If I just pop them in periodically? Thanks so much.'

Without waiting for an answer I bestowed yet another warm smile on her, turned, and pushed out through the glass swing doors. I made off down the long corridor. Off to collect my daughter. On the way I passed plenty of waiting mothers hovering outside classrooms, some of whom I knew, and some of whom, quite possibly, already knew of my predicament. My head was high, though, and my chin well up. Thanks Mum, I thought, my heart pounding as I strode along. Thanks for the tip, but actually, I can go one better.

Chapter Seven

Days passed and Nanette's dinner party loomed. On the day of the actual event, I tried to get out of it a few hours beforehand by coughing wretchedly into a bloodstained hanky, but Claudia wasn't impressed.

'Alf saw you do that in the kitchen with the tomato ketchup bottle,' she informed me sternly as I sat on my bed clutching hanky to mouth. She had her back to me at my open wardrobe and was riffling through my hangers. 'We all thought it was pretty sad of you, actually. Alf was on the phone to Vi at the time, and when he told her about it she said that you should definitely get out more and had you thought of taking Prozac? What's Prozac?'

'Jesus!' I flopped back on the pillows. 'Now my labourer's wife is pitching in with her two pennyworth, is she?'

'Don't say Jesus, Mummy – Oh! Hang on. What about this?' She pulled out a hanger and threw a short red dress at me.

'Oh, don't be ridiculous, Claudia. I haven't worn that in years! Not since puberty. Ooooh . . . God.' I shut my eyes and clutched my forehead. 'I do feel rotten.'

'Mum, I told you, the game's up. We all know you're faking it. Oh look, what about this one then?' Some equally ancient miniskirt came winging my way. I snatched it up, then threw it on the floor, swinging my legs round to get up.

'Claudia, if I'm going out at all I'm wearing my black, and that's final – *if* I'm going out.'

'Oh, Mummy, not your black *again*,' she wailed. 'You always wear that; you look like Batman.'

'Rubbish. I look thin and mysterious,' I said, wiggling into black trousers and a velvet shirt.

'And old and tired.'

'Thank you *so* much, my angel.'

'Well, you could at least wear chunky jewellery or something, like Nanette does.' She leapt up on my bed and bounced up and down in her nightie, a packet of crisps in her hand, 'or that pashy thing.'

'My pashmina—' I reached for it.

'No, not the grey one, the red one, and look, you tie it like this . . .'

'Yes, I know how to tie it.' I snatched it from her salty hands and sat at the dressing table to arrange it. Then I dropped it. Groaned. 'Oh God, what am I *doing* here? Dressing up to go to some godawful party of Nanette's to talk to some ghastly greasy Herbert she's lined up for me?'

'How d'you know he's going to be greasy? How d'you know he won't be absolutely gorgeous? And if he is, for heaven's sake *smile*, Mummy, flash your rings, tell him you're a rich divorcee or something.'

I gazed at her a moment in the dressing-table mirror; turned. 'Claudia, what's the *matter* with you? Don't you want Daddy to come back? You can't want some slimy accountant sneaking about the place, surely?'

'Of course I don't. I've told you, Mum, this is tactics. Apparently you can bring a man to his knees by pretending to be in love with someone else, and Dad's got to see you're having a good time,' she insisted. She knelt up on the bed urgently. 'And even if you're not, you've got to pretend, Mum. I know you think I'm the only one in my class from a broken home – I've heard you wailing about it on the phone to Molly – but I'm not. Chloe Chandler's dad went off with a floozie, and d'you know what Mrs Chandler did?'

'No idea.'

'She went straight down to B&Q where lots of men hang about, followed a few around with power drills and things in their baskets, and when she found one she liked, she brought him back home and – guess what – Mr Chandler came back the very next day!'

'Claudia—'

'And it doesn't have to be a Homebase-type thing. Chloe says you can do it anywhere. For instance, you could go to a bookshop, Mum – you like books – or – or yes, a garden centre! Mum, go to a garden centre! There's bound to be some there. They're everywhere!' She opened her eyes wide. 'Men are everywhere!' she repeated with awe. She flopped back dramatically on the bed, arms wide like a starfish.

I shut my eyes. 'Claudia, I am not popping down to B&Q for a DIY enthusiast, nor am I creeping round garden centres looking for a like-minded soil tiller, and neither, my love, is your father going out with a floozie.'

'Teacher then.'

I swung round aghast. 'How did you know that?'

'He told me last Sunday. Said in case I found out from someone else.'

'And how do you feel about it, my darling?' I got up and hastened anxiously to the bed. Hurt? Bitter? Murderous? Do you want to squash her peachy little face right into her blackboard? Poke chalk in her eyes? I know I do.

She shrugged. 'OK, I suppose. I'm glad she doesn't teach me, though.' I clutched my mouth at this horrific thought. She screwed up her nose. 'She's pretty average too, don't you think? I had a look at her in the playground. Not vampy and black-knickerish like I expected.'

I shut my eyes again. I didn't want to think about the colour of her knickers. Although I was sure they were white and came in a pack of three. I sighed. It never ceased to amaze me how much straight-talking children could take, and come back with too. Or was it just my child? My one and only, mature beyond her years.

'Daddy said you went to see her.'

'Oh yes?' My eyes snapped open.

'Said you were quite . . .' She puckered her brow.

'What?' I pounced.

'That word. What the missionaries do to the savages.'

My mind boggled. Missionaries? Savages? Had I tied her up, popped her in a cooking pot and boiled her to death, and let it slip my mind?

'Civilised.'

'Oh!'

I waited. 'Anything else?'

'Nope.'

I turned back and picked up my mascara. Well, whoopee. One tiny little brownie point from my estranged husband because I'd behaved well. I couldn't help thinking it was a better 'tactic' than shagging DIY shoppers, like Mrs Chandler, though.

'It was Granny's idea, wasn't it?' she went on, munching her crisps.

'What?'

'Granny told me she'd told you to be nice to her.' She leant forward eagerly. 'Granny also said there was a curse on all the women in this family, because Great-grandpa left French Granny, and Grandpa left her, and now Daddy's left you. D'you think that's true? D'you think it'll happen to me or d'you think I'll break it? Break the curse, fair maiden!' She raised both hands and plunged an imaginary sabre into the duvet.

I slammed down my hairbrush and spun round. 'Your grandmother talks far too much to a girl of your age! Curse, My Eye. You're to stop going there so much, Claudia!'

Her eyes widened. 'What, you mean I'm banned? Like Granny said you were banned from seeing French Granny?' She grinned. 'History repeating itself, Mum!'

I stared at her for a moment. Then I stood up, snatched up my pashmina and swept it around my shoulders. 'Don't be silly, I just said not so much, that's all.'

It hadn't escaped my notice that Claudia spent more and more time in my mother's company. Mum lived only a few roads away from the school and often picked Claudia up, taking her home for a cup of tea and a jam sandwich. When I went to collect her, I'd find Claudia lying on her tummy in front of the gas fire, engrossed in old letters and photograph albums, all of which had been locked away when I was a child. In those days I'd be told that it was none of my business, to go to my room, to be quiet. She was always irritable, like a bad-tempered terrier, always snapping at the heels of childhood. Sit still! Don't slouch! Get out of my kitchen! Not so with Claudia. How old were you when you got married, Granny? When did you first fall in love? Can I see the pictures? Oh, she'd grumble, sure, but she'd get them out, and talk Claudia through them, too. Was it just a mellowing of age? I wondered. Or was it simply Claudia's style – chirpy, probing, authoritative – taking life by the scruff of its neck, so unlike my own cowering self at that age? Well, I thought, striding to the door, they could dissect *her* broken marriage to their hearts' content, but I didn't want them delving into mine, and I'd tell Mum that, too; tell her to cut the chat.

'Claudia, I want you in bed by nine o'clock tonight.' I swept out to the landing.

She gasped. 'That is way, way too early!'

'I disagree.'

'Who's baby-sitting?' She snatched up her crisps and followed.

'Mac. He's downstairs in the kitchen, I think.'

'Not Spiro?'

I turned halfway down the stairs; eyed her beadily. 'No, Claudia. Not Spiro. Spiro is in the Fox and Ferret having a pie and a pint. He's twenty-four-years old, married with a child, and you, my darling, are ten.'

'I know!' She coloured dramatically. 'Just asking, OK?'

'OK. Just telling.'

'Oh!'

Her exclamation came as we both came barging through the kitchen door together, sniping at each other, arguing loudly, before the extraordinary vision before us stopped us in our tracks. A devastatingly attractive man, tanned, blond, with eyes nearly as blue as Johnny's and wearing black jeans and a white T-shirt, was sitting at the little scullery table eating a bowl of Frosties.

'Blimey!' Claudia added, just for good measure. 'A*don*is!'

He got to his feet in confusion. 'God, I'm so sorry. My father said you were out and that he was going to babysit or something. I had no idea – you must think I'm appalling, sitting here eating your food.' He smiled an apologetic but faintly winning smile.

'Good gracious, you must be Lance then,' I said, recovering, and coolly extending my hand. Would I extend a hand to Alf? I wondered.

He shook it warmly, grin still in place.

'That's it. I'm really sorry if I surprised you, but I've been travelling for about six hours and my father said you wouldn't mind.' He gestured to the bowl.

'No! No, not at all.' Heavens. My father? Not Dad? Pop? The old man? And when had any of my other workers ever got up when I'd come into a room? Most of them promptly sat down.

'We've got Coco Pops too,' piped up Claudia, 'if you prefer?' She dashed to the cupboard and flung it open, brandishing the packet, grinning rather too widely.

'That'll do, Claudia,' I said briskly. 'Go and brush your teeth, please.'

But Claudia didn't move. And after a moment I realised we were both just sort of staring at Lance. He really was very, very good-looking. Suddenly I came to.

'Right! Well, I must be off. I take it you're joining your da— father while he baby-sits for Claudia, so if you could just tell him I'll be back at about—'

'Right here, luv,' said Mac, coming in through the kitchen door behind me, wiping his hands on a rag. 'Just bin checking the generator down in the cellar, went a bit haywire the ovver day. You've met my boy then?' He nodded at Lance.

'Yes! Yes, indeed.' I smiled brightly. 'And I hope he's recovered from his journey.' I frowned. 'Was it really six hours, Lance? From Billericay?'

'Oh no,' he laughed. 'Florence. I had a couple of days off, you see, and I've got a bit of a thing about Botticelli so I went to have a look at those fabulous paintings in the

Uffizi gallery again. My God, that guy could wield a brush. Have you seen them?'

'Oh! Um, yes.'

'When, Mum?'

'Oh, years ago, darling, when you were a baby.'

'But I thought you said you'd never bee—'

'Now run along, Claudes, there's a good girl. Half an hour of television and then bed, OK?' I turned to Mac. 'You know where I am, don't you?'

'Number 32, down the other end. The sequinned busy-body.' He looked at me approvingly. 'You look smashing, by the way, luv, don't she, Lance?'

'I think that's something of an understatement,' grinned Lance. 'Have a good time.'

'Will do,' I managed as I scuttled to the door.

I shut it gratefully behind me. Phew. Feeling a bit hot in there, for some reason. Bit sort of sweaty-palmed. I tripped thankfully down the steps. Suddenly I stopped, wrapped my shawl dramatically around my shoulders, lifted one eyebrow and growled, 'I think that's something of an understatement.' I giggled, then tried it again as I turned left down the street, poshing up the accent until I resembled the Duke of Devonshire. Really, I mused, if it weren't for his obvious parentage I would never have guessed his provenance. One tiny clue, though, I thought with a grin, as I skipped along the cobbled street towards the Abbey, my heart feeling lighter and my step quickening by the second: Florence, the lifting of the bottom from the chair and the educated accent were all very fine, but if I wasn't very much mistaken I was sure I'd caught a glimpse of a gold chain nestling beneath that T-shirt. I'd also spotted a tin of Old Virginia and a packet of Rizzlers on the table, too. Still, I reflected as I reached Nanette's steps, the vast old Abbey towering right above me now, pale and golden in a beautiful evening sky, he might be more interesting than most labourers to have around. He was certainly more decorative.

Moments later Nanette opened the front door and my high spirits took a dive.

'Darling!' She stepped back for me to admire. She was dressed in an extraordinary sort of embroidered silk pyjama ensemble; her neck weighed down with heavy silver beads; her feet skippy in floppy gold sandals; her toenails bright red and dazzling. Rude not to comment.

'Nanette, you look . . . amazing.'

'Isn't it divine? Roger had the whole lot sent across from Hong Kong and I simply *had* to wear it. It's desperately see-through, of course, so I'm wearing a thong – Roger's idea – although he's devastated he's not here to see it. Poor bunny, he's still stuck out there in the Far East, I'm afraid. I can't *wait* to get him back and kiss him to bits!'

'Ah, so he's not here?' That was something of a bonus, anyway. Roger was her current amour, a computer sales-man: smooth, dark, and very, very softly spoken – a deliberate ploy, as I'd discovered to my cost one day, when I'd leant in close to catch his drift and a hand slipped up my skirt.

'No, still trying to screw money out of the slit-eyed nips, as Prince Philip would say, but I have got some *super* people for you to meet, Olivia. Come on, come on through!'

I followed her jangling beads and floppy sandals down her shiny parquet hall and into her ornate, swagged, dragged, beribboned and bowed drawing room. Four people stood in a silent, awkward circle around a glass coffee table, each clutching a glass of pinkish wine and gazing through the table to the carpet. Nanette clapped her hands prettily, as if to break up the bustling chatter.

'Everyone! Oo-oo! This is Olivia, my very good friend from just along The Crescent, and Olivia, these dear people are Cliff and Yolanda Blair, who are desperately old friends of mine—'

'No relation!' piped up Yolanda, 'but I'm a big fan of Cherie's!' She pronounced it like the drink, but it was clearly her habitual opening gambit so I smiled politely.

'—and Sebastian, who, actually, you *might* know because he lives in The Crescent.' Nanette always referred to The Crescent by its name, never 'the road'. 'And Malcolm here, who if I was a single girl I'd want to keep *all* to myself because he's a complete and utter cutie-pie and makes an absolute *fortune* at the BMW concession in Luton!'

I wanted to turn and run right now, but we all smiled and I shook hands; first with Yolanda, a broad-beamed lady, who managed to prise her hand from Cliff's arm for literally two seconds before firmly replacing it, then with Cliff who was tiny and frail and failed to meet my eye, then Malcolm who was very golf-club tie and belted grey slacks, and finally with Sebastian, tall, pale, with watchful slanting eyes and rather too long dark hair, and who, now you come to mention it, I did recognise.

When I'd first moved in here, Nanette had made it her business to bustle straight over with a kettle and a fruit cake. She'd introduced herself as 'a very merry widow' and swept around my scullery in a full-length fur coat. I later discovered that Nanette nearly always wore her fur coat, even in a heat wave, and even after the nasty incident in the high street when a militant youth had approached her shouting, 'And what poor creature had to die just so you could put that on your back!' To which she'd replied, 'Er, my mother-in-law' – yes, even after that little débâcle she kept it firmly round her bony shoulders, and on that, our very first meeting, had sunk down into it in my Lloyd Loom chair and proceeded to give me the lowdown on the entire neighbourhood. This one, Sebastian, was apparently, 'decidedly odd'. Not only, she'd hissed to me over the Nescafé and the fruit cake, did he pace up and down at his window all day long, waving his arms about, mouthing obscenities at anyone who passed and shaking his head like a mad dog, but he'd also been seen squeezing the grapefruit in Waitrose, wearing his pyjamas. Apparently he refused to answer if anyone spoke to him in the street, and at thirty-six, still lived at home with his mother. I'd already spotted his mother actually: a thin, pinched little woman who hurried everywhere, her head well in advance of her bent waist and her scuttling legs, always hastening back to her house with her shopping, slamming the door behind her and giving very black looks to anyone who caught her eye. They were Irish, apparently, had only been in The Crescent about six months, and according to Nanette, the *en dit* was that since they were only renting, most people were keen they didn't stay. In some small way, the son apparently taught at the boys' school in town, but Nanette reckoned it was just a way of integrating him back into the community. And now here he was, at my left elbow, staring distractedly at a spot somewhere above the top of my head.

'Now, you'll have a little drinky, Olivia?' Nanette fluttered her hand bossily in Malcolm's direction. 'Do the honours, Malc, there's a love. It's Kir, Olivia – I don't know if you've had that before? And then if you'll excuse me for just two secs, I'm going to put the finishing touches to the canapés in the kitchen. Don't fight over her now, will you, boys!'

Well, that surely put the kiss of death on any intelligent

conversation. We stood about a bit more in the awkward circle, and somehow, Malcolm and I managed to exchange a few, polite words about the traffic congestion in the city, Sebastian continued to stare above my head, and Yolanda persisted to whisper urgently – and in my view, rudely – in Cliff's ear. After several minutes of torture I made my excuses and escaped, on the pretext of helping in the kitchen.

'Nanette!' I hissed as she squirted some squiggles of pâté out of a tube and on to some tired-looking Ritz biscuits. 'What the bloody hell's going on here!'

She paused mid-squiggle, raised heavily made-up eyes. 'Sorry?'

'Well, isn't that the arm-waver in there? Are you trying to set me up with a nutter?'

'Ah!' She put the tube down. 'Yes, Olivia, listen – I was going to warn you about him—'

'It *is* him, isn't it!'

'Yes it is, but listen, he's fine, honestly. I had a chat to him in the street the other day and he was wearing perfectly ordinary clothes and I really think he's absolutely normal!'

'Oh, come on, you've changed your tune! You told me he was certifiable!'

'Well I know, but I really think that was just a phase or something. After all, we all get depressed, don't we? And when I saw him in the street I did just feel a tiny bit sorry for him, and anyway,' she went on hurriedly, 'Gerald cancelled at the last moment so I just sort of asked him, otherwise you'd have been the odd girl. He's terribly shy and lonely, Olivia. He just needs bringing out.'

'Well, not by me!' I hissed. 'I might bring out a lunatic!'

'Ssh, he'll hear you. Well, OK, Malcolm then? Christ, I gave you a choice! Malcolm's lovely, known him for years, he used to be in oil with my brother – hair oil, actually – but now he's with BMW. He's a complete catch, you know.'

'Nanette, I do not want to "catch" anyone! I wouldn't have come if I'd known you were matchmaking!'

'Oh, don't be ridiculous, Olivia. You can't hunker down like a hermit for ever. You've got to live a little. Johnny has to be shown that you're a very desirable woman!' And with that she picked up her plate of pâté and marched past me with her canapés into the drawing room.

If drinks were tortuous, supper was worse. I made a mental note to tell Imogen and Molly that my foresight had been extraordinary: it was far worse than an evening with Brenda Archdale. Malcolm, beside me, of hair oil and now BMW fame, told me in confidential I-wouldn't-share-this-with-just-anyone tones, exactly why the sixteen-valve fuel-injected 318IS was a superior machine to the 1SE, and how he could never go back to an eight-valve even though it was more competitively priced. He even hinted that if I played my cards right, he might take me for a test drive.

'You get sleeker body styling,' he murmured confidentially, ticking off the points on his fingers, 'you get alloy wheels, you get sports suspension, and you get all that for less spondulos than any other car in its class. What more could you want?'

'Very little,' I agreed. He had the most enormous open pores on his nose.

'And it does nought to sixty in 9.7 seconds, too.' He sat back in his chair and raised his eyebrows in awe. 'Incredible, isn't it?' He leant forward urgently again. 'And you see, the mistake you little ladies make is that you think you don't *need* something with that much poke, am I right?'

'Quite possibly,' I murmured, maniacally smearing

cucumber mousse around my plate, longing for oblivion, longing for going-home time.

'Take you, for instance, tootling off to the shops, taking the kiddies to school – what car do you drive?'

'Hmm?' I raised my eyes from the psychedelic pattern I'd created on my plate, and suddenly remembered Johnny's garage. My tired eyes flashed in their brave old sockets.

'I've got a Bristol and a Lagonda 3-litre Drophead Coupé.'

As he spat his cucumber mousse across the table, I turned coolly to Sebastian.

'I gather you're a teacher,' I said gently. After Malcolm I could be kind. I could bring him out, just an inch or two.

'Well, yes, occasionally. Just a couple of days a month really.'

Ah, so it was like day release.

'That's good. You must enjoy that?'

'Yes, I do.'

'It's nice to get out, isn't it?'

He frowned at this. Didn't answer. Too difficult perhaps. I persevered.

'And what is it you teach, exactly?' Even more softly.

He paused, perhaps trying to remember. 'Music,' he intoned eventually.

I clasped my hands and contrived to look enchanted. 'Music! Lovely! Songs, and things?'

'Um, some . . . songs, yes.'

'Super!'

A silence ensued.

'And do you play?'

'Sorry?'

'An instrument, you know, the violin or –' oh God, no – 'the recorder? I used to play the recorder!'

'Really.' Rather drily perhaps.

'Yes, at school. Not any more. If people ask "What do you play?" I just say, "Oh, the fool!" '

Suddenly I cringed. Oh God, you idiot, Olivia – the fool! He'll think you're taking the mickey! I cast around desperately.

'I – um, and – how is your mother?'

He turned almost 180 degrees to look at me. Really rather closely. 'She's well, thank you. How's yours?'

'Oh! Oh, fine. No, no the reason I ask is because I see her around quite a lot.'

'Who?'

'Your mother.'

He stared at me with his slanting, dark eyes, as if I had two heads, but happily Yolanda was causing a diversion on the other side of the table and the silence was averted. Nanette was bustling around her, changing plates.

'I'm *so* sorry, Nanette, it's such a bore, but they do say no liver, no blue cheese, no unpasteurised products and absolutely nothing that's been in the microwave. I take it the mousse had raw egg in? Ah yes, well, that's why I left it, and I'm afraid this hollandaise sauce is out, but if you scrape if off I can eat the salmon, and then what is it to follow . . . chocolate pots? More raw egg! Gosh, anyone would think you were doing this on purpose, you naughty girl! No, no, don't worry about me. Bumpy and me will be fine with an apple or something for pudding, won't we, bumpy?'

She patted what I now realised was a burgeoning stomach and smiled smugly at Cliff, the father, it transpired, of her five children. For these weren't newly weds who couldn't keep their hands off each other as I'd originally imagined, but a fabulously fecund couple who were about to inflict their sixth child on the world.

'I'll take the sauce off,' muttered Nanette, removing the plate.

'Oh dear, what a shame, and it looks so lovely, but one really can't be too careful and I'd never forgive myself if anything happened. Five perfectly healthy ones and then God forbid disaster should strike. Has anyone else got little ones here? Nanette, yours are all grown up now, aren't they?'

'Er, well. Not so grown up.'

'But teenagers, surely? At university?'

'Just.' Nanette ground her teeth and, as she replaced the salmon, I could have sworn she wiped a smear of hollandaise back on top.

Malcolm held up his hands and was quick to claim absolutely no offspring whatsoever, so no paternity suits, please, ho, ho, ho. Sebastian failed to answer and looked at her blankly, and I was forced into admitting I had one.

'Just one? A baby then, is it? The first?'

'No, she's ten.'

'Ah, I see!' Yolanda laid down her knife and fork for dramatic emphasis. 'Oh, I *am* sorry.'

All eyes were on me. 'Well, no, please don't be,' I stammered nervously.

'Oh, but I know what it's like.' She leant forward, all concern. 'Friends of ours have been to hell and back with it, haven't they, Cliff? All those blood tests, laparoscopies, Clomid injections, in and out of the infertility clinic – not to mention poor Bernard doing unmentionable things into a test tube with a porno mag – and all for absolutely no reason! You see, quite often, *just* like you, a child has already been conceived – as Bernard and Gill's child was – *totally* naturally, and there's no rhyme or reason why another one hasn't popped along after it! The one thing that everyone *does* say, though,' she confided, lowering her voice, 'is to relax about it. The more het up you get, the more it's just not going to happen, and d'you know, that's absolutely true. The number of couples I know who've adopted as a last resort and then – hey presto – the wife gets pregnant! They've stopped *thinking* about it, you see, stopped fretting, and another little tip – even more extraordinary – get a puppy. Sounds odd, I know, but it's the stroking apparently, the caring, the release of all your pent-up maternal instincts. You see, you're looking after something tiny and vulnerable and – what? Nanette, did you kick me? Am I opening my big mouth again? *Oh!*' Her hand flew to her big mouth. 'Oh gosh, I *am* sorry. Nanette did say, but I forgot.' She puckered her brow in consternation. 'You've had a sadness, haven't you?'

Naturally, I'd been busy blushing away throughout her weighty monologue, but this last remark really shot an extra bathful of blood up the back of my legs. A sadness. Christ!

'Well, no one's died,' I muttered.

'No, but didn't your husband—'

'Shall we all sit soft?' warbled Nanette gaily, getting to her feet and coming firmly to my rescue. 'Through into the lounge for coffee?'

Cliff was the first up from the table, but Yolanda sprinted to his side, then marched just ahead of him into the room. As I followed Cliff through, I noticed him grit his teeth and flick a quick V sign at her ample behind. It was a futile, childish gesture, and one that he'd meant to go unobserved, but one that I – after I'd got over my initial astonishment – applauded wholeheartedly. I hadn't categorised, or even noticed Cliff during the evening, except as a small, cowed appendage to his large, domineering spouse, but I began to realise that all was not quite as it seemed in that camp. Was Cliff unhappy? Was Cliff considering heading for the wide open spaces? And if so, how much better, I mused as I collected a cup of coffee from the tray, to be abandoned with one child than to be abandoned with six.

Cliff was settling himself down on a sofa in the corner, and I determined to have a word in his ear about the merits of the single life, about how Johnny was absolutely loving it, and how I was sure he'd thoroughly recommend it to him. God, I could even give him his telephone number. Yolanda, though, with bristling antennae, seemed to be alive to this possibility and as I sat down, scuttled to squeeze her large backside between us on the two-seater sofa. As we all sat squashed together, elbows in, she confided to me in a loud, pseudo-jolly voice that she never let Cliff go off on any sort of golfing weekend or boys' nights out because that, in her view, was where all the trouble started. It became clear that poor Cliff was a prisoner in his own home, purely there to procreate and pay the mortgage, and that any thoughts he might have of escaping had been crushed long ago.

'I don't let him out of my sight!' she warbled, nudging him gaily and spilling his coffee. 'Do I, darling? Heaven knows what he might get up to!'

Cliff forced a tight little smile, then resumed his contemplation of his coffee. Black and hot, he stirred it in measured silence, his eyes a trifle wild. Suddenly he got to his feet. I shrank back, half-expecting him to tip it all over his beloved's head, but he simply gathered some coats from a chair and spoke.

'The baby-sitter will be waiting, my love. We must be off.' Calm, measured, but gritted. The voice of a man on the edge.

At the mention of babies she was instantly galvanised, fussing about midnight feeds and bed-wetting and getting up at six to make breakfast, as Cliff helped her into her coat. His hands were shaking, though. Ah no, I reflected sadly, desertion was not on the cards for poor old Cliff. He'd never even make it to the wire, let alone send a postcard back from Blighty. No, no, this was a desperate man with only desperate measures left to him. And either way, he was facing a life sentence.

They left, and the evening limped on without them. Sebastian stood at the window, staring fixedly at a tassel on the curtains, Nanette snuggled up to Malcolm and explained in hushed tones exactly why a thong was so incredibly comfortable, and I threw the hottest coffee imaginable down my throat.

'Finished,' I gasped. 'Must be off, Nanette. Mac will be waiting.'

She followed me to the door, where I promised her that I'd had the most fantastic evening, that of course I'd come again, and agreed that Malcolm was indeed a complete honey.

'He really liked you,' she hissed, glancing back over her shoulder. 'In fact I think he might ring you!'

'Excellent,' I said, too tired to argue. 'Couldn't be more pleased.'

As I turned and walked back up the dark cobbled street, it occurred to me to wonder whether it was my knickers he was trying to get into, or my Lagonda.

Alone in bed that night I lay staring at the ancient brown William Morris wallpaper that still had to be stripped from the bedroom walls. Blue, Johnny had said, and I'd agreed, even though a pale yellow would have been more my choice. I swallowed hard. Nights were always the worst.

Still, I reflected, blinking hard, if I couldn't be with Johnny, at least I was alone. That was something of a solace. How much better to be here by myself than with a ghastly Malcolm, or a sad Sebastian, or anyone else you care to mention, desperate to start a relationship, desperate to get to the point at which Johnny and I had already been. That point of absolute familiarity, intimate honesty, that point that took years to get to and which marriages are made of. How could I contemplate embarking on that with someone else? Why would I want to? And even if I did, what was I supposed to do with the deep, abiding love I had for Johnny? Freeze it? Deny it? Stuff it under the pillow and suffocate it? I'd found my soul mate, found him years ago, grown up with him, married him, had a child with him. I'd never thought for a moment of looking for another.

I pictured him now, in bed with Nina, something I'd never yet allowed myself to do. The tears rolled down my face in torrents. I imagined that openness, that intimacy that was mine by rights, not hers. The pain was so great I had to sit up, gasping, pinch my arm hard to stop myself going further down that road. Then I lay back on the pillows feeling weak, staring at the ceiling. So how can you ever have him back? After that? a small voice asked. Oh, but I could. I knew I could. Scarred, damaged, as our lives would surely be, but I'd have him. The alternative, that which I'd glimpsed over the horizon tonight, was too horrific to contemplate.

Chapter Eight

The following Wednesday, Claudia and I bumped into Molly in the school car park.

'What are you doing here? You've got at least two years before Henry's eligible!'

'God, two years is nothing,' she said as she levered herself heavily out of her car. 'You have to put embryos down for some schools these days. No, I've left it late, and much as I'd like to just shove his name on a list, apparently I have to be shown around the wretched place first.'

I grinned. Molly was nothing if not relaxed. Some mothers liked to inspect the plumbing and shake hands with all the dinner ladies.

'Mrs Travis, apparently, I have to see,' she said, consulting a piece of paper. She held her side and puffed across the playing field beside me, the breeze flattening her denim dress against her huge stomach. 'God, it's hot. Where will I find her then, in the office or something?'

'She's the deputy head,' Claudia informed her. 'And she's totally sad.'

'She's sweet,' I assured Molly. 'I'll take you there. Bye, my darling.'

Claudia peeled off to her classroom and I escorted Molly

to the office. Passing the main hall, we discovered there'd been a catastrophe. One of the pipes had burst and both the head and the deputy head had been tasked off to deal with the water board, a distraught caretaker was trying to mop up a flood with a roll of kitchen paper – like sticking a finger in the Aswan Dam – and two dozen seven-year-olds were lined up outside in tutus, poised, whispering and giggling, to have ballet and tap in there.

'Oh, Mrs Piper, I'm *so* sorry,' twittered Audrey, the school secretary, wringing her hands melodramatically, when we got to the office. 'What *must* you think of us? *Such* a muddle, I do apologise, but there's simply no one here to show you around! I'd do it myself only I've been tasked off to take Mr Harty's French class and all I can say in French is *je t'aime*! They're always getting me to do this and I'm not qualified to teach a flea!' She flung her hands apart in silly-me appeal. A great advertisement to a prospective parent, I thought. 'You couldn't come back again tomorrow, could you? When we're a teensy bit more organised?'

Molly groaned. 'I could, it's just that it took me ages to arrange a child-minder for Henry, and I dread the thought of bringing him with me – not that he's not an angelic little boy, of course,' she added quickly. 'I couldn't just have a wander round on my own, could I? Peer in some classroom windows, put his name down and come back for a better look nearer the time?'

'Of course, of course!' Audrey fluttered, rummaging in a drawer for a list. 'Here, put his name down here.'

Molly grabbed the pen eagerly. 'How early do you take them?' she muttered, scribbling.

'How old is he now?'

'Nearly one, but he's very mature,' she said firmly.

Audrey looked taken aback. 'Oh, er, well, not for another eighteen months or so—'

'As much as that?'

'Oh, it'll fly by! I tell you what, why don't you just go to the nursery today? That's the first class he'll be going in to. Perhaps Mrs McFarllen would show you where— Oh!' Her hand shot to her mouth. Her cheeks flushed. 'I'm so sorry, Mrs McFarllen, I—'

'Don't be silly,' I said smoothly. 'Of course I'll take Molly to see Miss Harrison.'

'Oh, but I didn't mean to put you to any— I – I didn't think, I—'

'It's quite all right. Come on, Molly.'

I took her arm and we swept out.

'She knows,' muttered Molly as we marched along.

'Of course she bloody knows. Everyone knows, the whole bloody school knows.'

'But that's outrageous!' she gasped. 'It's so embarrassing for you. I don't know how you can bear it!'

'I don't know how I can bear it either,' I mused. 'But I do.'

As we approached the nursery, Molly suddenly stopped short. 'Livvy, I'm not sure I can do this.'

'What?'

'Well, be introduced to her by you when she's living with your husband! What – say howdy-doody when I know my goddaughter's father is having a ding-dong with her? No, thanks, I'll come back another day. In fact – come to think of it – I don't think I want Henry to be taught by her at *all*! How can I form a relationship with someone who's doing this to you? No,' she shook her head vigorously, 'he can go to the nursery in the village. Come straight into the reception class here after that, bypass Miss Whiplash altogether.

In fact, why don't you take me to see the reception teacher? I'm sure—'

'Don't be ridiculous, Molly. You know as well as I do this is the best nursery for miles around. Christ, they all sniff the Copydex at the one in your village. Come on.' I seized her arm. 'To tell you the truth, I don't mind this at all. I rather enjoy encountering her.'

She gave me a strange, sideways look, but it was true. I'd noticed recently that instead of going round the back of Claudia's classroom and out to the car park, which was my usual, quicker route, I made a point of coming through the main entrance and going right past the nursery doors. There she'd be, on her hands and knees with the teeny-tinies, doing jigsaws, playing with sand, her backside often presented to me as she leant forward on her elbows. It was wider than mine, but not huge. Small cervix too, I bet. She'd get up, drift across to help another child, the rhythm of her rolling buttocks in her long skirts languid, hypnotic, like a black girl's. If I had a small silver pistol I could draw it from my bag, aim, and shatter her coccyx, I was sure. I only got a quick glimpse each morning, of course, didn't stand and stare, but it was enough. Like a fix, it set me up for the day. Why? I wondered. Was I stalking her, for God's sake? Sometimes I horrified myself. And why did I want to hurt myself every morning? Because there was no doubt about it, that's what it did: gave me a short, sharp stab of pain. It was almost as if I didn't want that pain to go away, like daily opening up a sore. I've often heard that when someone dies, the grief-stricken, the left behind, want to mourn constantly. They don't want to feel better, don't want to stop crying or stop poring over photographs, because by feeling better, they'd be distancing themselves from the deceased. That was how I felt. I wanted to keep that distance short between me and Johnny, and Nina was my link.

She was sitting on one of those miniature chairs, showing a little blonde girl how to draw around a stencil as we approached. Molly hesitated but I pushed straight on through those glass doors, like barging into a saloon. When she saw me, she stood up hurriedly, knocking over a jar of crayons. She flushed scarlet. Molly glanced awkwardly out of the window.

'Oh, Miss Harrison, Mrs Travis is having a terrible time with a burst pipe in the hall and Audrey asked me if I'd bring Mrs Piper in here to see you. She's thinking of bringing Henry here in – what would it be, two years, Moll?'

'Um, yes, about that,' admitted Molly, scuffing her toe. 'He's two in August next year.'

'Oh, er, yes, well, I'd be glad to show you around.' She shot me a quick, nervous look. 'Um, I don't know if you want to wait here, Mrs McFarllen, or—'

'Hmm?' I raised my eyebrows, deliberately misunderstanding. And I wanted her to have to say that again. The Mrs McFarllen bit. I ran my eye over her quickly and noticed her T-shirt was pink today, but slightly see-through again. Did Johnny like to see her bra straps or did she just buy cheap tops, I wondered?

'Well, I just thought you could either have a chair here, or—'

'Oh no, no, don't worry about me, I'll wait outside. I'll see you in the car park, Molly. Oh – incidentally, more letters!' I produced a bundle from my bag with a flourish. 'Just like Christmas, isn't it! Would you be an angel and pass them on? How is he, by the way?'

A feather could have dropped audibly in the silence.

Molly and Nina cringed to their toes.

'Fine,' she gasped eventually.

'Good, good. He hasn't got his hayfever, then?'

'Um, a bit,' she admitted, staring at the floor.

'Oh God, what a bore. Those antihistamine pills I gave you the other day should help, though, and what I meant to tell you was that he never used to have a down pillow at home. The feathers tended to set it off, so I bought him one of those squashy ones – you know, with a bit of foam inside. I could bring it in, if you like. Still,' I mused, peering out of the window, 'they do say it's going to rain soon and that usually sorts him out, gets rid of the pollen. I must say, my garden could really do with a good downpour. It's as dry as a bone! Is yours?'

Now I couldn't have been nicer, could I? I wasn't patronising her, I wasn't picking on her, I was just making chatty conversation, and still the pair of them cringed and blushed.

As I left them to it and walked to the car park, though, I had to delve into my handbag for a tissue. The palm of my hand was bleeding. There were deep nail marks in it.

Later, when Molly reappeared from her interview, she stalked straight past me in the car park.

'I don't know how you could have done that, Livvy,' she muttered, making for her car and putting her key in the lock.

'Done what?' I followed her.

'Prattled away like that about Johnny. It's so – so demeaning! God, I thought you were going to offer to make their bed! Dig their garden for them, pop out for some more hayfever pills – or condoms!'

'I want her to think I don't care,' I said slowly.

'But she knows that's not true!' She rounded on me

fiercely. 'She knows it's an act – don't you see? You're making a fool of yourself! I mean, fine, I agree with your mother, you don't have to spit in her eye or get her sacked, but you don't have to pretend she's your new best friend either!'

'Oh, so what do you suggest I do, avoid her? Go out of my way not to go near her, so everyone thinks – poor Olivia, she can't bear it?'

'No, but you don't have to go the other way! You don't have to offer to bring bouncy bedding in for them! What about a bit of silent dignity?'

I stared at her. Started to blink. 'It helps,' I said shortly. 'It helps me to know how he is.' A lump came to my throat. 'The thing is . . . I sort of pretend . . . that she's just a friend of his. Our mutual friend.'

She stared. 'Oh, Livvy!' She flung her arms around me and hugged me hard. I stood like a stone. Gulped.

'I'm in trouble here, aren't I, Moll?'

She drew back and put her hands on my shoulders. 'Maybe you should see someone,' she said gently. 'A counsellor or something, I don't know. And maybe you could go together? Would he come?'

I shook my head. 'Don't want to. Too real somehow, too painful. What – raking through our lovely marriage with a perfect stranger? He'll come back, Molly, you'll see. It's just a phase.'

She narrowed her eyes at me. 'I'm worried about you, Liv.'

I nodded. 'I know.'

She took my hand. 'So's Imo. She wants to know if he's mentioned divorce.'

'Divorce!' I gave a cracked laugh. 'Don't be silly, we're not that far gone! No, no, we're – well, we're not even officially separated. Just estranged. We don't want a divorce.'

'Have you asked him?'

'Of course not!' I said, stricken. 'Why would I want to force the issue?'

'So that you'd know. So that you'd be in the driving seat for once. I kind of feel that you've gone backwards these last few weeks. Your first reaction was downright bloody fury, and rightly so – how dare he? Let's get the bitch sacked immediately – and now you're much more . . .' she hesitated.

'Pathetic?'

'Accepting of the situation.'

'Deluding myself it'll be all right? Some day?'

'Well, yes, and you could be helping yourself, Livvy!'

'How!' I wailed.

'By grasping the nettle a bit more, turning the tables, confronting him. When did you last talk to him?'

I shrugged. 'When he last picked Claudia up. Two seconds at the front door. When he rings I pass her straight over to him.'

'But what do you do about practical matters – finances, the house, school fees, paying the builders? How d'you sort all that out?'

I shrugged again. 'I just do. We've always had a joint account. I just pay the necessary out of that as usual. It hasn't come up.'

She sighed. 'It's as if none of this is happening, isn't it? As if you're in denial, no decisions to be made, and meanwhile you carry on renovating that bloody house. I mean, have you talked about that? About whether you should stop? Sell it?'

'Of *course* not, Molly!' I said aghast. 'God, it's – it's our dream, our project! We wouldn't sell it. We love it!'

Molly sighed, rubbed her forehead. She shook her head sadly as she started to get in her car.

'But don't you see, Moll,' I urged, leaning into her open door, '*he's* not doing anything either! I'm just following his lead! If *he* doesn't want any major decisions to be made, why should I force his hand? He doesn't want to rock the boat, does he? Otherwise he'd be saying, "Come on, let's sell" or, "Sign this decree nisi, Livvy" – but he's not, so that must mean he's coming back!'

'Or it could mean,' she said darkly, 'that he's a complete and utter coward and can't face telling you, can't face the truth. It's as if you're both putting your lives on hold, warding off reality.'

'There's only so much reality a person can take,' I said sadly as I shut her car door. 'Maybe he's had his fill of it too.'

As I drove home I was ambushed by tears. They fled down my face in torrents, and whilst one hand whipped them away like a hysterical windscreen wiper, the other gripped the steering wheel hard. 'Oh God, you complete and utter bastard,' I muttered to the dashboard, 'look what you've done to me.'

When I'd recovered some equilibrium I stopped off at Waitrose. I wanted to feel normal again, like a normal housewife cruising those aisles, shopping for her family. Cheese, I thought decisively, striding in, proper smelly cheese – I haven't had that for weeks. But when I got to the cheese counter I realised I didn't know what to buy. Parmesan, Johnny always had to have, in a huge chunk, and Roquefort too, but now – I didn't know. Didn't know what I liked. I suddenly felt panicky as I stood there clutching my numbered ticket, the girl behind the counter in her white hat and apron raising her eyebrows patiently. I dropped my basket and fled from the shop. Out in the car park, as I tried to open the car door, I realised my hands were shaking like crazy. I touched my forehead. God, perhaps I did need something. Perhaps Vi was right, Prozac maybe. I took great gulps of fresh air instead and, after a minute, got back in the car and drove home.

As I drew up to the house I realised there was a car in my usual parking place. I knew this car, this blue BMW. I drew up behind it and sat for a moment. Well, it had to happen, but right now, on what could not, in all honesty, be classed as a good day, it was all I needed.

After a moment I got out and walked past it, noticing a huge dent in the front wing. That looked nasty. I trailed round to the back door to give myself a moment to compose myself before I went to the sitting room where I was sure she'd be but, as I turned the corner, I realised my mistake. It was a beautiful day and, of course, the party was taking place in the garden. Down by the stream, under the spreading cedar tree, draped in various positions about my white, wrought-iron garden furniture, my builders were At Home.

Alf was standing pouring tea from a china pot, Spiro sat cross-legged on the grass, Mac relaxed in a deck chair and Lance was mixing what appeared to be a large gin and tonic. Sitting centre stage, looking radiant in a crisp white shirt and brown linen trousers, her copper-coloured hair shining in the sun, was Angie. I smiled in spite of myself. Wherever Angie went, people flocked around. Not that my builders needed much excuse to flock.

'Livvy!' she called to me, raising her hand in a wave, just as if nothing had happened. As if her son hadn't left me. As if she'd seen me since. I bit my lip and walked towards her, down the gravel path edged with lavender bushes, under the rose arbour, stooping, as I reached her, to kiss her cheek.

'Angie, it's lovely to see you.' I suddenly meant it; felt almost choked at the sight of her.

'Darling, forgive me for not getting up but look what I've done to my stupid foot! Too maddening.'

I glanced down and noticed her shoe was off and that her foot was badly swollen. Spiro – whom I seemed to remember attending to my own feet very recently – was lifting it gently and wrapping a wet towel around it.

'Should be in hospital,' he muttered grimly. 'I say so, but no one listen.'

'Some lunatic pranged into me just as I was coming round your corner – didn't even stop!'

'Oh Angie, how awful. I saw your car but didn't realise you'd just done it!' I dropped down on the grass beside her. 'Are you OK?'

'No, she not,' growled Spiro.

'I'm absolutely fine, and this dear boy is doing wonders. I just banged my foot on the pedals, that's all. In fact *all* these boys have been absolute sweethearts. Thank you, Lance.' She looked up and took her gin with a smile.

'I just thought something stronger than tea might do the trick,' he explained. 'Angie directed me to your drinks cupboard. Hope you don't mind.'

'This is my second one,' she admitted with a wink. 'But the boys are on tea.'

'Of course I don't mind.' Heavens, it had certainly all been very matey here, hadn't it? First-name terms and buckets of gin.

Angie swirled the ice around in her glass and giggled. 'I was just telling Lance here about that time when you and I flew to Paris for a shopping weekend, remember? And that woman beside us on the plane said to the steward in a very imperious tone, "I'd like a G&T, please. That's a gin and tonic to you." And he retorted, "Ice an' a slice, madam? That's a bit of frozen water and piece of citrus fruit to you." Her face! D'you you remember, Livvy? God, how we laughed!'

'I do,' I smiled, remembering.

'Oh – and Lance has been showing me all his marvellous bits and pieces!'

I boggled. 'Has he?'

'Yes, didn't you know? He makes coffee tables, chess boards – all kinds of things, and all with the most marvellous inlay and marquetry – terribly talented. Has he not shown you his portfolio?'

'I only arrived the other day,' explained Lance quickly, looking slightly embarrassed, as well he might. Yes, he'd only arrived the other day and so far I'd seen him do little more than eat my cornflakes, drink my tea and mix my gin.

'There hasn't really been time, has there, Lance?' I said smoothly, but Angie caught my tone. She looked around.

'Well, boys, now that Mrs McFarllen's back, I'm sure I'm going to be absolutely fine,' she said, beaming. 'Thank you all, *so* much.' Despite her charm, there was no disputing the fact that this was a directive for them to leave. Even Mac, who'd been falling asleep in his chair, got to his feet, yawning widely, and as was his wont, scratched his balls. 'Come on, lads, back to work,' he muttered. 'Let's leave these ladies to their tinctures.'

'Oh, Livvy darling, you haven't got one,' said Angie. 'Lance, would you—'

'Sure.' He turned to go but I stopped him.

'Thank you, Lance, but I'll stick to tea. I'd be grateful if you'd take a look at the waste pipe under the scullery sink, though.' I eyed him beadily. 'I think it's sprung a leak.'

Let's get things straight around here, I thought as he wandered off, hopefully put in his place.

'Nice boy,' murmured Angie, to his departing backside. 'Reminds me of David Gower. And, as I say, very talented. More of a cabinet-maker than a chippy. Strange to think he's the fruit of his father's loins.'

'Strange to think anyone would consider utilising Mac's loins in the first place,' I muttered irritably, getting up from the grass and sinking into his vacated chair. Why the hell were we talking about Mac? Intuitively, Angie stretched out and squeezed my hand.

'How are you, my dear?'

I delved into my bag for my sunglasses and put them on quickly. 'Pretty good, normally, but for some reason I'm having a bit of a bad day today.'

Spiro put his head around the French windows. 'Lance found a very big leak!' he announced importantly. 'It's all gone slippy-sloppy up your back passage.'

Angie snorted with laughter. 'Heavens – what a ghastly thought!'

'Shall I mop it up?' he went on.

I sighed. 'I'll come, Spiro.'

'No, let him.' Angie put a restraining hand on my arm. 'Yes, please, Spiro!' she called. 'And tell Lance we've changed our minds, we'll have that other gin and tonic after all!' She dropped her voice. 'You look like you need it, Livvy, and we might as well make use of the extra hands about the place.'

'Yes, except that I seem to be paying fifteen quid an hour for the privilege.' I blinked behind the shades. 'Feel I'm losing control a bit here actually, Angie. Feel I'll come home one day to find they've done the washing up, cooked my supper, and that one of them's tucked up in my bed or something.'

'Well, just so long as it's not that one,' she muttered as Alf, bending to pick up some bricks, gave us the classic builder's behind. We giggled, but then a silence ensued. I waited for her to speak, not trusting my voice.

'The garden looks lovely,' she said conversationally, sipping her gin, but not looking at me. 'You've made a super job of those borders, which, let's face it, were rather dull and conventional. I love the way you've contrasted those mauve campanulas with the Boule de Neige. It works beautifully with the *Alchemilla mollis* at the front and the dark foliage behind.'

'It's my refuge,' I said quietly. 'I've lost interest in the house, but this is where I get rid of all my angst. Blow out my passion.'

She nodded. 'I remember when Oliver died, I had this strange compulsion to have my hands in the soil at all times – remember? Sometimes I'd find myself out there in the middle of the night, pulling away at the weeds. It made me feel closer to him, somehow. At first I thought it was because we'd buried him, so there I was in the dirt with him, earth to earth, as it were, but now I think it had something to do with control. Which you mentioned earlier. Controlling nature when I hadn't been able to control someone else's. Hadn't controlled Oliver.'

Another silence broke over us. Suddenly I could bear it no longer.

'Have you seen him?' I blurted out.

'I have.'

'So – he's told you?'

'He has. A couple of weeks ago.'

A couple of weeks ago. But she hadn't come to see me.

'I didn't want to intrude, Livvy,' she said gently. 'Hoped you'd come to me.'

'Well, I – just wanted to be on my own for a bit. You know.'

'I understand.' She patted my hand.

'Did you . . . meet her?' I managed.

'Yes.'

God. Already. 'Where?'

'Johnny and I met for lunch. She just came for a drink first.'

'And so . . . what did you think?' Vocalising it was awful.

She turned to face me fully for the first time. 'Well, if I was being kind I'd say she was a sweet little thing, but as you and I both know – since it appears that by some horrific coincidence she teaches at Claudia's school – that's generous. She's *très ordinaire*. What the devil's he up to, Livvy? I expected Claudia Schiffer at the very least but, good heavens, that bosomy little nobody – and to leave you for her!'

I sighed. 'I know. Defies belief, doesn't it? And there was I thinking you might be able to shed some light on it, tell me he'd always had a penchant for plain, buxom women.'

'The only light I can shed is the little I gleaned when she left the restaurant – which she tactfully did when she'd had a drink.'

'And?'

'Well, it seems . . .' she hesitated, 'it seems he'd been rather unhappy.'

I jumped. 'Here? Did he say *I'd* made him unhappy?'

She shifted in her chair, looked uncomfortable. 'Not in so many words, my darling, but—'

'Yes?'

'Well, he said . . . said he was tired of you always trying to please him.'

I stared at her. 'What?'

'Said it bothered him that you had no life of your own.

149

That everything you did revolved around him, that he wished you'd do something for yourself.'

'He said *what*?'

'Apparently you were always running around after him, fixing up treats, weekends away, with his friends, not yours. Accommodating him.'

'But – but I thought he liked that! Jesus, he'd go into a steep decline if I didn't do all that, and that made *my* life unbearable! I *had* to think of things to do! Christ, and I bust a gut doing it!'

She sighed. 'I know. There's just no pleasing some people. I'm not judging, Livvy, just reporting back.'

'Jesus!' I slumped back in my chair in disbelief, eyes wide, staring. 'Hang on, let me get this straight. I made *him* unhappy by being too nice to him? Is that it?'

She leant forward. 'Think about it, Livvy,' she urged. 'What sort of people are we attracted to? Not ones who hover around us solicitously, but ones who impress us, ones who make things happen!'

'And what does *she* do that's so bloody impressive!'

'Oh, apparently she does all sorts. Ran the marathon a couple of years ago – God knows how, with that bust – wants to swim the channel one day apparently, does a lot of deep-sea diving. Oh – and they go off on mountain bikes together. She bungee jumps too, if you're interested.'

I stared at her incredulously. 'Bike rides and bungee . . . Angie, are you telling me he gave up on our marriage because I wouldn't fix a bit of elastic to my back and jump off the Tamar Bridge?'

'No, I'm not saying that,' she said patiently, 'but what I am saying is that maybe, subconsciously, you've put your life on hold because of him. Because of that huge personality of his – and, believe me, I know what I'm talking about.

I had it with Oliver too, and how. In that grand racing world I could quite easily have slipped under the quicksand of money and glamour and beautiful women, but I made a conscious decision early on that I wouldn't just be Oliver McFarllen's wife, that I'd go my own way. And I always did. He ran around me.'

I thought back. It was true. She'd always been elusive, never at his beck and call, and he was always anxious about *her*. Striding in from the stables – 'Is Angie OK? Has she got enough help in the kitchen? Are you girls lending a hand? How about someone laying the table. I don't want her tired, we're going out tonight.' No, Johnny had never been like that. But then I'd never been like Angie. God, only a few months ago I'd turned down a job at the Chelsea Physic Garden, thinking it would clash with the building works, with family life.

'You're too flipping considerate, Livvy, that's your problem,' she went on. 'You're even being considerate about Her, too, which, incidentally, Johnny cites as being totally typical of you.'

'Oh, *does* he,' I seethed. I was dimly aware that Angie was deliberately trying to rouse me to anger, and that she was doing a damn good job of it.

'Yes, he said, "You see, Mum? She's even making a friend of Nina. It's unreal!" '

I jumped up. 'Oh, *is* it bloody unreal, well, we'll soon see about that!'

'I think he needs a bit of a shock, Livvy.'

'He'll get one!' I hissed, pacing around my chair.

'I think he needs to see that you're not just sitting about waiting for him to come back.'

'Too bloody *right* I'm not!' Lance approached down the garden with my drink.

'That you're your own person—'

'Of course I am!'

'Still a very attractive woman—'

'You *bet* I'm attractive! God, I'm – I'm fucking gorgeous!'

'Still highly desirable—'

'Yes!' I shrieked, banging the back of the chair with my fist, 'yes, yes, *yes*!'

'And I think he needs to see—'

'A man!' I interrupted, eyes wide. 'That's it: he needs to see a man!' I swung round wildly, looking for one, just as –

'Lance!' I seized his arm. 'Lance – you'd be perfect! Absolutely perfect! Just like David Gower!'

'Sorry?' he blinked.

'Lance,' I breathed, 'listen. I – I need to borrow you, not for long but I—'

'Er, thank you, Lance,' Angie said hastily, prising my fingers from his arm and taking the drink. 'Mrs McFarllen's just a little overwrought. It's the heat. Thanks so much for the drink.'

Lance looked startled, but turned and went on his way.

'Perhaps you could be a little subtler than just grabbing the nearest builder that comes to hand!' she hissed.

But I was well away. 'And a job,' I breathed. 'I need a job. I'll ring the Chelsea Physic, see if that's still up for grabs, tell them I'll take it on any sort of salary.' I paced up and down, gripping my gin. 'Yes, it has to be in London. And clothes – I must buy clothes, expensive ones. Clothes, a job, a man – that'll do the trick, that'll show him!'

'Now slow down, darling, slow down,' said Angie anxiously. 'Don't forget you're doing this for *you*. It sounds to me as if you're plotting all this for him again, to paint a picture for him!'

I stopped in my tracks; stared at her. Then I sat down slowly, the wrought-iron seat cold beneath me. 'Well, yes I am. Of course I am.' She was right.

'Make sure it's what *you* want,' she insisted, sitting down beside me. I stared at her even harder. Blinked.

'But I don't know what I want. I've been pleasing him for so long, Angie, I don't know what I want any more. You're right. He's right. I'm just a frigging please machine. Press my buttons and I'll please you. I don't want a job or new clothes, I just want my husband back. Is that totally sad, as Claudia would say?'

'No, it's totally understandable,' she said slowly. 'All I'm saying is . . . enjoy the process. Enjoy the means to the end. Because, believe it or not, if you approach it that way, you may enjoy the means, even more than the end.'

I thought about this. 'Unlikely, but I take your point. I also agree that it's got to be more fun than sitting around waiting for him.'

'Of course it has!' she squeaked. 'That's the spirit!'

I blinked at her. 'It is?'

'Of course! Fun!' She raised her glass. 'You, Olivia McFarllen, are about to have some fun!'

I looked at her excited face. A slow smile spread across mine. 'OK,' I said raising my glass too. 'Here's to fun then.'

She crashed her gin enthusiastically into mine, spilling both. 'Attagirl!'

Chapter Nine

The following morning, I rang Imogen. 'D'you know any nice men?' I demanded.

She paused, taken aback. 'What sort of men?'

'Attractive, sexy, single men, of course. Come on, Imo, you must know loads!'

I felt her switch the phone to her other ear, give a little cough and shuffle her chair around. Perhaps the gallery was busy. 'What d'you want one for?' she muttered.

'I want to make Johnny as jealous as hell, of course. What d'you think!'

'Ah, right. That old chestnut. I wondered when you'd come round to that way of thinking. Hang on, I'll get my address book.' She broke off for a second. 'Right, now, let's see . . .' I heard her flipping through the pages. 'Well, there's Giles, of course, who would have been perfect . . .'

'Yes?'

'But sadly he's come out. Such a waste.'

'Oh.'

'So then there's James, who's gorgeous, but then he's rather gone the way of the Brompton Oratory brigade, bit pious now, so . . .' more page flipping, 'Ah – hang on, Rollo! Yes, now Rollo's lovely. He'd be very suitable. Works for the foreign office, frightfully rich, terribly

155

intelligent, just split up with his girlfriend – he ditched her – fabulous flat in South Kensington—'

'Sold,' I purred. 'Perfect, Imo. He sounds totally perfect. Invite me to dinner tomorrow. Then I'll invite him back here this weekend.'

'Tomorrow! God, you must be kidding. For a start he's in Russia at the moment, and for another thing I couldn't possibly suggest anything for his diary without a couple of weeks' notice.'

'A couple of weeks!' I shrieked. 'God, that's no good. I need him on Sunday!'

'Sunday. Gosh no, I'm sorry, I don't think I'd be able to deliver the goods by then, Livvy,' she said doubtfully. 'There's Simon Franklin, I suppose – he likes to do things fairly impulsively – but even he gets pretty booked up, although he might have a space for dinner in July—'

'Never mind, never mind,' I said quickly. 'Forget it, Imo. Thanks anyway.'

'Sorry, but, listen, I'll tell you what. I was going to take the parents to that big concert they're doing in the Abbey next week on the fifteenth. Dad really wants to go and Rollo's a real music buff. Why don't I fix that up anyway? You could come with us? It's something to have in reserve if nothing else.'

'What big concert?' I said dully.

'You *know*. God, it's on your doorstep, for heaven's sake. Faulkner's new orchestral piece. It's going to be absolutely packed.'

'Is it? Oh, OK, fix it up as a stopgap, but meanwhile I need some more immediate crumpet. Speak to you soon, Imo.'

I put the phone down. Clearly Imogen's friends were so rarefied and sought after there'd be no getting into their

Filofaxes, or indeed anything else, this millennium, and that was no good; I needed results and I needed them now. By Sunday actually, three days' time. I gritted my teeth. Malcolm. It would have to be Malcolm. Oh God, could I really bring myself to? Yes. Yes, I could. This was an emergency, and needs must. Before I could change my mind I hurried to the back door, slipped on my old garden-ing boots, which were all I could find, and hastened round to Nanette's for his number.

Was he really so unattractive? I tried to remember as I scurried across the cobbles. No, quite good-looking actu-ally, average height and with rather a lot of dark hair, I seemed to recall – hopefully it wasn't a toupee – no sign of a paunch, reasonable teeth – yes, he'd do fine. I'd have to light him properly, I reflected as I hurried along – subtly, you know, in a dark corner of the sitting room. Thank God for dimmer switches, candles even – and if his clothes were too appalling I'd lend him something of Johnny's. Yes, brilliant. Johnny's old dressing gown or something – that would really set the cat amongst the pigeons, and he could be naked underneath. Suddenly I felt sick. The thought of Malcolm naked apart from a toupee made me stop, clutch a lamppost. I hung on to it for a moment and breathed deeply, tried not to think about it. When I'd recovered, I went on up Nanette's steps, and rang her bell.

Nanette answered the door with Roger, beaming away behind her, clasping her from behind, as it were, both in matching kimonos and both looking very post-coital. Ah, so he was back. She was nearly sick with excitement when I told her my mission.

'Oooh, I just *knew* you two would hit it off! Didn't I say so, Rog? I'm *so* glad you liked him, Olivia! He's such a poppet, dear old Malc, and a great mucker of yours too, isn't he, darling? Hey, perhaps we could all go out as a foursome sometime!'

The very vocabulary set my teeth on edge, but I nodded gamely. 'Great!'

'The old dog!' hooted Roger. 'Getting his feet under your table in double-quick time, eh? Blimey, Malcolm and his trouser snake pop up in the most unlikely places, although I wouldn't have thought he'd have the class for you, Olivia!'

'Oh, heavens, I thought he was totally charming.'

'And now you can't wait to get your hands on him, eh? Ha! Terrific! Well, I must say, I thought it was more the form for the boy to ring the girl, but then I don't know many emancipated women, do I, Pumpkin?' He nuzzled Nanette's ear. 'Lucky dog!'

'To be honest, Roger, I'm not that emancipated myself, but this is a bit of an emergency,' I said grimly. 'Thanks, Nanette.' I took the piece of paper she'd scribbled the number on, hurried down the steps, and back home to my telephone, fingers itching to dial. Time was of the essence.

Malcolm seemed delighted, if astonished, to hear from me. I could almost hear him loosen his tie, lean back in his chair and work up a bit of a sweat from the plate-glass office of his Luton car showroom.

'Sunday? Er, yes, sure. Shall I book a table somewhere? What sort of time – eight thirty-ish?'

'Eleven o'clock in the morning,' I said firmly. Johnny would be arriving at eleven thirty to take Claudia out.

'Oh! Right. At your place?'

'That's it.'

'And then lunch?'

'Er, no. No, I've got to go out to lunch, I'm afraid.' God, I couldn't cope with him for any longer than was absolutely necessary.

'Ah. Right. So – what time are you going out?'

'Oh, about twelve. Thirty,' I added charitably. Didn't want to seem mean.

'So . . . you want me to pop round for about an hour and a half. On Sunday morning. Is that it?'

'That's it,' I agreed brightly.

'OK . . . fine. And then we'll take it from there, shall we?'

'Yes, why not?' I agreed blithely. 'Oh, and, Malcolm, um – what will you be wearing?'

'Sorry?'

'Well, just so I have an idea myself. Casual? Smart?'

'Oh. Well, smart-casual, I suppose. The blazer perhaps—'

'No, no, not the blazer,' I said quickly. 'What about a T-shirt and some chinos?' I suggested, catching sight of Lance through the window, looking good in something similar, sawing boards on a work bench in the garden. But what would Malcolm look like in a T-shirt? No, ghastly, like Tony Blackburn probably, I dithered.

'A suit,' I said firmly. 'Have you got a nice suit?'

'On a Sunday?' He sounded bewildered. 'Just for coffee?'

'Yes, you're right, you're right, too over the top. Just a shirt and trousers will be fine.'

'Right,' he said faintly. 'See you then, then.'

'Excellent, Malcolm, see you then.' I replaced the receiver. I hoped to God he wouldn't overdo the aftershave – he looked the type who might – but I was sure I could kill it with something stronger, outblast him with Chanel, perhaps. But otherwise – perfect. I nibbled my thumbnail nervously. So. Three days' time. And meanwhile all I had to do at the appointed hour was look totally alluring, very much in love, and as if I was having the time of my life.

The following day I raced into London and took Knights-bridge by storm. I flew around Harvey Nichols as if my life depended on it, charging in and out of changing rooms, sending curtains swishing back and forth on their rails, wriggling into far tighter and sexier outfits than I would normally entertain, finally rejecting them all, and instinctively settling on a very elegant cream linen dress with capped sleeves and a pair of kitten-heeled, navy mules. If I say so myself, with my short dark hair and my eyes – which as my face got thinner, were getting huger and hungrier by the minute – the whole effect was very fey. Very *Roman Holiday*.

That was Friday, but the complicated bit of the plan revolved around Saturday. It dawned and, as I sat at the scullery table in my old jeans, cradling my tea, ignoring my breakfast, and drumming my fingers on the old Formica, I grew thoughtful. The thing was, I didn't particularly want Claudia around, a) to see Malcolm and double up with mirth, b) to witness any potential shit hitting the fan depending on whether Johnny, i) hit the roof, ii) hit the road, or iii) hit Malcolm. So. I drummed some more. She was due to go to her best friend Lucy's house for the day, and had originally been asked for the night, too, but I'd refused on the grounds that Johnny would be coming to collect her on Sunday morning. However, a quick call to Lucy's mother could change all that . . .

I was just replacing the receiver, when Claudia sat down for her cereal. She was showered and dressed and ready to go, and hurriedly shook out a bowl of Frosties, sloshing milk on top. I hovered next to her.

'Still going to Lucy's?'

'Mm-hm.' She nodded, mouth full. 'Can you drop me

there in about ten minutes? I want to get there really early. We're going to make a ouija board.'

'Sure. Is anyone else going?'

'Lottie and Saskia. *They're* both staying the night.' She glared at me as she munched away.

'Are they? Well, darling, I've been thinking – seeing as it's become a bit of a party, why don't you stay too? You could see Daddy next Sunday. I'm sure he wouldn't mind.'

She nearly dropped her spoon. 'Really? Oh, cool, Mum! Oh, that is totally cool! They're going to see a film on Sunday morning, and have lunch in Café Rouge. Can I do that too?'

'Of course.'

'Of *course*? Good grief, what's happened to you? This is brilliant! I'll just go and pack a bag.' She jumped up.

'I've done it, darling. There.' I pointed to her rucksack at the bottom of the stairs. She stared.

'Oh! Great. Did you put my inhaler in?'

'I did.'

'But – hadn't we better ring Lucy's mum?'

'I've done that too,' I smiled.

'Oh, Mum, you are awesome this morning!' She ran to pick up her bag, then stopped. Turned. 'Oh – but what about Daddy? Will he mind?' She looked anxious suddenly.

'Of course not, my darling, and I'll explain that it was a very special sleepover, planned ages ago. He'll be fine!'

'OK,' she said doubtfully. 'And give him lots of love. Oh – I know, why don't I ring him and tell him? Would he like that?'

'No, no,' I said quickly, 'I'll do that. I've got to ring him anyway about something else. You just get your jacket and we'll be on our way.'

'Thanks, Mum. Hey,' she turned and looked at me

suspiciously as we got to the front door, 'you're not by any chance seeing anyone tonight, are you?'

I flushed. 'Of course not. Why?'

She grinned. 'Just wondered. You seem awfully keen to get me out of the house, that's all.'

'Don't be ridiculous!' I spluttered as I ushered her through the door. 'The very idea! Now get in that car, young lady, before I change my mind!'

Sunday dawned even brighter and sunnier than the previous few days. Ninety-four degrees was predicted in old money; twenty-seven in new. Either way, the heat was on. As I came in from the garden and went up to the bathroom to have a shower, I paused at my bedroom to gaze out at my handiwork. I smiled. Under the cedar tree, down by the stream, I'd put a small round table, covered it with a red gingham cloth, and placed two French café chairs either side. A posy of white roses was set just so already, but in an hour or two, when Malcolm got here, I'd add a basket of warm croissants, a jug of orange juice, fresh coffee, and a pot of raspberry jam. There Malcolm and I would be, talking intimately and laughing softly, so that when Johnny arrived for Claudia, rang the bell, got no answer because, of course, I could pretend I hadn't heard it from the garden, and walked round the back, he'd be presented with an arresting tableau: his wife and a strange man, sharing not just a tender moment, but what could only be construed as a very late breakfast. A breakfast after the night before. A lovers' breakfast. (At this point I'd reach out and clutch Malcolm's hand, or something equally appropriate.)

Yes, OK, I couldn't do the subtle lighting job on Malcolm that I'd previously envisaged, but I could at least put him in deep shade with an old Panama hat of Johnny's –

quite familiar, I thought, to lend him that – pulled down over his eyes. Right down.

I was just about to move away from the window and hop into the shower, fizzing with nerves and excitement now, when something stopped me. I stared. To my horror, I saw the caravan door open. Good grief, hadn't they all gone home for the weekend? It was Sunday, after all. Did they have to live with me permanently? The door stayed open, but no one appeared. Oh terrific, I seethed furiously. All my sylvan scene needed was Mac, belching and scratching his balls, Alf, bending down for bricks and showing us half his backside, and Spiro, sobbing away in a corner somewhere – Jesus! I watched in fury as finally Lance came down the steps, dressed in shorts and a T-shirt, his tool bag under his arm. Suddenly I remembered he'd said he was going to work this weekend because Mac wanted to get the Aga in next week and the cabinets had to go in first. Damn. I didn't particularly want him ligging around, sniggering behind his hand at me and Malcolm, but at least, I reasoned, he was less obtrusive than the rest. And if he was ensconced in the new kitchen with his lathes and drills going, and Capital Radio blaring, he probably wouldn't be any trouble. I followed his journey up the path, under the rose arbour, across to the terrace and – ah, that's exactly where he was headed for. Good. He shut the kitchen door behind him, and, relieved, I hopped in the shower.

As I lifted my face up to the warm water I felt nervous, but strangely excited too. Gosh, perhaps Angie was right. This taking control lark was rather stimulating, and if Johnny took the bait, heavens knows what sort of passions and jealousies could be aroused. I wondered briefly if the posy of flowers was a bit too much... No. Why not?

Flowers were always delightful, and what about a straw hat for me? Very Vita Sackville-West in her garden. Or was she a lezzie? She was certainly very Bloomsbury and blue-stockinged, but I couldn't quite remember which way she'd leant . . . forget the hat. The garden was stunning enough anyway, just at its most magical at the moment, with the Albéric Barbier in full flower, the lavender borders brimming over and – Damn. I paused mid-scrub as the telephone rang from my bedroom. Swearing and dripping I grabbed a towel and ran to get it.

'Hello?'

'Hello, Olivia? It's Malcolm.'

'Malcolm! Hi!' Gosh, I was almost delighted to hear from him, almost as if he really were my lover. I could quite get into this role-playing.

'Olivia, I'm awfully sorry, but something's come up.'

I blinked. 'What?'

'Well, I'm so sorry, but I've just realised I'm supposed to be somewhere else this morning. I do apologise, but I'm afraid I'm not going to be able to make it.'

I stared, horrified and dumbstruck, into the mouthpiece. What did he mean, he had to be somewhere else? Where else could a man possibly be on a Sunday morning, apart from church, the pub or a car-boot sale, for God's sake? I sat down heavily on my bed, aghast.

'Malcolm, I don't believe it. Where have you got to be?'

Silence.

'Malcolm?'

There was another pause, then I heard him clear his throat. 'Olivia, am I right in thinking you're separated?'

'Yes.'

'And you have a young daughter?'

'Yes.'

'Who, presumably, your husband has visiting rights to on a Sunday?'

I licked my lips. Couldn't speak. My tongue seemed to be entwined with my tonsils.

He sighed. 'Olivia, when you've been single as long as I have, you get to know the ropes. A lot of the girls I know are gay divorcees, but some are not so happy about it, and the Sunday morning routine is an old one. I don't particularly want my lights punched out by your estranged husband, if it's all right by you.'

I was speechless. All my plans, my schemes, dripped off me, evaporated into the duvet. But a small part of me felt awful too. There'd been a sadness in his voice. A jaded resignation.

'Malcolm, I'm so sorry. I feel dreadful now, and I really did like you.' I crossed my fingers hard here. 'I didn't ask you over just to – well to—'

'Use me?'

I gulped. Licked my lips. 'Um, look. Maybe – maybe we could get together some other time?' I said generously.

'I don't think so, do you?'

'Er, right. No, no, maybe not.'

'Goodbye, Olivia.'

'Goodbye.'

I replaced the receiver. Stared at it. Bugger. Bugger, bugger, bugger! Now what the hell was I supposed to do? God, Johnny would be here in – I glanced at the clock – an hour. I'd got the linen dress laid out on the bed, the croissants poised ready to be warmed in the oven, Claudia was away for the night – gosh, that had been difficult enough to arrange – I couldn't waste all that effort! Couldn't do it all over again next Sunday, could I?

I paced about the room wrapped in a towel, racking my

brains madly. For an awful heady moment I wondered if I could borrow Roger. He was in Insurance or something, wasn't he? Could I possibly ring and ask Nanette if he'd come over and take a look at my policy? No – no, he'd probably rape me in the undergrowth hooting 'Lucky dog!' before hoovering up all my warm croissants and, anyway, I had a feeling Johnny had met him once so he'd know he belonged to Nanette. He'd also know he was a complete prat. No, that was no good. So what on earth was I going to do!

I wrung my hands wretchedly, gazing out of the window at my perfect table, my flowers, when suddenly, right underneath my window, from out of the kitchen door came Lance. I stared down at him. He was wearing old khaki shorts, a faded pink T-shirt, and was carrying a couple of skirting boards, destined, no doubt, for the workbench, which he'd set up outside the back door. I blinked. Of course! Why didn't I think of it before? Lance! Hell, in anyone's book he was completely bloody gorgeous, far more gorgeous than Malcolm – and certainly Roger. Yes, yes, Lance was perfect! But the only problem was, I thought, chewing my lip maniacally now, how to organise it? How on earth could I set it up without him suspecting anything, and without him – heaven forbid – thinking I fancied the pants off him? I chewed my lip even more furiously, paced about the room a bit more. I glanced nervously at the clock. Ten o'clock. I didn't have much time. Suddenly I remembered something. Quick as a flash I got dressed in the cream dress, the navy shoes, the pearl earrings, brushed my hair, tucked it neatly behind my ears, added lipstick and mascara, and went downstairs.

Out in the garden Lance was planing away, his broad

back bent low over the bench as he worked, his shoulders rippling under his T-shirt, the blond curls curling at the nape of his brown neck, just slightly damp with sweat as he— Blimey, I'd be sweating myself soon; I was rather warming to this idea.

'Hi!'

He turned. I gave a breezy smile. A dinky little wave.

'Oh, hi there.' He looked me up and down. 'You going out?'

'Um, no, just sort of, felt like a change from jeans, really.'

'Oh, right. Very smart. Not much good for your usual grovelling about in the flowerbeds, though.' He turned and went back to his planing.

'No, I suppose not.' I walked round the bench so that I was facing him. 'Um, Lance?'

'Yes?' He paused, looked up.

'I was having a look at that brochure of yours just now. You know, the one you showed Angie the other day, with all your tables and chairs and things in it?' I produced his portfolio from behind my back.

'Oh right,' he brightened.

'Yes, and I was just wondering, would you have time to make Claudia a bedside table? Nothing fancy –' keep it cheap – 'it's just that – well, she's got nowhere to put her books and things and I'm sure she'd love it.'

'Sure, I can do that. Which one caught your eye?' He moved across to take the book from my hand. I held it back.

'Well, I was wondering if we could discuss it later. You know, have a sort of meeting. At about eleven thirty?'

He shrugged. 'OK, but I can talk you through it now if you want. I'm not that busy.'

'Er, no, that's all right. I've got to – do the washing-up.

But I thought, if we could catch up later, ooh, let's see, say under the cedar tree? Over there where the table is?'

He turned and followed my gaze. Slowly he took in the two chairs, the checked tablecloth, the flowers, the jam, the coffee cups. He looked startled for a moment, then his face cleared. As he turned back, his eyes glinted, as though he'd just had a brush with possibility.

'Sure,' he grinned. 'Under the cedar tree it is. Shall I have a rose in my teeth?'

'Don't be ridiculous,' I spluttered. 'But – you might put some trousers on.'

He blanched. 'Sorry?'

'N-no – nothing,' I hastened. 'Forget it.' God, so *stupid*, Olivia. Why on earth should he change his shorts, for heaven's sake?

He gazed down at his shorts. His mouth twitched.

'You don't like my legs?'

'Don't be ridiculous. I've never even looked at them!' I could feel myself blushing.

His brow wrinkled. 'But you think . . . Ah yes, that's it, you think that if you *do* look at them, *and* my brochure, you'll be so overcome, you'll start panting and have to loosen your clothes?'

'Idiot!' I spluttered. 'Forget I said it. I'll see you by the tree at eleven thirty, wear what you bloody well like. Now if you'll excuse me I've got jobs to do.'

I turned and stalked off, hopefully with dignity, towards the back of the house. But after a moment, just as I was crossing the terrace, his voice stopped me in my tracks.

'What time's Johnny coming?'

I turned. Flushed.

'What?'

'I said,' he strolled towards me, hands in his pockets,

'what time is your husband coming?'

'I – don't know what you mean!'

'Oh, I think you do, Olivia.' His voice was gentle now. Less flippant.

He gazed at me, blue eyes very intense. I took a deep breath. Raised my chin. After a long moment, I spoke.

'Eleven thirty. And yes, Lance, how clever of you, how sharp. You've seen right through my little plan. I did want to make him jealous, wanted a reaction from him, but unfortunately, the candidate I originally picked for the job also smelt a rat and cried off ten minutes ago, so I panicked and asked you instead, satisfied? You see, naïve and new to this game as I am, I thought I'd hit on an original formula. Thought – I know, I'll pack Claudia off to a friend, be caught by my husband having a cosy *à deux* with my lover under the tree and then, terribly flustered, say, "Oh, Johnny, I'm so sorry! I was so caught up with lover-boy here, I forgot to ring and tell you Claudia wasn't here!" ' I smiled ruefully. 'Little did I know I'd picked a well-worn, sad divorcee's path, one that all you predatory, prowling, single men can sniff out at twenty paces. Forget it, Lance. I'll still have the bedside table, if you don't mind, but I'll just mark the brochure and give it back to you later.'

I turned and started to go towards the house, tears already pricking my eyelids. Just short of the French windows, he caught up with me.

'Hey, hang on. Don't go off in a huff!'

I walked on.

'I just think you could do it better than that, that's all.'

I stopped. Turned to face him. 'What?'

'You want to make him jealous, right?'

'Well, yes I—'

'And is sipping tea with some stuffed shirt under the cedar tree really going to make him see red?'

'Well I thought it might just—'

'What time did you say he was coming?' he interrupted.

'Half eleven.'

He glanced at his watch, interrupting. 'He'll be here in ten minutes. Right. We have to get a wiggle on. Now, what we need are a couple of these,' he walked across to the washing line, reached up and grabbed a couple of towels, 'and a rug, possibly – have you got a rug? Oh yes, I know. I've seen one in the cloakroom.' He marched inside and, as my heart began to beat faster, reappeared a moment later with it under his arm. He laid it on the grass with the towels.

'Now,' he frowned, 'let's see . . . I'll take off this—' he whipped his T-shirt over his head – 'and these—'

'No!' I squeaked as his hand went for his flies.

He grinned. 'Only teasing. No, I'll just lie down like this, I think.' He settled back on the rug, arms locked behind his head, legs stretched out, brown chest, with its smattering of golden hair, bared. His merry blue eyes squinted up at me, into the sun. He shaded them with his hand.

'You look ridiculous, if you don't mind me saying so. If you'd just had a romp with your lover you'd hardly be prissed up like that. You look like you're going to the Tory Party Conference – all you need is a frigging hat – and apart from anything else, it's eighty-five degrees. Go on, go and get your kit off and put your cossy on. Oh, and grab some suntan lotion while you're at it. Come on, chop chop, we haven't got much time!'

I gazed down at him incredulously. Get my kit off? Suntan lotion?

'But—'

'What?'

'Well, he'll hit the roof, won't he? Seeing us laid out out here, all sort of—'

He raised himself on one elbow. I have to say, he looked completely gorgeous. 'All sort of . . . naked? And isn't hitting the roof the general idea?'

I gulped, hovered tremulously for a moment, but didn't make the mistake of hesitating again. He might change his mind. As a wave of hysteria threatened to engulf me, I ran inside, up the stairs, across the landing and into my bedroom, pulling out drawer after drawer, riffling around for my costume. My costume – oh God, could I do this? My hand stayed abruptly. I shut my eyes tight. Thought of Johnny. How I wanted him. Yes, I bloody could.

What I actually came down in – rather sheepishly – was something of a compromise: a bikini top and shorts, not quite having the nerve to go the whole hog which would involve exposing my thighs, which, since I lived in shorts, were horribly white and, as Claudia put it, 'rather porridgey'.

I crept nervously to the rug. He was still prone, hands locked behind his head and eyes – thankfully – shut. I was grateful for that small amount of tact, for not looking me up and down as I slunk down beside him.

'Got the Ambre Solaire?'

'Yes,' I whispered, my heart going like a bongo drum.

'Good. To be applied later. With vigour. Now, what would you like me to be, a solicitor? Architect? Famous artist? And shall I change my name to Jeremy?'

I giggled. 'Oh, well, now let me see . . .' I paused. 'How about Lance, the cabinet-maker?'

He grinned across at me, seeing me for the first time with not a lot on.

'That's very loyal of you, Olivia, but actually, I think it would be better if I wasn't a chippy or anything too manual and close to home. It would look a little slutty of you to have bonked one of your workforce already, don't you think?'

His eyes danced at me. I shaded mine to see him more clearly. I could never quite tell if he was laughing at me or not. Slutty? Would it? Well yes, of course it would! I inched away from him hurriedly on the towel, suddenly having severe second thoughts about this charade, when at that moment, the doorbell rang.

'Shit!' I squeaked, flipping over, face down on to the towel. 'He's here!' I shoved my fist in my mouth. 'Oh God, Lance, I'm not sure I can do this. I think I'm losing my bottle!'

'Don't be ridiculous, of course you're not. Here –' he passed me the Ambre Solaire – 'have this one. Now, sit up and rub it into my shoulders. Firmly, please, I don't want any namby-pamby business.' I hesitated. 'And don't forget, Olivia,' he murmured into the towel, 'I'll bet he's just given that Nina of his a right good seeing to.'

That did it. I knelt up, emptied half a bottle on to Lance's back, and got stuck in. His skin was soft and velvety, already warmed by the sun, and I could feel my heart pounding for various reasons as I kneaded the lotion in. A silence prevailed. Just my heavy breathing and a couple of swallows, warbling away in the treetops. Then the bell rang again. I was almost shaking with nerves now – in fact, I had a feeling I might have to run for the loo in a minute. Thank God I had my back to the side passage and wouldn't see his face immediately. All went quiet. For ages.

'Oh God, he's not coming round!' I hissed, panicking. 'He's going to go away!'

Lance raised himself up on his elbows. 'Quite normal,' he whispered. 'He feels he doesn't live here any more, you see, so he wouldn't presume to come round the back. I'll go and see him.' He jumped nimbly to his feet.

'Lance! No, you can't! What are you going to say?' I gasped.

'Oh, I'll say you're in the bath, soaking, and that in all the excitement you forgot to ring and tell him Claudia was away. I might yawn a bit too, scratch my sleepy head, and then as he goes, I'll turn and walk back upstairs to the bedroom.'

'Lance!' I shrieked, but it was no good. He'd gone.

I flung myself down on the towel and stuffed the corner in my mouth. *Omigod omigod!* He'd freak! He'd go insane, he'd – he'd hit him! Would he hit him? I took the towel out of my mouth. I had a feeling Lance was just a little bit bigger, and Johnny wasn't a fisticuffs sort of man but, oh Lord, the fur would most certainly fly. I shut my eyes tight and counted – one elephant, two elephant – like Claudia did to will the seconds by.

'Enjoy that, did yew girl?' A voice came sailing over the fence. I shot up on my elbows. Mr Jones was grinning at me from his garden.

'Sorry?' I whispered, clutching the towel to my bare-ish bosom.

'I said, did yew enjoy that, like!' He winked salaciously.

'Enjoy . . . what?' I flushed.

'The cucumber!'

'Oh!' Oh, the relief. 'Delicious,' I assured him. 'Really, really yummy.' God, go *away*, Mr Jones! I craned my head and peeked nervously round the side passage. Still no sign. Couldn't hear anything either, no voices.

'Good, good,' he purred. He gazed thoughtfully at the

spot Lance had just vacated. 'Like 'em young and firm, do yew, girl?'

'What?' I gasped.

'I said, yew like 'em young and firm! Best way. Leave 'em in the greenhouse too long and they're past it, see? Start to droop at the end; can go a bit soggy too, like!'

I gulped. Heavens. What a thought.

'And I'll have some bewtiful ripe tomatoes for yew soon!'

'Oh! Oh . . . good!'

Happily he seemed to have had his say, and his head disappeared as he went on his way, back to his greenhouse to urge on his bewties, no doubt. I flopped back on the towel, and just as I was thinking I might actually faint from a combination of frayed nerves and heat, Lance reappeared. He strolled back through the house, out through the French windows, hands in his shorts pockets, whistling merrily. He sat down beside me with a grin.

'Well?' I breathed, sitting up.

'He's gone,' he smiled.

'And?'

'And, he seemed most put out. Astonished. Stunned even, and,' he frowned, 'yes, very taken aback.'

'What did he say?' I squeaked, kneeling up.

'Oh, well he spluttered fairly incoherently for a bit – particularly when I explained how exhausted you were – but then he finally said something about ringing you later.' He grinned. 'I said that m-i-ght be all right, but to give it a while because you really were shag— shattered and would probably still be asleep.'

'Oh!' I squealed, clutching my mouth. 'You didn't!'

'Yes, and as he turned to go I said that if he hung on for a minute I'd walk with him because I had to pop out for more baby oil. He scarpered like a scalded cat.'

'Oh, Lance, that's a bit over the top!'

'Not at all. I always put baby oil in my bath.'

I lay back nervously on the towel. Blimey, what would Johnny think? Well, he'd think naked massaging, that's what. I felt a bit queasy now, but then abruptly my blood boiled. After all, that was probably what *he* got up to, wasn't it? If not worse! Why should I feel guilty? Serves him bloody well right, I thought fiercely.

Lance lay down beside me. I shut my eyes, feeling the sun beating down. At length, he murmured something.

I turned and shaded my eyes. 'What?'

'I said, so you definitely want him back, do you?'

'Of course I do,' I muttered. 'He may be a bastard, but he's my husband, Lance.'

So we'd given him a nasty shock, had we? Good. Excellent news. Yes, see how that feels, Johnny, a nice sharp jab in the heart. I'd been having those coronary pains for months now, although, I realised with relief, I felt stronger now than I had for ages. Of course. Control. That was it.

'But he's poking another woman.'

I turned my head. Squinted. 'What?'

'I said he's been unfaithful. Doesn't that bother you?'

'Of course it does. Of course.' I frowned. 'But he's not a serial philanderer, Lance, that's the difference. It's a one-off. He's never done it before, and once he's back, he'll never do it again. You're looking at it from the idealistic, hearts-and-flowers, single person's point of view,' I reasoned sensibly. 'And I probably thought exactly like you before I got married, but real life, grown-up life, isn't like that, Lance. Some marriages do go through a blip like this. You can't just ditch twelve years for one indiscretion.'

'But it's not an indiscretion, he's still doing it,' he

persisted. 'It's not like he's been caught with his trousers down and – oops, up go the hands, fair cop, big disgrace, been a naughty boy but home he goes with his tail between his legs. It's still going on. I think most affairs, or blips, as you call them, end in the guilty party slinking home, but he seems to have chosen to stay away. He's chosen her, Olivia.'

I wasn't quite ready for this amount of straight-talking, and whether or not Lance knew this and was deliberately shooting from the hip to shake me, I don't know, but I found I couldn't answer him. Had neither wind nor words to draw on. He's chosen her. Yes, that was enough to knock the stuffing out of me. A few well-chosen words designed to bring a lump to my throat, tears to my eyes, and a ruddy great boulder to sit on my heart. Thanks, Lance.

When I'd gulped down all the detritus, I turned my head back to him, trying to think of ways to explain to a fine young chappie like this what twelve years of marriage, three homes, numerous holidays, friends, commitments, responsibilities and a child of our own felt like. How I couldn't give it up. But his eyes were shut now, and his breathing, slow and measured. Eighty-five degrees in the blazing sun and no worries. Morpheus had swept him away.

As he slept, I gazed, uninhibited now, on those fine features; that straight nose, full lips, the dark lashes brushing his bronzed face. Of course, I reasoned, if one was going to have an affair, this was exactly the sort of man to do it with. Single, uncomplicated, just a spot of undiluted fun to get the blood coursing through the veins, make me feel vibrant and sexy again. But that wasn't what I wanted.

I turned my face back to the sky and shut my eyes against the scorching rays. No, it wasn't what I wanted, not right now. I felt the sun on my eyelids, my skin soaking up this heat. Unlike Lance, worries I most certainly had, but the eighty-five degrees were getting to me now, making me drowsy. I mustn't drop off, though, I thought sleepily, my skin would absolutely scorch out here. Just two minutes, then I'd get up.

Some time later, I was woken by the doorbell. It was ringing and ringing. I opened my eyes and sat up, startled. Lance was still kipping deadly beside me, snoring away. It rang again, then again, sharp, and insistent.

'OK, OK!' I muttered, staggering to my feet. I weaved sleepily up the garden, through the French windows – hanging on briefly to the doorframe for support – then propelled myself towards the front door. When I reached the hall, I caught sight of myself in the mirror. My face and chest were a livid red, and my hair, wet and sweaty, plastered to my head. I groaned. Oh no, how could I have fallen asleep like that? With my skin? The bell went again.

'I'm bloody *coming*!' I shrieked, as I reached for the doorknob. I swung it back with irritable emphasis.

There, on my doorstep, stood Johnny.

'Johnny!' I gasped, taking a step back. I wrapped my arms protectively around my bare midriff.

'Hi, Livvy.'

'Wh-what are you doing here?'

He frowned. 'What d'you mean?'

'Well – did you – forget something? Come back for something?'

'Come back? No, I've just arrived. Sorry, I suppose I am a bit late, but the traffic was appalling.'

'Late for what?'

'Well, I've come to collect Claudia, of course.'

Chapter Ten

I stared at him, aghast. 'But – you came earlier!'

'What?'

'Didn't you come earlier?'

'What d'you mean?'

'Well – someone came!'

'To collect her?'

'I don't know, I didn't speak to him!'

'So who did?'

'Lance! He's my – my cabinet-maker.'

'Your cabinet-maker?' He blinked. 'Blimey, exactly how rarefied are these builders getting, Livvy? You'll be telling me you're employing gilders next. OK, so where's Claudia?' He peered behind me.

'Oh! Oh no, she's not here!'

Johnny paled. Stared at me. 'You mean . . . you let her go? With this person? This person who came to the door, spoke to your cabinet-maker and – and handed over my *child*?'

'No! God, no.' I pushed my hands desperately through my sweaty hair. 'She's at Lucy's, you see. She stayed the night there, and I meant to ring you and tell you, Johnny, but – well, I forgot.'

His eyes widened with comprehension. 'Ah.' He nodded.

179

'Right. So . . . I've just sat on the sodding M1 for two hours, in greenhouse conditions, when you could have made a quick phone call, is that it?'

'Well I *meant* to ring, of course, but I've been so busy, you see!' God, this was desperate. All I'd done was make him angry.

'Clearly,' he said drily. 'Well, don't let me hold you up any longer.' He glanced behind me, through the French windows to the garden beyond, where Lance was spread-eagled on a towel, mouth open, snoring loudly.

'I take it that's the master craftsman?'

'Yes,' I hesitated, 'that's – Lancelot.'

He snorted. 'Lancelot! Blimey, that's a good one. So – let me guess – you're Guinevere? Lots of "Aye, my lord, and wither my wimpole? Chase me round the Round Table"?'

I regarded him for a moment. He looked totally irresist-ible, of course, this love of my life, this ache in my tubes, this short fuse to my heart. Tall, tanned, his blond hair sun-bleached, standing on my doorstep in his ancient shirt and shorts that I knew so well, had washed, hung out, and ironed so many times. After a moment, I folded my arms and raised my chin at him.

'Johnny, do I poke fun at your relationship? Do I make derogatory remarks about your fluffy, winsome, bosomy little teacher? Or do I make an effort to be as pleasant and as civilised as possible about this horrific situation I find myself in?'

He looked suitably chastened. Nodded. 'No, no, you're right. Sorry, that was cheap.' He scratched his head sheep-ishly. 'Sorry, Livvy. You're behaving very well. Much better than I am.'

Oh, this was worse, far worse. A lump came to my throat, and as his blue eyes apologised, I wanted to throw myself on him, hug him to bits, smell that shirt, his hair, his skin, say, 'But I don't want bloody Lancelot! I don't want to be standing here going through the motions of this ridiculous charade. I just want you!' But I didn't. Because isn't that the truth? There's always something to behave about.

'So,' he scuffed his Docksiders on the doorstep, 'it is a relationship, then?'

Ah, so he'd picked up on that. Gone after that little word I'd tossed him like a dog would a bone. Even sounded a mite territorial about it. Good. I gave a dismissive little shrug.

'I'm not sure yet. It's still early days.' Play it cool, Livvy, dead cool.

He nodded. 'Right. Well, anyway, it's none of my business,' he said hurriedly. 'I'll be away.'

'You don't want to –' I stood aside to let him in – 'get a drink or anything? I mean, if you've been in the car for ages—'

'No, no,' he said quickly, glancing at Lance. 'No thanks.' He gave a wry smile. 'I don't think I'd be quite as civilised as you, Livvy.'

I smiled back, tears filling my eyes. 'It doesn't come naturally, I can assure you.'

He nodded. 'I know.' As he turned to go, he glanced back. 'Incidentally, I should put something on that chest. You're going to be as raw as hell in the morning. And give Claudes my love. Tell her I'll see her next week.'

I nodded. Couldn't speak now. He walked to his car and raised his hand in a final salute as he got in. I waved back, watched as he drove off, then sat down on the bottom step of the stairs and burst into tears. Damn him. Damn him for being all I'd ever wanted.

After a while I wiped my eyes and blew my nose

violently. Get a grip, Olivia. I peered in the mirror again. God, I couldn't have looked more awful, though, could I? I thought with awe. Bright red skin, sweaty hair – I hardly presented a seductive spectacle, and actually, I felt a bit cold and shivery now. I grabbed a cardigan from the banisters, threw it on and went out into the garden. Lance wasn't exactly looking his best either, I thought ruefully, snoring away like that, mouth open, catching flies. Shame Johnny had had to see him like that, but then again, if he'd met him at the door, it appears he might have resorted to some uncivilised behaviour, which was something, anyway, I conceded grudgingly. But then – oh God! Who *had* met Lance at the door? My hand flew to my mouth. I hastened across the lawn to wake him.

'Lance! Lance!'

I crouched down and shook him hard. '*Lance!*'

He came round sleepily. 'Hmm? What?' He raised himself up on one elbow and peered blearily at me. 'Christ,' he muttered, 'what time is it?'

'Almost twelve. We fell asleep. Listen, Lance, you know the guy who came to the door?'

He sat up and yawned widely, scratching his head. 'Johnny?'

'No! No it wasn't Johnny! Johnny's just been. He got stuck on the M1!'

'Oh. Really?' He frowned, looked bewildered.

'Yes, really, so what the hell did he look like?'

'Who?'

'The other guy!'

'Oh.' He peered into the middle distance, trying to remember. 'Well – quite tall, I suppose, longish dark hair, and sort of . . . yes, slanty eyes.'

I stared. Sat back on my heels. Tall . . . long dark hair . . .

slanty— 'Oh God!' I clutched my mouth.

'What?'

'Oh no, I think I know who that is! Did he look slightly . . . not quite there?'

'He looked completely not quite there, especially when I gave him the baby oil bit.'

I groaned. 'Oh no! Oh God, Lance, I think that was Sebastian, from down the road! And there you were, socking it to him in graphic detail, telling him I was recovering from a monumental seeing-to and douching away upstairs! Didn't he try and stop you?'

Lance shrugged. 'I suppose I didn't give him much of a chance. I was giving it plenty of verbal, see, and all the time, hopping from foot to foot, getting ready to dodge in case a fist came flying my way, although,' he paused, 'I must say, he didn't seem inclined to do that. He just gazed at me sort of—'

'Vacantly?'

'Well, speechlessly, anyway. Blinked a bit, too.'

I stuffed my feet into my deckshoes and groaned. 'Oh God! Now I'll have to go and bloody *see* him, won't I! Have to explain, apologise, do *something* otherwise it'll be all round the flaming neighbourhood – how the abandoned wife at Orchard House spends her Sunday mornings. Nanette will have a field day!' I stood up and chewed my lip thoughtfully. 'I know, I'll say you're my brother or something, and – and you're staying here, and that your wife's just had a baby – hence the oil – and that the reason I was soaking in the bath in the middle of the day was because – oh, because I'd been doing some heavy gardening. Digging. Something like that.'

He shrugged, locked his hands behind his head and lay back. 'Could do, but I don't know why you have to bother.

What does it matter if he thinks you're a goer? It's no bad thing.'

'Isn't it?' I gasped.

'Of course not. Contrary to what you might think, us men like girls with a bit of oomph, with a bit of weh-hey about them. Listen,' he sat up, 'up to now he's just thought of you as yet another up-tight housewife from down the road. He'll probably look at you in a completely different light now!'

'Lance,' I hissed, lowering my face to his, 'I do not wish him to see me in any other light than that of a neighbour, OK? He's the local oddball, for heaven's sake! In all probability he's as mad as a meat-axe. The last thing I want is some nutter turning up on my doorstep looking for a bit of "weh-hey"!'

'Is he?' he frowned. 'A nutter? Blimey, he looked all right to me.'

'Oh, what would you know?' I snapped as I buttoned up my cardigan. 'You think all single women should behave like prostitutes, have a bit of oomph about them – except your wife and your mother, I presume, who you'd no doubt like strapped into their pinnies and welded to the stove. It's the classic madonna-whore syndrome. You're probably as barking as he is!'

'Right. Sorry I spoke,' he muttered, settling back and shutting his eyes again.

I ignored him and marched off round the side of the house, out on to the road. I strode off along the cobbles, needing to go while I still felt brave, while I was still fired up, and practising my apology as I went. Happily it didn't matter that my face was the colour of a tomato since I was about to blush heavily anyway. How about if I started with something like, 'Sebastian, good gracious, what must you think? Do let me

explain. You see, my brother and his wife are staying and—'
Oh, I don't know. Something like that, anyway.

I climbed the steps to his tall, elegant town house,
peering first into the basement below, which in Nanette's
house was the kitchen. No lights on, no sign of life. I rang
the bell and gazed for an inordinately long time at the red
front door. I was just about to go away when his mother
opened it. Just a fraction. She peered at me around the
two-inch crack she'd conceded, almost as if she'd come up
from the bowels of the earth and hadn't seen daylight
before. I'd never seen her close up before, and I nearly
gasped. She was sensationally ugly: her upper teeth protruded and were slightly pointed, making her look like a
small, anxious rodent, and her steely grey hair was tied
back in a bun so tight, it pulled her eyebrows up, giving her
a startled ferret expression.

'Yes?' she whispered.

'Oh! Um, hello!' I smiled brightly. 'I'm Olivia
McFarllen, from down the road. I've, um, seen you around,
but we've never actually been properly introduced!' I held
out my hand matily. She glanced at it, shot out a white hand
and almost touched my fingers. Almost.

Oh God, had he told her already? Was I a Scarlet Woman
in her eyes? Not to be touched? I flushed.

'Well, I really came to see Sebastian. Is he in?'

'No, he's not.'

'Ah, right. Will he be long? D'you think?'

'I've no idea. I'm going out myself now, though, so if
you'll excuse me . . .' She made to shut the door.

'Oh, well, it's just that he knocked on my door. About an
hour ago. And I just wondered – what he wanted.'

She frowned. Opened the door a bit wider. 'You didn't
answer it?'

'Um, someone else answered.'

'But didn't come and get you?'

Not so stupid, this old bag. Superior thought processes were apparent. 'Er, no. You see, I was very busy. Very involved.' Oh, no, not *involved*, Olivia!

'Well, I wouldn't worry. I don't suppose he specifically wanted to see you. He was out delivering leaflets.'

'Oh, leaflets! Lovely!' I enthused. 'Getting out and about then?'

She narrowed her eyes at me suspiciously, declined to answer. No, quite right. Probably fiercely protective.

'Well,' I hastened on, 'when he comes back, perhaps you could just say – that I'd love to have a chat? When he's around?'

'I'll give him the message.'

She shut the door and left me staring at the paintwork again. God, what an old harridan, I thought as I turned and went slowly down the steps. Poor old Sebastian. Heavens, it was no wonder he was like he was with a mother like that. She probably smothered him as a child, hadn't let him play with any rough boys, probably hadn't even let him go to school. I'd hazard a guess she still ironed his pants for him, tucked his pyjama top into his bottoms at night. It was years since I'd seen it, but she reminded me of that nutty mother in *Psycho*, the one at the top of the house in the rocking chair, which I suppose made Sebastian the creepy son . . . although now I came to think of it, hadn't the son dressed up as the mother? Yes, that's right, there hadn't been a mother at all. I glanced back nervously. Could that have been— Oh, don't be ridiculous, Olivia. She's half his size! None the less, I thought with a shiver, no showers for me until I'd safely explained away Lance's sexual marathon story. I didn't want him thinking we were poking fun at his own sexual inadequacies; didn't want him meat-cleaving his way round to my place.

I slowed my pace as I approached my gates and stopped. Hesitated. It was funny, but now that I was out, and it was such a beautiful day, I didn't much feel like going back. I also didn't feel like facing Lance. However accommodating he'd been this morning, now that it was all over I felt slightly foolish. I wanted to distance myself from him. Wanted to get back to that more formal employer-employee relationship we'd had yesterday, forget the cosy, reclining-about-on-rugs-half-naked relationship of this morning. I always kept a ten-pound note in the car in case of petrol emergencies, so not wanting to pop into the house, I stopped by to pick it up. I shoved it in my shorts pocket and strolled on. Yes, that's it: I'd go into town, buy a bar of chocolate, get the papers, wander around for a bit – why not? And with any luck, by the time I got back, Lance might just have eased himself up from his supine position on the lawn and gone back to making cupboards for my bloody kitchen – which, let's face it, was what he was contracted to do in the first place, I thought (a little uncharitably, perhaps, under the circumstances). I joined the footpath, walked on through the park and out on to the steep hill that led to the high street.

Being Sunday, the town was fairly empty – just a few tourists, sitting around in cafés and wine bars, studying guidebooks, heading no doubt for the Roman ruins. I bought the Sunday papers, and suddenly realised I was starving. I hadn't eaten since breakfast, which I'd hardly touched, so I stopped off in one of the sunnier watering holes and sat down outside, under a shady umbrella. As I shook out the review section of the newspaper, for one startling moment I felt a delicious sense of freedom. No

Sunday lunch to cook, no Johnny to worry about, no volatile moods to pander to; no joint to wrestle out of a steaming oven, no apple sauce to make, no pudding – which I never ate but which Johnny and Claudia liked – to spend half the morning preparing. Just me, a glass of chilled white wine – I studied the menu, and – yes, a Caesar salad. I snapped it shut and smiled up at the rather attractive Italian waiter who was hovering, and gave him my order. Well, I thought, lighting a cigarette, which Claudia would have objected to, with dire threats of 'death, Mummy, really slow and lingering, and me an orphan, with no one to look after me.' Well. I smiled into the sunshine. This really wasn't so terrible, was it? A beautiful day, with no one to please but myself. Yes, in theory, I would have had it differently, but actually, in reality, it was not so unpleasant. Was I even warming to it? This single life?

When I'd finished my lunch and read most of the papers, I paid the bill and strolled back, taking a short cut through the West Gate of the Abbey and down a cobbled side street. I passed the Abbey nearly every day of my life but never failed to be moved by it. I stopped now and stared up at the square, red tower, which had been built in something unbelievable, like 1080, from Roman tiles that had already been hanging around for – ooh, about eight hundred years. In anyone's history book, that made it pretty ancient. I strolled on round to the more recent, Gothic façade, but stopped short at the door.

When we'd first moved here, I'd gone in quite a lot, marvelling at the vast painted ceilings, exploring the nave, the crypts, the chapel of the first martyr, enjoying the history, the architecture. Claudia loved it too, and I occasionally accompanied her to evensong, which she liked, but never with Johnny. Having been quite a strict Catholic, he'd suddenly taken against it all, declaring it a load of papist mumbo jumbo – which was odd, because in London he'd chivvy us all into going at least a couple of times a month. Now he no longer went at all. Too much to confess, I thought bitterly. And to be honest, with no one to bully me into it, I didn't choose to worship much either. It didn't bother me that this church wasn't my denomination – and, anyway, they did hold Catholic services here. It was just that I'd always felt attendance a duty, an onerous one, to be done under duress. But as I stood there on the main steps, worn down by centuries of pilgrims' feet, I realised I missed it. It was imbued in me, this religious ritual, whether I liked it or not. A combination of my mother, the nuns at school and, to a lesser extent, Johnny and his family, had seen to that. I missed the contemplation, the peace of prayer. In truth, I missed that still, small voice of calm that I'd kicked against all my life.

On an impulse, I stuffed the rather gaudy Sunday papers in a bin and walked in, abruptly conscious of my shorts. I pulled the turn-ups down a bit. The morning service had finished and the tourists had taken over, swarming about the place. On the South side, orchestra stands and chairs were also being noisily assembled, possibly for a rehearsal of the concert Imogen had mentioned. I stopped, disappointed. Something pompous about not causing a commotion in my father's house came to mind, but in truth, I think the bustle annoyed my romantic sensibilities more than my religious ones. It was at odds with my vision of myself as a young Sophia Loren-like figure, alone in a huge cathedral, black headscarf tied under chin, kneeling to ask my maker for guidance, for forgiveness, whereupon a rather sexy young curate would approach, see my bent head – and, of course, my sylphlike figure and finely chiselled profile – sit beside me and place a hand on mine.

'You look troubled, my child.'

'Yes, well,' I'd sigh. 'You'd be troubled if you'd been left for a complete bimbo, and were having to contend with the builders, not to mention—'

At this point my fantasy lost any religious fervour it might have possessed and plunged into mediocrity. I grinned. Just as well the place was packed, I decided, as I came out through the Chapel door, and I couldn't attempt my prayer/fantasy. Who knows where it might have ended, and anyway, declothing vicars was a rather serious offence, I believed.

I smiled as I rounded the bend into my road, admiring the roses that cascaded over my garden wall. Madame Alfred Carrière was such a good doer. It didn't last all summer, of course, like the modern hybrids, but, my goodness, that flash of splendour made up for its brevity. I was also pleased to see the back of Lucy's mother's car parked outside: the Range Rover lookalike, with its spare wheel giving free advertising to the garage of purchase, that badge of the upwardly mobile, school-running mother. Ah good, Claudes was back then. I realised with a guilty pang that I hadn't really missed her at all, as I usually did. Too preoccupied, no doubt. As a treat, I thought, I'd make her pancakes for supper. Let her eat them in front of the telly, in front of *Ballykissangel* – or *Ballykissarsehole*, as Johnny used to call it – with a packet of Jaffa Cakes between us for pudding, as was our wont.

Lucy's mother, Amanda, was sitting in the front seat. When she saw me in her rear-view mirror, she shot out of the car. I saw her face and stopped short, as if I'd hit a barrier.

'Is she with you?' she called. I'll never forget the sound of her voice. 'Have you got her?'

Her face was pale, strained. I made myself go on, broke into a run.

'What?' I called stupidly, knowing.

'Claudia, is she with you?'

'Of course not! She's with you, isn't she?'

Amanda's face crumpled as I reached her, her hand clutched her mouth.

'Oh God, Olivia, this is all so awful and it's all my fault! I'm so sorry.' Her voice cracked as she reached out and gripped my arm. 'Claudia's gone missing!'

Chapter Eleven

'What d'you mean, gone missing?' I felt my stomach heave, my heart leap into my throat.

'Well, she wanted to come back, you see, this morning,' Amanda fell over her words in her distress, 'and so I brought her back because she seemed so anxious, and then, of course, you weren't here and – and stupidly I left her because she said she'd be fine, and then I panicked and rang and you still weren't back and *she* wasn't here either and – oh God, Olivia, I'm so sorry!' She hid her face in her hands and burst into tears.

Feeling sick to my stomach but knowing I had to stay calm, I sat her on the garden wall.

'From the beginning, Amanda,' I said trembling. 'Slowly. Tell me exactly what happened.'

She wiped mascara from under her eyes with the tips of shaky fingers. Nodded. 'Sorry.' She seemed to pull herself together for a moment. Took a deep breath. 'Well, she was fine last night. I let them have pizza in front of a video and then they all slept on mattresses on the floor in Lucy's room and giggled for ages. Claudia was as cheerful as the others, had a great time – midnight feasts, dancing to pop music, that sort of thing – but then this morning at breakfast, well, she seemed rather quiet. The others were still shrieking away, very overexcited and hyped up, but she wasn't, and she didn't eat anything either. I asked her if she was OK and she said she was fine, and then a bit later on, I dropped them off at a ten o'clock matinée of *Titanic*. When I picked them up outside, the other three were larking about as usual, but Claudia was still withdrawn, so I took her aside and asked her what was wrong. Her eyes filled with tears. She said she normally saw her daddy on a Sunday, but she'd chosen to come here instead, and now she felt awful because she thought he might be upset, think she'd chosen her friends instead, that she didn't want to see him.'

'Oh, Claudes!' My hand flew to my mouth.

'So I said, well, OK, what time did Daddy normally come round? And she said, oh, about lunchtime, I think, so I said – well, look, Mummy's probably put him off, but d'you want to go home and check, and maybe ring him to see if there's still time to see him? Well, her face lit up at that, and she said she did.' Amanda paused for breath, took a huge gulp of air. 'Anyway, I said, OK, that's fine, I'll drop you off, so we all piled in the car and drove straight over, but you weren't here. There was a note on the door from someone called Lance who said he was in the Fighting Cocks if you wanted to join him, but otherwise the place was deserted.' She gave a tremulous sob. 'Except that the back door was open, and Claudia said that if you'd left it open like that you wouldn't be long and you'd probably only popped to the shops, and that, in any case, the builder would be back soon.' Amanda raised her chin to hold back tears. 'Anyway, the other three were going on and on about how I'd promised them Café Rouge and how they were starving, and Claudia was insisting that she didn't want to come, and then the baby started screaming and – oh God, Olivia, in the end I just left her here!' She turned guilty eyes on me.

I nodded. 'It's OK, Amanda. I might well have done the same.'

'So off we all went for lunch and, of course, sitting there in the restaurant, I worried, so I rang to make sure you were back but there was no answer. Then I really panicked. I hurried the girls through their pudding but it took ages to get the bill and then I dropped them all off with my neighbour before dashing back over here. The back door was still open and I looked all over the house and the garden and she just wasn't here. Then I looked down the road and then I thought – well, maybe you'd come back and you'd both gone out together and I'd missed you or some-thing, but then you came back and – Oh God, Olivia, I feel sick!' She held her hand over her mouth, eyes full of fear. 'What are we going to do!'

She felt sick. I swallowed. Right. So she'd searched everywhere and Claudia wasn't here. My head told me that she was very sensible for her age and that she wouldn't be far, maybe across the stream in the thicket at the back, or maybe even next door with the Joneses, but my heart told me that she was ten years old and she was on her own somewhere, had been for two hours, and I didn't know where.

'Should we ring the police?' trembled Amanda.

'Not yet. You go and ask next door. I'm going to check out a few places near the river.'

I flew round the back of the house and down the garden. Most people assumed the stream was our boundary, but our land – such as it was – carried on over the other side. Amanda wouldn't have been down here. I ran over the bridge and into the little thicket where Claudia had her tree house. Oh, please let her be sulking up here, I begged as I climbed the rope ladder, please let her be reading a comic, cross that I wasn't around to get hold of Daddy for her, please! I reached the top and peered in. Empty. I clattered back down again and ran to the back fence. My hands clutched the black railings. There was a park beyond with wide pathways where we sometimes went roller-skating up to the lake. I shaded my eyes. No sign. Just a few teenage girls immobile on the grass with skirts pulled up, and an old couple asleep in deck chairs. I ran back, across the bridge, then veered off left to the caravan. I flung open the door. Nothing. I felt panic rising, but made myself stop and rack my brains. As I shut the door I had a thought: the note on the door from Lance. If she'd read it, and thought – oh, Mum's gone to join him in the pub – then she'd surely come and find me there! Of course! And there was a garden there too, so she was probably on the swings, or having an orange juice and a bag of crisps with Lance, happy as Larry!

I ran breathlessly back to Amanda in the drive.

'She wasn't next door!' she shouted.

'No, it's OK, stay here in case she appears, but I think I know where she is.'

'Oh, thank God!' She clasped her hands. 'Where d'you—'

But I didn't wait to explain, I was gone. The Fighting Cocks was only a couple of hundred yards from our house, at the end of The Crescent, and in the summer it teemed, mostly with teenagers having their first illicit pint, loafing around on the grass, laughing loudly as it reached the relevant parts, or even just hanging out on the wall with an orange juice. The garden was heaving when I arrived. I glanced at the swings, but they were being ridden by much older children, showing off, standing two to a swing, facing each other, making them soar in the air. I spun around, squinting against the sun to spot her. There were children everywhere, running amongst the tables, eating chicken nuggets with their parents – but no Claudia. Then suddenly I spotted Lance. He was sitting at the end of a long table he was having to share with a multitude of others, one hand holding his mobile phone to his ear, the other, shading his eyes as he gazed, rather grimly, at the table. My hand shot up.

'Lance!'

I dashed across. 'Lance – is Claudia with you?'

He glanced up quickly from his phone. 'Speak to you later,' he informed someone abruptly. He snapped it shut. 'Ah! You made it at last.' He smiled. 'D'you want a drink?'

'No!' I shrieked, gripping the table with two hands. 'Is Claudia with you!'

The rest of the table caught the hysteria in my voice and paused, drinks and sandwiches halfway to mouths.

Lance got up. 'No, she's not, why?'

'Oh, Lance, she's missing!' I gasped, rapidly losing control. Vocalising it was so awful. My baby. Missing. He came round the table, took my arm and led me away.

'When was she last seen?' he muttered gently.

'Lucy's mother brought her home – I think about an hour and a half ago. We must have both just left the house!'

'You mean, she left her there?'

'Yes, because she thought I'd be back in a minute!'

'Well, an hour and half's not long. She must be around here somewhere.'

'Yes, I suppose, but where!' I wailed, spinning around, as if vainly hoping to see her sitting at another table, with another family perhaps, tucking into a ploughman's, grinning and waving a fork at me. We pushed our way through the throng to the gate. 'Where?' I repeated hysterically.

'Now don't panic. She's a sensible girl, and it's not as if she's a baby, for heaven's sake. She's probably just popped round to see a friend or something.'

'No.' I shook my head, knowing he was talking about a different world. A friendlier, latch-key world, an every-mum-in-the-street-is-an-auntie world, not the closeted, privately educated, socially divisive world Claudia belonged to. 'It's not like that, Lance. She doesn't go to the local school, none of her friends live round here, she gets ferried everywhere by car. Oh God, where is she!'

I started to run up the road, my eyes darting about, heart pounding. I didn't know where I was running, I just knew I couldn't walk. I belted down a side street, stopped, spun around and dashed back again. Lance was waiting.

'Why did she come home?' he said, walking fast to keep up with me as I started running back up our road. 'I thought she was staying for lunch?'

'She was, but she wanted to see Johnny. She felt bad about going to Lucy's when she usually saw him on a Sunday.'

'OK, so then wouldn't she have rung him? Possibly gone to find him?'

'What – in London!' I shrieked, stopping dead in my tracks. Suddenly I saw her. At Piccadilly Circus, on the steps up to Eros, lying with the homeless in a cardboard box, hair matted, eyes dark and hollow, syringe hanging out of her arm, predatory pimp hovering.

'OH CHRIST!' I roared. I had to hold on to Lance's arm for support.

'Steady – *steady*,' he insisted nervously. 'No, I doubt if she'd actually *go* to London – she's not silly – but she might try to contact him, surely?'

'Yes! Yes, you're right, she might!' Hope flooded back

for a second. 'I'll ring him.' I hurried on. 'And the police?' I threw over my shoulder. 'Should we ring them too?'

'No, not yet,' he said firmly, jogging to keep up. 'I know you're worried but I think it's a bit premature. Let's explore all the possibilities first because, let's face it, that's all the police will do.'

Amanda came running down the road to meet us. 'Well?' she shouted.

I shook my head.

'Oh God, this is awful!' She clutched her mouth. 'And it's almost *more* awful for me because it's someone else's child!'

She was getting hysterical, and actually, I didn't want to hear about how awful it was for her. I felt like giving her a good slap. She was sobbing now, and Lance was trying to calm her, leading her to her car, knowing she was doing me no good at all, talking to her in the voice one reserves for – who was it now? – yes, that's it, the bereaved. Send her home, send her home, I prayed. She was nodding as he cajoled her into the front seat, and I saw her reach, sniffing, for the ignition key. As I watched her drive off, I wondered if I was actually here at all. Wondered whether this was real, or if I was actually in a hospital bed – I felt sick enough – coming round from some ghastly anaesthetic dream which would disappear just as soon as the gas wore off. Lance came back to me.

'I gave her a job. She's going to ring all the girls in Lucy and Claudia's class, just to make sure she hasn't tried to get hold of one of them. That sent her packing.'

I was in the hallway now, front door open, looking desperately for Johnny's number on the hall table. I felt incredibly dizzy.

'So they'll all know,' I trembled. 'All her friends will know she's missing.'

'We can't keep it a secret, Olivia. We have to find her, that's all that matters.'

I touched my forehead. Of course that was all that mattered. What was I thinking of? Losing face amongst the class mothers?

'Now, Johnny?' He picked up the receiver, raising his eyebrows expectantly.

'Yes, I know but I can't find the bloody number!' I sifted through papers, lifting them up and letting them drop with hopeless hands.

'Well, what's it written on?'

'The back of a milk bill, I think – ah! Here!' My trembling fingers pounced on the scrap I'd jotted it down on, not wanting the number in my address book. Too permanent somehow. I dialled. Nina answered.

'Is Johnny there?' I barked. No niceties now. And she knew it was me. Didn't bother to ask. Yet I'd never rung there before, he always rang here. He came on.

'Livvy?'

'Johnny, is Claudia with you?'

'Of course not. I've just this minute got back from you, why?'

I explained in a quavering voice. He was silent. I waited for the storm to break, the how-could-you-have-let-her-out-of-your-sights, the recriminations.

'Oh Christ, this is all my fault,' he said quietly. 'I've put her in this mess. This is my doing. She came back to see me.'

I was stunned, but I rallied. 'Of course it's not your fault, Johnny, but we must find her. Ask Nina, has she tried to ring while you were out?'

He turned and I heard him talk to her. I had to close my eyes, clench my teeth, so painful did I find the sound of their murmuring voices. He came back.

'No, she hasn't. Livvy, I'll come down. Ring the police and I'll come down.'

'No, Johnny, she may be coming to see you! She's got your address, remember, and you won't be there!'

'Nina will be here in case she arrives. I have to be with you on this one, Livvy.'

I shut my eyes again. He had to be with me. But he'd qualified it. *On this one, Livvy.*

'OK.' I put down the phone, swung round to Lance. 'She's not there. Now I'll ring the police.' As I went for the receiver, his hand closed on mine.

'In a minute. Just check first – has she taken any money?'

'Oh!' I dropped the receiver. 'I don't know ... Wait!'

I raced upstairs two at a time, dashed into her room and seized her china pig. I pulled out the plug. I knew she had about thirty pounds, enough to get her to London and back. It was still there.

'No!' I screamed as I crashed back down the stairs. 'It's still there – that's good, isn't it?' I panted, hanging over the banisters, pleading for confirmation. Surely it meant she wasn't in London, and what on earth could happen to her round here?

'I think it is,' he said slowly. 'I think it means she isn't far away. Nanette?'

'Oh God, of course! Nanette!'

I jumped the last few steps and lunged again for the phone. Roger was in, Nanette was at her mother's, and no, he hadn't seen Claudia. I could feel my courage draining.

'Who else?' demanded Lance. 'Your mother?'

'Yes – brilliant, my mother! But she'd need money to—'

'Ring her anyway.'

I did. She was out. Her answer machine was on. Lance paced up and down the hall, biting his lower lip, eyes narrowed. I watched helplessly.

'What would she do,' he muttered, 'on a normal day, on a normal Sunday morning? What would she do?' He swung round, his eyes interrogating me. I fought to think.

'Read maybe, or – or go upstairs and play on the playstation, write an E-mail to a friend.'

'OK, but if she was outside?' he urged. 'If she was out in the garden?'

'Well, her bike, I suppose, or— Her bike!'

I ran out of the front door and round the side passage to the shed. Lance followed.

'It's gone!' I yelled. 'Her bike's gone!'

'Right,' he breathed. 'Now we're getting somewhere.'

'Oh, Lance, she's just gone for a bike ride! That's all, isn't it?'

'Hopefully. And Lucy's mother's ringing all her classmates because there's a good chance she'd ride to one of them, isn't there?'

'Well, not normally. She's not allowed out of The Crescent, but—'

'OK, so where else did she ride it? With you, maybe, but today she tries it on her own. Think!'

'In the park,' I said quickly. 'We'd both ride together up to the lake, and also along the tow path by the stream; it runs along the back of The Crescent.'

'Right. I'll take the park and the lake, you take the tow path. If we meet back here with no joy in ten minutes, we'll call the police.'

'Shouldn't we do that now? They could take a description of her and—'

'Time,' he interrupted. 'All of that takes time, all those

questions, forms to fill in – and the chances are, if we're quick, we'll catch up with her.'

'OK,' I agreed, 'but back here at –' we glanced at our watches – 'quarter to.'

Off I raced, back down the garden, but this time, with a slightly lighter heart. She wasn't on a train, she wasn't in London, she wasn't doing drugs in a squat. She was just pootling about on her bike, waiting for Mummy to come home. Oh, thank God. I crossed the bridge and turned right along the tow path. I liked to go the other way, where the trees dipped into the water and the moorhens gathered underneath with their broods, but I knew Claudia preferred this way. This was her beat, with lots of rises and dips to pedal up fast, and shoot down again. As I hurried round a bend, I nearly mowed down an old lady walking her pug.

'Oh – sorry!' I steadied myself, holding her shoulders. 'Have you seen a girl?' I panted. 'Of about ten, riding her bike?'

'I haven't dear,' she said, startled. She adjusted her cardigan where I'd held her. She made to move on, but as I broke into a run again, she called me back.

'Oh – I say!'

I swung about.

'There is a bike, though. Further along, in the hedgerow. I noticed it as I came round.'

I stared at her. Couldn't speak. She raised her walking stick in salute, and went on her way. A bike. In the hedgerow. Full of fear and foreboding I raced around the corner – and there it was. Claudia's bike. Pink, too young for her she'd insisted recently, too Barbie doll, with a basket on the front, and in her basket, an apple and a book. No Claudia.

My eyes shot about. 'CLAUDIA!' I screamed, my heart pounding. Silence.

'CLAUDIAAA!' I felt bile rush to my mouth. My eyes darted back to the bike, abandoned on its side, front wheel at an acute angle, like a silent distress signal. Oh God, she must have been dragged off the path, into the bushes! A strangled sob reared up my throat. Through the bracken I crashed, sobbing now.

'CLAUDIA! CLAUDI-AA!'

Low branches tore at my clothes and face as I plunged off in all directions, going round in circles, always coming back to the same spot, glancing helplessly at the bike before tearing off again.

'Oh God, oh God,' I sobbed, stumbling further down along the tow path. A couple of amorous teenagers, arms and tongues entwined as they walked blindly towards me, eyes shut, were suddenly confronted by a mad woman, face scratched and bleeding, sobbing wildly.

'Have you seen a girl!' I cried.

'What?' The spotty youth unstuck his lips and blinked, startled.

'A girl! Look, there's her bike back there – about ten, in red shorts probably – have you seen her?'

'Nah, sorry, luv.' He made to move on.

'Oh yeah, hang abou'.' His girlfriend held his arm. 'Yeah, we did, remember? What about the one wiv that man, Gary? You know, the one back there?'

'What man!' I roared, voice hoarse but nearly fainting with fear.

Gary shrugged. 'Dunno.'

'Yeah, he was, he was wiv one,' she insisted. She turned to me. 'A little girl. She was wearin' red shorts an' all, and he 'ad her by the arm.'

Oh God. Oh dear Jesus and God. 'Which way?' I choked.

'Over there.' She pointed behind me. I swung about. She was pointing across the other side of the stream, back to The Crescent, to the row of back gardens.

'She was cryin' an' that, too, weren't she, Gary?'

'Dunno.'

'Yeah, she was, an' I watched them go, 'cos I fought it was funny, wasn't sure if he was her dad, an' he took 'er up that parf, into that house there.'

'Which one?' I breathed.

'There, that one wiv the green back door, over there.'

She jabbed her finger. I followed it. Stared – then froze with horror. My heart nearly stopped completely. Oh God. Oh dear God Almighty. Sebastian. It was Sebastian's house.

Chapter Twelve

I flew across the footbridge and down the path that led along the back of The Crescent gardens. Sebastian's house was in the middle, tall, and red brick at the back, in contrast to its white stucco façade, and with a strip of immaculate lawn stretching down to wrought-iron railings and a gate at the bottom. With a pounding heart I ran along the path to the gate. He'd forced her through here, sobbing, the bastard. Had her arm in a vicelike grip. The gate was still open. I ran through, then, realising the French windows at the back of the house were also wide open, veered left and shot behind a shed. I flattened myself against it for a moment, panting hard. I had to get her out of there, but I had to be careful. If I charged in, all guns blazing, he might put a kitchen knife to her throat, hold her hostage or something. Oh yes, I thought, my mind racing, it was all becoming very clear now. He was obviously taking some sort of warped revenge for having my sexual exploits thrust in his face by Lance. Perhaps he was impotent, or – or maybe he had designs on me himself, was plucking up the courage to ask me out and had come to the door on the pretext of delivering leaflets, but then had had to listen to Lance's account of me, wallowing in Radox, bug-eyed with sexual exhaustion. Well, that was enough to send anyone remotely remedial into a complete lather, enough to make him bide his time, wait, watch, and then take revenge. Enough to make him take my baby. A sob tore up my throat. I gulped it back down, clenching my teeth.

Peering cautiously round the shed, I narrowed my eyes. I could just about see into the drawing room, but the bright sunlight made it too dark for me to determine if anyone was in there. I had to make an angled dash across the lawn, aim for the outside wall of the house, flush with the French windows, and hope for the best. Head down and bent forward, I went for it, leaping an immaculate flowerbed and making it to the relative safety of the wall. I flattened myself against it, heart going like a bongo drum. Slowly I inched my way along the doorframe and peeped round. I could hear noises, voices, and for a moment I thought there were a few people in the room, until I realised the television was on. I couldn't see anyone, except – yes. Suddenly I realised that that was Claudia, sitting hunched in an armchair at the back of the room. Except I hardly recognised her. Her hair looked lank and too dark, and she was wearing a dressing gown. A man's dressing gown. *His* dressing gown. A little yelp escaped my lips and I could bear it no longer. A garden rake was propped up against the wall beside me. I seized it and charged in.

'CLAUDIA, GET BEHIND ME!' I shrieked, spreading out my arms and brandishing the rake at the rest of the room. Claudia looked up from the television in astonishment.

'Mum!'

'Get behind me!' I yelled.

'But—'

'JUST DO IT!'

Claudia, never having seen me in totally-lost-it mode,

208

waving a rake, leapt up and scuttled behind me.

'Why?' she whispered.

'Where is he?' I barked.

'Who?'

'Sebastian!'

'Oh well, around, I think.'

Around. I swung about, pushing her behind me, still shielding her with my body, glancing furtively in corners, waiting for him to pounce out from behind one of those dark pieces of furniture at any moment.

'Now, back,' I hissed.

'What?'

'Back! Go backwards, out of the French windows!'

Catching the madness and urgency in my voice, Claudia obeyed. Clutching her dressing gown to her, she started reversing out, wide-eyed. I backed with her, eyes darting everywhere.

'Did he touch you, my love?' I whispered brokenly.

'What d'you mean?'

'Well, did he –' I choked back a strangled sob – 'hurt you in any way?'

'Of course not!'

I swung round to see her staring in astonishment at me.

'But he took your clothes?'

'Yes, but—'

'The bastard!' I spat. 'The rotten, dirty, filthy bastard. How *dare* he – *aha*!'

A figure materialised from the shadows. A figure coming through the far door, bearing a tray of tea and biscuits. Sebastian, in a white shirt and faded brown cords, blinked in surprise as he confronted a scratched and bleeding woman in his sitting room, legs planted wide apart and bent at the knee like a sumo wrestler, hands gripping either end of a horizontal garden rake, kung fu style.

'*Aha!*' I cried again, bracing myself, head stuck forward and moving slowly from side to side, like a bull facing a matador. 'So! You've finally slunk out, have you, you little piece of filth! Come one step closer and I swear to God I'll— *Stay where you are!*'

Sebastian stopped, astonished. 'Good Lord, what on earth—'

'Don't you Good Lord me,' I hissed, 'you dirty, scummy degenerate – *Keep backing away, Claudia!*'

Claudia, who for a moment had popped her startled head out, hastily obeyed and began making her way out to the garden.

'Now run!' I yelled over my shoulder. 'Run home and I'll cover you. I'll follow later. Now! GO!'

Claudia didn't wait to argue with a mother in this mood. She took to her heels and scampered off, scared witless, no doubt.

'Mrs McFarllen, are you taking drugs?' enquired Sebastian calmly.

'How *dare* you?' I breathed as I slowly followed my daughter, backing out, but keeping my rake rigid at chest level. 'How dare you abduct a poor defenceless child? You're not just a harmless halfwit like everyone says, you're a bloody pervert! The lowest of the low! D'you know what happens to people like you in prison? Hmm? Do you? Do you know what your fellow inmates will do to you?'

'Good god,' he muttered. 'You need help.'

'Help!' I barked derisively. 'Ha! You're the one who needs help, you little creep, and I'll see that you get it – in spades! You were seen,' I hissed, curling my lip, 'by a decent, upright young couple out walking, seen dragging an innocent child, screaming, *sobbing*, on her knees practically, into *your house*!'

'This is outrageous!' His face clouded and he came towards me.

'NO CLOSER!' I bellowed, swinging the rake so it pointed straight at him. I brandished it at his chest. 'No closer or I'll—'

THWACKK! As he took another step I jerked the rake up, slamming it under the tray and sending it flying. It performed a neat somersault, and steaming Lapsang Souchong and garibaldis leapt high in the air – then splashed straight down in his face.

'Christ!' he clutched his eyes.

Temporarily blinded, he staggered about a bit, and I took advantage. I flung down the rake, shot one last look at the stumbling, gasping figure with his face in his hands – then fled. Up the immaculate lawn I tore, leaping the flowerbed, through the gate, down the towpath, through our own wrought-iron gate, then back down the garden, through the French windows – and home. I slammed the glass doors shut behind me, shooting bolts across at top and bottom with quivering hands. I spun round.

'Claudia!'

No answer.

'CLAUDIAAA!'

'In here,' came a flat, dead-pan voice.

I flew off in its general direction and found her, sitting with Lance, at the kitchen table. She was still huddled in the dressing gown and drinking orange juice straight from a carton. I dropped to my knees beside her.

'Darling, oh, my poor darling,' I sobbed, hugging her knees. 'Are you all right? Shall I call the police?'

'Don't be ridiculous, Mum. You've made a complete and

utter pill of yourself,' snapped Claudia, shaking me off. 'I'm so embarrassed. He didn't hurt me at all, he just hauled me out of the river.'

My mouth fell open. I sat back on my heels, then stood up. 'Wh-what?'

'My bike hit a rut and I went in headfirst, bumped my head on a rock. He was at an upstairs window and saw what happened. He came out to help me. I was absolutely soaking so he lent me a dressing gown and put my clothes in the tumble dryer.'

'But – they said you were crying,' I gasped. 'And being held by him!'

'I *was* crying. I cut my knee, look.' She lifted the dressing gown to show a newly bandaged knee with blood still seeping through. 'It hurt like anything, and he wasn't holding me, he was just helping me 'cos I was limping so much. I could hardly walk. I've never been so embarrassed in all my life, Mum. He was so kind and put a bandage on, and made tea and everything, and then you appear like bloody Boadicea, looking totally insane, screaming and hollering, with blood all over your face and twigs and things coming out of your head, and a *rake*, for God's sake. You looked like such a spasmo.'

'Oh God.' I sank down on to a chair. 'You mean he didn't—'

'No, of course he didn't, and I'm really disgusted by your mind sometimes, Mum. You thought he was showing me his privates, didn't you?'

'Well I—'

'I'm going up to change.' She got up and stalked out.

I sat, staring after her for a minute. Then slowly, I leant my elbows on the table, pushed my hands into my hair, clutched my head and groaned.

'Oh Lord!' I whispered. 'Oh Lord, Lance, I went berserk. She's right. I went totally, indescribably, doo-bleeding-lally berserk! I was like a mad woman in there! Called him names, all kinds of terrible – oh Christ – *ghastly* names and – oh God –' my head shot up and my eyes bulged with horror as I remembered – 'I threw hot tea all over him! Scalded him, gave him third-degree burns! He'll probably have me up for assault!'

'Probably,' Lance agreed calmly, pouring me a cup from the pot he'd just made. 'But I'm sure we can get you off with a decent brief and some cock-and-bull story about it being the wrong time of the month and you being emotionally unstable or something. Tends to work. Anyway, the main thing is, Claudia's back.'

'Yes,' I breathed, leaning back in my chair with relief. 'Yes, you're right, thank God. Helped out of a river by Sebastian.' I raked my hands desperately through my hair again, punishing it. 'Oh Lance, I must go back,' I groaned. 'I must go straight back – yet again – and apologise, sort things out. Poor, simple, decent, innocent man! I've probably scarred him for life!'

'What, with the tea or the insults?'

'Both! Oh, how appalling of me, Lance. Imagine what that could do to a man like that? I must make it up to him somehow. Maybe I could take him and his friends on an outing? To the zoo, or something? Hire a minibus?'

'Olivia, I'm not convinced he's as— Oh-oh.' He broke off suddenly, glancing out of the window. 'Forget the Whipsnade trip, I think you'll have to go and make your neighbourly peace some other time. Right now you have a visitor.'

I glanced out of the window.

'Johnny!' I breathed, as the old yellow E-type screeched

to an emergency halt outside. 'Oh God, I'd forgotten about him. I should have rung him on his mobile, told him she was OK! Blimey, he got here in double-quick time; must have driven at a million miles an hour!'

'I'll make myself scarce,' muttered Lance, getting up and making for the back door.

Johnny's face when he got out of the car was very pale, his mouth set in a taut line. I jumped up and raced out to meet him. I knew that every moment of thinking she was missing was torture, and that if I ran, I could spare him one or two.

'It's OK!' I cried as I flung open the front door. 'She's back! She went for a bike ride and fell in the stream, but she's fine!'

He stopped still at the gate. His face cleared. 'Thank God. Oh, Livvy, thank God.' He broke into a run, and as I raced out to meet him, he swept me up in his arms and caught me to him. As he held me tight, my face pressed into his chest, my arms round his warm shoulders, I could feel his heart pounding. I shut my eyes. I wanted to sob. It was like a drop of water to a parched soul.

'Where is she?' he said, releasing me, holding me at arm's length.

'Upstairs, changing. I'll tell her you're here. Oh, Johnny, I'm sorry, I should have rung you on your mobile. You've had to come all this way again on a wild-goose chase!'

'Wild-goose chase?' He stared. 'Don't be silly, I'd have wanted to be here anyway. She's my daughter, Livvy.'

'Yes. Yes, of course,' I nodded meekly, humbled. 'Sorry.' I hung my head.

I seemed to be getting it all wrong today, didn't I? I was all over the place, apparently. We turned to go in, just as, clattering downstairs, in leggings and a pink T-shirt, and framed in the open front doorway, came Claudia. She yelped with delight when she saw Johnny. He ran, and she leapt the last few steps into his arms.

'Hello, pixie,' he muttered into her hair. 'I hear you've been having huge adventures. Lone bike rides and falling into rapids, very Enid Blyton. You'll have to let me come with you next time.'

'Daddy,' she pulled back from him, 'I'm – I'm sorry about this morning, about not seeing you.' Her voice cracked and it broke my heart. I don't imagine it did much for Johnny's, either. He held her gently by her shoulders, gazing at her.

'Don't be silly, Claudes. That wasn't your fault, it was mine. Why should you have to choose between me or your friends? You should be able to have both – see me when you get up in the morning and then go out to play with your friends. I've done this to you, it's my fault. I made you choose.'

I found myself nodding boisterously behind him and had to arrest my neck muscles. Steady. Don't want your head to drop off into the flowerbed, Livvy. All the same, it sounded encouraging, didn't it? Sounded like he'd seen a degree of light. Perhaps this misadventure of Claudia's was going to have a little morality tale at the end of it? Be a bit of a catalyst for a happy ending? Encouraged, I followed them inside, but as they made to go into the kitchen, Johnny turned.

'Livvy, d'you mind if I have a quick word with Claudes? I just want to get one or two things straight in her mind.'

I blinked. 'Sure! No, gosh, good heavens, you go ahead. You, um, go in there and I'll – well, I'll wait in the sitting room.'

They disappeared within and the door closed.

215

I stared at the white, panelled door. Frowned. What? I wondered. What was it he wanted to get straight in her mind? And what did he want to say that he couldn't say in front of me? That he'd fallen out of love with Mummy? That he was sorry if it inconvenienced her, but that was what happened to grown-ups sometimes? Their sudden closeness surprised me too. I felt very . . . well, excluded. More so, I suppose, because it hadn't always been thus. Claudia had always been very much a mummy's girl. I vividly remembered a time when she was about three, in London, and Paddy, our beloved tabby cat, died. I'd dreaded telling Claudia, but finally had sat her down and broke the news. Oh dear, what a shame, she'd said, before skipping out to play. I'd been surprised but relieved, but the following morning, had found her sobbing inconsolably in our cleaning lady's lap, because Vera had said how sad it was about Paddy. 'But, darling,' I'd said, dropping to my knees beside her, 'I told you yesterday. I told you Paddy was dead!' She'd raised an anguished, tear-stained face. 'I thought you said Daddy!' Johnny had roared with laughter when I'd told him, but I'd noticed, thereafter, a tendency to come home from work slightly earlier, to make it through the door at bathtime, to read her a story at bedtime, and I suppose it had worked. At some stage, they'd bonded closely, only for Johnny to test that bond now, some seven years later.

I inched a few steps closer to the door, inclining my head towards it. I could hear muffled voices within, but nothing clearly. Then I went the whole hog and put my ear to it. Johnny said something about loving her just as much as ever, and Claudia said something I couldn't make out, and then Johnny said in a loud voice, 'Livvy, d'you want to come in?'

I gasped and leapt away.

'We can see your feet, Mummy,' explained Claudia. 'Under the door.'

'Oh! Oh no. I – I was just wondering if you wanted a cup of tea?'

'Well, we can make it ourselves, can't we?' came back Claudia, witheringly. 'We're the ones in the kitchen.'

'Of course, darling, sorry,' I trilled back. Crikey, she sounded so – chilly. Still cross, I suppose, for humiliating her in front of Sebastian.

I crept shamefully off to the garden to wait; picked up my trug from a bench. Well, they could only be talking about me, couldn't they? I reasoned bitterly. What else was there to talk about? I went to the end of the garden and buried myself in the herbaceous border, savaging a piece of ground elder that had seeded itself around the delphiniums, taking advantage of my abstraction these past few weeks. As I straightened up to chuck it on the lawn, I saw movement through the caravan window. I squinted. Ah, so Lance had made himself scarce in there, had he? Well, that showed a degree of tact, anyway. In the dim, distant past of all of three hours ago, I seemed to recall that he was supposed to be my lover, my boisterous young lothario, but in the light of a missing child, I didn't think having a spare lothario about the place was necessarily a good thing. I heard the back door open and crouched down again, busying myself amongst the earthworms where I belonged, waiting for them to come to me.

'I'll be off then, Livvy,' said Johnny from a short distance.

I gave a little jump, just to show I'd been totally absorbed. As I turned, though, his blue eyes held me. Squeezed my heart. He shaded them with his hand against

the sun. I wiped my perspiring face with my hand and
realised it was covered in mud. Yes, yet again, I thought
bitterly, I'd dressed up for Johnny. Scratched and battered
by brambles, and now covered in earth, I'd made myself
utterly desirable. I thought longingly of the cream linen
dress and my kitten-heeled shoes upstairs.

'Bye, then,' I said with a cheery grin. 'See you in a
couple of weeks.' I went to go back to my border.

'Look,' he took a step closer, 'I'm just going to pop in
and thank that chap down the road. It seems he did Claudia
a really good turn.'

I swung back. 'Oh! Hang on, no, don't do that, Johnny!'
'Why not?'

Claudia strolled up beside him. I shot her a nervous
glance. Had she . . .? No, bless her, she clearly hadn't told
him about the bellowing harridan episode.

'Oh, well,' I faltered, 'because—'

'Because Mum wants to. Don't you, Mum?' She eyed me
beadily. 'We thought we'd go together.'

'Yes, that's it,' I breathed. 'Take some flowers, do it
properly, you know.'

He shrugged. 'OK. But be sure you do, won't you?'

'Of course I will,' I bristled. God, anyone would think I
was a child.

'Bye then.'

'Bye.'

He hesitated, and for an awful moment I thought he was
going to kiss my cheek. Like social acquaintances. I quickly
bent down to collect my trug, concentrating on separating
weeds from stones. By the time I'd straightened up, he was
on his way – back up the lavender walk, through the rose
arbour and round the side of the house. I watched him go.
Claudia had gone with him, and I could hear her now,

clattering about in the kitchen. I picked up my trug and walked slowly back to the house. Whatever happened, I thought, I mustn't ask her what Johnny had said in the kitchen. That would be an intrusion on her privacy and on her relationship with her father. I put the trug by the back door, breezed in, humming a little tune, and put the kettle on. She was reading an old *Beano* annual at the kitchen table.

'All right now, darling?'

'Yes, thanks.'

My hand went for the tea caddy. I paused. Turned. 'Um, Claudes?'

'Hmm?'

'What did Daddy say?'

She glanced up from her book. 'What?'

'You know, your, um – little chat.'

'Oh. Oh, just stuff about wishing it didn't have to be this way. Hoping I'd understand when I was a bit older. The usual bollocks.'

'Claudia!'

'Sorry. Just a bit fed up with it all at the moment.'

She got up and left the kitchen. I dithered for a moment, then hastened after her into the sitting room.

'Claudes, how about helping me make some pancakes? And then when we've eaten them, we could trough our way through a packet of biscuits in front of the telly!'

'No thanks, I'm going upstairs. I've got some homework to do.' She reached for her book bag behind the sofa and brushed back past me again. I bit my lip.

'Claudia, I'm sorry. I've said I'm sorry. I was worried about you, that's all.'

She turned. 'Well, I'm worried about you, Mum. You really lost it today. You've got no brakes.'

'Of course I've got brakes!'

'You haven't, you're out of control. I was talking to Lucy's mum about it.'

'Claudia!'

'No, she was really helpful.'

'Was she indeed!'

'Yes, she said that she got a bit unhinged after her last baby. Said maybe you should take up yoga.'

'Yoga!'

'Yes, Lucy's mum does yoga and she's really calm. Really tuned in.'

Is she, by jingo? Well, she wasn't so flipping tuned in today. I nodded thoughtfully, though, pretending to take it on board. At least it wasn't the men in white coats. 'Right, yoga. Yes, that's sounds fun. I might look into that.'

'You should. Lucy's mum can put her ankles behind her ears.'

Diverted that this should calm me down and not have me screaming for the fire brigade to come and unhook me, I nodded again. 'Right. And . . . you think that might help me, Claudes? Feet behind the ears?'

She shrugged. 'It might, you never know. Might stop you overemoting.'

My mouth hung open as she turned and mounted the stairs. Overemoting? Christ! She was ten! Bloody ten! Where was she *getting* all this? I gazed incredulously after her.

Later that evening I rang Molly.

'Where's it all coming from?' I whispered, aware that Claudia was still working upstairs. 'Do the teachers feed them this rubbish, d'you suppose?'

'I blame the media. You only have to open one of those innocent-looking *My Little Twinkle* comics to find it's full of psychobabble. 'Dear Tina, I feel a bit depressed at the thought of having to do my homework ... Dear Jessica, have you thought of getting some counselling?' Honestly, they'll all have disappeared right up their backsides by the time they're teenagers. Why's she so concerned about you, anyway?'

I confided the details of my hideous day, graphically depicting the ghastly Sebastian episode.

'Well, I'm not so sure you weren't right,' she said slowly. 'In fact, I'm not convinced you didn't do exactly the right thing. I mean, why did he take her back to his house? Why not your house? It's just as close. And I don't like the idea of her handing over her clothes to him, either.'

'Don't you?' I yelped, reaching for a cigarette.

'No, but having said that, I'm quite prepared to accept that I'm totally paranoid and I've only got like this since I've had children. If you'd told me that story three years ago I'd have said, "Gosh, what a perfectly sweet, helpful man," but now I've got Henry I see paedophiles at every corner. I can't read him *Fireman Sam* without wondering if Sam's waving his hose about in a rather provocative manner. It's biological, I'm afraid. Once you've had children all that a-stranger-is-a-friend-I've-yet-to-meet crap goes right out the window. A stranger is a potential child molester. It's symptomatic of our overprotective natures.'

I sighed. 'Perhaps, but you should have seen me, Molly. I was like a mad woman in there. I reckoned if I'd had a knife in my hand instead of a rake, I'd have stabbed him with it.'

'So he was lucky then. Just the tea and biscuits. I really don't know what you're worrying about, Livvy, and I'd certainly forget about the flowers. That might put all sorts of ideas into his head. In fact, I wouldn't even bother to apologise in person. Just pop a little note round saying you're sorry if you got the wrong end of the stick. But make sure you keep that "if" in there. Because if ever I heard an iffy story, it's this one.'

Chapter Thirteen

The builders were back the following morning, and with them, an uncharacteristic air of doom and gloom. As they unloaded their spluttering, terminal lorry and dragged in the usual hundredweight of cable, copper piping, planks, bags of plaster, bolts and brackets with which to decorate my kitchen, their faces were long, their voices muted.

'What's up?' I whispered to Mac as I staggered in with a steaming tray of tea, the first of many morning cuppas.

Mac glanced round to make sure we were alone. 'Alf's wife's left him,' he confided soberly. 'He got back on Friday night to find a note on the kitchen table. Said she'd had enough of him, and don't try to find her 'cos she ain't never coming back.'

'No!' I set the tray down, aghast. 'Vi? But they're on the phone night and day. I thought they adored each other!'

'Oh, he adored her orright – couldn't please her enough – but she bossed him around somefing chronic. She always had the upper hand, like, and he's done as he's told all his bleedin' life, and now she's up and left him, ungrateful bitch. Gone to Spain.'

'Spain!'

Mac took his cap off and scratched his head. 'Yeah, well, she's always bin on about wanting to live on the Costa

Brava, run a bar an' that, sit in the sun wiv all those fat gits wiv gold chains, knockin' back jugs of Sangria, but Alf's never bin for it. He won't go furver than Margate, Alf won't – needs his family about him, and who can blame him? She don't give a monkey's about anyone's family, though. She's a right cold fish, that Vi, and I've always said so. She don't need nobody, never even wanted kids, and that's not natural, is it?'

'Oh, so there are no children?'

'Nah. Alf would have loved 'em, dotes on his nieces and nephews, he does, but she wouldn't have it. She likes her own company and she's welcome to it. Got it in spades now, hasn't she? Fancy buggerin' off just like that! Took the video an' all.'

'Gosh, poor Alf.'

I glanced across at his huge sorrowful bulk as he passed by the window, head bent, water sloshing from his buckets.

'So, is he very—'

'Gutted,' said Mac, averting his head politely and spitting dexterously to the concrete floor. 'Totally gutted. He's given his life to that cow and then she ditches him wivout so much as a by-your-leave. Silly tart.'

Spiro sidled up beside us with a piece of skirting board on his shoulder. 'I theenk she go with another man,' he confided. 'I smell rats. I don't theenk she go alone, I theenk she go off to do Olé olé and Viva España with a toy of a boy.'

'You may well be right, Spiro, my son,' agreed Mac soberly. 'She's certainly stupid enough, but then I can't see any man in his right mind wantin' to give her one. She's built like a bleedin' matchstick, not an ounce of flesh on her, tits like teabags. Reckon she'd snap in two as soon as look at you, but then my Karen says she had enough black undies in her bottom drawer to sink a battleship, and that Bernie Mundy down the offy said she was always in there buyin' her Baileys and giving him the eye, so who's to say, eh?' He blew his nose, took a peek at the contents of the handkerchief, and replaced it in his overall pocket.

'He so sad,' muttered Spiro, shaking his head. 'He cry in the lorry today.'

'No! Oh, Spiro, how awful!'

Spiro got out his hanky. 'He say his life is over.' He blew his nose noisily. 'He say – he say that now it all gone pear-shaped he has nothing left to live for, and I theenk to myself – oh, bleeding heck, eet is just like poor Mrs McFarllen. All alone and lonely weeth nothing to live for either!'

Crikey. I blinked.

'And he say he want to die. He say – he say – oooooh!' Emotion overwhelmed him, the woolly hat came off and he dabbed at his streaming eyes. 'And you all so nice!' he sobbed.

I patted his shoulder. 'Come on now, Spiro, you're diluting the tea. Be a good chap and—'

'Get a grip boy,' growled Mac. 'We've got a lot to do today. I don't want any fairies sobbin' down their tutus. I want that concrete plinth put in for that Aga toot sweet and I want it six by four, an' I want that stove plumbed in by tomorrow, no messin'. Now get mixing, Zorba my son. We've got work to do!'

Spiro hastily replaced his hat and shuffled over to the mixer. Through the window I could still see Alf, bent over his plaster palate outside. I went to see him, approaching tentatively. His face was hidden as he concentrated on stirring the soggy pink mess with a trowel.

'Alf, I'm so sorry,' I said gently. 'Mac told me.'

He nodded, but I could tell speech was going to be difficult. Even more so than usual. He didn't raise his head and kept on mixing. I was about to tiptoe away, when finally he managed, gruffly: 'You're orright,' which I'd come to learn was East London for anything from, "No, thank you, I don't take sugar in my tea," to, "Yes, please, I'd adore to be King of the Pygmies."

I left them to it. Mac seemed to be marshalling his troops with a power and a vigour hitherto unseen, barking out orders and strutting about like a mini masonic tyrant. Lance appeared from the caravan and fell in seamlessly, greeting me with a low 'Have you heard?' – to which I nodded back my sympathies, and then the three of them scurried around under Mac's direction, hammering, mitring and plastering like whirling dervishes. Presumably Mac thought that if he got them working flat out it would take their minds off their troubles, and who was I, the mere recipient of their labours, to disagree?

Work had been occupying my mind lately, too. I was dimly aware that I'd promised both myself and Angie I'd write to the Physic Garden, offering my services. The trouble was, though, that every time I sat down to draft a letter, I'd wonder why on earth they should even consider me, rather than the hordes of fresher, cheaper, younger graduates who flooded out of Cirencester's gates each year, or even the older, far more experienced gardeners whose seamless careers were uninterrupted by childbirth, house restoration, or even marriage restoration. And what about all those smart young London gardeners, fingers on the horticultural pulse, who exhibited at Chelsea and charged a grand for a morning's consultation? Why me? At this point I'd gulp insecurely, doodle a bit, sigh even more, gaze out of the window, screw up the paper and finally wander out to my own little patch, where, I told myself, at least I was improving my practical skills, even if I was only dead-heading the lilies or restraining the Rambling Rector from strangling Madame Hardy.

On this particular morning, I dutifully sat down for the obligatory doodle, sigh, gaze and screw, but as I got up guiltily from the writing desk, pushed open the French windows and ambled out into the blazing sunshine to till my soil, it occurred to me to wonder why on earth I would even *want* to slog to London on an overcrowded commuter train, and spend a back-breaking morning in a stifling greenhouse tilling someone else's soil, before slogging back home again? It wasn't as if I needed the money – although of course it would come in handy. No, it was the independ-ence, I told myself sternly. I knelt down amongst the frilly and abundant *Alchemilla mollis* and tugged at a dandelion root. Who was it said that work was the only dignity? Scott Fitzgerald, or someone equally dissolute, but he had a point and, let's face it, I was pretty short on personal dignity at the moment. I shuddered as I remembered yesterday's débâcle. And of course the ability to write my own cheques without drawing on the joint account would certainly show Johnny. Show him I was making my own way. And then, of course, there was the stimulation, I thought wearily, reach-ing for my trowel. I sat back on my heels for a moment. Yes, let's not forget the sodding stimulation, eh? What did that really mean, I wondered? When people bandied that word around? Did it mean talking to people? Because I could talk to my friends, who were far more intelligent than a lot of the gardeners I knew. Using my brain, then? Well, surely a good book would do more for the grey matter than pricking out dahlias? No, what it really meant, I decided, was no longer feeling guilty about doing nothing. It gave one a badge to wear, a tick to put by one's name. Olivia McFarllen has a job. She occupies her time with more than her house, her garden and her child. She stood up and she was counted. And, of course, at the moment, it was more important than ever that I was seen to have a life, because I couldn't even include 'getting my husband's supper and ironing his shirts' in the domestic equation, as Claudia had so succinctly pointed out to me on the way to school this morning.

'Mrs Chandler's got a job now,' she'd informed me sternly, 'and Mr Chandler was really impressed by that. Said it was more than his increasingly expensive strumpet had.'

I cast my mind back, at the same time trying not to go up a lorry's backside. 'Mrs Chandler? Chloe's mother?'

'That's it.'

'Whose husband left her?'

'Yep.'

'But . . . wasn't she the one that went off with some loose-limbed youth from B&Q, whereupon Mr Chandler came back with his tail between his legs?'

'Ah yes, he did,' she twisted excitedly in her seat to face me, 'but you see it's all changed now. Mr Chandler *did* come back, but then his strumpet—'

'Must you say that word, Claudia?'

'Yes, I like it – his Strrrr-umpet,' she trilled, 'mounted a huge campaign, cycled past his factory gates with her shirt undone and no pants on, that sort of thing – and he went back to her.'

'Right,' I'd said weakly, negotiating a roundabout. 'So, then Mrs Chandler got herself a job, in – don't tell me—'

'B&Q.'

'Naturally.'

'And now she's selling rotary saws and that type of thing, and all on commission, Mum. Chloe said she made an extra eighty-four pounds last week.'

'Excellent,' I said faintly. 'And, um, her young man?'

'Oh, well, Mrs Chandler claims she got bored with him and gave him the boot, but Chloe says she was sitting in the back garden with him only last week and Mrs Chandler came out in a bikini to sunbathe looking *really* hideous – you know, flabby white tummy, saggy underarms and those spongy bits on the tops of the legs, like you've got, Mum, only much worse – and Chloe said that Len – that's his name – took one look, made a face like he was going to be sick, and legged it. They've never seen him since.'

'But . . .' I struggled with this information as I swung into the school gates, 'but surely he'd seen Mrs Chandler before?' I was dimly aware I shouldn't be having this conversation with my ten-year-old daughter, but couldn't quite stop myself.

'What, you mean nudey?'

'Well, yes.'

'No, because Chloe says they always did it with the lights off.'

'How would Chloe know?'

'Because she peeped through the keyhole, der-brain. Crikey, Mum, get real. We've got to get *some* sort of sex education before we go up to the upper school. If it wasn't for Alice Cassidy's parents, who are practically naturists and wander round the house naked and do it in the conservatory, we wouldn't know *what* was going on.'

I pulled to a halt in the car park. 'Well, three cheers for Mr and Mrs Cassidy. Sorry Daddy and I were never so obliging. I hope you don't feel too deprived.'

She shrugged as she got out. 'I'll survive. Oh – it's OK,

Mum,' she said quickly as I went to get out my side, 'I'm a bit late so I'll just run in. Oh, by the way, that letter's for Sebastian. Can you put it through his door? Plus the one from you, too,' she added meaningfully.

I glanced down at the note she'd left on her seat as she scampered off. So. My daughter no longer wanted me to accompany her to the classroom door. Didn't want me to make a fool of myself, no doubt. A bit of a loose cannon, these days, Claudia's mum, and, of course, what with her husband's mistress up there, who knows *what* she might do. I sighed and picked up the letter. It was sealed, of course; show me a child who doesn't lick an envelope. I turned it over and wondered what she'd written. Sorry about my barking mother? She really should get out more, sell a few rotary saws and cycle round St Albans with no pants on? I sighed again, put it down. No, she was right. I must pop it through his door, and add sincere apologies of my own, too. I riffled around in the glove compartment for a bit of paper. No point going home and agonising over the Basildon Bond, I'd write one in the car right now, on any old scrap of paper, pop it in, and then that would be the end of it.

I finally found an old shopping list on the floor under my seat, scribbled out 'Domestos, butter, Immac', and wrote on the back –

Dear Sebastian,

I'm *so* sorry. What must you think of me? I got totally the wrong end of the stick yesterday, made a complete fool of myself and couldn't be more ashamed.

Best wishes,
Olivia McFarllen

There. Short, gushing, and to the point. Perfect.

On the way home, I stopped outside his house and ran up the steps. I slipped Claudia's note through the letterbox, and was about to add mine to the doormat when I suddenly realised I was being watched. I glanced down and saw the mother, her toothy, ferrety face pale and watchful, staring up at me from the basement window below. I hesitated. My note wasn't actually in an envelope, and she'd most certainly read it, and then what on earth would she think? Why was I so ashamed? So foolish? What stick, exactly, had I grasped the wrong end of? And on a scrappy old shopping list, too. No no, I thought hastily, I'd go home, write it out again, do it properly and then drop it by later.

I tucked it in my pocket and glanced down nervously. I couldn't actually see her now, but I was sure she was still there, hovering about in the shadows. I hurried back down the steps, feeling those sharp grey eyes in my back all the way to my car. I shivered as I got in. Perhaps Molly was right. Perhaps there was something 'iffy' about that whole setup there; perhaps she was his accomplice or something. She certainly looked like she could have been an embalmer in a previous life. I shot off down the road, scurried up the drive to my house, ran in, and shut the door fast behind me. Home.

The day limped on, and by mid-afternoon, the temperature had hit the nineties. Claudia was dropped home by a friend, and lay in a cool bath for half an hour before taking to her bedroom. I, meanwhile, wilted restlessly on the terrace, listening to the sounds of banging and crashing as the boys ploughed on. At one point Lance and Spiro beetled off for more supplies, but other than that, relentlessly, unceasingly, through the heat, with no radio blaring, no chatting, no whistling, no breaks for tea, no stops to execute the perfect roll-up on an upturned milk crate – on they toiled. I was astonished, but deeply impressed. Later, when they'd finally drooped back to the caravan to collapse, I crept in to inspect their handiwork. I was even more impressed. Golly, I thought as I gazed around in wonder, all this in one day. Just shows what they can do when they really pull their fingers out.

The flapping blue tarpaulin had gone, and in its place, the ceiling and walls were pink and plastered. The soggy concrete floor had also been replaced, by a gleaming, reclaimed wooden one. At the far end of the room, the huge, concrete plinth was in situ, ready for the Aga to be enthroned, and around the perimeter of the room, some of Lance's carefully sculpted oak cupboards were already in place. I scurried across the shiny floor and pulled out a drawer. Smooth as silk. I spun around, a delighted smile slowly spreading across my face. My goodness, yes, it was really taking shape, and it was perfect! Just perfect. And just as I'd imagined, too. Finally, after all these months, it was beginning to come together.

The old sash windows had been restrung, deep skirting boards were nailed in and ready to be painted, granite work surfaces were propped up waiting to be fixed, but what really surprised and pleased me was that I could get pleasure from it. Yes, even without Johnny here beside me, admiring it too, it made me smile, and I'd thought that would be impossible, you see. Thought it was all tied up with him, this dream house, and I was astonished to realise it might not be. Was I actually getting stronger then, I mused as I wandered around, or was it just time healing, as people so often – and thoughtlessly – told one it would? Perhaps a bit of both.

By way of celebration, I went back to the old scullery,

poured myself a glass of chilled Sancerre from the fridge, and strolled out to the garden, making for the cedar tree where I always sat on a summer's evening. Claudia was tired and had gone to bed early, and all was quiet. The garden seemed to breathe at me, to open its arms, and I sank contentedly into its embrace, the air heavy with the musky whiff of tobacco plants and trailing jasmine. Soft cascades of broom brushed my skirt as I sauntered down to the seat beneath the tree, but as I got close, I realised – damn. On the opposite side of the stream, directly in front of me, the lads had spilled out too. Out of their caravan and on to the grass, lying stretched out or propped up on their elbows. I hesitated. I could hardly sit here drinking just a few feet away, could I? Perhaps I should sit on the terrace? But on the other hand, I wanted to sit here. I always did. And this was my garden, damn it. I sat, firmly. Mac turned and caught my eye. I raised my glass.

'Kitchen looks great!' I trilled merrily.

'Yep. It's coming along.'

Silence. I smiled inanely into my lap.

'You like yer war?' he ventured.

'Sorry?'

'I said, d'you like yer floor?'

'Oh yes, very nice!'

Lance glanced across, smiled. I smiled back. Looked down into my lap again. I shifted uncomfortably. Heavens, this was ridiculous. They were only a few feet away, and the whole point of sitting here was to gaze into the sylvan scenery, not at them.

I cleared my throat. 'Um, listen,' I called. 'This seems rather silly. D'you want to come across and have a celebration drink? There's some wine and beer in the fridge?'

It was as if I'd cast a magic spell. As if I'd snapped my

fingers and – abracadabra – they were across. The stream was leapt – or in Spiro's case, waded – and in an instant they were beside me; sitting on the grass around my chair, grinning up at me like delighted pixies. Lance instantly became barman.

'Right, lads,' he said, rubbing his hands together, 'beer or wine, or shall I bring both?' He looked at me for confirmation.

'Please do,' I purred.

Christ, I felt like Lady Bountiful now, sitting here under my cedar tree with my faithful swains about me. I slid my bottom off the chair and shifted down to the grass. That's better, I thought, hugging my knees, chummily. Much less us and them.

Lance disappeared, only to reappear moments later with a tray of glasses, a bottle of wine wrapped in a fabric cooler that he'd found God knows where, a six-pack of cold Stella, and a huge bowl of Hula Hoops. Crikey, he really was Mr Fixit, wasn't he? I thought admiringly as he set it all down on the grass, and looking particularly attractive this evening in khaki shorts and a baggy white T-shirt. Clean, too, I noticed, as actually, I realised, glancing around, they all were. Did they have a power shower in that TARDIS of a caravan, as well as satellite TV and beds that came whizzing out of the wall? I must ask Claudia.

A moment later the air was filled with snapping and fizzing as ring-pulls were zapped back and a cork was popped, then the happy sound of contented glugging as Stella went down dry red necks, and a cumulative – 'Aaaahh . . .' as the business of thirst was attended to. Even Alf looked slightly less wretched as he downed his can without troubling a glass, and lay down to shut his eyes.

'How is he?' I whispered to Lance.

He shrugged. 'He's OK. It's the shock more than anything, and I think that's starting to wear off. And he's not so bad here, you see, working with the boys. It's just at home. Empty kitchen, bedroom, you know.'

I took a slug of my wine. Oh yes, I knew. And how.

'Ees so very, very like you, ees it not, Meesis McFarllen?' said Spiro, on my other side, muscling in on the conversation and warming to his theme again.

I groaned inwardly.

'And always it happen to the good people,' he mused. 'Nice people, smiley people, like you and Alf. He just like you, always if I ask – can I have a ciggy, Alf? – he say yes, or – can I borrow radio, Alf – he say yes, yes!'

'Well, maybe that's the problem, Spiro. We're too free with our yeses.'

'And you know,' he hissed in my ear, 'he only forty-eight! Ees incredible, no? And he still very fit and able to do things.' He smiled at me, flashing perfect white teeth, and suddenly, I saw the way Spiro's mind was going. Alf, my fit and able labourer, my eighteen-stone, glass-eyed, flatulent of bottom and gushing of armpit bricklayer, was being offered in my general direction. Alf, good, Alf, *smiley* Alf, Alf, the man who liked to say yes, was being proffered for my delectation by his friend, the woolly-hatted, perpetually sobbing Greek.

I leant towards him. 'No, thank you, Spiro,' I said firmly.

Lance stifled a giggle beside me.

Spiro looked puzzled. 'You no like him?'

'Oh, no, I like him very much, but just not in that way, savvy?'

He sighed, nodded. 'Savvy.' Then he paused. 'So . . . perhaps you like the younger man, yes?' His eyes drifted past me to Lance. They sparkled excitedly. 'Perhaps you like—'

'Spiro,' I interrupted urgently, 'what I'd *really* like is another bottle of wine. Would you mind getting one, only this one seems to have mysteriously evaporated.' I waved the empty bottle in his face.

He sighed, took it resignedly, and got to his feet. 'OK. I go.'

'Attaboy,' grinned Lance, as Spiro retreated up the garden path. 'What you have to realise,' Lance went on in my ear, 'is that Spiro comes from an island called Mexatonia.'

'Where's that?'

'Exactly. No one's ever heard of it. It's a tiny disputed territory just off Albania. It's so minute that when the goat-herder dies, his widow automatically marries the fisherman instead. So instead of sex, cooking and mucking out the goats, it's sex, cooking and mending nets, that's all.'

'Right.' I nodded thoughtfully. 'So instead of sex, cooking and Eurobonds, I'd get sex, cooking and my plumbing sorted, is that it?'

'Exactly.'

We giggled companionably, and for a moment I felt ridiculously, absurdly happy; lolling about here with my boys, sharpening our wits, cracking a few jokes, the mayflies buzzing about us, dancing in the low beam of the evening sun. I glanced contentedly about me. Alf was beginning to exhibit signs of sleep. Another can of Stella had done its worst, and he was snoring softly now.

'What happened to his eye?' I asked Mac, who had stealthily usurped the Greek beside me.

'Our stepfather stabbed him wiv some scissors when he was a nipper.'

'Good God!' I sat bolt upright. Felt sick. 'How *terrible*!'

'Yeah, dreadful. I was six at the time, and he was about four. We bofe went off to boarding school after that.'

'Boarding school. Heavens, I wouldn't have thought . . .' I tailed off, about to say – you'd be able to afford it.

'Barnardo's,' he offered helpfully.

'Oh! Right.' I took a slug of wine. Fell silent for a moment. 'Gosh, Mac, you and Alf, you've – well, you've had a pretty traumatic time then.'

He shrugged. 'Could be worse. We've always had each ovver, and we've always looked out for each ovver.'

'You mean, you've always looked out for him,' Lance put in softly.

'Yeah, well, you do, don't you? If you're brovers. Anyway, it weren't that bad. We could have been brung up in Kosovo, couldn't we? Could have had bombs dropping on our beds, could have had—'

'Coo-ee!'

Any extension of this incisive, sociopolitical discussion was brought to an abrupt halt by a loud trill. We all turned in its general direction and saw Nanette, up on my terrace, on the steps of the French windows, wobbling about on pink high heels, wearing the skimpiest of miniskirts, and waving a bottle of champagne.

'Is it a party? Can I come down? I've brought my own bubbly!'

Well, she was coming anyway. Before the "Of course!" was out of my mouth, she was teetering across the lawn towards us.

'I spotted you all out of the bathroom window,' she called, 'having a little drinky, and I thought – well, I'm damned if I'm going to celebrate up here on my own. Why not go and join them?'

'Why not indeed,' I said, getting up to greet her and give

her a kiss. 'But what are you celebrating, Nanette?'

'Oh!' she gushed, clasping her hands together, eyes shining. '*Too* exciting. Roger's asked me to marry him!'

'Oh Nanette, that's wonderful!' I hugged her.

'Isn't it just? And it was such a surprise! There I was, on my hands and knees polishing the parquet floor because Brenda makes such a frightful mess of it, and he just walked in the front door and popped the question! Then he said, "Nanette, I can never resist a woman who goes down on her knees for a man, so while you're down there . . ." Isn't he awful! Oh Lord,' she clasped a jewelled hand to mouth, 'and here I am pouring out all my personal effects, and we haven't even been properly introduced!'

'Sorry, Nanette.' I turned hastily. 'Um, well, you've probably seen these boys around because they're my builders.'

'I have indeed,' she purred, 'but I haven't seen this one.' She plucked admiringly at Lance's sleeve.

'Ah, well, this is Lance, he's quite new, and this is Mac, his father, who's the foreman, and Spiro from Greece, and Alf, who's sleeping it off on the grass.'

'Nanette,' she purred, 'as in Newman, but I don't have to do the washing-up!' She gave a tinkly laugh as the boys regarded her blankly. 'I say, this is all so thoroughly modern of Olivia, isn't it?' she beamed at them. 'All socialising together? So egalitarian, hmm? I do think you're lucky to have an employer like this!'

'And I think you're lucky to have any teeth!' beamed back Mac, quick as a flash, but as she blinked, uncomprehendingly, Lance stepped in quickly.

'Er, can I open that bottle for you, Nanette?'

'Oh, thank you, young man, and bring me a glass too, if you would.'

'Of course,' said Lance, his mouth twitching as he turned.

'Now he's *nice*, Olivia,' she whispered to his not quite retreating backside. 'For a bit of rough, I mean. Obviously he's not in the same league as Roger, but he's quite nicely spoken. You could do worse, you know.'

'Jesus.' I raked my hand despairingly through my hair.

She frowned. 'Sorry, have I said something?'

'No, it's just – well, everyone seems intent on . . . Never mind. Sorry, Nanette. Tell me about Roger. When are you getting married?'

'Christmas,' she said happily, 'just a quiet little ceremony, we thought, except that of course he is Jewish, so we might have to stamp our feet a bit and pin money on our clothes or whatever they do.'

I laughed. 'Sounds fun.'

'Did you know?' she pounced. 'I mean, could you tell?'

'What?'

'That he was Jewish?'

'Er, no, but then I've never really thought about it.'

'Oh yes, he is, frightfully.' She nodded. 'You can tell by the way he parks in The Crescent, just leaves it slap bang in the middle of the road. And of course his mother's an absolute nightmare, but then they always are, aren't they? And *her* mother, who's barely alive, is even worse and still speaks with a ridiculous Polish accent, although I swear she puts it on. But I do love their warmth and culture, don't you? I mean, I think they're pretty much accepted over here now, don't you?'

I frowned. 'Who, the Poles?'

'No, the Jews!'

I looked at her in astonishment. 'Well, of course they are, Nanette!' I spluttered.

'No, no, just checking,' she said quickly, 'only I *am* prepared for people to be a tiny bit – you know – funny. After all, it is a mixed marriage, and you'd be amazed how narrow-minded some people can be, still thinking they're a load of tight-fisted, big-nosed—'

'Um, where is Roger?' I interrupted, looking round nervously. Heaven forbid he should overhear his bride's views on his chosen people. 'Is he coming over?'

'Oh no, he's had to go to some sales conference or other with a load of men in brown suits, too dull for words. You know, it always amazes me how interesting Roger is when he works with such dreary people— Thank you, young man.' She beamed this last up at Lance as he handed her a drink. She patted the grass beside her. 'Now, come and sit beside me and tell me how you know Olivia.'

'I work for her. I'm a carpenter.'

'Of course you are, I keep forgetting! You simply don't look like one, that's all! He's very like Malcolm, don't you think, Olivia?'

She leant back to survey him with narrowed eyes as he dutifully sat beside her.

'He's nothing like Malcolm!' I spluttered, and was about to expand on their striking physical differences, when I realised Nanette had introduced Malcolm simply to inform Lance – softly, so he had to lean in close to hear – exactly where I'd gone wrong with Malcolm. I sighed and sipped my drink, pretending not to care, and actually, I discovered I didn't. Occasionally I'd catch snippets like: '. . . *rang* him, for God's sake, came on much too strong,' or, '. . . doesn't exactly *look* desperate, but you know, it starts to *show*.'

I smiled. Night was stealing up on us now. I leant back against the ancient cedar and gazed into the midnight-blue vault of the heavens. Stars were beginning to twinkle down, and I thought, with a wry smile, what an eclectic gathering we were in this warm, airless summer night: Alf, fast asleep, curled up in the foetal position, thumb practically in his mouth, his face sad, even in slumber; Mac, beside him, quietly sipping his beer, watching over his brother, half his size but with twice his brain power – who knows what horrors they'd been through together? Spiro, far from home, and far from his wife, who perhaps even now was standing at her open doorway in her village, her baby in her arms, gazing up at the same stars but in a different sky; Nanette, from Dagenham, who'd pulled herself up from her roots by her bra straps, who thought that keeping a man and her figure was a sufficient lifetime accomplishment, but who'd fallen in love with a man who every nerve and sinew of her narrow-minded, prejudiced body resisted; and beside her, Lance, blond, beautiful, and generous of spirit, who was letting her flirt and prattle on, instinctively knowing that Nanette was one of those people for whom a response is not important, just an inert body, and then, of course, there was me . . .

After a while, Lance stood up, stretched.

'Night, all.' He raised his hand and wandered off towards the bridge, back to the caravan. I watched him go with regret. Breaking up the party, eh, just as I was beginning to enjoy myself. Nanette seemed peeved too, and gave a little wriggle of her buttocks, a regrouping gesture.

'I'm going to take you shopping,' she hissed, still watching Lance, but leaning against me now, mouth drooping dramatically at one corner. Her eyes were glazed and I realised she'd drunk most of her bottle herself. 'I came through your kitchen just now and saw your bra in the laundry basket. Nobody's going to be driven crazy by that, Olivia. What you need is one of these.' She pulled down her top and shoved her well-upholstered bosom under my nose. 'Plunge and lift, see? Not squash and separate. Get a grip, Olivia. I'll take you to Pollyanna's in Harpenden next week.'

She prattled on about silks and pads and gussets, but she was right, I mused, as I watched Lance disappear through the caravan door, I must get a grip. Not on my underwear, but on my life. The door closed behind him and I looked beyond, into the dark horizon. The great weight that had been gathering for weeks in my chest was still there, but tonight, for the first time, I felt as if it wasn't sitting so tight, and that, were a strong gust to shift it westwards, clearer skies might follow. So was it in my making, I wondered, to shift it? Or would it take something more magnificent to send it scuttling away? The stars twinkled knowingly above, but I couldn't tell.

Nanette was still talking beside me. 'Roger says I should floss more,' she confided. 'Says it's terribly important.' I gazed out at the lilies on the riverbank. Tall, strong and optimistic. 'He has lovely gums,' she said dreamily.

Mac offered me a cigarette and I took it. I hardly smoked at all these days, yet I'd smoked like fury when Johnny left. Fury. That's what had gone. Or was going, anyway. I dragged the smoke down deep. It was strong, and made me feel slightly ill, but I liked the strange, groggy feeling, mixing with the scent of the tobacco plants and the warm night air. So, I wondered dreamily, was this just a transitory blurring of the senses I was experiencing? Or could it really be that, at last, my continued existence on this planet was not causing me quite so much dismay?

Chapter Fourteen

Imogen rang the following morning.

'Right, I take it you're still on for tonight?' she said briskly.

'What's happening tonight?'

'The concert, remember? In the Abbey?'

I put down the glass of Alka-Seltzer that had been halfway to my dehydrated lips and pulled my dressing gown around me.

'Oh. Right.' Well, yes. OK, somewhere, dimly, at the back of my fuddled mind, it rang a bell; something about rustling up a bit of crumpet for me. In fact I believed I might have even instigated it, but right at this moment I didn't feel quite so instigatory, if that was even the word. I leant against the scullery wall and rubbed my throbbing forehead.

'Um, listen, Imo, if it's all the same to you I had a bit of a heavy night last night,' I mumbled. 'Bit of a session. I wouldn't mind just curling up on the sofa with Joanna Trollope and a Horlicks.'

'Oh no you don't, and it's not all the same to me! It's taken me ages to organise this and get seats and everything, and Rollo's coming especially for you!'

'Rollo?' I blinked. I wasn't sure I could take anyone with a name like that entirely seriously. 'What, as in

Rollo-me-over-lay-me-down-and-do-it-again?' I giggled. A mistake.

'That's the spirit!' she enthused brightly. 'Honestly, you won't be disappointed, Liv. He's totally gorgeous, and so excited about meeting you.'

'If he's so gorgeous,' I said suspiciously, 'why aren't you going out with him?'

'Oh, I know him far too well,' she said airily. 'Shared a house with him at Oxford. He's like a brother to me really. Come on, Livvy. You've got to come. Mum and Dad are dying to see you too.'

'Oh all right,' I caved in pathetically, although why anyone should be excited about meeting a recently separated, neurotic, single mother unless she'd lied through her teeth about me, I had no idea.

'Great. Parents' place for drinks at seven o'clock and we'll go on from there, OK?'

'OK, OK,' I agreed wearily. I could tell Imo was in no mood for shrinking violets.

Imogen's parents lived some distance from the city. Twenty minutes to the west, in fact, in a glorious, unspoilt part of the Hertfordshire countryside, where, on a summer's evening, with the swallows swooping and calling to each other across the valley, and with the wind in the right direction deflecting the low hum of the M25, you could almost believe you were in Devon. Tonight was just such a night, a sultry, misty evening, and as I drove up the bumpy track to their house, a low, rambling, Elizabethan farmhouse complete with beams and gables and tiny leaded lights glinting in the evening sun like shining eyes under the brows of the eaves, I couldn't help feeling a surge of pleasure. I'd spent a lot of time in this house as a child, had some happy times, and I was quietly confident it wouldn't have changed one jot.

Inside it had always been shabbily chaotic; very dark so one fumbled around a bit, and I remember following Imo around in our school uniforms, feeling along walls and stumbling over books, papers, and stacked-up files, all piled up on the stairs, to get to her bedroom. Imogen's father was the headmaster at the local boys' school and her mother, an elegant, but slightly eccentric don at Oxford. The written word was a priority in this house, but food wasn't, and mealtimes here had always been something of an eye-opener for me and Molly. In the first place nothing was prepared, nothing cooked. One was simply invited into the rather grubby kitchen to view the freezer and choose an individual M&S meal, which Mrs Mitchell then shoved in the oven. So, for example, I might be having a chicken Kiev, beside Mr Mitchell who was tucking into salmon en croute, opposite a brother demolishing a lamb biriani, and another brother with turbot in a white wine sauce. Sometimes Mrs Mitchell decanted them from their foil containers, and sometimes she didn't, depending on how the mood took her. Reading was pretty much mandatory, though, and Imo, her brothers and her parents would all drift to the table with whatever happened to be clasped in their hands – anything from Kierkegaard to *The Hobbit* – prop it up against a handy pepperpot, and munch away distractedly. I'm fairly sure this rule didn't apply if proper guests were present, but as a school chum of Imo's, I clearly didn't count. My mother, of course, had been horrified when I'd told her.

'You see what comes of overeducating children? They think they're all so flaming clever, but let's face it, it's no better than a telly supper!'

She had a point, but then my mother always had a point,

and generally, a disparaging one. It sprang from insecurity, of course. I very much doubt if Jeffrey Archer had ever been propped up at the Mitchells' table.

As I walked up the path to the front door tonight, Ursula Mitchell, a tall, elegant, faded blonde with a rather hawklike nose, and wearing a bright red shot silk ensemble, was outside greeting her guests and directing them round to the terrace, where I realised drinks were being served by caterers to twenty or so people. Quite a party.

'Olivia!' She took both my hands in hers and swooped for a kiss from her great height. 'I'm *so* glad you came!'

'I'm glad too,' I smiled up at her, and I was. It was years since I'd seen these lovely people.

'Come and meet everyone,' she insisted, linking my arm in hers. 'I'm bored with standing sentry at the door so I'm going to show you off. You look simply marvellous, my dear, and I must say, your Rollo seems rather divine too. I hadn't met him properly before tonight, but I assure you, he's quite a dish!' She winked. 'So isn't that perfect?'

As she beamed conspiratorially at me I nervously smoothed down the cream linen dress which had finally got an outing but had creased disastrously in the car. My Rollo, eh?'

'And Imo?' I asked, as I followed her through a wrought-iron gate, noticing her hair was quite grey at the back now, but that her ankles were still worth watching. 'Does she have a dish of the day?'

'Oh, my dear, haven't you heard?' She stopped, turned, and for extra emphasis, touched my arm confidentially with cold fingertips. 'The conductor, Hugo Simmonds! He's on the podium tonight and he's absolutely mad about her! He's been here for dinner a couple of times because Gerald got quite involved with the organisation of this concert, and d'you know, Olivia, I have to say he couldn't take his *eyes* off her!'

'I think quite a lot of men have that problem,' I remarked with a smile.

'Well, quite, but does she give them half a chance? No! They're all nuts about her and then they're lucky if they last two weeks! To be fair, the vast majority are no-hopers anyway, but I worry about her, Olivia. What's wrong with the child?' She frowned petulantly. 'And, you know, she's not getting any younger; time is marching on.'

'Mrs Mitchell! And you an ardent feminist – I'm shocked!' I laughed.

'Feminism be damned,' she grinned, taking my arm again, 'I'm a mother first and a feminist when it suits me, and it's Ursula, Olivia, although I know childhood habits die hard.' She sighed as we walked down the stone steps to the crowded terrace together. 'I *do* worry about her, though. She never seems to give anyone a chance, and Hugo *is* rather special. She'd be mad to pass him up. Darling, have a word if you can, would you? Tell her how scrummy he is?'

I laughed. 'I'll try,' I promised. 'Is he here?' I looked around.

'No no, he's limbering up with his baton at the Abbey. You'll see him later, and it's to be hoped that when she sees him strutting his stuff her heart will melt and – ah, now here we are – Imo! Imogen darling!'

She called to her daughter, who was talking to a tall, slim man on the other side of the terrace. Imo turned. Her pale, golden hair was piled up on her head with tendrils escaping and curling at the base of her neck, Grecian style. She wore a simple, black shift dress, pearls, was lightly tanned, and looked amazing.

'Livvy!' She came over, simultaneously catching the tall

man's sleeve and dragging him with her. 'God, *finally*! I had a nasty feeling you were going to do a bunk. You look terrific, by the way.'

'Thanks,' I grinned, 'so do you.'

'Oh Livvy, this is Rollo. Rollo, Olivia McFarllen, who together with Molly Piper, who *should* be here but is predictably even later, is my dearest friend.'

I shook hands with him. 'Molly's coming?' I said delightedly. 'I didn't think this would be her sort of thing?'

'Of course it isn't, I bullied her into it. Told her a bit of culture would do her good instead of gormlessly watching *Friends* and *Frasier*, who she's beginning to believe *are* her friends, she's so welded to that sofa of hers. Anyway, I've got to go off and relieve Mum at the door, so I'm going to stop wittering on, dear hearts, and leave you both in peace. Toodle-oo!' And with that she gave a dinky little wave and off she skipped. Just like that.

I gazed after her. Blimey, don't make it too obvious, will you, Imo? And couldn't you at least have given us a starting point? This is Rollo, he's in conglomerates, or – even better – this is Rollo, he's an incredibly wealthy polo player?

'Imogen's tact is legendary, of course,' said the tall man, smiling down. 'She once had the hots for a friend of mine in the diplomatic service, but I told her she'd make a disastrous diplomat's wife. You can't just plonk John Prescott next to the King of Tonga, tell them they've got a weight problem in common and then swan off hoping for the best.'

I laughed. But first, I had to wipe my face. Because good-looking though Rollo undoubtedly was, with his toffee-coloured hair, which rather cunningly matched his toffee-coloured eyes, set wide apart in an endearingly boyish face – he had a problem. He spat. I took a discreet

248

step backwards, lobbed up a social 'And what do you do?' and studied him closer.

Yes, it was the front teeth, I decided as he prattled away happily about the foreign office. Too big, and too far apart. Way too far, as Claudia would say. I reached for a canapé and made a mental note, as I munched and smiled politely, occasionally managing, 'Oh really?' out of the side of my mouth, and, 'Gosh, the South African desk, that must be interesting,' that Claudia must have as much orthodontic treatment as she needed, as soon as she needed it, whatever the cost. I didn't want her growing up with an impediment like this and, let's face it, it *was* an impediment. I reached for another canapé, a tray of which had been handily placed on a table beside me. God, I was starving. I really must make an effort to eat properly now I was on my own. Trouble was I couldn't be bothered, especially in the evening when— Bugger. He was gazing expectantly at me.

'Um, sorry?'

'I said, what do you do?'

'Oh! Oh nothing much.'

He raised startled eyebrows.

'I mean, nothing much now,' I hurried on. Crikey, I'd forgotten he was Imogen's friend and that 'nothing much' was tantamount to admitting you sucked worm's blood. 'I mean, I used to garden, you know, pre-children. Professionally, I mean. I used to do garden design.'

'Terrific!' he brayed. 'Gosh, I'd love to do something creative like that. You should keep your hand in. Did you ever do Chelsea?'

'Er, not as such.' I reached nervously for more food.

'Shame. Great mate of mine exhibited there every year, as well as at Hampton Court. You might know her actually – Saskia Soames?'

A giant prawn, centimetres to my lips, froze. Saskia Soames had had an unfortunate effect upon it. On top of the prawn, perched and glistening, sat a huge, shiny globule of saliva. I lowered it carefully.

'Er, no, I don't know her.'

'Oh, you must meet her, she's such a gas. I'm surprised actually, because Imo knows her. We must get you both together!'

'Yes, we must.' I looked round desperately for a handy dog, or a bin. Could I chuck it in the flowerbed? No, of course I couldn't.

'I'm sorry – you're eating,' he said, following my gaze, 'and I'm bombarding you with questions. Pop it in and I'll shut up for a minute.'

I gazed. Pop it in? Are you kidding? I stared at it hard. 'Is this fish?'

He peered at it, then up at me, incredulously. 'Yes, it's a prawn.'

'Is it? Heavens! I can't eat fish!'

'But – you've just eaten about six!'

'Have I? Good God, I'll come out in the most almighty rash tomorrow. All over!'

At this unattractive concept Rollo palpably flinched. 'Golly, poor you,' he muttered. 'Oh well,' he brayed, recovering, 'it's clearly my fault. I must have been distracting you! Disarming you, even! Ha, ha!'

'Yes, clearly!' Prat.

'Tell you what, I'll have it,' he offered, opening his mouth gallantly.

I didn't hesitate. In fact I more or less chucked it in, and then we both beamed delightedly as he munched away. There was something pleasingly apposite about it I felt, back to its maker, as it were. Suddenly my hand shot up.

'Molly!' Oh, the relief. 'You made it!'

'Finally,' she hissed, coming over and kissing me rather damply as she reached into her shirt to hitch up her bra strap. 'Bloody baby-sitter was late and then Henry sodding well threw up over me as I kissed him good night – do I stink?' she asked anxiously.

'No,' I promised, then realised she did. 'Here,' I handed her my bag. 'There's some Chanel No. 19 at the bottom, and do your other eye – you've only got one made up.'

'Have I? Damn. Thanks,' she muttered, grabbing the bag, and was about to scuttle off when she spotted Rollo, hovering territorially. She raised her eyebrows and shot me a quizzical glance.

'Oh! Sorry, Molly Piper, Rollo . . .?'

'Somerset,' he offered toothily, complete with ocean spray. Molly flinched but, quick as a flash, I'd turned to kiss Hugh, her husband. All yours, Moll.

Hugh, small, clever, and very theatrical, was gazing about him at the crowd, blinking with mock wonder. 'People,' he muttered dreamily. 'People talking . . . socialis-ing . . . yes, yes, I remember now, it's all coming back.' He sniffed his drink. 'Alcohol too.'

I giggled. 'You're not about to tell me you don't have a life any more, are you, Hugh?'

'Oh, but I don't, my love, I don't,' he said, putting an arm round my shoulders and leading me away. 'Just a pukey little toddler and a soon-to-be-podding wife, and wait till that one pops out: you won't see us for years. We'll come up for air, ooh, in about ten years' time I should think, when hopefully the world will still be turning and those who we chose to call our friends will still be out there, smiling and offering us a glass.' He gazed blankly into his champagne. 'You know, I really can't imagine why we all embark on this procreation lark in the first place, Livvy. Vanity, I suppose. An insatiable desire to recreate in our own image, and look where it gets us? Sunk in the mire of shitty despair.' He knocked back his glass in one go and smiled abruptly. 'You, on the other hand, dear heart,' he said, waggling his glass at me, eyes twinkling, 'seem to have it all worked out. You manage to make this whole childcare business look graceful and effortless, and all on your tod now, too, I gather. Tell me,' he added more gently, 'is it a mid-life crisis, or has he just gone blind? You've never looked lovelier.'

I smiled. 'He's a bit young for a crisis, isn't he, Hugh?'

'Lord no, everyone's doing things so much earlier these days. Life's become so accelerated, you see. Girls of eleven are having babies and sexually speaking one's finished at forty. Johnny's obviously doing a spot of panic-buying while he can still get it up, and making a total dick of himself in the process.' He grinned. 'His loss, not yours. Oh, excuse me, young man.' He grabbed a passing waiter. 'That was so delicious, I believe I'll have another.' He put his empty champagne glass on the tray, plucked another full one, and emptied it in one, smacking his lips. 'Yum yum.'

I giggled. 'Hugh, I'm not convinced this is quite the place to get plastered.' I glanced around at Ursula's cronies.

'Oh, but it is, my love, it is. Not only have we got all these stiffs to talk to here, but we've got the wretched concert to get through yet. If I drink myself to a standstill, with any luck I'll sleep through it. Oh, by the way, I'm armed.' He slipped a hand in his pocket and brought out a hip flask. 'Stick by me, kiddo, and you'll be OK.'

I giggled as Molly came charging up, still half made up. 'He spits!' she reported in horror.

'Doesn't he just?' I agreed.

'Bloody hell, don't I get enough bodily fluids at home without being subjected to more at a party?' She wiped her cheek. 'Outrageous! Is he supposed to be yours? What is Imo thinking of? Send him back!'

'Shh, he'll hear. Oh Christ – look out, we're being hounded.'

We smiled sociably as Ursula Mitchell bore down on us. She swooped, encircled our shoulders with bony arms, then confided in hushed tones, 'The seats *are* numbered, my dears, but it's better to get there early, otherwise it's such a crush. If you youngsters wouldn't mind making a move to the cars then I think the others will take the hint and follow. I just thought that if we got there in good time, Imogen might manage a few moments with Hugo, you see.'

Out of the corner of my eye I saw Imo, in no rush, still happily chatting away, and I wanted to say, 'Look, Ursula. Knowing Imo as we all do, don't you think that nothing is going to make her run a mile more than this sort of pressure?' But I didn't. She was happy and excited, and dreaming of a society wedding in New College Chapel, orange blossom tumbling from the pews. So instead I dutifully followed Molly and Hugh to the loo, to the coats, to the door, to the cars, and thence, to the Abbey.

Any qualms I had about venerable old cathedrals being used as venues rather than places of worship were quashed as I joined the glittering throng that waited outside to enter the Abbey. It looked fabulous, lit up and glowing in the clear night sky, and the chattering, excited crowd that jostled politely to get through the huge oak doors couldn't have been more appreciative, ooh-ing and ah-ing as they strained their necks to get a glimpse of the vast, vaulted ceiling. I suppose if The Man Himself were to burst through the double doors and demand to know what the devil we were doing, tanked up, bejewelled – armed, even, in Hugh's case – and awaiting entertainment, we might have had our work cut out convincing Him, but tonight I was happy enough to join the ranks of the great and the good – who were no doubt pious to a man, and who were out in force. I spotted the High Sheriff, the local MP, a brace of High Court judges with their wives, but also quite a few students, eager to hear the London Symphony Orchestra doing their stuff.

'Blimey, I had no idea,' muttered Molly, reading a poster as we went in.

'Me neither,' I admitted. 'No wonder it's so packed.'

As I went up the steps, dutifully escorting Rollo, I couldn't help noticing the young couple ahead of us. They were no more than seventeen probably, in duffel coats and college scarves, close, but shy, as they studied a programme together. He bent his head to hear what she was saying, as she, blushing into her straight fair hair, enthused falteringly about the pieces we were about to hear. He nodded, smiling, turned shining eyes on her, encouraging her. I felt a stab of pain. They were only just embarking, but already they'd found each other. And how lucky they were. For finding is everything.

In the area just within the doors, people milled about talking loudly, waving programmes above their heads to friends they'd spotted in the crowd, and despite frantic attempts of officials to try to guide them to their seats, there was a general unwillingness to move on. This was too much of a social event to hurry, too much of an occasion. With elbows tucked in, and taking tiny pigeon steps, our party gradually made its way through the chattering throng, with Ursula, beckoning us on madly from the front like a wild-eyed scout leader, keen to get front-row seats. As I nudged through – 'Excuse me, so sorry, oops, can I just squeeze through,' – I stopped suddenly. The back of a woman's head, a few feet away to my right, looked terribly familiar somehow, but I just couldn't place her. I peeled off from Rollo for a minute, took a quick peek around the side – and gasped. Stopped dead in my tracks. It was my mother. Except that I hardly recognised her. Her face was lightly made up and shining as she smiled and chatted. She was wearing a peach linen coat dress with peach lipstick to match, and her hair, which had been lightened and subtly streaked, was swept off her face in waves, tucked behind her ears, before curling softly at the edges. At her throat was a turquoise necklace which matched the bracelet on her wrist, and, I noticed, the sparkling gems in her ears. There was no dark helmet of hair, no pale, dramatic make-up, no navy-blue shift dress, and not a pearl in sight.

'Mum!' My mouth, literally, hung open.

She turned. Saw me. 'Oh, hello, darling. I wondered if you'd be here.' She kissed my cheek. I stared. For a moment I simply couldn't utter. Then I untwisted my tongue.

'M-Mum – what are you doing here!'

'Hmm?' She looked surprised. 'Oh well, I was invited, of course!'

'Really?' I looked around. The women's group? Or the church perhaps. 'But, Mum, this isn't our church, so—'

'Oh no,' she laughed, 'no, not the church, darling. Howard asked me.'

'Howard?'

It was then that I realised there was someone standing right beside her, right by her arm. I just hadn't connected them. He was mid-fiftyish, tall, with a hint of a paunch, silver-grey hair and a moustache to match, and he was smiling proprietorially down at my mother.

'Howard, this is my daughter, Olivia.'

'Oh!' I gazed, shook his extended hand, but couldn't speak.

'At last,' he grinned. 'I've heard so much about you but, I must say, I was keen to meet the real thing. You get a great press from your mum. Talk about proud mother and all that!'

'Oh!' I said it again, gormlessly too, aware that my mouth was still open.

'Howard's a doctor,' offered Mum, helpfully. 'We met when I took my usual stack of old magazines into the hospital.'

He grinned. 'The nurses kept telling me about this glamorous lady who was keeping them, not only in English *Vogues*, but in French and Italian ones too. I'm ashamed to say they plotted our meeting in an orthopaedic waiting room and I was an entirely willing participant!'

I gazed. Don't say 'Oh' again, you moron, just don't. 'S-so you're a doctor then?' I stammered.

'Well actually, I'm a urologist.'

I racked my brains. 'Ears?'

He laughed. 'Not even close. If I said that renal canals were a speciality, would that help?'

'Oh! Yes, it would!'

We laughed. *Mum* laughed. Mum, who couldn't even mention a front bottom without pinched lips, was laughing at renal canals? I gaped at her. And the *peach* number! I just couldn't help it.

'Mum – the clothes!' I blurted out. 'I mean – I've never seen you in anything remotely like that, ever!'

She laughed. 'I know, isn't it strange? But Howard said he couldn't be doing with all that navy blue. He bullied me out of it, said it reminded him of one of the sisters on his ward.'

'A particularly repressed one,' put in Howard, with a sly grin. 'Rumour has it she keeps a cane in the dispensary cupboard, to whip the other nurses into shape.'

I giggled. I loved him. Oh God, I loved him already.

'So what d'you think?' Mum glanced at me shyly and for a moment I thought she was asking about Howard. She smoothed down her coat.

'Gorgeous!' I enthused. 'I love it, Mum. You look fab! I just can't wait to tell Claudia. She won't believe it!'

She laughed, blushed a little too. 'Go on, darling, catch up with your party. I saw Imogen go past ages ago.'

I turned, realising that the rest had gone on, but that Rollo was still hovering, not exactly beside me, but quite close, studying a programme. I hesitated. No, I couldn't introduce him, not after Howard. It would be such an anticlimax.

'See you later, Mum.' I kissed her warmly and beamed at Howard. 'Goodbye, *so* good to meet you.'

'You too,' he smiled, and I'd swear he winked too.

'Sorry, Rollo,' I muttered, as I fell in beside him, 'got – caught up.'

'That's OK,' he smiled, tucking the programme away.

We walked on in silence. Maybe I should have explained. Explained that that was my mother, only I hadn't recognised her because she'd changed beyond all recognition and I'd been too astonished to introduce him. I realised, with a pang, that I hadn't seen her for ages. Oh, I'd spoken to her, sure, but hadn't seen her for – what, golly, weeks now, probably. I'd been so preoccupied lately, I hadn't even stopped to think how she was. But then, she was always . . . the same. I turned back and caught a glimpse of them finding their seats, Howard ushering her along a row, his hand gently guiding her peach linen elbow, handing her a programme as she straightened her skirt beneath her to sit down, both chattering away the while, smiling. I turned back, shook my head in wonder. My God. For years now my mother had been pained, irritable and bitter. Could it be that one man was changing all that? Could it be that one, single, beating heart had caused her to transform herself, to come alive again? What power! Just as one had snuffed her out, all those years ago, another, years later, was lighting the blue touchpaper again. I didn't know if that depressed or elated me, because whilst it was wonderful to see her like this, all those wasted years hurt. So many years! And wherein lay the moral for me? Was it that I'd better move fast? Turn those years into months, at the very least? Seize the disastrous dental arrangement beside me, or maybe the blond Adonis back in the caravan, or even the slick sales-man lurking in the BMW showroom – pick one of them up and run with it? Make the best of it? God Almighty! I shuddered. And what about a career, a child, both of which my mother had had – shouldn't all *that* have been enough? Shouldn't that have filled the need? Or was it simply that, in the words of The Beatles, love is all you need?

I wandered on, lost in thought, and almost walked past her, I was so distracted, until I realised she was actually plucking my sleeve.

'Olivia!'

It was Angie.

'Oh – hi!' I peeled off from Rollo once again.

She was looking stunning in a pale, silver-grey suit, and as I went to greet her I realised two of her daughters, plus husbands, were with her as well. I glanced around fearfully. Surely not Johnny too? I couldn't help it being the first thing I said as I kissed them all.

'Johnny isn't here, is he?' I murmured anxiously to Angie.

'I'm afraid he is, my dear.'

'But not with us,' put in Serena quickly. She squeezed my arm. 'We couldn't stomach him being in our party, told him to sod off on his own. I'm sure you won't see him. They're way down at the front.'

'They?' My mouth dried.

She nodded, tight-lipped. Hugged me hard. 'Bastard,' she muttered in my ear.

Lovely Serena, quite the prettiest of all, with her husband, Angus, who laid a sympathetic hand on my arm. Gosh, it was almost as if he'd died, wasn't it? And for a moment, I wished he had. It would be so much easier to bear, somehow, so much more clear cut, and I could have had some dignity as a widow. Instead of which, half the county was crammed into this church – many of whom I'd grown up with, many of whom were bound to know us – and he'd seen fit to bring her along, to what – to torture me? To humiliate me? I lived two seconds away, for Christ's sake; there was an odds on chance I'd be here, surely? In an instant Imogen was beside me. I held her arm, felt genuinely giddy.

'He's here,' I whispered.

'I know, I've just seen him. Came to find you.'

'Imo, I'm not sure I can do this. I'm going to slip out.'

'Don't be ridiculous,' she hissed. 'He might have already seen you and you can't just disappear, it looks wet. Stick that head up high and walk with me. I've seen her, and she looks like a dog's dinner and you, my darling, have never looked better. Come on.'

I took a deep breath and walked down the aisle with her.

When we got to about four rows from the front, she bundled me in, sandwiching me between her and Rollo, who'd already taken his seat.

'Where is he?' I gasped, as I sat down.

'Other side of aisle, about two rows ahead of us to the left. I'll tell you when to look.' She paused. 'Now.'

I shot my eyes across and saw Johnny, in a dark suit, blue shirt, spotty tie, tanned and very handsome, of course, his blond head bent with hers over a programme. She, Nina, had her hair pushed back in a velvet hairband, very average blue shirt, grey skirt too short for her legs, twenty denier tights. All of this I took in in a nanosecond, then looked away. Their heads. Touching like that. I had to breathe very deeply. Felt sick, physically sick.

'OK?' Imo squeezed my hand.

I shook my head. 'No.'

'You're fine. You're doing fine.'

I watched in a daze as the orchestra, high up on a specially constructed platform in the nave, tuned up. Tears threatened. I raised my eyes to the heavens and concentrated hard on the intricate painted panels of the choir ceiling. I'd read in a guidebook somewhere that years ago, they'd been restoring this particular area of ceiling, and whilst they were up there on ladders and scaffolding, carefully cleaning away, they'd discovered this, an older, much more beautiful ceiling with a medieval painting on it, underneath. I tried to imagine the excitement that must have caused, the shouts of joy from way up there as the restorers unearthed the vision I gazed at today, and gradually I felt the bile go down. I swallowed hard, slowly lowered my head. Happily, Rollo was engrossed in his programme.

'But this is very exciting,' he was muttering as he read avidly. 'It says here that this is the first time this piece of

Faulkner's has ever been performed.'

I nodded politely, couldn't speak. He leant across to Imo.

'Imogen, is that right? That this is the first time this symphony's been performed in this country?'

I spread my programme across my lap to catch the drips. Imo leant in eagerly for a meeting of minds.

'Yes, apparently he wrote it some time ago but recently changed it, and has only now allowed it to be performed.'

'But that's amazing, because he hasn't written anything of any note since that marvellous overture, has he?'

Despite my turmoil I was dimly fascinated to observe that Imo wiped her wet face without even appearing to notice. They were on a higher intellectual plain, of course, where things like personal hygiene were too trivial to worry about.

'No, nothing at all,' she said excitedly, 'and of course that was premiered at the Festival Hall with Simon Rattle conducting, remember? We all went in our final year. Gosh, this is such a treat!'

A treat? Really? They sat back, on tenterhooks, and I reached resignedly in my handbag for a tissue. I wiped my programme with deliberate ostentation, but he didn't appear to notice. Oh yes, I thought bitterly, tucking the hanky away, such a treat. Particularly for me, of course, to be closeted here with my husband and his floozie, for all the world to see – maybe even my mother, I thought with a sudden pang – and with my consolation prize of Spitty Dicky beside me. I caught Molly's eye further down the row and she grimaced sympathetically in Johnny's direction. I nodded and raised my eyebrows indicating that yes, I too had clocked them.

Suddenly there was a hush, and then a roar, as Hugo Simmonds took the podium to tremendous applause. He greeted his orchestra, then turned to the audience and smiled. Out of the corner of my eye I saw Ursula Mitchell straighten her back as she clapped madly. Actually I could see her point. He had quite a presence, if you liked narrow, pale faces with high foreheads, swept-back fair hair, and slightly hollow cheeks. There was something very English, very clever, and extremely intense about him. His sharp grey eyes darted about the audience, quickly searching the rows until he'd found what he was looking for. His gaze fell on Imo, beside me. I could almost feel the residual heat. Cool as a cat, Imo acknowledged him with a slight inclination of her blonde head and a Grace Kelly smile. She didn't blush or squirm as I would have done; she wasn't embarrassed to be singled out before hundreds of people; she was gracious, she was relaxed. I marvelled, briefly, but then again, I reasoned, she was used to it. If every time you batted an eyelid it started a stampede, you would get used to it. If every time you stood up, a queue formed, you'd get to take it in your stride.

Satisfied, if not satiated, Hugo turned his back on us, and faced his orchestra. His raised arms paused briefly in mid-air, then came down with a flourish, and the music began. I sank back in my chair and let it wash over me. Modern, explosive occasionally, but at the same time strangely melodic, whatever it was, it was a relief, and I was thankful for it. Thankful for its blanketing effect, for being able to shut my eyes and hide behind it.

So many thoughts churned through my head. I thought of my mother and Howard, meeting in that hospital waiting room, and of Howard, with his twinkly, northern charm, somehow asking her out. How on earth had he managed it without getting the cold shoulder? I thought of Angie too, alone, yet never lonely, surrounded as she was by her huge, loving, extended family. But most of all, I thought of Johnny. I remembered his head touching Nina's, and then, all of a sudden, I had one of those awful, monstrous flashes that I'm subject to occasionally, of the two of them entwined in bed together. An obscene vision, it lurked like some dreadful, leering Caliban at the back of my mind, awaiting its chance, always keen to spot a gap and roar in. I held my breath and stared furiously at the stained-glass windows on my right until it passed, until I was breathing normally again. The urge to look to my left, though, across the aisle, was becoming more overpowering, and as the music went on I found I did – continually, compulsively, couldn't help it – until eventually the inevitable happened. She looked too. I caught her eye, looked away, and realised she'd tell Johnny I was here. In that split second, knowing he'd glance across, I dived my head playfully into Rollo's shoulder, gazing up at his face. He glanced down, surprised but pleased, and as I turned back, I was just in time to see Johnny turn away, a slight flush on his cheek. Good, I thought viciously. I hope that hurt.

Rollo, on the other hand, was far from hurt. Hugely encouraged, he nestled in close, and every so often he'd peer round at me with a questioning little smile and an alarming look in his eye. I groaned inwardly. Oh hell, I didn't want him getting the wrong idea. I hesitated, then armpit dived him again, only this time made damn sure my face was upturned to the glorious ceiling.

'It's lovely,' I breathed by way of explanation – unfortunately, just as the trumpets sounded.

He looked surprised, then smiled. 'Thank you,' he whispered.

I froze. Thank you? Christ, did he think I'd said 'You're lovely'?

I cleared my throat. 'The Abbey,' I muttered quite loudly. 'The lovely ceiling, the way they've lit—'

'Shhh . . .' He silenced me gently, as one or two people turned and frowned. He smiled, put his finger to his lips. 'Later,' he whispered excitedly, squeezing my arm.

I sank back in horror. Later? God, did he think I was rampant or something? Couldn't wait? Was sitting here twitching away in an agony of erotic anticipation? I shook my head in disbelief and listened on in silence.

On and on. Interminably. No interval, of course, I discovered gloomily from my programme, so held in thrall were we all supposed to be by this sodding symphony. Oh no, an interval would no doubt be deemed to break the mood, spoil the atmosphere. Just the two hours of purgatory then, looking rapt and cultured with an aching heart and an aching bottom, waiting for the agony to end.

Finally, of course, it did, and to my astonishment, the applause was deafening. There was a sudden roar of approval, tremendous clapping, and then the audience got to its feet as one. Dropping my handbag and programme I hastily followed suit, catching Molly's eye as she nudged Hugh awake and he too got up, rolling his eyes at me in mock horror at the ordeal. All around, people were calling out in rapture, and some, like Imo and Rollo beside me, even stamped their feet which I thought was a bit childish, but by all accounts, judging by the flushed, enthusiastic faces of those in the know, it had been a towering success.

Hugo Simmonds, flushed, elated and dripping with sweat, raised his hands and gave us his orchestra. They stood and bowed, as Hugo, with elaborate gestures, singled out the stars: his leader, his flautist, his brass section, his percussion, before finally, turning himself to bow to thunderous applause. He soaked it up for a moment, stood, waved, then turned and disappeared off stage, only to reappear a moment later and receive the same treatment. But still the applause went on. Louder now, and more insistent, as if something was missing, some need waiting to be gratified. Hugo Simmonds smiled, nodded knowingly, and flicked back his damp fair hair. Then he simply gestured to someone near the front of the audience to come up. For an awful moment I thought he might be looking at Imo, but then a few rows ahead of us, a tall, dark man in a dinner jacket stood up with his back to us. As people craned their necks to see, murmuring, 'There he is!' I realised it must be Faulkner himself. He brushed back his hair, and slid along the row to the end, where he went to the front to mount the stage. As he got to the top step and turned to the audience, there was a deafening roar of approval, and for the first time I saw his face. My hand shot to my mouth.

'Bloody hell!'

I gaped in horror, unable to take in what I was seeing. Unable to quite believe my eyes. For up there on the podium, smiling shyly but delightedly, bowing, and waving occasionally to acknowledge the tremendous applause, was Sebastian.

Chapter Fifteen

I gaped, wide-eyed and frozen with horror. The vaulted ceiling, the medieval panels, and all the ancient Roman tiles above it, seemed to fall in on my head. Sebastian. Sebastian was . . . Faulkner? How on earth could that be? Despite the pressure of several tons of masonry on my shattered skull, what was left of my brain strung the names together. Sebastian . . . Faulkner. God, yes, of course, even I, with my modicum of classical music knowledge, had just about heard of him. I flushed to my roots, jaw hanging, boggling at him up there on the podium, bowing and smiling.

'Christ,' I murmured.

'What's up?' yelled Imo into my ear, above the applause.

'I know him,' I muttered.

'What?'

'I said I know him!'

'No!' she squeaked, swinging excitedly around to face me. 'How come?'

I opened my mouth to speak, but happily, didn't have time to elucidate, as in a matter of moments, Ursula was upon us, bustling importantly along the row, knocking into people's knees, sending programmes flying, eyes shining.

'My dears, *such* a thrill,' the breathed ecstatically. 'Hugo Simmonds has conveyed to us by means of a sweet note,

267

that he'd be delighted to have us all join him backstage for a small celebration. Imagine, Imo, we'll meet Faulkner too!'

'Oh, but Olivia already knows him,' said Imo excitedly, 'don't you, Livvy?'

'Er, well,' I gulped, 'sort of . . . ish.'

'No!' Ursula gasped. 'My dear, why didn't you say?' Her eyes shone alarmingly. 'Is he *totally* enchanting?'

I swallowed, and it was on the tip of my tongue to explain that I wasn't the best person to ask since the last time I'd seen him I'd brandished a rake and cast aspersions on his moral character, so the chances of him being overly enchanting to me backstage were minimal, but instead I edged away, smiling nervously.

'D'you know I'm – not sure, Ursula, because to be honest I don't know him terribly well, and – and actually, what with the baby-sitter waiting I really must be getting—'

'Nonsense,' she insisted, seizing my wrist urgently, the possibility of a personal introduction gleaming in her eyes. 'Imogen was telling me how wonderful your builders are, always stepping in to help you out. They won't mind another hour. Come!' She called me to heel, dragging me firmly by the arm. 'How absolutely splendid to make an entrance with someone who's actually acquainted with him,' she squeaked. 'I can't wait to tell Hugo! How exactly do you know him, my dear?' She swooped, hawklike, her sharp nose level with mine as she propelled me from the nave, through the crowds, bumping into people's backs with no regard at all as she made for the back of the Abbey in a frenzy of excitement.

'Um, he lives in my road,' I muttered, glancing around desperately for a convenient side exit.

She stopped, clapped her hand to her forehead. 'Of course he does! In The Crescent! Which is precisely why he wanted the first rendition of this work to be performed here, giving something back to his city, rather than it going straight to the Festival Hall!' She marched on again. 'The powers that be were dead against it of course – wanted it in London – but he was absolutely adamant – and what a success! Tell me,' she breathed, 'right there at the end, throughout that final recapitulation, did you or did you not have goosebumps literally all over?'

'Um, yes.' Not a lie, but from fright rather than ecstasy, and actually they were beginning to reform.

'Come along, my party!' Ursula threw back imperiously over her shoulder as we marched on, glancing round to check that Imo, Rollo, Molly and Hugh were all trailing dutifully behind. Suddenly Ursula stopped.

'Damn. Wait here,' she hissed, parking me by a pillar, but never for a moment loosening the grip on my arm.

She turned and beamed delightedly. 'Charles! Sonia! So good of you to come! Did you enjoy it?' This she addressed to a rather mousy, elderly couple who'd followed, a trifle bemused, in our wake. 'I'm *so* pleased,' she enthused without waiting for an answer. '*Lovely* to see you again,' and with this she kissed them with a definite air of finality.

But Charles and Sonia, camel-coated and seventy-odd, were slow to catch her drift. They were inclined to linger, chat a little, become expansive, come with us even, and Ursula was going to have her work cut out explaining that they were the last people on earth she wanted cluttering up her backstage salon; just the young, the vibrant, the chic and, of course, me, the sick at heart. I glanced about wildly for a handy escape route or even just a pew to hide behind, but I was comprehensively hemmed in on all sides now: Ursula to my right, her hand on my arm, a pillar behind me, and Rollo, quivering with excitement and hopping stupidly from foot to foot, to my left.

'What fun, a party!' he squealed as he pranced skittishly.

Berk. I regarded him with complete disdain. Total, utter, berk. I'd really gone off him in a major way. He was the sort of intellectual giant who clutched his sides when the fool pranced on in a Shakespeare play, the sort who pooped a stupid horn at the last night of the Proms, wearing an oh-so-funny Union Jack hat. Hugh sidled up to me, elbowing Rollo out of the way, and found my ear.

'What's going on?'

'Party, backstage,' I muttered. 'Ursula's idea, but I'm out of here.'

Hugh brightened. 'You mean we get another drink? Splendid, I'm game.'

'Why don't you want to go?' asked Molly as I slipped behind Hugh, past Rollo, and then behind another pillar.

'Because,' I hissed flattening myself against it, 'that chap I told you about, the one who lives down my road and I thought had abducted Claudia – turns out to be bloody Faulkner! It's bloody Sebastian Faulkner!' I inched sideways, spotting, with relief, the Chapter door to my left.

Hugh's eyes widened. 'Faulkner abducted Claudia? I didn't hear about this.' A *Daily Mail* exclusive lurked alarmingly in his eyes.

'No! Of course not, but I thought he had! I made a mistake, but I can't possibly go in there now, it'll be excruciatingly embarrassing! Now for heaven's sake go away and stop talking to me – I'm trying to be discreet, for God's sake. Cover me or something useful.'

I scurried off to the side door, with Molly and Hugh dutifully turning back and shielding me, helped by Molly's huge bulk. Seizing with relief the high iron handle on the old oak door, I turned it. Rattled it dementedly, in fact. Damn, locked. As I swung around frantically, about to leg it to the main entrance, I saw Ursula bearing down on me, with Molly shrugging helplessly behind her. My deodorant was beginning to let me down.

'Wrong way, Olivia!' she called. 'They're using the refectory for the party!'

She linked my arm and made to pull me away, but I dug my heels in hard.

'Ursula, listen,' I said desperately. 'I'm – I'm awfully sorry but I can't come. I feel terribly ill. In fact, I think I'm going to be sick.'

'Oh, I know, it is frightfully stuffy in here, isn't it? Terribly close. But once we're out of this madding crowd you'll feel heaps better, I promise!' She yanked my arm.

'But I—'

'Listen, Olivia, I'll be honest with you.' She dropped her voice dramatically and lowered her head. 'I didn't get a note from Hugo, although I rather hoped I would, but then again he is terribly shy. All the same, I know he'll just be dying to see Imogen, but it would help enormously if you came too. Just to sort of ease our path through the stage door, seeing as how you're a personal friend of Mr Faulkner's and all that.'

I gaped. 'N-no, but listen, Ursula, I'm not, I—'

'Mum, what *is* going on?' Imogen came up looking totally bewildered. 'Are we supposed to be going backstage or not? Everyone's waiting!'

'Yes, of course we are, darling. We're just coming, aren't we, Olivia?' She turned pleading eyes on me. I stared. Looked at Imo. Back to Ursula. Nodded dumbly. 'Excellent!' she breathed. 'Come along now!'

Her iron grip once more took up position under my

elbow, and as she marched me, lamblike to the slaughter, along the ancient stone passages, beaten almost hollow with age, I realised where Imogen got it from – this desire to be first; to be top; to be the best. As long as I'd known her she'd striven for perfection, which of course was laudable, but it also meant she couldn't settle for anything less. And Imo had yet to settle.

'Here we are!' Her mother stopped suddenly, raised her knuckles, and gave a sharp tap at the refectory door. It was instantly opened by a lackey.

To my relief, the room was packed. Teeming, actually, full to the brim with the orchestra, presumably their friends and relatives, and various sundry hangers-on. Ursula looked momentarily disappointed since we clearly weren't the chosen few – let alone the chosen multitude – but, happily, Hugo Simmonds was close to the door. He spotted her instantly and, raising his glass above the crush, came squeezing across to greet her.

'Ursula!'

'Hugo! My dear I hope you don't mind us barging in, but Olivia here knows Sebastian *terribly* well and we just wanted to pop by and congratulate you both! Imo – say hello to Hugo!'

'M-mind? Heavens, I'm d-delighted!' he said, flicking his hair back nervously. He almost came out in a muck sweat as Imogen diligently obeyed orders and kissed him on the cheek. His glasses all but steamed up.

'It's l-lovely to see you, Imogen. D-did you enjoy it?' he stammered. I was stunned. Was this the same commanding man of moments ago?

'It was wonderful,' Imo enthused warmly, 'really wonderful, Hugo.'

'Thank you,' he gasped. 'I'm s-so glad you came. I

w-wanted to ask you but w-wasn't sure if you'd . . . I-I must say, Imogen,' he gulped, 'you look absolutely marvellous.' His grey eyes roved admiringly over the Grecian curls, the tanned, smooth shoulders, the slim brown legs and for a moment, he forgot to stutter. 'An absolute vision,' he declared roundly.

'He wants to give her one right now,' muttered Hugh in my ear. 'Behind the choir stalls. Can't wait. And I'll tell you something else, old Ursula Mitchell wouldn't mind if he did.'

I giggled, but I was simultaneously scanning the room nervously for Sebastian. Ah, there he was, right over the other side, thank God, with his back to me. His dark head protruded a couple of inches higher than the swarm of people he was talking to. If I stayed right here by the door, had a quick drink and slipped away in two minutes flat, I'd be fine. I'd done my duty, got old Ursula in; yes, I could be away. I kept my eyes firmly on that head lest it should suddenly turn, took a glass of champagne from a tray as it passed by, and sipped and stared. As I did, I grew more and more incredulous. I simply couldn't believe it. Could *not* believe who he was. Christ, I mean, he'd never said, had he? Never mentioned it, and he'd had ample opportunity, surely? Had he, though? I racked my brains, trying to remember where I'd first met him. Of course, at Nanette's. God, bloody Nanette, who knowing no better had billed him, first as a lunatic, and then as a *teacher*, for heaven's sake. What planet was she on?

'I think he's rather cute,' murmured Molly in my ear, crunching a pistachio nut. 'Can't think why you thought he was certifiable.'

'Molly, you thought so too!' I hissed. 'When I told you about Claudia turning up in his house, you said I shouldn't apologise in person because it all sounded very iffy! I distinctly remember!'

'Yes, but that was before I knew who he was, before I'd seen him in the flesh. Anyone can see the man's totally normal. In fact,' she squinted, 'he's really rather handsome.' She inched round to get a better view of the side of his face, pulling me with her. 'You told me he was a long-haired loner who ran about in jim-jams.'

'Yes, well, he's wearing a dinner jacket now, isn't he, and he's had his hair cut.'

I had to agree, though, that with a good couple of inches off his hair so that one could see those dark, slightly slanting eyes which ran parallel with high cheekbones, he looked a different person. Quite a presence.

'He's got such a sensitive face,' she murmured.

'Oh rubbish,' I scoffed. 'If anything he's got an arrogant face. You're only saying that because you know he's a composer. If he was a doctor you'd say he had a caring face, and if he was an artist you'd say he had an artistic face, and for heaven's sake stop staring, Mol. He'll see us!'

I realised in panic that we'd drifted away from the door, and that our exit was now blocked by a few more newcomers. I desperately tried to fight my way back, simultaneously scrabbling in my bag for my car keys. Time to go. Definitely time to go.

'He can't see us, Livvy,' Molly said as I rooted about in my bag. 'He's far too swamped by all those luvvies. Just look at them fawning. They're practically kissing the hem of his jacket.'

Having at least found my programme in my bag, I used it to shield my face and peep over. She was right: people were literally queuing up to talk to him.

'Was he nice when you went over?' she whispered, eyes glued.

'What?'

'When you went round to apologise, what did he say?'

'Oh, I didn't go round in the end. I did as you said, I sent a—' Christ. A note. Had I sent a note? My mind fled back. I'd written one, certainly, and failed to drop it in because of his mother, so then I'd gone home to write another, but . . . I went cold. 'Oh God!'

'What?'

'I forgot to write a letter!' I clasped my mouth. 'Oh, Molly, I forgot to do it! Forgot to apologise!'

She looked at me in horror. 'You mean . . . he still thinks – that you still think—'

'I've got to get out of here, Mol,' I said urgently. 'Got to, before he sees me. Come on,' I turned and lunged for the door.

'Too late,' she muttered in my ear.

I swung my head to see – Sebastian Faulkner, pale-faced, stony-eyed, who had not only seen me, but was making determined strides in my direction, pushing fixedly through the madding throng, his dark eyes as hard as a couple of flints.

'Help!' I squealed, as I pushed for freedom, but we were three deep from the door now, and Molly's heavily pregnant state made it nigh on impossible to shove through. I felt like a fox being hunted, the hounds right on my tail, but as I glanced back, panic-stricken, I suddenly saw Ursula Mitchell step out right in front of him, blocking his path.

'Mr Faulkner, *might* I say how absolutely marvellous I thought that was!' she gushed. 'I honestly don't think I've enjoyed a piece of music so much since I heard Pascalle conduct Beethoven's Fifth with the Berlin Philharmonic in

Rome, which I was privileged enough to go to last year with a great friend of mine Lady Farqurson, and I have to say, that even *that* occasion, momentous though it was, didn't *quite* send shivers up my spine the way that *your* symphony did tonight! Truly magnificent, maestro!'

He gave a small bow. 'Thank you,' he muttered, and made to sidestep her, his eyes still fixed and predatory, but dear old Ursula hadn't finished. She blocked his way – bless her – and gave him another earful, just as I, managing to barge past Molly and make a desperate lunge for the door, arrived to find that the only obstacle between me and freedom was Rollo, leaning laconically against it, and holding forth about Faulkner to a couple of credulous college students.

'. . . such powerful stanzas, yet such insight into the common lot. One feels almost humbled by his power, his presence, his— Ow!' he yelped weedily as I barged up. 'That was my foot!'

'Move,' I hissed shamelessly, elbowing him roughly.

'Sorry?'

'Move out of the way!'

'Sorry?'

'Oh, for Christ's sake get out of my way and stop bloody spitting at me!' I shrieked, wiping my face.

He frowned. 'Olivia, are you all right? You look a bit—'

'Tra-la-la-la-la-diddly-dah!' trilled a loud soprano behind us. I jerked my head back to see Ursula, who, much to Imo's embarrassment, was now giving the composer her own cringe-making rendition of her favourite bits, still blocking his path. 'That's the phrase I just adored,' she beamed, 'at the beginning of the second movement. *So* bewitching with that lovely lilting melody, and such a contrast to the first movement. In fact, I was saying to someone . . .' She tried desperately to catch Sebastian's eyes, which were not on her at all. 'Mr Faulkner, I was saying to—' she gave up and followed his gaze. 'Olivia! I was saying to Olivia, who, of course, you know!'

In one bony swoop of her arm, like python snatching its prey, she lunged out, plucked my arm, and pulled hard, sweeping me into her inner circle. I felt like a child being hauled before the head. My knees began to knock, and my eyes, when I finally dared to raise them, found his: cold, dark and forbidding. He gave me a look that froze my spine.

'You *do* know each other, don't you, Olivia?' insisted Ursula, in case I'd made it up.

'Yes, we, um, do.' I faltered.

'Unhappily,' he barked sharply, and I could see his hands clenching by his sides.

Ursula's social smile quivered. 'I-I'm sorry, did you say—'

'Oh, thank God!' shrieked a shrill voice behind us. Suddenly Molly burst through, pushing people out of the way, clutching her huge stomach, eyes wild. 'I've got the most frightful pains, Livvy, terrible stomach cramps, and Hugh's too drunk to drive! I've been looking everywhere for you. Would you be an angel and take me home?'

'Oh, my dear!' Ursula was all consternation. 'Are they labour pains, d'you think? Are you about to have it? Do you need an ambulance?'

Molly staggered about a bit, enjoying herself hugely. 'Noo, noo,' she gasped bravely, 'I think I'll be – AAARGHHH!' She clutched my arm suddenly and sank to her knees. Ursula jumped back in horror. 'No, I'll be fine, really,' she gasped, straightening up, face racked with simu-lated pain. 'I'm sure it's too soon, not due for days yet, it's just that I must lie down, you see, put my feet up and—

Hugh!' She gasped with relief as her husband pushed his way through. 'Oh, Hugh darling, so sorry, ghastly pains. Livvy's going to drive us home! Bye, all, thank you *so* much Mrs Mitchell, lovely party, lovely concert!'

She'd played her part perfectly, and we'd undoubtedly have made a seamless exit were it not for Hugh, who, loving a drama, and having not worked in one for a while, was delighted to stumble across this one. He threw himself into it shamelessly.

'Darling!' he cried. 'Oh God, darling, are you all right? Shall I ring Mr Kenny?'

'Mr Kenny?' Ursula blinked. 'Isn't he the Queen's gynaecologist?'

Hugh straightened up. 'He's my wife's gynaecologist,' he informed her soberly. 'What he does in his spare time is his own affair, we all have to make a living. Come, my dear.' He supported Molly's bulk as she collapsed, groaning, on to his shoulder. 'Come, I'll help you to the— Christ!' Hugh leapt back theatrically as there was a sudden splash on the floor between Molly's legs. Everyone gasped.

'Oh God, it's your waters!' cried Hugh, a mysteriously empty glass in his hand, insanity in his eyes.

Molly looked genuinely horror-struck. 'Good God.' She stared down at the puddle. Blinked. 'I didn't even feel it!'

'Ah well, that's mother nature for you,' muttered Hugh, manoeuvring his wife expertly through the gaping throng, which was parting like the Red Sea now, and towards a hurriedly opened door. 'It eases you into it gently, lulls you into a false sense of security but, mark my words, it'll be the stirrups and the forceps for you before the night is out. You'll be biting through my hand, kicking innocent bits of furniture and being sensationally abusive to the medical team. It'll be just like Henry all over again! Come, Livvy, to the hospital, please, and don't spare the horses! Mind your backs, good people, mind your backs. Bye all, wish us well!'

'Bye!' I managed to squeak as Hugh ushered us out.

As the door shut behind us, we fled down the corridor. Back through the nave, we raced, down the side aisle of the empty Abbey, our feet echoing wildly on the flagstones. Hugh and I were on either side of Molly, who, the size of a barrage balloon, was running for England. Down the steps we clattered, through the huge oak doors and out into the garden, where, under a leafy tree and the safety of darkness, we threw ourselves on to a bench, collapsing in an hysterical, giggling heap.

'Oh God,' I gasped, as we fought for control. 'Oh Molly, you were marvellous. I didn't know you had it in you! You should be the one out there treading the boards. I thought you were going to have it right there and then!'

'Bloody hell, so did I!' she gasped. 'It took me a moment to realise my waters hadn't gone!'

'Ah me,' sighed Hugh, wiping his eyes happily, 'I haven't enjoyed myself so much since I was a spear carrier in *Hamlet* and Ophelia sat on my spike. Did you see Ursula's face? Horrified that Molly might be about to commit the ultimate social sin of *dilating in public*! I was about to offer to have a quick peek at your cervix, Mol, but I thought that might be going too far.'

'Far too far,' I agreed sternly, mopping my eyes, 'the Frascati on the floor was bad enough.'

'Ah, but we saved your bacon, eh, Livvy old girl?' Hugh slung an arm round my shoulders as we struggled to our feet. 'Christ, he was going to have you for breakfast! I've never seen such murder in a man's eyes. It damn nearly wiped the smile off my face, I can tell you, and it takes a lot to do that. He was hopping mad.'

'But justifiably, surely,' I said more soberly, as we made for the car park. 'Don't you think? I mean, after what I'd accused him of?'

'God, I should say,' agreed Molly warmly. 'I'm surprised he didn't just biff you on the nose and have done with it.'

I stopped. 'And then he had to witness our ridiculous charade. And I'm sure he knew it was a charade. I saw his face at one point. He knew I was trying to slip through the net again, so once again I've done him a disservice, haven't I?' I bit my lip. 'I didn't go and apologise when I should have done, and I couldn't even stand my ground in there and do it then.' I swallowed.

Molly looked at me in horror. 'Livvy, you're surely not thinking—'

'Liv darling, he'll have your guts for garters,' interrupted Hugh gently, taking my arm. 'And not just for garters. He'll make suspenders out of them, believe me. The man's world famous, he has a name to protect and, God, even if he hadn't, even if he was as small a fish as I am, he'd be so bloody furious about being accused of— Well, Christ, if anyone said that about me I'd – I'd – bloody . . .' For once he was lost for words.

'Precisely,' I said quietly. 'So don't you see? I have to go back. It's so awful, what I've done, and now I've made it worse. I have to go back.' I turned.

Molly caught my arm. 'Wait a bit,' she urged. 'Hang around out here and wait until everyone's gone. Catch him on the way out. At least then he won't be surrounded by all those bloody sycophants.'

I shook her off. 'No, I'm going. If I don't go now I'll never pluck up the courage, and then I'll never do it.'

They watched in silence as I walked away from them. I

retraced my steps, up into the Abbey, down the side aisle that we'd just this minute raced through, bubbling over with laughter, down towards the altar. I tracked right through the nave, past the tombs, the monuments, round the vast painted column at the far end, and then, full of fear and dread, went down through the great gothic arch and the wooden steps to the refectory. I stopped for a second, my hand on the handle, heart pounding. There was still plenty of noise coming from inside, chattering and laughing – and for a moment I almost lost my nerve. Molly was right: I didn't have to do this. Not here. Not now. Some other time perhaps. Then – damn it. Get on with it, Livvy. I turned the handle and walked in.

The room was still crowded, but not nearly so tightly packed. It had thinned out a little and it was possible to walk around. I slid along the sides, my eyes darting, searching, until quite quickly I found who I was looking for. He saw me at exactly the same moment. Broke off abruptly from talking to the cluster of ten or so people around him who were listening intently. I wouldn't say you could hear a pin drop, exactly, because the rest of the room was still buzzing, but certainly as the group around Sebastian fell silent, it provoked something of a ripple effect. I noticed Imogen and Ursula to the right of me, staring.

'Excuse me,' muttered Sebastian to his neighbour. He came towards me, a muscle going in his cheek.

'Mrs McFarllen,' he said in a low voice, 'you've made your way back to my party. Is that wise? Are you so deprived of social engagements that you seek out even those where you are clearly unwelcome?' His voice was soft, but bitter and scathing, and it seemed to me that at this point, the rest of the room caught his tone and went quiet.

In an instant Ursula and Imogen were beside me.

'Olivia, what is it?' hissed Ursula. 'What's going on?'

I cleared my throat. 'I've come to apologise,' I said, looking up into his stony face. 'I made a very foolish mistake the other day, and accused you,' I made myself meet his cold brown eyes, 'of a dreadful thing.'

'What? What dreadful thing?' urged Ursula, just a little too agog.

'She accused me of being a child molester,' said Sebastian in a level voice. 'A paedophile.'

A horrified gasp went round the room.

'No!' someone breathed, Then, 'Good God!' and, 'Slanderous!'

'Olivia, how could you!' gaped Ursula.

I felt incredibly giddy and a bit light-headed, but I managed to meet his eyes.

'How could I?' I said. 'Because I was frightened. Terrified, actually. I don't know if you have children, Mr Faulkner, but let me tell you, the most frightening thing in the world is losing them. I lost my child,' I said, forcing myself to look round the room, to catch anyone's eye who was interested, 'last Sunday. My ten-year-old. She slipped off on her own on her bike, and when I followed the route I imagined she'd taken, through the woods, down by the river, I found something that confirmed my worst fears. Her bike, dragged into the bushes, and abandoned. When I asked a passer-by – no, screamed at a passer-by – if she'd seen a little girl in red shorts, she said yes, going into a nearby house, sobbing, and being taken by a tall man. This tall man.'

Even Ursula looked slightly askance at this. She shot a look at Sebastian, who was still staring at me.

'So without stopping to think, and imagining only

horror, I stormed into that house, all guns blazing, to find my little girl, sitting in this same man's house, and wearing nothing at all, but his dressing gown.' I paused. 'Now what would you have thought?' I asked, trembling now. 'Ursula, what would you have thought?' I turned demanding eyes on her.

'Well I – I . . .' she floundered, turning bewildered eyes on Sebastian.

'Exactly. You'd have thought the same as me. But you'd be wrong, as it happens, and that's why I'm here. To apologise. I apologise, Mr Faulkner.'

There was a stunned silence.

'S-so what happened?' stammered Ursula. 'I'm confused, I mean, if he didn't—'

'Claudia fell in the river,' I said. 'She hit a rut on her bike and went headfirst into the stream, banged her head on a rock. Mr Faulkner saw from an upstairs window and rushed out to help her. He dried her clothes, gave her a dressing gown, and made her some tea. I have a lot to be thankful for. She had a pretty bad bump and had he not seen her, had she been floundering about in the river for longer, it could have been a different story. I might even have lost her. As it was,' I turned back to Sebastian, 'I called you every foul and vile name under the sun. In my defence I might say that I had no idea who you were, although I doubt that would have made any difference. To an enraged mother a famous composer is just as culpable as a man in a dirty mac. But I was wrong.' I was aware my voice was beginning to wobble so I speeded it up. 'Very wrong. I slandered and insulted you and I'm deeply sorry and ashamed. I'd like to thank you for being so quick-witted and helping Claudia, and – and I deeply regret,' I rushed on, 'any pain I've caused you. I'm sorry.'

With that I turned, and without waiting to hear his, or
Ursula's views on the subject, walked out of the room. I
went back down the Abbey, and out into the night, whereupon I promptly burst into tears.

Chapter Sixteen

That night I slept fitfully. I dreamt I was up on the Abbey stage, a key member of Sebastian's orchestra, performing his masterpiece with a vast, outsized cello clamped between my legs. As I screeched and scraped away hopelessly, making a terrible din and ruining the symphony, the front row of the audience became mutinous.

'Off! Get her off!' they yelled.

I glanced up from my bow, sweat pouring off me, to see Angie, Howard, my mother, Imogen, Ursula, Johnny and Nina, their faces all contorted with rage, shaking their fists, baying for my blood.

'She never could play!' yelled Johnny, on his feet now. 'She's a fraud!'

In the row behind, Alf, Mac and Spiro, still in their work overalls, feet up, and swigging Stella from cans, were booing and making obscene gestures involving strenuous wrist action. A can came flying my way. 'Off, get 'er off!' they jeered.

Finally Sebastian stalked on from the wings, enraged. 'Mrs McFarllen,' he spat, 'in the words of the great Thomas Beecham, you have between your legs something that can bring pleasure to millions, and all you can do is *scratch* it!'

'I can't play!' I wept. 'I never said I could, I—'

'Mummy, Mummy!' I was being bounced up and down now, my head nearly coming off my shoulders as it rocked back and forth.

'Aaggh! Don't! I'll learn, I swear to God I'll learn, I'll – Claudes!'

I opened my eyes to see Claudia, astride me, dressed in her stripy summer school uniform, bouncing me up and down on the bed. The sun was streaming in through the windows.

'Learn what?' She frowned down at me.

'Oh my God,' I breathed, blinking sweaty eyelids and pushing back my hair. 'What a nightmare. What a godawful, terrible, horrific, nightmare. I feel sick. What time is it?'

'Twenty to eight, and I've got my ballet exam today.' She yanked the duvet off me. 'Oh yuk! You're all sweaty!' She dropped it back in disgust.

I sat up and clutched my head. She was right, my hair was plastered to my scalp, my T-shirt sticking to me. I shot my eyes to the bedside clock.

'Christ! Your ballet exam! You're supposed to be there in twenty minutes!'

'I know.'

'All tutu'd up with a hairnet on!'

'I know.'

I stared. 'And you deliberately didn't wake me earlier because you don't want to do it! Claudia, you are such a devious, mendacious little—'

'Don't say the F word.'

'I wasn't about to say the F word!'

'It shows lack of character. And, anyway, what's the problem? I'm waking you now, aren't I?'

'Claudia, I'll give you lack of character!' I seethed,

leaping out of bed and grabbing my jeans. I plunged my legs into them. 'Just get your tail downstairs *now*, grab your tutu and get in that car and I'll join you there in two minutes! *And don't forget the bloody hairnet!*'

Three minutes later, unwashed, dying for a cup of tea, mouth like the bottom of a budgie's cage and armpits decidedly pongy, I was nevertheless reversing at high speed out of that drive. I can move when I feel like it and, amazingly, I thought, glancing smugly at the clock, we'd made it. She'd be in that exam room in precisely ten minutes, strapped into her pointes and doing the dying swan if I killed us both on the A41 in the process.

'You'll make it,' I snarled as she sulked beside me.

'Yeah, I know,' she sighed, resignedly. She'd had a go, but I'd had a better one.

I caught sight of myself in the rear-view mirror and pushed desperate hands through greasy hair. 'Oh, Claudes, *look* at me! Pass me my—'

'Here.' She'd already reached into the glove compartment and found my dark glasses.

I shoved them on. 'Thanks.'

'And this?' She picked up an old baseball cap from the floor.

'Please.' I rammed it on.

She was still rummaging around. 'Mint?'

'Definitely.' I opened my mouth and she popped in a Polo. I sucked for a bit, then shot her a sideways glance. Winked.

'Heavy night?' she offered sympathetically.

'Terrible,' I groaned, sucking hard. I rubbed my forehead with my fingertips, remembering. 'Oh gosh, *really* terrible, actually.' What an evening. What an absolutely, awful evening!

287

'I had a great time last night, Mum.'

'Good, good,' I murmured distractedly, shooting straight across the top of a mini roundabout, four wheels off the ground. God, what a disaster! First Johnny and Nina all snuggled up together in hand-holding cosiness, and then bloody Sebastian! Up there on the *stage*, for heaven's sake! I shook my head in disbelief.

'It started off really badly 'cos Alf was so sad and grumpy and still upset about Vi, but then Spiro came over from the caravan and said that their telly wasn't working so did I think you'd mind if they all came over and baby-sat with Alf. I said you wouldn't. You wouldn't, would you, Mum?'

'Hmm?' Oh God, and *Molly*, practically giving *birth* like that!

'Mum?'

'What, darling?'

'Watching the telly?'

'Yes, no fine. Lovely.'

'Oh good. So anyway, they all came over and we got loads of pizza and stuff out of the freezer and they drank lots of beer – *lots* of beer, actually – and Spiro got really happy and larky. Oh Mum, it was so funny. He was doing Greek dancing on the table and throwing plates and catching them – we used those big Spanish bowls you've got – and I was doing it too, all in my nightie!'

'Excellent, excellent, my love,' I murmured distractedly, as I remembered yet another shaker. What about my mother? Turning up with a *man*, for goodness' sake!

'And then in the middle of being really happy, Spiro suddenly got really sad because he missed his wife and son so much – you know how he cries – so I had a brilliant idea and said, why didn't he ring her up! You don't mind, do you, Mum?'

'Hmm?' Unbelievable really. My mum. God, after all those years. All those arid years.

'Mum?'

'What, darling?'

'Using the phone?'

'Of course you can use the phone.' Heavens, and talking of mothers, what about Ursula! In fine ambitious form, throwing Imo to that conductor like a Christian to the lions.

'So anyway he rang and talked for ages, all in Greek, of course, and then because he was so cheered up and happy, we decided to have a disco, and we turned the music up really loud and Mac was the DJ and he did all the rapping stuff, you know, and Alf – oh gosh, Mum, Alf was *so funny*! He was like, really, really drunk – could hardly stand up by now – and he was burping and everything, and then he started doing this striptease dance – you know, like in *The Full Monty* – de da de da de da!'

But it was Sebastian who was really making my toes curl in their trainers this morning. I cringed down low behind the wheel, hiding under my baseball cap. I'd never forget his face, gimlet-eyed as he pushed through that room towards me. I glanced across at Claudia, who for some reason was slipping her blazer off one shoulder and rolling her eyes like Shirley Bassey. 'Put it on, darling. You know Mr Harty likes you to at least turn up in it.' I hoiked it back up. Yes, crikey, those *eyes* of his – wouldn't like to come across them in a dark alley. I shivered.

'And then he got up on the sofa and was mucking about and sticking out his bare tummy, which was really fat and hairy like a dog's, and he was rubbing it and everything, and we were laughing and laughing, and suddenly – he was sick! But *luckily* Spiro held out a bowl, so most of it – "Puyaka!" – went in the bowl! Wasn't that lucky, Mum?'

'Hmm? Christ!' I just managed to screech to a halt as a lollipop lady stepped out in front of me. 'What?'

'I said wasn't it lucky it went in your Spanish bowl?'

'Oh. Yes. I expect it looked nice.'

Claudia frowned. 'No, it didn't look nice. But, anyway, we chucked it down the loo and Alf had another beer and said he felt better, and then we did this brilliant kanga – you know, de-da-da-da-da-da – DA! De-da-da-da-da-da – DA! – all holding on to each other in a line all over the house. We even went upstairs and tramped all over the beds – it was brilliant!'

'Good . . . good.' And then to try and escape like that with Molly and Hugh, like – like flipping adolescents! What must he have *thought* of us? But at least I'd gone back, I thought, with a degree of relief as I swung in through the school gates. That was something, anyway. Imagine how I'd feel this morning if I hadn't!

'And while we were up there, in your bedroom, some undies of yours were lying on a chair, and Alf put your bra on, and it was *so funny*, Mum. He had this great big hairy tummy and teeny tiny bosomy things and he was doing a really silly dance and singing, ". . . with-a-little-bit-of-this, and-a-little-bit-of-that, and-shake-your-bum, just-like-your-mum." '

'Bottom,' I said vaguely, recalling Sebastian's face visibly pale as I'd gone back into that room.

'What?'

'Bottom, not bum.'

'Oh right. Well, anyway, then Lance came back from the pub—'

'Lance?' I swung around.

'Yes, he'd been at the pub all night, hadn't been with us, you see, and he got really cross!'

290

I stopped the car in the car park and frowned. 'Why?'

'Exactly!' She shrugged incredulously. 'I have *no* idea! I mean, you're not cross, are you?'

I shook myself. 'Cross? Should I be?'

'Well, anyway, *he* was.' She rolled her eyes dramatically. 'Livid. He went absolutely doolally, kicked the others out of the house and back to the caravan—'

'But . . . what were they all doing there? Wasn't Alf baby-sitting?'

She groaned and reached on to the back seat for her reading bag. 'I *told* you, Mum, their telly broke so they came over. *And* he told me to go to bed—'

'Who?'

'Lance, when it wasn't even him that was baby-sitting, it was Alf.'

'Well, darling—'

'*And* he turned my light out without even letting me read!'

'It was probably well past nine o'clock.'

'Huh!' She slammed her door and came round the front to my open window.

'Bye, my love, have a good day. I'm shooting off now.'

'Because you haven't got your make-up on and you don't want to bump into Nina.' She grinned.

I pulled her straw boater down over her eyes. 'You're too sharp for your own good, young lady.'

'I know, just call me Razors.'

I smiled. 'Well, here's something I'll bet you don't know, Razors.'

'What?'

'Granny's got a boyfriend.'

'No!' Her eyes widened with disbelief. '*Granny!* Brilliant! Since when? How d'you know?'

'Since I don't know, but I met him last night, at the concert.'

'Cool! A boyfriend! What's he like?'

I suddenly had a vision of Claudia's idea of a boyfriend, something young and blond, something out of Steps, maybe.

'Well, he's about her age,' I said quickly.

'Oh!'

'But *very* nice and smiley.'

'Handsome?'

'Mmm, Claudes, he's *her* age. Tubbyish and grey, but kind-looking. Stares at her a lot, you know, into her eyes.'

'Oh yum!' She was excited by that. 'Can I meet him?'

'Of course. I thought we'd ask them for tea on Sunday, and listen,' I added quickly, 'whatever we think, Claudes, it's lovely for her, don't you think?' I asked anxiously.

'Oh *yes*. And I think if Dad doesn't come back it would be lovely for you too, Mum, even someone tubby and grey. Think how you've worried about Granny all these years, wished she hadn't been so lonely. Well, that's going to be *me* worrying, if you're not careful!'

I ground my teeth. 'Claudia, shall we discuss this when you're twenty-five and have been worrying for fifteen years, and not, perchance, when you're ten and have been worrying for all of two months? Anyway, you're a child, for goodness' sake, you don't need to worry about me!'

'Children feel things very keenly,' she informed me soberly. 'Don't you know that? Esther Rantzen knows that. She says it a lot on Childline. Don't keep me talking, Mum, I've got a ballet exam to get to.'

'Oh Christ, your exam!' I yelped, clutching my head in horror. 'I'd forgotten again – go – GO!' I pushed her. 'Why aren't you running!'

'I'm going, I'm going,' she said as she turned and trudged wearily across the car park, the weight of the world on her shoulders, dragging her bag and her feet. I watched her go, aghast. Heavens – her exam! That's why we'd been rushing! Oh God, I was losing it. I shook my head hopelessly as I shoved the gears roughly into reverse. There was no doubt about it, I was really, really, losing it.

And I must keep more of an eye on that young lady, I reflected sagely, making for the exit and still watching her in my rear-view mirror. I wasn't sure I was entirely happy about her spending so much time with the builders when I was out. It seemed to be putting all sorts of precocious ideas in her head. And she needn't think she could pull the wool over *my* eyes either, needn't think I didn't know what was going on. Reading after nine o'clock, indeed! I swung out of the gates with a knowing little sniff and headed for home.

When I got back, I made some tea and took it into the new kitchen where, despite their rather splendid surroundings of which they should have been justifiably proud, I found a pretty subdued bunch of boys beavering away. Mac and Alf didn't seem to be able to drag their faces out of the Aga fuse box to look me in the eye, and Spiro had his hat pulled right down over his eyes as he crouched to fix some skirting boards. I frowned as I looked around for somewhere to set the tray.

'You all right, boys? You all look a bit peaky this morning.'

Lance appeared from behind the larder door and took the tray from me. 'Claudia tell you about last night?'

'Last night?' I tried to remember. 'Oh, about coming over to watch the television?' Suddenly I realised they felt they'd overstepped the mark and that a strict line should be taken. I straightened up. 'She did actually, and listen, guys, you know I don't mind if I'm here, but I do draw the line if I'm out, OK?'

'OK,' they mumbled quickly, heads down. I turned to go. Hesitated. It was unnervingly quiet.

'Did she stay up late?' I demanded suddenly.

'A bit,' admitted Mac, quietly.

'And did she watch anything unsuitable?'

There was a long and tremulous pause.

'Not . . . on telly, no,' said Lance, finally.

'Good.' I nodded. 'That's all right then, but another time, please remember she goes to bed at nine o'clock.'

I turned to go, but Mac straightened up to face me for the first time that morning.

'I'd say we'll be out of your hair in a couple of weeks, luv.'

'Really?' I was startled. 'What, finished?'

'Yep, 'bout ten days.'

'Gosh, as little as that.' I realised, with a strange pang, that somehow I'd thought they'd be here for ever.

'Well, now that the Aga's in and the cupboards are nearly there, we've only got the new bathroom suite to plumb in upstairs and you're laughing.'

'Yes. Yes, I suppose I am. Yes, you're right, that'll be it then,' I said, cranking up a smile. I walked across and stroked the top of the shiny, navy-blue Aga which had finally gone in yesterday. Its concrete plinth built, it had been ceremoniously set, then plumbed in upon it, and was heating up nicely now, enthroned and radiating warmth like some plump, benign king of a South Sea island.

'You'll be glad to see the back of us,' said Mac. 'Bet you can't wait to have the place to yourself!'

'Yes!' I laughed, but it had a hollow ring to it. 'I expect everyone's glad to see the back of you, aren't they?'

'Too right they are!'

'Still,' I said softly, 'it'll be quiet without you.'

I drummed my fingers on the hob cover. There didn't seem to be an answer to that. I turned, and as I went, caught Lance's eye. He looked away quickly. Well, of course he would. An embarrassingly sad housewife who was admitting to a flicker of regret at seeing her builders go? Crikey. Most people hung out the flags! Declared it a day of celebration! I wandered through to the front hall, biting my lower lip. And not just regret, I realised in horror, also – yes, I felt a wee bit panicky, too. Alone then, in this house – apart from Claudes – for the first time since . . . well, you know. And you see, because of the boys, I hadn't actually been alone, yet. There'd always been someone to talk to, to share a joke with, to take a cup of tea to.

I stopped and picked up the mail from the mat, marvelling at myself. Good grief, I *was* sad, wasn't I? Genuinely pathetic. Actually admitting that the place wouldn't be the same without a rusty old cream caravan blocking the view of the cherry tree, or a clapped-out lorry monopolising the driveway. Why, only yesterday I'd met Alf, backing out of my downstairs loo – the Portaloo apparently being occupied – and squirting a cheap, lavender spray in a desperate attempt to veil the sensational whiff he'd left behind, the result being a sort of lavender-bush-with-dog-poo-on-it aroma. Well, I could do without that, couldn't I? And what about the constant stench of roll-ups and Pot Noodles, the blaring radio, the empty crisp packets that went forth and multiplied on a daily basis – I wasn't going to miss any of that, surely? I stared out of the window at the bright blue morning-glory that had wound itself around the frame, bursting into transitory flower. Don't answer that, Olivia.

Instead, I turned briskly to the letters I'd picked up, and

opened a bill from Barclaycard – before dropping it hurriedly on the mat again. Heavens! Really? As much as that? Were they talking lire? And for what? I peered down, kicking it around so I could see the print. Oh, OK. Wretched linen dress and kitten-heeled shoes. I hated them already. I leant back against the front door and flicked through the rest of the post. And OK, I conceded, I *would* answer that previous question. What I'd miss, all right, what I'd miss, apart from the jokes and the banter, was the feeling that they were on my side, that they were with me, rather than against me, which frankly, was becoming a rare commodity these days. I mean, take last night for instance. Crikey, if all my enemies had conspired beforehand they couldn't have planned it— Hello, what's this? I stopped flicking through, and turned over a rather smart cream envelope, addressed to Mrs Olivia McFarllen, and penned with something of a flourish. No address or stamp, so hand delivered. I ripped it open quickly. Inside, in the middle of a piece of thick, expensive paper, in italics in black ink was written:

Dear Olivia,
    That was a brave thing you did last night. Come for drinks tonight at seven, if you can.
    Yours,
        Sebastian.

I stared. Read it again. Brave thing. Me. Drinks. Tonight. Me brave. Him Sebastian. Thing. I did. Blimey!

I lowered it for a moment, and stared. How sweet. How very, very sweet, and how – well, forgiving. And, gosh, yes, of course I'd go, but . . . I gulped, golly. Talk about going back into the lion's den. But then again, he didn't sound very lionlike, did he? I raised the paper and read it again. No, more dovelike. More dove with olive branch in beak, in fact. I turned and walked slowly upstairs, one hand trailing thoughtfully on the banister rail, one still clutching the note, then sat, my heart hammering slightly, on the edge of my bed.

So ... off to Sebastian's, eh. Bound to be a terribly smart and sophisticated affair; what on earth should I wear? I jumped up abruptly, and hastened to my wardrobe, flinging the doors wide. I riffled through the hangers with a vengeance, tail up, nose twitching, sniffing my way along. Now ... let's see ... which of my lovelies ... I got to the end of the hangers, blinked in surprise, then went back to the beginning again. Eventually I stood back, folded my arms peevishly. Well, what on earth did one wear for a bevy with a famous composer, for heaven's sake? And was it just me, or would there be others? Because if it *was* just the two of us, anything more than trousers and a shirt would be over the top, but if, say, it were a celebration, a post-concert party perhaps, then something a bit more stylish would be called for. Maybe – maybe this? I pulled out a little black number I hadn't worn in years. Stared at it. What are you thinking of, Olivia? This is drinks with a neighbour, just down the street, not cocktails with a crown prince at St James's Palace. And anyway, why are you so excited?

I hung the black dress up slowly, went back and sat down on the bed. I'm not excited, I reasoned, just – flattered. That's all. And relieved. That he's no longer angry. I raised my chin. Got up and went across to the cheval mirror. But I'm not *excited*. Hell, no. I smiled at my reflection, tucked my hair back behind my ears. Why, only the other day I was calling him Sad Sebastian, for goodness' sake; he was still the same person now, wasn't he? Why should I be any more interested? Quite.

I shut my wardrobe door firmly and turned to my chest of drawers. From the bottom drawer, I shook out a pair of khaki Gap trousers – a bit creased and faded, but perfectly serviceable – and a white shirt. I gazed at them. All the same, that huge talent, that masterful way he clearly had with quavers and semiquavers – you couldn't deny that had a certain glamour, a certain cachet? I mean, Jeremy Paxman wouldn't be the same without his masterful way with dodgy politicians, and what about Alan Titchmarsh's masterful way with turnips, or Imran Khan's— No, OK, Imran Khan would be absolutely delicious whether he was masterful with a cricket bat or not. I sighed and pushed the bottom drawer in with my foot. But there had definitely been something commanding about that man's presence last night, hadn't there? And not just because the luvvies were simpering around him either. No, there was something very . . . watchable about him. Of course, I reasoned, a dinner jacket always helps, and a few inches off those wayward, gypsyish curls . . .

I shook myself and went back to gaze at my reflection in the mirror again. Golly, I looked old. I peered closer. Older still, close up. I put my fingertips on my cheekbones and pulled the skin back. Much better, shame I couldn't hook it behind my ears, took ten years off me. Couldn't smile, of course, but you could see why people fell for it. I dropped the skin and my face fell with a shudder, now resembling a Van Gogh self-portrait. Ah well, perhaps he was an ankles man? I gazed down at them ruefully. It was pretty much all there was left, these days. I glanced back up at my face sharply. Oh, don't be ridiculous, Olivia, the man's an intellectual, he won't be looking at your ankles or your cheekbones, he'll be interested in your mind! I nearly buckled at the knees in terror at this thought, and hurriedly racked my brains to think of any famous pieces of music I could talk about. 'What do you like?' he might well ask. Yes, well, he might well ask. Um . . . Wasn't the theme from one of Claudia's old Disney videos something memorable – *Sleeping Beauty*, was it, or . . . oh yes, the music from the Hovis ad, with the lad trudging up the cold northern hill? I mulled it over for a moment, but fearing that the next thing to spring to mind might be so staggeringly prosaic I'd even horrify myself and be forced to decline the invitation, I abandoned my mind, and instead, with a sigh, went downstairs in search of chocolate to appease my body.

Chapter Seventeen

When I finally ran out of the house at half-past seven that evening, I was hot, flustered, out of control, and not at all in the cultured, sophisticated frame of mind I'd intended. For a start, there had been huge hassles over the baby-sitting. When I'd popped into the kitchen to see the boys and ask Spiro, seeing as it was his turn, I'd been met with such flushed faces and a horrified silence, I was taken aback.

'What? What's the matter?'

Finally Spiro found his tongue. 'Oh, Meesis McFarllen, I feel so badly, I fall on your breast with shame. I theenk you not know, but last night, I seen your shreddies, I seen your jugs jacket, I see—'

'Hang on, seen what? Jugs what? Spiro, what on earth do you mean?'

'I think what Spiro means,' said Mac, stepping in smoothly, 'is that we thought we might go out for a curry tonight. Didn't we, boys?'

They nodded to a man. Beaming with relief until I thought their faces would split in half.

'Yeah, that's right,' agreed Alf happily. 'A curry. Need to get out, see, have a bit of a vindaloo.' He rubbed his stomach and grinned even wider. I feared for my lavatory pans.

'Oh! Oh, well, that's a bit of a blow.' I frowned. God, it

was a blow, actually. Suddenly I saw my sophisticated evening disintegrating. Where the hell was I going to get a baby-sitter at such short notice?'

'Perhaps I could ask Nanette,' I wondered aloud. 'I think she might be on her own this week.'

'And if she can't,' put in Lance quietly, 'I'll do it. I'm not that desperate for a curry.'

'Oh, Lance, that's awfully kind,' I beamed. 'You're an angel. I tell you what, I'll keep you in reserve.'

'You do that,' he muttered with ill-concealed sarcasm. I glanced at him, startled. Now what the hell did he have to be peeved about? His face betrayed nothing, though, so I shrugged. Oh well, I couldn't cope with sulky builders right now. I had bigger fish to fry.

I hastened over to see Nanette, who was indeed Roger-less, and who declared that she'd be delighted. She and Claudia liked nothing more than a girly nail-varnish-and-highlights chat, and they'd already had a couple of cosy evenings together, painting toes, putting face packs on and wading through *Hello!* Magazines searching for Posh and Becks, something Claudia complained she didn't get enough of from me.

'Where are you going, anyway?' called Nanette, hanging out of an upstairs window which she'd pushed open when she'd heard the doorbell. She was jangling armfuls of bangles and clutching a duster in her nails.

'Sebastian's,' I muttered, glancing nervously down the street.

'*Sebastian's!*' she shrieked. 'I don't *believe* it!'

'Nanette, you were totally wrong about him,' I hissed, 'he's not a nutter, or a teacher, he's a world-famous musi-cian! A composer for heaven's sake – he's Sebastian Faulkner!'

She frowned. Shook her head. 'Never heard of him. Who?'

'Oh, never mind. Let's not discuss it at the top of our voices in the street. I'll see you later, OK?'

'Be there at seven o'clock.'

'Great.'

Except, of course, that she wasn't. Seven o'clock came and went and I paced about the garden for a bit. Then, when it got to twenty past, I rang her.

'Nanette, are you coming?'

'Of course, darling. Just getting ready.'

'Nanette, you're *baby*-sitting! You don't have to get ready, just come over, please! I'm going to be late!' I wailed.

'Okey-doke.'

Five minutes went by. Then ten, so I rushed off to get Lance.

'She *is* coming,' I yelled through the caravan door, 'but she's going to be late, so I just wondered— Oops – sorry!' The door opened and he appeared with just a towel around his waist, fresh from the shower. I covered my eyes and carried on talking. 'I just wondered, could you possibly come over just till she arrives?'

'Sure, and you can uncover your eyes too. I'm perfectly respectable, you know. You mustn't be so uptight, Livvy.'

'Right, yes. Sorry.'

I dropped my hand and he dropped his towel.

'*Lance!*' My hand shot to my eyes again.

'Sorry, I dropped it,' he laughed.

'Oooh, *God!*'

Seething now, I turned and raced back to the house to find Claudia, lying on the sofa reading a teenage magazine.

'Darling, it's half-past seven,' I panted, checking my hair

in the mirror, 'and I must go. Lance will be up in two ticks followed by Nanette, OK?'

'Fine. Can I watch *The Simpsons?*'

'No you *can't* watch *The Simpsons*. Do some flipping homework for a change why don't you!'

She looked up from her mag. 'Mum, you're nervous.'

'What?'

'I can tell when you're nervous, you always get stroppy. Take a deep breath and think –' she turned back to her magazine and read – ' "I can do this. I can trap this man. I'm gorgeous." '

'Oh, for God's sake!' I snatched the comic from her hands, reached into the bookcase, flung *Anne of Green Gables* at her and stormed out. All of which was not particularly conducive to feeling calm, confident, and collected as I beetled across the cobbles in shoes that frankly, could have come out of Nanette's wardrobe. I hadn't worn anything like these mules, or the peacock-blue pedal pushers I'd squeezed into, since I was about twenty, but I had a feeling the place might be teeming with trendy arty types and I didn't want to look frumpy. I wondered, as I ran along, tucking back my hair, if I looked too frivolous, though, and tried desperately to look serious and intelligent. Oh, and musical. I hummed a little tune. Abba. Hopeless, Olivia, just shut up. As I ran up the steps to the front door and teetered on the top one to ring the bell, it occurred to me to wonder if mother would be in. I did hope not. I wasn't convinced she'd be conducive to the artistic atmosphere within, unless, of course, it was some dismal, gothic novel, sort of way.

Two seconds later, well-heeled heels came drumming down the hall, and the door was thrown back to reveal – not mother, but Sebastian. Such was my relief, I beamed.

304

'Hi!'

His face, which I realised had been on the point of holding back some reserve, relaxed at my smile.

He grinned. 'Hi, come in.'

He stood aside to let me into a huge, smoky-blue hallway, covered in prints and drawings, with a vast iron and stone staircase which swept up and up, curling finally to an enormous round glass lantern in the roof, storeys high.

'Gosh!' I stared. 'I had no idea these houses were so big!'

'Deceptive, aren't they?' he agreed, following my gaze. 'That's what I liked about it when I saw it. Very understated on the outside and full of surprises within.'

He turned back to me, and I suddenly realised that I was exactly the reverse. Very overstated on the outside in these ridiculous peacock-blue trousers, and no surprises at all within. Why hadn't I worn something grey and subtle to match the chaste good taste of this house, instead of something more at home in Nanette's all white shag pile? Sebastian himself was wearing ancient cords – the badge of the intelligentsia – and a blue Boden shirt. I did notice, though, that he'd clearly just washed his hair because it was still a bit damp at the edges. We stood there smiling at each other.

'I just wanted—'

'Olivia, I—'

We laughed. 'Go ahead,' he said, scraping back short dark waves, 'you go first.'

I felt my meagre supply of words dwindling but ploughed on regardless. 'Well, I – I just wanted to say how sorry I was. You know, about all that ghastly business with Claudia and then gate-crashing your party last night when I should have known better. I've – well, I've been a total imbecile and I'm sorry.'

He smiled. 'Forget it. God, I meant to say forget it in the note – did I not say that? Come on, let's go through and sit in the garden. It's too stuffy in here.' He guided me through the house. 'Anyway, apart from anything else, you apologised quite enough last night, explained yourself perfectly, and very eloquently too, definitely had the crowd on your side. I got a bit nervous at one point, thought I was going to be lynched, and it made me realise that had I been in your shoes, I might well have thought I was the mad flasher-mac man, too.'

'Really?' I gazed about as I found myself on an elegant terrace, spilling over with urns of ivy and dusty white geraniums. I sat down on the French café chair he held out. Clearly it was just the two of us and I felt hugely relieved.

'Really,' he confirmed, as he sat beside me, a tiny iron table between us, 'I'd forgotten about that tigress instinct mothers have, but looking back I seem to remember mine was just the same. When I was about eight, she once saw me talking to a strange man in our road and came tearing up, demanding to know if he'd offered me sweeties or anything. As the poor man opened his mouth to speak she beat him about the head with her handbag. She wasn't to know he was my housemaster, I suppose.'

'Oh God!' I giggled and took the beautifully chilled glass of Pouilly Fumé he offered me. 'Is she here now?' I glanced nervously around.

'Who?'

'Your mother.'

He put down his glass, sat back and regarded me curiously. 'You know, the first time I met you, Olivia, you showed an inordinate amount of interest in my mother. She lives in Dorset, with my father. Why on earth would she be here?'

'In Dorset! Oh! So – so who's that – that woman then?' I jerked my head back housewards. 'With the hair,' I scraped mine back to demonstrate, 'and the teeth.' I stuck mine out rattily.

'Maureen? She's my girlfriend.'

I dropped my hair. Stared. 'You're kidding!'

He laughed. 'Of course. She's my housekeeper.'

'Oh!'

'Because I live on my own and I'm fairly hopeless on the domestic front, she cleans and puts food in front of me now and again. She's got a flat in the basement. Why on earth did you think she was my mother?'

'Because Nanette said—' I stopped, flushing, as I remembered what Nanette had said. She clearly hadn't a clue, but wanting to appear informed, had creatively filled in the gaps on the strength of very limited information.

He folded his arms, mouth twitching slightly. 'Yes, what exactly *did* Nanette say? I'm keen to learn, if only to discover why, at that godawful dinner party of hers, you addressed me so slowly and distinctly and in words of only one syllable. At first I thought it might be because you were brain-dead, but then when you miraculously recovered your powers of speech to address the rest of the party, it occurred to me that you might imagine I was, am I right?'

I flushed and picked at an imaginary speck of dust on my trousers. 'Oh God, Sebastian, this is all so horribly embarrassing,' I mumbled. 'You see – well, the thing is, Nanette told me you were a bit . . . unhinged.'

'Unhinged.' He mulled the word over, nodding soberly. 'Right. Why so, exactly?'

'Oh, such silly reasons, too stupid to even—'

'No no,' he interrupted, 'I insist on being enlightened. It might happen again you see, and I need to know how to

307

curb my derangement in public. Do I twitch maniacally? Inadvertently sing, at table, suck my thumb and twiddle with my hair during pudding?'

I giggled. 'Well, OK she said –' I gazed at my trousers – 'she said you stood in front of your window all day long waving your arms about like a windmill.' I glanced up. 'Oh, and she also said you ran around the streets in your pyjamas.'

'*A la* Wee Willie Winkie?'

I grinned. 'I suppose, but listen, Nanette's hopeless; she gets everything wrong and—'

'No, not, not at all. As a matter of fact, our Nanette is very observant, and I fear I might well have to plead guilty on both of those counts, but would you first like to hear my defence, before you actually send for the men in white coats?'

'Oh, heavens no,' I said hastily, 'please don't bother. I mean we all have our foibles, Sebastian, and to be honest I've got some very odd habits so—'

'The arm waving,' he interrupted, 'is perfectly legit, and stems from me conducting as I compose in my head. Before it gets to the piano, and before it makes it on to paper. Does that make sense?'

'Perfectly,' I beamed.

'But the pyjamas . . .' He scratched his head. 'I can only assume it was that time I ran into her in Waitrose when I was probably wearing some comfortable old stripy trousers I picked up in a market in Afghanistan. I tend to work in them – oh, and a crumpled old T-shirt that probably looked – to our manicured Nanette – like I'd slept in it. And of course I always look appalling when I'm working and haven't had a haircut for months. Mad, probably. Will that do? Or do you need further and better particulars?'

'No no,' I laughed, 'that will do.' His brown eyes were merry and far from steely now as they met mine over the white wine. He had one of those thin, intelligent, Jeremy Irons type faces that leant naturally to the serious, but when animated, was very attractive.

'And the teacher bit?' I blurted quickly, realising I was staring shamelessly. 'Nanette had some crazy idea that you were let loose on small boys on your day release from the institution.' I laughed, then stopped abruptly. 'Oh – hang on, in fact *you* told me that too, I remember, at dinner!'

He nodded. 'Well, it's absolutely true, although teaching's probably overstating it somewhat. But I do go to the High School about once a month to talk to the boys.'

'Oh, right. What about?'

'Table tennis.'

I blinked.

'Music, Olivia,' he said patiently. 'Composition and theory, that sort of thing.'

'Oh! Of course!' I laughed nervously, but flushed dramatically. God, you *moron*, Olivia, you must stop sounding so inane. And why are you sitting here like some fearless, probing breakfast TV reporter, getting this world-famous musician to explain why he's yet to be locked up and have the key thrown away? Who d'you think you are, Judy Finnigan? Oprah Winfrey, even? I shut up for a moment, and gazed instead at his immaculate walled garden, the one I'd zigzagged across, apache style, just a few days ago. It was very well designed, in a tasteful, white-flowers-and-greenery sort of way, and since I so often feel that gardens reflect their owners, I wondered if this was the man. Controlled, precise, safe. For some reason, I felt it might not be. One thing was for sure, though, he certainly wasn't a gusher. He chose his words with care, whilst I tended to choose mine with reckless abandon. I tried to think of something intelligent to say.

'I loved your music last night,' I lied.

He smiled. 'Thank you. Was it your sort of thing? I mean, is that what you like to listen to, as a rule?'

I hesitated, sensing a sure-fire way to ingratiate myself, but could I then bluff my way, musically speaking, for an entire evening? I licked my lips.

'Um, listen, Sebastian, could I possibly retract that last remark? Only, the thing is, it was a bit of a fib. I was so preoccupied last night I didn't actually listen to a note.'

His eyes widened. 'Oh. Right.'

'I mean I'm quite sure it would have been my thing,' I hastened on, 'I'm sure I'd have loved it, but the reason I wasn't listening was because my husband turned up with his girlfriend, and I had trouble concentrating on anything other than taking a pot shot at the pair of them.'

'Dear me,' he stammered, scratching his head. 'Yes, that must have been very – difficult.' He reached for the bottle and looked awkward.

Ah, well done, Olivia. You're embarrassing the socks off him now, airing all your dirty linen in public. But something told me to plough on. Something told me that in order to establish any sort of channel here, any sort of rapport, all small talk had to be banned, even if it meant making a monumental fool of myself in the process. The refined good taste of our surroundings somehow made it all the harder.

'He left me a few months ago, you know.'

'Yes, I had heard. Nanette, you know . . .' He hastily refilled his glass, eyes lowered.

'Went off with a teacher at Claudia's school. Of course, that was pretty hard to take, pretty gut-wrenching, but I guess I'm more or less used to it now.' I nodded bravely. 'I guess I'm getting over it.' God, I sounded like I was in therapy now, spilling the beans to some New York analyst – and when had I ever said 'I guess'? Twice!

He smiled, put the bottle down. 'From my experience, Olivia, it takes a lot longer than a few months to get over something like that.'

'Your experience?' I pounced. Ah, now we were getting somewhere.

'Oh, very limited,' he said hastily. 'We weren't married, like you are, and no children, so . . .' he shrugged dismissively.

'But it was serious?'

He paused. 'Very.' There was another long pause, but I kept quiet, knowing that was the only way. That he'd go on only if he wanted to.

'We met about five years ago. Quite late to fall in love, I suppose – I mean, properly, for the first time. I'd got to the ripe old age of thirty-two thinking it would never happen.'

I did some quick mental arithmetic and filled up his glass shamelessly, even though it was practically brimming over, keen to hear more. He cradled it and narrowed his eyes, gazing pensively over his green enclosure. Leaves dipped and danced against the high brick walls in the long evening shadows. He turned, looked directly at me.

'It was doomed, right from the start, actually. Madness when I think about it now. We were both too set in our ways, too long in the tooth perhaps, and too attached to our customs, our countries—'

'Our countries?'

'Lara's Russian. She plays in the Russian National Orchestra and we met when one of my symphonies was being performed over there. I went across to oversee rehearsals; she was a first violinist.'

'Oh!'

Gosh, how romantic could you get? My mind flew to a rehearsal room somewhere, and in the front row of the orchestra, a beautiful violinist, one arm cradling her instrument, the other bowing beautifully, revealing slim arms, a perfect figure, long blonde hair – I was sure – eyes, full of passion for the music, meeting the dark eyes of the handsome composer over the music stands, as she made his dream, his masterpiece come to life. And Lara! It had to be Lara, didn't it, Zhivago's lost love, calling to her desperately as he crawled through the snow – 'Lara! Lara! Lara!' No doubt she looked just like Julie Christie too. I sighed.

'How romantic. Didn't you try to make it work?'

'Oh, sure. I spent two years in Russia and she spent a couple over here, but I hated the place and couldn't compose there. Musically speaking I dried up completely, and England had pretty much the same effect on Lara. She missed her family, friends, her language – that's what she missed the most, actually, not being able to chatter away, ever, in her own tongue. It's not like being French or German and living over here, because there are plenty of other French and Germans too, but not many Russians, and Lara got very lonely. Felt terribly isolated. She stopped playing, stopped going to the orchestra even.'

'Gosh, how sad! So she went back?'

'Fourteen months ago. Precisely. Which is why I say to you, Olivia, don't expect the scars to fade so quickly. I've been at this lark much longer than you have and mine are still there.'

'I know,' I said in a small voice. 'I was being flippant when I said I was used to it. Of course I'm not. It's like getting used to having your arm chopped off. I don't think I'll ever be whole again.' I took a big shaky breath. 'I miss him so much.' I stared into my lap. Oh God, was I really doing this? I couldn't believe I was. I concentrated hard on a chipped paving stone.

'I know,' he said quietly. 'I know how you feel. And some days are better than others, aren't they? Some days you can kid yourself you're all right, that you're actually staggering from the depths towards dry land, and then just as you reach the beach, a bloody great tidal wave crashes over your head and drags you back in again.'

'That's it,' I wobbled, 'that's exactly how it is. It's like I'll never reach that bloody beach.' To my horror and eternal shame, a great tear ran down my nose and plopped into my lap. I brushed it away furiously, not sure if he saw, but if he did, to his credit, he tactfully pretended not. There was a silence for a while.

'Right,' he said suddenly, standing up, 'enough of all that. Goodbye to all that, in fact. Come on, let's get cracking.' He rubbed his hands together briskly, smiling down at me.

I blinked, nervously. 'Cracking?'

'Oh,' he scratched his head sheepishly, 'sorry, I do that. Think of things without saying them and then go one step further and carry them out.' He grinned. 'Comes from living alone, I think. No, I just thought – well, since you missed out on so much music last night, I'd play you something wonderful tonight. Bach is my big passion at the moment, but I'm open to Schubert on a beautiful evening like this, or perhaps you'd prefer something – I don't know – more joyous? Scarlatti, perhaps?'

'Oh!' I smiled. 'Well, that would be great, but couldn't we listen to something of yours?'

'Of mine?'

'Yes, since that's what I missed last night. Has that

Abbey thing been recorded yet?'

He grinned. 'That "Abbey thing" hasn't, as yet. It'll have to be something else, but then again they're all pretty similar.' He turned and went inside through the French windows, crossing the drawing room to the CD player. 'I churn out the same old rubbish, as a rule.'

'What rot,' I said warmly, picking up my glass and following him in. 'Everyone says how marvellous you are!'

'Ah, yes, everyone,' he said scanning his CDs, his back to me. 'Everyone who's desperate to embrace modern music, determined not to seem backward-thinking, keen to be progressive and avant-garde. It's rather like the art world – critics rave about the latest Damien Hirst or whatever, but do they really like it or are they just terrified of not seeming hip?'

'Perhaps they don't understand it,' I said, making what I considered to be my first intelligent contribution that evening.

He turned abruptly. 'D'you know, I really object to that assumption. That's just the sort of obnoxious, smug, pretentious twaddle the darlings of the creative world like to peddle. Art and music are there to be enjoyed, not understood!'

'Oh, er, yes I quite agree. I was just, um, repeating what someone else said.'

'Oh, right.'

'Yes, um. Ursula Mitchell,' I lied disloyally. 'She's terribly sweet,' I added with a surge of guilt, 'it's just that, well, she longs to be part of that arty milieu.' Oh good *word*, Olivia.

He shrugged. 'Well, I don't really know her, but I can imagine. I know the type. Anyway,' he slipped the CD in, 'here goes. Oh, by the way, I'm assuming you'll stay for supper? Maureen put some sort of casserole in the oven. She's a disastrous cook but she's been with me for years now and I haven't the heart to tell her. Would you care to join me in picking the gristle out of her goat's bladder stew?'

I giggled. 'That's the most attractive offer I've had in a long time. I'd love to, but I might just ring home. I told Nanette I'd only be about an hour or so.'

'Sure. It's in the hall.'

When I got back from the phone, Sebastian was sitting up rather straight in a high, wing-back chair on one side of the fireplace, remote control in hand, fingers tapping impatiently. He looked up. 'Ready?'

'Oh, yes, sure!' I hastened to my chair, realising that this wasn't background schmaltz we were about to listen to. We weren't going to chat above it either, or even have it on while we had supper – no, we were going to sit here and listen. I perched rigidly on an identical chair the other side of the marble fireplace and clasped my hands on my knees. What was I supposed to look at, for heaven's sake. Him? Or should I shut my eyes? Or would that be considered smug and obnoxious again? Christ, I hadn't really been educated for this. I hoped I wasn't going to fart in the slow movement or something terrible. His hand went to flick the switch, then abruptly – paused. He frowned.

'I say, this is awfully pretentious of me, isn't it? Asking you round then foisting my music upon you?'

'Don't be ridiculous. You didn't foist anything on me, I asked!'

'Yes, but if I were an acrobat or something, and suddenly on a whim I rolled back the carpet and performed my double backflip, or – or a plumber insisting you inspect my S-bends, or—'

'Oh, for God's sake, Sebastian, just get on with it and put it on!'

'Righto.'

He gave a mock salute and obliged with a grin, but that little exchange had relaxed me. I felt that the somewhat academic atmosphere had been purged. I leant back in my chair and crossed my legs.

'Well, this particular piece is played by the Berlin Philharmonic. It's called *The Rigorous Judgement*.'

Blimey, *The Rigorous Judgement*. I sat bolt upright again. Perhaps I'd been right about that garden, after all. Perhaps he was into order and control. I braced myself and waited.

The Rigorous Judgement, however, began sublimely. Breezy flutes and other pleasant windy things piped softly and wistfully and I imagined we were somewhere – oh goodness, somewhere pastoral and sylvan, with a bird perhaps – a piccolo was it? – lifting the melody. I gazed contentedly into the empty grate, letting myself be lulled along, cajoled by gently rising passages until, abruptly, the mood changed. The bird seemed to cry out in alarm, there was a shriek, and suddenly, it seemed the woods were upon us. Dark, base notes sounded ominously, one after the other, coming like footsteps all the time, and simultaneously terrified piping noises whirled overhead, swooping and crying as the strings gathered momentum. The intensity built, and as drums and cymbals joined the violins, there was a sudden sprawling change of key, as horns and trumpets heralded some sort of procession, some kind of parade. I sat up a bit. Braced myself. More and more triumphant waves unfolded until there was a great orchestral wall of sound, and then suddenly – it stopped. A single flute piped on, to a clearing, perhaps, where the strings started up again, softly. They played quietly for a while until, finally, they too faded away, as the picture faded too, leaving nothing behind, but a tantalising afterglow.

I stared at Sebastian in silence for a moment, realising I was actually on the edge of my seat. For a while there I was speechless. I felt my cheeks flush red.

'Good heavens, that was beautiful!' I finally managed.

'Really?'

'God, *really*!' I gasped. 'I mean, well, I've never sat down and listened properly to that sort of music before so I'm not the best person to ask – a complete philistine, in fact – but I could *see* it, Sebastian, and *feel* it too! I had no idea music could do that to you, had no idea you got pictures with it!'

He laughed. Stood up. 'Good.' He rubbed his hands together briskly. 'Well, come on, let's go down and get some supper, before you start reminding me of some of the more pseudy music critics I know.'

He caught my eye and I laughed, but I could tell he was pleased, and as I got up and followed him down the steps to the basement kitchen, it was with a considerably lighter heart. That music, dark and forbidding though it had been in parts, had somehow changed the mood of the evening. All guards were off and all defences down; it was as if he'd said, 'OK, this is me. Like me or loathe me,' just as I, I thought suddenly, could walk him round to my back yard, swing my arm towards my intricate beds, paths and borders and say, 'OK, well, this is me, too.'

As he struggled to get a huge, red-hot casserole out of the oven, he directed me to a drawer where I found some knives and forks, and I set about laying the table. Uncannily relaxed now – to my amazement he even flicked Capital Radio on – I sat down, as he manoeuvred the heavy Le

Creuset across from the stove to the table, and lifted the lid. We stared into it for a moment in silence, then at each other. His mouth twitched. I swear to God, not even a dog, not even a ravenous Labrador, would hoover up that honking, heaving pile of bones.

'Bloody hell,' muttered Sebastian under his breath, and on an impulse, turned and tipped the whole lot in the bin.

He then had a surge of guilt about Maureen's hurt feelings, and giggling wildly, we had to lift out the steaming bin liner, wrap it in three more, and then take it to the dustbins outside. Whilst Sebastian was getting rid of the evidence, I managed to rustle up a mushroom omelette, find some rather good Brie lurking at the back of the fridge, and Sebastian came back and opened another bottle of wine. Finally, we sat down. The wine and the conversation flowed, barriers were lowered – I knew his past, or the important bits anyway, and he knew mine – and it seemed that we could now get on with the business of discussing friends, family – both subjects complicated – work, children, this single life – anything, in fact, of great, little, or no importance that sprung to mind. It was easy, it was relaxed, and later, as I toyed with the cheese, laughing as he recounted some musical anecdote, I even forgot to answer him.

'What?' he demanded.

I looked up. 'Sorry?'

'What were you thinking?'

I grinned. 'I was just thinking how different you are from that night when I first met you at Nanette's. I don't think you said more than two words to anyone, just stared fixedly at the curtains as if you were contemplating eating them or something.'

He wiped his mouth on his napkin. 'Ah yes, the dinner

party from hell, with the used-car salesman, the couple who wanted to talk us through all eighteen of their home births, and the strange woman beside me, keen to hear about my macramé classes.' He grinned and I smiled back at him over the table. The kitchen clock ticked on in the silence. Suddenly I glanced up.

'Sebastian, I must go. It's way past twelve, Nanette will be pacing up and down.'

'Is it?' He looked up. 'God, and I've got to do some work tomorrow. Come on, let's get you out of here otherwise I'll be too wide awake to sleep and start tinkering with that wretched piano, composing whatever springs to mind well into the small hours, and then tomorrow I'll feel like death, when I should be wide awake and concentrating hard on doing some proper, paid, commissioned work.'

I laughed. 'Is that what you're like?'

'Oh, totally. It's compulsive, this music lark, I'm afraid, but only when I'm doing what I want. I'm surprised Nanette hasn't observed me tearing my hair out at four in the morning, mouthing obscenities at passers-by, called the police, even.'

We got up and he walked me to the door, opening it on to the warm, dark night, at which point, the first awkward moment of the evening arose. I turned, smiled.

'Good night then, and thanks, Sebastian.'

He scratched his head, which I'd noticed he did occasionally. 'Night, Olivia.'

We hesitated, and then I sort of lunged cheekwards, whilst he, unfortunately, lunged the other way. We laughed as we crashed noses, tried again, and finally accomplished a dignified social peck on the cheek.

'I should walk you back,' he called as I tripped down the steps into the street.

'Don't be ridiculous, you can *see* me back from there.'
He laughed. 'True.'

As I walked across the cobbles in the warm, still air, a crescent moon was rising over the tower of the Abbey, and I was aware and pleased that he was indeed watching me. As I got to my gate, I turned and waved, smiling. He raised his hand back in salute, and then the red front door closed as he went in. My smile faded and I stared at the door for a moment. Swallowed. Yes, that's what I miss, I reflected. Having a laugh. A giggle. Having – well, the companionship of a man. Oh sure, I had masses of girlfriends but I missed – yes, I missed maleness. I sighed, looked up at the stars. It wasn't the same as being with Johnny, of course. Nobody could make me roar like he could, make me literally throw back my head and hoot with laughter, and nobody could make me come alive as he did too, make me want to dive impulsively into bed with him, stay there all day. I absently dead-headed a day lily beside me. In a way, then, I realised sadly, this evening had been something of a poisoned chalice. It had made me realise what I missed: being the female part of a team, moving around the kitchen with a man, getting his perspective on things, laughing at his jokes – but it had also made me realise that nice as Sebastian was, he could never be Johnny. That no one could ever be Johnny. And up to now, that had never been so glaringly apparent, because up to now, I'd only met pretty second-rate men. But this one was first rate, and still he couldn't match up. I stared up at the stars finding the plough, its handle, the pan. Where did that leave me then? Sad and alone for twenty years, as Claudia kept doggedly reminding me, finally tottering into some dentist's waiting room with my gardening mags and seeing the light in a white-coated, middle-aged man's eye as he prepared to

320

repair my molars, as time, finally, did its repair work, too?

I sighed and crunched up the empty drive to the front door. Mac's lorry was missing, so no doubt the curry evening had turned into eight pints and some sampling of the local nightlife, too. There'd be hangovers in the morning.

I put my key in the lock and heard the television quietly humming.

'Nanette? I'm back,' I whispered, shutting the door softly behind me.

I went into the sitting room, but the sofa was empty – no Nanette. She must be in the kitchen then. I turned the television off and went in to look. Apparently not. I tried the loo. 'Nanette?' I called quietly, knocking softly. I pushed open the door. Nothing.

Where was she? Slightly panicky now I dashed upstairs, first into Claudia's bedroom where to my relief, she was fast asleep, breathing peacefully, and still hugging her old blue rabbit. I smiled, pulled up her duvet and tucked her in. Then I frowned. Bloody hell, where on earth was Nanette? Crashed out on my bed? I went next door. No. In the spare room then, having decided it was so late she'd stay the night? I opened that door. Empty. Well, how very peculiar. I stood on the landing, frowning. Had she gone home? I'd told her I'd be late, for crying out loud. Surely she wouldn't do a thing like that? Leave Claudia here on her own? But then again, if Roger had suddenly rung up, announced he was back, been panting to see her . . . there was no knowing with Nanette. I stared out of the landing window. Suddenly it came to me: of course, the garden! It was a warm night – a sultry one, in fact – so she'd be down there, by the river, where we'd all gathered the other evening, sitting under the cedar tree armed with a drink and a magazine and gazing periodically at the stars. I know that's where I'd be.

I ran downstairs and went out, walking confidently down to the river. There I stopped, bewildered. The seats under the tree were deserted, as was – I swung back – the terrace. I turned around, biting my thumbnail. The caravan was in darkness across the stream, but on an impulse, I went across the little bridge towards it anyway. Perhaps Lance hadn't gone for a curry, after all; perhaps he'd know where she was. As I approached, though, I stopped dead in my tracks. Well, how odd . . . I peered. How very extraordinary. That really was the weirdest thing. The caravan was moving. Rocking, and bouncing up and down of its own accord, as if it had a momentum all of its own, as if it was, well, as if it was possessed! I ran up and flung open the door.

'Lance!'

'Shit!' came a voice from the shadows. Lance's voice.

Instinctively I flicked on the light.

At the other end of the caravan, where the beds pulled down from the wall, two naked bodies were caught, mid-writhe, on a lower bunk. Frantic bare arms scrabbled for the duvet on the floor, and as they hiked it up over their heads, naked legs and buttocks were still glaringly apparent below. Two tousled heads shot out from under it, and two pairs of startled eyes blinked at me in the brightness, like rabbits caught in headlamps. Lance's eyes, and Nanette's.

Chapter Eighteen

'Nanette!'

We stared at each other for a second, then I quickly slammed the caravan door.

'Oh, for God's *sake*!' I shrieked furiously at it.

Two seconds later she was out, hair standing on end, and hurriedly tying up a white nylon dressing gown with the legend 'Plasterers Do It Plastered' emblazoned on the front.

'Oh Lord, Olivia, what must you think?' she gasped, raking a hand through dishevelled hair. 'I'm so sorry, can't think *what* came over me!'

'Rampant hormones, I should think. Christ Almighty, Nanette, you're supposed to be baby-sitting my daughter, not shagging my builder!'

'Cabinet-maker,' she correctly quickly.

'And what if Claudia had come downstairs? What if she'd come outside and found you! Talk me through *that* charming little scenario, if you will!'

'Oh no,' she assured me earnestly, clutching my arm, 'I made absolutely sure she was fast asleep. I wouldn't have *dreamt* of doing anything untoward if there'd been the slightest chance she'd come down, really.'

'Don't be ridiculous,' I scoffed, 'you were probably so revved up it wouldn't have mattered if she'd been sitting right beside you on the sofa! Taking notes!'

'Well, at least we made it to the caravan,' she said peevishly, pulling the dressing gown around her. 'That was Lance's idea. He was being frightfully responsible, you know; you really mustn't blame him.'

'Responsible!'

'Well, I don't know why you're so upset, Livvy. It's not as if you wanted him, did you, so why shouldn't I?'

I gaped at her, speechless. 'What the hell has *that* got to do with anything!' I spluttered finally. 'The reason I'm upset, Nanette, is because I'm concerned for my daughter's welfare, and *you* were supposed to be looking after her! I couldn't give two hoots what you do with Lance in the privacy of your own home!'

'Oh no, I couldn't do it there.' She shook her head vehemently. 'It wouldn't be fair on Roger.'

'Roger! You're still planning on being fair to Roger, are you? Jesus! Well, what would he think about all – all this!' I flicked my hand despairingly at the caravan behind us.

'Oh, I think best not to tell him, don't you?' she said, glancing about nervously. 'I think we'll just keep it between ourselves and put it down to premarriage nerves, eh?'

'You didn't look very nervous in there!' I jerked my head back.

'No, no, I wasn't actually,' she agreed guilelessly, eyes wide. She lowered her voice and glanced back at the door. 'If you must know, Olivia,' she whispered, 'I was absolutely *fan-tastic*! Had him positively *squealing* for more, and we did it four times, and the fourth time his teeth nearly went through the duvet like a tatty old sandwich!'

'Nanette, I really don't—'

'And as for him!' She rolled her eyes dramatically. 'Boy, is he *heaven*. I swear to God, Olivia, you don't know *what* you're missing, and listen –' she clutched my arm as I tried to interrupt – 'I'm really happy to share, honestly. It's frightfully greedy of me, what with Roger as well, and as far as I'm concerned Lance is just a delightful diversion with a cute little backside, but you could really *do* with him, darling. Make you feel *loads* better, I swear, and I'd hate to think I was hogging the lion's share or anything.'

'Ah,' I said folding my arms grimly as Lance appeared, doing up his jeans. 'The lion himself.'

'Oh er, hi, Livvy,' he said rather sheepishly. I must say he looked all in, utterly exhausted as he staggered down the steps.

'Lance, I was just explaining to Nanette here, that with an impressionable ten-year-old about I'd rather you didn't enliven her sex education with practical demonstrations in my back garden, OK?'

Lance shrugged. 'Your back garden, but our caravan, surely?'

'Then move it,' I hissed. 'Tow it to Waitrose car park next time you feel the urge, but *don't do it in my back yard*!'

He regarded me with a quizzical smile. 'I really don't know why you're so upset. Claudia was fast asleep.'

'Yes, and alone! Anyone could have walked in!'

'Oh, come on, being in the back garden doesn't exactly constitute leaving her—'

''Ello 'ello 'ello! I feel like PC Plod breaking up this happy gathering. Wha's going on then?' Mac elbowed his way roughly into our heated little circle and flung a drunken arm round my shoulder. 'What's up, luv? Wha's occurring?'

'Ah, good, Mac, you're back,' I said, relieved. 'I was just explaining the house rules, *vis-à-vis* sexual activity, to Lance and Nanette here, hoping to keep it off the premises, as it were. I'm sure you'll back me up.' I folded my arms grimly.

Mac looked from Lance to Nanette. He blinked in astonishment, then a slow, beery grin developed. He took a deep breath, raised a finger, and seemed on the point of making a profound statement, when round the corner Spiro and Alf suddenly lurched into view, arms round each other's shoulders, singing their respective national anthems in their respective tongues, at the top of their voices. As they approached, they stopped singing, slowed down, and came to a halt in front of Nanette. They swayed a bit, and looked her up and down with considerable interest. Nervously clutching the neck of the dressing gown, Nanette turned and scuttled back into the caravan. Alf turned to me and raised startled eyebrows.

'Orraaghff?' It was half belch and half interrogative, and roughly translated from troglodyte, I imagine it meant – Good evening, Mrs McFarllen, so what the devil's your neighbour doing in my dressing gown then? I shuddered. Christ! And to think I'd thought I'd *miss* them!

'You bin a naughty boy, then, Lance?' grinned Mac with road-map eyes, wagging a crooked finger at him. 'You bin a bit of a lad? You dirty devil, you! You see?' he hissed alcoholically in my ear, 'I told you he was a one wiv the birds. Can't keep 'em off him, like flies round a pile of shite they are. Looks like you've missed yer chance there, though, luv. Looks like No No Nanette has turned into Yes Yes Nanette and got in there first!'

I noticed Lance watching me carefully.

'Oh, you conceited idiot!' I hissed. 'You actually think I mind, don't you? You actually think that I'm gnashing my teeth here, cursing my bad luck, because instead of having a delightful supper down the road with an eminent musician,

I could have been getting my leg over your "cute little backside" in your SQUALID LITTLE CARAVAN!'

'MUM!'

I froze for a second – then swung round in horror to see Claudia, hanging out of her bedroom window in her nightie.

'Mum, what's going on?' she called sleepily. 'Why are you shouting like that? You woke me up!'

'Sorry, darling, sorry!' I called back in a hoarse whisper. 'Go back to bed, I'm coming!' I made to go towards her, then stopped in my tracks, turned. I took a step towards Lance. 'This is never, *never* to happen again, got it?' I breathed. He gazed at me with strange, heavy eyes, but didn't answer.

'Oh, for God's sake!' I spluttered impatiently, before beetling back up the garden path towards the house, towards my daughter.

I raced in through the back door, through the kitchen, and took the stairs two at a time, arriving to find her kneeling up in bed in her nightie, rubbing her eyes.

'What's happening? What's going on?'

'Nothing, darling, nothing at all. Lie down now and I'll tuck you in.'

'But what was all the fuss about?' murmured Claudia sleepily as I pulled the duvet back over her.

'Oh, nothing really. It was just – well, a fox got into the garden, that's all. Went down the rubbish bins, made a bit of a racket. Now go back to sleep.'

'Oh.' She turned over to face the wall. 'Mum?'

'Hmm?' I paused, mid-creep to the door.

'What's – getting your leg over?'

I paused. Turned. 'It's . . . a riding expression. It's, you know – how you mount a horse.'

'But why were you talking about it just now?'

'Oh, because . . . because Mac was thinking of chasing the fox. On horseback.'

There was a brief silence. 'But we don't have a horse.'

'Exactly,' I breathed, 'which is why I told him it wasn't such a good idea!'

She turned back, stared at me as I went to shut her door. 'And a horse has a cute little backside?'

I swallowed. 'That's it!' I agreed brightly.

She smiled, turned back to the wall again. 'Nice try, Mum. Really nice try. Very creative.'

I shut the door and groaned. Leant back against it for a moment, eyes shut. Oh God. Sometimes I despaired. Sometimes I really, really despaired.

A moment later I came to, shook my head wearily, and went off down the corridor. To my own room. To bed. And for once, I thought, slamming my bedroom door behind me, I was grateful for the solitude that awaited me there.

The following morning I was decidedly frosty as I delivered the elevenses. As I banged the tray down on the side and made to stalk out, Alf stared in dismay.

'What, no bourbons?'

'Alf, I have to be in an *extremely* good mood to deliver bourbons, and if you must know, I'm feeling distinctly below par today.'

'Ah. Too many late nights,' he offered sagely.

'I don't think so,' I muttered as I turned to go.

''Ere, hang on, luv. Lance has got somefing to say to you, haven't you, Lance?' put in Mac quickly, digging his son in the ribs with a chisel.

'Thanks, Dad,' muttered Lance sheepishly. 'I can speak for myself, and actually I thought I might do this without an audience.'

'Oh come on,' I said, turning to face him, folding my arms. 'I wouldn't have thought that would affect your performance in any way?'

He paused. 'All right.' The eyes that met mine were clear, blue and steady. 'I was out of order last night and I'm sorry. It shouldn't have happened. I've got no excuses besides a couple of beers inside me and the fact that you've got an extremely provocative neighbour, but I shouldn't have risen to it.'

Alf tittered dirtily.

'All right, Lance,' I sighed. 'Let's forget it.'

'I'll say she was provocative,' put in Mac. 'Lance here says she had all the gear – you know, corset, suspenders and stilettoes an' that – had it all on under her jeans, just for comin' round to babysit!'

I gaped. 'You're kidding.' So that's what she'd meant by 'getting ready'.

'Nah, straight up, inn't that right, Lance? Said one minute she looked perfectly normal, sitting beside 'im watchin' *Coronation Street*, an' the next, she'd leapt up, whipped all her kit off, an' bugger me if he didn't have Miss Whiplash standing in front of him, legs astride, hands on hips, all in black lace an' rarin' to go!'

I groaned. God, no wonder she'd accepted with such alacrity. She'd probably been waiting for just such an opportunity, planned the whole seduction. She'd certainly had her eye on him ever since that first meeting down by the river.

I licked my lips. 'Yes, well, I'm sure you didn't stand a chance, Lance, and I accept your apology, but at the end of the day it takes two to tango, and before you tell me –' I raised my voice above a cry of protest – 'that you were putty in her hands and what's a poor boy to do—'

'Too right!' cried Mac.

I grinned. 'I'd say we just drop the subject and make sure it doesn't happen again, OK?'

Lance tugged his forelock and grinned. 'It'll never happen again, Miss,' he said soberly.

'Excellent.'

I bent to pick up the empty tray, hiding my smile, glad to be back on bantering terms with the boys, but also, I realised, glad about something else, too. In a funny sort of way, I was grateful to Nanette. I'd like to think I'd never been seriously tempted by Lance, but having said that, he was, let's face it, extremely decorative, and fun to have around, and sometimes, in my lowest moments, I'd found myself looking at him with something approaching wantonness. It would be fun, a little voice in my head had assured me more than once, and fun is exactly what you need right now. A bit of uncomplicated coupling, some warmth, some tenderness, but no strings, no commitments, a place where the body and not the heart is the only participant. But seeing Nanette emerge from that caravan last night, crumpled, dishevelled and deeply undignified, made me realise it was just what I didn't want. Casual sex was not something I'd ever gone in for, and to embark on it now, feeling vulnerable and insecure, would make me feel, I was sure, in the aftermath of the event, even more frayed at the edges, even more alone.

As I went to take the tray out, Mac called me back. 'Oh, by the way, luv, I forgot to mention, you had a visitor last night.'

I turned back. 'Oh really?'

'Yeah, just before we went out for a curry. Alf was monopolising the karzy in the garden, right, having a wash and brush-up, so I went for a Jimmy Riddle in the garden.'

'Do I need to know this, Mac?'

'Oh, not in yer 'erbaceous border or anything crass, luv – I'm not a complete heathen – no, I was just takin' a leak in the shrubs round the side. I'm conducting a little experiment, see, 'cos did you know that urine can change the colour of a hydrangea? Straight up, pee on a hydrangea and it goes from blue to pink. It's the acid see, and—'

'Mac, the visitor!'

'Oh. Oh yeah.' He paused. Scratched his head. 'Yeah, well anyway, there I was, havin' a— Well anyway,' he hastened on, 'round the side of the house, as I said, out of sight, like, when stone me if someone doesn't cough behind me. Well I swung round, right, which was dangerous, like, in my predicament – lucky I missed me shoes – and saw this bird sitting on your terrace. The one at the side which you never sit on 'cos it don't get the sun.'

'A bird?' I frowned. 'What, you mean a girl?'

'That's it.'

'Well, who?'

'Well that's just it, I don't know, 'cos I didn't recognise her, see. But I knew it wasn't one of yer Mollys or Imogens 'cos I know them, right, but when I'd tucked me old man away and asked her what she was doing – politely like, 'cos I imagined she was a friend of yours – she said she'd seen Spiro here in the front drive, on his way out to get some fags, and he'd told her you'd only gone for a quick drink down the road and wouldn't be long, so why don't she wait?'

I turned confused eyes on Spiro.

'Ah yes,' he piped up, remembering. 'She look so tired, you see. She walk from the station, no car, so I say – ah, I so sorry, she not here, but you wait inside, she not be long, but she say – oh no, I no do that, but I seet in garden if OK.

And I say – sure, ees OK, Mrs McFarllen, she so kind, she no mind!'

'But hang on, who was she? What did she look like, Spiro?'

He shrugged. 'Pretty, I think, but not so much. Blondie hair, a skirty.' He shrugged again. 'I don't know.'

'You know what I think?' said Mac suddenly. 'I think it was his woman. His fancy piece.'

'Whose fancy piece?' My heart lurched.

'Johnny's, your ovver half.'

I stared. 'Why d'you think that, Mac?'

He frowned. 'Dunno.' He shrugged, suddenly all Inspector Morse'd out; reached for his hammer. 'Just a feeling, really.' He put the hammer down. Second thoughts puckered his brow. 'Something . . . about the way she was, through,' he said carefully. 'Really nervous, like she shouldn't be here. Sitting bolt upright on that terrace an' clutching her handbag. Shit scared too, definitely, eyes dartin' about everywhere, and she didn't say who she was neiver, 'cos I asked, and said I'd take a message an' that, but she just said she'd popped by on the off chance, hoping you'd be in.'

'And she didn't say what it was about?'

'Nah,' Mac shook his head. 'And she went soon after, too, just up and left. But if you ask me,' he wagged his hammer sagely, 'it's her guilty conscience rearin' its ugly head!' He nodded triumphantly.

'What d'you mean?'

'Bet you anything you like she'd come round to explain herself. Listen, luv, she knows she's nicked your husband, but it's been a few months now, so the glory's wearin' off a bit and her conscience is beginning to prick her. She don't want to be forever branded as the Scarlet Woman or what have you, 'specially since she teaches at the school an' it all gets about, so she's come to get – what is it the Pope deals out?'

'Er, dispensation?'

'Nah.'

'Redemption?'

'That's it. She's come for a bit of that, come to make it cosy an' above board, get it all off her chest. I know you women,' more hammer wagging, 'you don't like skulkin' about bein' disliked, do you? You want to be over the garden fence again, eh? Like as not she's thought to herself – blimey, she used to be friendly to me, at the school an' that, an' I didn't take her up on it. I could go now, explain myself, then we could be all chummy and everyone wouldn't think what a cow I was. Mark my words if I'm not right.' He grinned, pleased with himself.

'Really,' I said drily. 'Yes, well, thank you for that penetrating insight into the female psyche, Mac. I had no idea you were such an expert.'

'What, wiv five daughters an' her indoors? Do me a favour! There ain't much I don't know about the female mind – or the body, come to that!'

Cue much raucous, dirty laughter, which I took as my own cue to leave. I went, shutting the kitchen door firmly behind me.

Funnily enough, though, I reflected as I abandoned the tray to a sideboard and wandered out gardenwards, I'd be loathe to admit it, but I had a sneaking suspicion Mac might be right. Recently, when I'd taken Claudia to school, I'd sensed that our Miss Harrison had deliberately made it her business to seek me out. I'd spot her lurking near Claudia's classroom, quite out of her normal infant territory, searching furtively for some nonexistent nursery book in the junior bookcase, or on some other equally spurious mission.

I wandered thoughtfully down the lavender path, pulling idly at the fragrant heads and sprinkling the seeds. Likewise, I remembered with a jolt, when I'd gone to watch a ballet display the other day, there she'd been again, making it her business to be bustling around with extra props for the show. She'd obviously been alive to the fact that I'd be turning up, and had tried to catch my eye as I'd walked in. These days I hadn't felt much like catching it, and had swept on in, head high, to take a seat.

I paused for a moment under the apple tree. And now she'd been here, had she? Looking for me. I glanced back to the side terrace and for a moment, my blood boiled. She'd sat here, in *my* garden, on *my* sacred territory. She'd taken in the glorious delphiniums, the stocks, the jasmine round the door, smelt the nicotiana placed carefully in pots around the house for night scent, seen my secret patch on a summer's evening in all its glory. How dare she?

And the reason she'd called unannounced, of course, I realised, pulling savagely at a leaf from a low bough, was because she knew that if she telephoned, I might slam the phone down, tell her to bugger off, inform her I had nothing whatever to say to her. I walked on down to the water's edge and stopped for a moment, gazing across to the other side, to where the dragonflies were darting in and out of the bulrushes, under the heavy boughs of the chestnut tree. I narrowed my eyes into the sun. Nice to know she'd been a bag of nerves, though. I turned and walked back. Yes, good. And she could prepare to get even more nervous, because actually, I was getting stronger by the day. I wasn't the cringing, cowering creature of a few weeks ago, grateful just for a glimpse of her skirt because in some warped way it brought me closer to Johnny. No, she'd had that phase, and she'd blown it. No, no, *these* days, she'd find it much harder to track me down. Harder still to confess her sins and hope for— Golly, what exactly did she want? I stopped still for a moment, dazed. An amicable arrangement or something? A civilised atmosphere, an understanding that Claudia could go to their flat – which I'd point-blank refused to let her do – and for her, Nina, to maybe join Johnny on trips to the zoo with her? For Claudia to treat her as some sort of stepmother or something? To be a nice, big, happy, dysfunctional family?

I felt my cheeks flush with anger as I walked smartly back to the house, ducking under the rose arbour as I went, brusquely dead-heading it on the way. Oh, dream on, Miss Harrison, dream on. You see the last thing I'm feeling right now – I crushed a perfectly good rose bud viciously between my fingers – is papal.

Chapter Nineteen

Days passed. The weather, if it was possible, grew even warmer and Claudia's school term began to draw to a close. It occurred to me, as I took her in one baking hot Monday morning, that I only had three more days of avoiding Miss Harrison's eye before eight weeks of summer holidays, followed by Claudia passing on into the senior school in September, which, although in the same grounds, was in a totally separate building. It also occurred to me, as it had on many occasions, that being at the same school until the age of eighteen was a hell of a long time, and that although I'd rather lackadaisically assumed she'd stay, it might be time for a change. Maybe the High School in town? It was only round the corner and would certainly make life easier for me – in more ways than one. I resolved to talk to Claudia about it.

On the afternoon that Claudia broke up, by way of celebration, my mother and Howard came for tea. Claudia and I had gone to town; making scones, biscuits, a chocolate fudge cake, piling bowls high with strawberries and cream, and setting it all out on a table under the cedar tree. Deeply giggly about 'Gran and the Man' as Claudia called them, we sat and waited, with Claudia speculating furiously about what he'd be like – a rather twinkly Des Lynam type, she'd decided, with a bristling moustache – and me, fervently hoping Mum wouldn't be too nervous.

Half an hour later they breezed in, arm in arm, and it was Claudia and I who were rendered speechless. Far from nervous they held court, recounting stories of how they'd met, teasing each other and giggling like a couple of children, as Claudia and I sat and stared, our heads going back and forth from one to the other, like the centre court crowd at Wimbledon.

'I finally plucked up the courage to ask your mother to a hospital dinner dance, you see. Well, you should have seen the assembled company's faces when "Poor Old Howard" turned up, not only accompanied, but glamorously accompanied!' He squeezed her hand and grinned.

'Poor Old Howard, my eye – you were the life and soul of the party and clearly had been for years! "A guinea a minute" the sister beside me informed me you were!'

'Nonsense, a shy retiring chap like me? No, no, I was brought out of my shell that night.'

'Well, I didn't exactly need a tin opener, did I? I'd hardly finished my coffee when you were on that dance floor, dragging me up!'

'Ah, but I could sense you were itching for a canter, my love. Those dancing feet of yours had been tapping away under the table from the moment the band started up and, my goodness, what a mover! What rhythm! I could hardly keep up; thought I was going to have a coronary!'

'You'd be in the right place for it!'

'Don't you believe it. Some of those colleagues of mine shouldn't be allowed to operate on a rabbit.'

'Oooh, I'll tell them you said that, Howard!'

'Do,' he twinkled. 'That way I'll lose my job and we

could *both* take graceful retirement. I could potter about in the garden, digging up plants instead of weeds, tramp mud through the house and get under your feet all day. I'd probably drive you mad!'

'Stark staring, and there's no "probably" about it!'

'Hey – we'd be demons at cribbage, though, wouldn't we, love?' He nudged her. 'We could play all day!'

'Howard,' she laughed, 'we practically do that anyway!'

Well, Claudia's mouth simply wouldn't shut, and as I followed her back into the kitchen with a pile of empty plates I had to tell her to stop staring.

'I don't see why. They don't notice. It's as if we're not even there! Mum, it's so extraordinary, it's like she's a totally different person. It's like – well, like she's possessed or something, like someone's cast a spell! And her hair! All sort of blondie and swept back and – and white jeans, for heaven's sake! Granny doesn't even wear trousers, let alone jeans! And now they're talking about going on a cruise. Granny would have said that was s-oooo . . . what's the French word she says?'

'Bourgeois.'

'Exactly! "Too bourgeois for *words*, darling" – can't you just hear her? Jesus, I just can't *believe* it!'

'Shh, they'll hear you, and don't swear.'

'I'm not swearing, but, Jesus!'

'Claudia!'

She stared at me, eyes still wide. Then she gave herself a little shake. Came to.

'Well, I think it's brilliant,' she said soberly. 'In fact, I think it's more than brilliant, I think it's wicked. But just think, Mum, she could have been like this all along, all sort of fun and larky! Isn't that awful? That it was all lurking inside her and we didn't know?'

I smiled sadly, began wiping up. 'I know. That's exactly what I thought when I saw her the other day.'

'Hey!' She caught my arm. 'D'you think he's got a son?'

'I think he has, actually. I know he's a widower and I'm sure he said he had a boy. Why?'

'For you, of course! Maybe it's in the genes; maybe he could work the same magic for you!'

I put the tea towel down. Turned to face her. 'Claudes, am I a bore? Do I lack fun? Am I a grouch, now that Daddy's gone?'

'Of course not, Mum.' She plucked a strawberry from a bowl and sailed out through the back door. 'You were like that before he went!'

Later, when Claudia took Howard off to see her guinea pigs and Mum and I were alone, side by side in deck chairs and straw hats, mopping our brows periodically – me, hastily averting my incredulous gaze from the pink canvas deck shoes Howard had 'impulse bought her in Harrods' – I shaded my eyes into the distance, to where Claudia and Howard were, down at the hutches.

'Mum, d'you think Claudia's had enough of that school? If she goes on into the seniors she's got seven more years of it.'

'Hmm?' She came back from smiling at Howard's back. 'Oh, she's talked to you then?' She licked some cream from her fingers and set aside her strawberry bowl.

I stared. 'No, why, has she talked to you?'

'Oh yes, she rang the other night. We had a nice long chat. Yes, she's bored there now. She'd be happy to go.'

I sat forward, gaped at her open-mouthed. 'Well, why the hell doesn't she tell *me* that!'

'I don't know, darling.'

'And where does she want to go? To the High School?'

She gave me a sideways glance. 'No. She wants to go to boarding school.'

I stared at her, aghast. '*Boarding* school! No! Why?'

She shrugged. 'Because she thinks it would be great fun, as I'm sure it would.'

I felt very sick suddenly. 'She wants to get away,' I breathed shakily. 'She's had enough of living in a broken home with a distraught, neurotic mother and – oh God – she wants to get out of here!' I clutched my mouth but a small sob escaped. My baby. Wanted to leave home. My only child.

Mum laid a hand firmly on my arm. 'Which is precisely why she didn't tell you. She knew that was how you'd react, so she wanted to sound me out first, and that is absolutely *not* why she wants to go. She's an only child, Olivia; she needs the company. She's read all the books – *Mallory Towers*, Angela Brazil – she thinks it would be a hoot, and so it would!'

I swallowed. 'I never meant her to be an only child. I still think . . . maybe . . .'

'I know you do, I know, and believe me, you'll go on thinking that until your menopause.'

Of course. Like she had, too. Hoping against hope that my father would come back, and me, knowing full well I was destined to be an only child, as Claudia surely did too. And dying to get away. I remembered reading all those books, dreaming of midnight feasts in the dorm, pillow fights, shrieks of laughter, a world away from the sourness that pervaded my childhood. Financially it had been out of the question, of course, but I'd deliberately worked my little socks off at school, dreaming of university when finally, *finally* I could escape. It gave me an actual physical pain in my gut to realise Claudia felt the same way. I breathed deeply, blinking back the tears.

'Think about it,' Mum said, as Claudia and Howard came slowly back up the lawn. 'There's plenty of time. She doesn't have to go this year. She's not eleven for a couple of months, she'd be quite the youngest in her class. She could go next year.'

'But – I'd miss her so much. I'd miss her!'

'Of course you would, but you know, boarding schools are so different now. She'd be back practically every weekend.'

I couldn't speak. But she'd be gone. Effectively, she'd have left home. And she was all I had.

'Promise me you won't talk to her about it until you've calmed down, OK?' muttered Mum urgently.

'OK,' I whispered, for they were back, bearing guinea pigs.

'Howard likes Edward best,' announced Claudia, holding a speckled one aloft. 'But the only thing is, he says he's not Edward at all, he's Edwina, which might explain why, cooped up with Pandora all day, they've never had babies!'

'I knew my medical training would come in handy one day,' laughed Howard. 'If only for sexing guinea pigs!'

Later, when they'd gone, I gave Claudia a big squeeze as she went off for her bath, burying my face in her hair. She stepped back in alarm.

'M-u-um! My shell necklace!'

'Sorry.' I took the broken bits from her. 'I'll mend it.'

She shrugged. 'It's OK, I didn't really want it any more.' She ran up a few stairs, then halted, turned, her hand on the banister. 'I didn't mean what I said about you being a grouch, you know. You're not.'

I managed a grin, but couldn't speak. Nodded instead. My chin wobbled. She was waiting for me to answer.

'I know,' I whispered.

She stared. 'Mum!' She jumped down the last few steps and I dissolved. Hands on face, ambushed by tears. Stupid. Couldn't help it. Didn't want to.

'Mum!' she cried in alarm. I sat on the bottom step and she sat beside me, hugging my neck hard.

'Is it Dad?'

'Yes!' I sobbed, grateful for that. 'Yes, yes, it's Dad.'

She sighed, and hugged me some more, but then abruptly, her arm froze.

She sat back. 'It's not Dad, is it? Gran told you, didn't she!' She wriggled free and moved along the stair so she could see my face properly.

Damn, I rooted in my pocket for a hanky, this was so awful! So like I'd sworn I'd never be, loading guilt on to children, so like my mother – never, never, never! I sat up straight and blew my nose.

'Don't be silly. This has nothing whatever to do with that. I'm just a bit tired and overwrought, that's all.'

'I'm not going,' she said vehemently, shaking her head violently. 'No way, no way. I'm not going. I *knew* this would happen, knew that's what you'd think! You think I want to get away!' she wailed.

My tears dried up the moment hers started. 'Now, Claudia, listen. We must think about it.' I wiped my nose determinedly, stuffed the tissue back in my pocket. 'We certainly mustn't rule it out, and in fact the more I think about it, the more I think it's a very good idea. You're on your own so much here, and now that Daddy's gone—'

'*No!*' She sobbed wretchedly. 'You think I don't love you! You do, you think I don't love you, and it's just not true!'

Well, that set us both off. Tears streamed in torrents

down our faces as we hugged, kissed, wailed, reassured each other, said how marvellous we both were, how incredibly special, then wailed some more, until finally, totally spent, we sank back on the stairs, exhausted. Somewhat dazed and startled by our mutual hysteria, we stared into space for a while, sniffing a bit. Then we sat up, blew our respective noses, got to our feet, and arm in arm, went as one to the fridge for the chocolate fudge cake. Setting it between us on the little scullery table we dragged up stools, and armed with a spoon apiece, dug straight into the middle, sniffing loudly. Naturally, in time, our equilibrium recovered, as naturally, in time, our blood sugar levels were raised.

'We'll see,' I said sternly, between dripping chocolaty mouthfuls, back in mother mode again. 'We'll go and have a look at one or two, and then we'll see, OK?'

'But not too far away,' she warned, waving a spoon bossily at me. 'It's got to be close, and back at weekends.'

'Agreed.' I nodded.

We pitched back into the calories again.

'Becky's going,' she said licking her spoon, 'and she's taking her pony. Maybe I could have one too?'

'Becky's going?' I looked up, surprised. Becky was a great mate of Claudia's, and one I thoroughly approved of. A sweet girl with an incredibly close-knit, happy family.

She regarded me wisely over a spoonful of chocolate. 'Mum, you don't *have* to be orphan Annie to go to boarding school, you know.'

I blinked, surprised. 'No. No, I suppose you don't.'

The following day Molly came round. As we basked, beached-whale-like on sun-loungers on the terrace – Molly, considerably more whale-like than me, tossing and turning uncomfortably in the shade, groaning, and swigging intermittently from a strange bottle of chalky white liquid which allegedly assuaged the heartburn and wind – I told her about Claudia. Henry was splashing happily in an ancient paddling pool I'd found, as Claudia dashed inside to find some boats for him to play with. Still such a child, I thought desperately, as she ran back out, armed with the boats. Too young to go, surely?

'It'll be good for her,' pronounced Molly roundly. 'She's incredibly sociable and she'll have a terrific time. God, I never wanted to go, far too cringing and pathetic and tied to Mummy's apron strings, but think how you would have loved it!'

'I know,' I said sadly, knowing precisely why. I gazed at my daughter sailing the flotilla in a circle round Henry, ducking them occasionally and making him giggle.

'Of course, the only one who'll lose out here is you,' said Molly abruptly.

'Precisely.'

'On your own.'

'Thank you, Molly, it had crossed my mind.'

She narrowed her eyes thoughtfully. Was silent for a moment.

I cleared my throat. 'Molly, I do hope you're not about to say, "Perhaps you could get a dog"?'

'No, I wasn't, but – well, how's Sebastian?'

'Oh, thanks!'

'No, but seriously, I thought he was terribly nice.'

'Molly, you met him once, and then you nearly had a baby on his feet.'

'Ah, but I liked him,' she nodded unconvincingly, lips pursed. 'I could tell he might be right for you.' She puckered her brow. 'He had, well, he had, um . . . kind eyes.'

'Nonsense, he was all sort of glowering and wall-punching when you saw him.'

'Yum-yum.'

'And, if anything, he's got a particularly steely gleam to his eye. You couldn't even pick him out of an identity parade. You obviously haven't the faintest idea what he looks like.'

'Even so,' she persisted, sitting up, 'I *feel* I know him.' She cupped her hands around an imaginary crystal ball, shut her eyes and contrived to look mystical, mouth twitching. 'And I feel . . . yes, I feel he could make you . . . very happy . . . my dear.' She reached out and clasped my hand.

'Bog off,' I said, snatching my hand away as she giggled wildly. 'And don't wee on my sunbed, please. It's a new one.'

'I wasn't about to – have to be hysterical for that – and, anyway, it's the wind that seems to ambush me these days.' She shifted uncomfortably on the bed. 'You know, there's a lot to be said for elective Caesareans. Quite apart from anything else you get them two weeks early – which considering I'm likely to be two weeks late, would mean a month less of this malarkey – and if I'd gone down that route I'd have had the bloody thing by now, straight out of the sun-roof.' She reached into her handbag and lit a cigarette. 'You know in Brazil – first one this week so stop looking so disapproving – in Brazil, no self-respecting Brazilian beauty would *dream* of having a natural birth. What – and get your precious birth canal all shot to bits? Good heavens, what would your average, swaggering, polo-playing husband think about *that*? That's not what it's there for at *all*.'

'Bit late now, isn't it? You told me Henry came out like a human cannonball. Nearly knocked the midwife out.'

'Well, quite, so there's no hope for me,' she said gloomily. She beamed, suddenly. 'So back to you. Back, via birth canals, to Sebastian, in fact.'

'You are so disgusting, Molly Piper.'

'But didn't you say you'd seen him recently?' she persisted, twisting round to face me.

I sighed. I had. More than once, actually. Twice, to be precise. After our supper I'd phoned him to say thank you, and he'd asked if I'd like to see a film with him later on in the week. Naturally that had led to supper in a little bistro afterwards, and then walking home, we'd spotted a poster advertising an open-air concert in the park, which naturally we'd gone to too, a few days later. (On both of these occasions incidentally – and much to Claudia's horror – Maureen had stood in as baby-sitter. I could tell at a glance that nothing would get past those sharp eyes – particularly Lance and Nanette – and after a couple of evenings with Maureen, Claudia had become really quite proficient at needlepoint, which, I thought, on balance was better than oral sex.) But I digress. Yes, Sebastian liked me, that I could tell, and I don't say that with any degree of smugness or insensate conceit, either. It's just that I'm not the sort of girl men instantly fall for, so when it does happen it's all the more apparent. And I liked him too, but not in the same way. I liked his dark, intelligent good looks, he made me laugh, he was droll and dry, and I liked the rather quizzical gleam he got in his eye when he was about to say something amusing. In fact I couldn't fault him but, at the end of both evenings, I was left with that same hollow, empty feeling I'd had when I'd come back from his house that first night. After the concert in the park, I cried when I shut the front door. It was me, of course, I knew that. Not him. I never asked him in for a coffee because I felt it wouldn't be fair, and he never made a move in that direction because he hadn't been given so much as a smidgen of a sign that it would be acceptable. Lately, though, I wondered if I should, just for the hell of it. This wasn't Lance, after all; it wouldn't be *that* casual, would it? This was a man I liked enormously, but whom I just wasn't in love with. Surely then, it couldn't hurt? In fact, it might even help – might help me to fall in love, be better again. I so desperately wanted to be better. To be normal, not to be living in this ghastly limbo land, waiting to see what would happen next.

'Yes, I've seen him,' I sighed.

'And?'

'And . . . well, he's very nice,' I said lamely.

'Thought so,' she retorted smugly. She sat up and pursed her lips. 'Right, tell you what, why not bring him round for supper? Better make it sharpish, though, otherwise I really will have this baby on his feet. How about Friday?'

I turned to look at her properly. She was being suspiciously determined about all this. 'Sure, I could bring him,' I said slowly. 'But what's the rush? Why the indecent haste?'

She was quiet for a moment. Put her sunglasses on, sat back and gazed out at the view, which, with the sun glancing off a riverful of floating water lilies, was carrying on like an Impressionist painting.

'They're going away together, you know that, don't you?' she said quietly.

I swallowed hard. 'I . . . suspected,' I muttered. Johnny had indeed telephoned to say he was going away for a while and couldn't see Claudia for a bit. He hadn't elaborated and I'd foolishly hoped it might be a business trip, but since it fitted in quite seamlessly with the start of the school holidays, it seemed unlikely.

'Where are they going?' I said in a small voice. Molly was friendly with a few of the nursery mothers, so I knew she'd know.

'St-Jean-de-Luz.'

I sat bolt upright. 'St-Jean-de-Luz! That's where we went for our honeymoon!'

'I know.'

I breathed deeply, bit the inside of my cheek hard. 'Tell me the worst, Molly. I know you know, and I deliberately never ask.'

She shrugged miserably. 'I don't really know much, actually, because apparently she's very private, but Tessa Jarvis says – well, she says they're very close at the moment. Nina's told her how incredibly happy she is, how she never thought anything like this would ever happen to her, never thought she'd get someone like Johnny—'

'OF COURSE NOT, BECAUSE SHE'S SUCH AN AVERAGE LITTLE TART!' I bellowed. 'My bloody husband! Never thought she'd – "*get*" – my gorgeous bloody husband! How bloody *dare* she?'

'Breathe,' Molly commanded, reaching out and clutching my wrist. 'Come on, you've gone all purple now, breathe – in . . . out . . . in . . . out . . .'

I sank back and obeyed. God, he had such a weird effect on me, it was like releasing demons. And my language became so exotic too, like that girl in *The Exorcist*. Next thing I knew my head would be rotating.

'Anyway,' I snarled, simultaneously breathing deep, 'Tessa Jarvis doesn't know her arse from her elbow, she's got a huge mouth on her, and *her* bloody husband is the pits! Pinches bottoms at school fêtes, and I should know!'

'Well quite,' she agreed hastily, 'she's a terrible old gossip, but I'm just telling you what I've heard, that's all.

Because I think you should be prepared.'

'For what?' my heart stopped.

'For . . . any serious developments.'

I stared at her. There seemed to be two of her. Two pairs of sunglasses. Two curly heads. I couldn't speak for a while.

Then, at length: 'She came to see me, you know.'

'What, here?' Molly whipped off her glasses, aghast.

I nodded. 'But I wasn't in. She hasn't been back since and I've avoided her at school. Obviously, though, she had something to tell me. Something . . . burning.'

Molly nodded thoughtfully. 'I'd say you might be right,' she said quietly. 'And maybe Johnny didn't want to be the one to say it. Or couldn't say it.'

A long silence prevailed. Eventually, I took a deep breath.

'Molly, we'd love to come.'

She frowned, miles away now. 'Hmm?'

'To dinner, Sebastian and I.'

'Oh good!' She brightened. 'Friday then?'

'Perfect.'

'Spag bol in the kitchen, I'm afraid. It's about all I can manage these days. Oh God, is that all right?' She looked suddenly alarmed. 'He's probably not used to that sort of thing, is he?'

'No, Molly, he only dines at the Connaught. Don't be ridiculous, he's perfectly normal, he even picks his nose like the rest of us, he just happens to be good at music, that's all.' I got to my feet. 'Gin and tonic?'

She consulted her watch and blinked. 'Lord, Livvy, it's only ten thirty for God's sake!'

'I'll take that as a no, then,' I said evenly, as I marched inside, crossed to the sideboard, and with a shaking hand, poured an extremely large one for myself.

Chapter Twenty

Supper on Friday began somewhat inauspiciously. Having assured Molly that Sebastian couldn't be more relaxed, I did actually sneak him a sidelong, nervous glance as we stood for what seemed like an eternity on the doorstep of the Pipers' little flint cottage, getting absolutely no answer at all from their cranky old bell. Finally we tried the door, pushed tentatively through, and happened upon a sitting room that looked for all the world as if it had been burgled. We glanced at each other, startled. There was an astonishing lack of sofas, chairs, tables – or indeed any sort of furniture at all – and all that remained on the rather grubby carpet were piles of books and magazines, a few mouldy coffee mugs, one of Molly's maternity bras, and a brace of apple cores festering quietly on the fender. Neither Molly nor Hugh was anywhere to be seen.

'Looks like they've moved out,' muttered Sebastian, gazing around. 'The thought of me coming for supper was clearly too much for them, they've done a runner, put their possessions on their backs like Kurdish refugees and fled. We'll probably find them halfway down the road, wild-eyed and desperate, dragging an astonished donkey and making a break for the border.'

'Either that or the bailiffs have been,' I said nervously.

'Which, believe me, is entirely possible with Molly and Hugh. They've clearly forgotten we're coming, anyway. Come on, let's go.' We turned hastily back to the door.

'Well, bugger off, then, oh ye of little faith!' cried a voice behind us and we swung round to see Molly, sweeping through the French windows in a billowing maternity smock, like a ship in full sail, a plate of garlic bread poised in her hand.

'We're out here in the garden, and we've got no garden furniture to speak of so we dragged all our stuff outside.' She threw her arms around her barren sitting room. 'Welcome to *Lifestyles of the Poor and Disgruntled!* Makes a refreshing change, don't you think? You don't mind being outside, do you? We thought we'd have a barbecue so Hugh can wear stupid clothes and do macho things with tongs and baked potatoes.' She grinned and kissed me on both cheeks, then beamed up at her guest.

'Ah, Sebastian, what must you think of me? Did I behave *quite* appallingly the other night?' She twinkled merrily at him.

He grinned. 'Quite appallingly, but with remarkable aplomb and presence of mind too. You're obviously a dab hand at rescuing damsels in distress from sticky situations. I only wish I could stash the big-with-child card up my sleeve to deploy in similar circumstances.'

She chuckled. 'Ah yes, privilege of my gender, I'm afraid, and I do like to make the most of my fecundity. It has very little else going for it, believe me. Now,' she linked both our arms with a squeeze and turned us gardenwards, 'come and meet the man responsible for my condition. You can't miss him, he's the one in the vest and the shorts who thinks he looks like Bruce Willis in *Die Hard.*'

We strolled outside with her where, sure enough,

scattered about the long, unmown grass and the daisies, was the sitting-room furniture – a sofa, two armchairs and a coffee table – all looking a bit tipsy and off balance, and slightly embarrassed to be outside. And in the middle of this al fresco furniture showroom, was Hugh, in what looked like his underwear, behind a wall of smoke, fighting desperately with a furious, flaming, spitting cauldron that was more reminiscent of Sputnik than a barbecue.

'Remember these, Moll?' he cried, waving a huge pair of barbecue tongs. 'I borrowed them from the maternity ward. They'll be needing them back when you go in!' He clamped them to an imaginary head and pulled hard, rolling his eyes maniacally like Doctor Death. 'Oooh, aahhh!'

'*Au contraire*, my darling,' she sang, 'they'll be needing them back for your vasectomy, for when I have your balls off. Sebastian, this is my husband, Hugh, who you met very briefly last week. He's an out-of-work actor, and as the evening wears on, you'll appreciate why.'

'Not at all,' smiled Sebastian, shaking Hugh's hand, 'I thought your performance in the supporting role of "tense father" the other night was masterful. It was method acting, I take it?'

'But of course,' grinned Hugh, taking a deep bow. 'There's always method in my madness. No offence taken, I hope?'

'None at all,' smiled Sebastian.

'Excellent! Now – a drink! Good God, Molly, call yourself a hostess? These good people haven't even got a bevy!'

A jug of Pimm's was discovered lurking under a table, the flies were ceremoniously picked out of it, then Hugh poured four huge, lethal tumblers, and the evening slipped happily along. And as we sat, laughing and chatting, slumped in their comfortable old chairs with the springs bursting out of their arms, in their tiny, magical cottage garden, surrounded – more by accident than Molly's design – by hollyhocks, flocks and lupins, our toes in a daisy-strewn lawn, we gazed on to a veritable Constable scene of traditional English haystacks in the fields beyond. As Hugh waved his tongs in a final triumphant flourish we then ate our traditional English barbecue: charred spare ribs, sausages that were black on the outside and raw in the middle, vast baked potatoes that were as hard as bullets but no one seemed to mind, and a salad, that much to everyone's mirth, I insisted on rushing to the flowerbed to decorate with borage and nasturtiums, as meanwhile, the drink and the conversation flowed on.

Molly and I discussed the chaotic state of her garden, as was our wont, with her promising to put into practice all my handy hints, and me, knowing full well she wouldn't, whilst Sebastian and Hugh chewed the arts long and hard, alternately eulogising or rubbishing every single play, film, festival or concert they'd ever been to, disagreeing as much as they agreed, and enjoying themselves hugely.

'So what sort of thing do you do yourself then, Hugh?' asked Sebastian finally, picking the charcoal from his teeth.

'When you're not poisoning your guests,' I added, flicking raw sausage off my plate.

'Oh, quite a lot of telly, you know, that type of thing,' Hugh said airily, waving his arm about vaguely.

'He does sanitary towel ads,' said Molly grimly. 'If we're lucky.'

'Sanitary – but surely . . .?' Sebastian looked perplexed.

'Wrong gender?' Hugh offered brightly. 'No problem. I change sex; after all, I am an actor! No, seriously, dear boy, I am, as my wife so kindly reminded me, in the current ST ads, but I don't wear them myself. No no, I'm the fresh-faced lad playing volley ball with our padded heroine on the beach. Voila!' He jumped up to demonstrate, punching an imaginary ball, a frozen smile on his lips. He held the pose. 'Recognise me?'

'Er, well . . .' Sebastian smiled.

'I'm the gorgeous young buck she bounds confidently up to in her skimpy white shorts – for thanks to Panty Pads, our lass *can* wear skimpy white shorts – and whose shoulders she playfully straddles – for our lass *can* straddle shoulders with no embarrassing repercussions – and whose hair she playfully ruffles. I'm the git who lollops across the sands with the silly cow's arse wrapped round my neck, like so.' He turned to show us his hunched back. 'Recognise me now?'

'It's all coming back to me,' grinned Sebastian as Hugh staggered about under a colossal imaginary weight, like the hunchback of Notre-Dame.

'And, um, when you're not doing important feminine hygiene ads? Dare I ask?'

'He lolls about at home, scratching his bum and getting in my way,' said Molly, preparing to throw the rib bones to her two Border terriers, who were sitting bolt upright, quivering with excitement.

'What my dear wife means,' said Hugh, leaning conspiratorially towards Sebastian, 'is that when I'm not making passionate love to her on a sultry afternoon amongst the buttercups, I am in fact, rehearsing for my play.'

'Ah, and that is?' Sebastian brightened.

'Oh, dear boy, sweet of you to ask, to take an interest and all that, but it's very much a fringe thing. On a considerably lesser stage to the one you inhabit, playing to seriously dwindling audiences, and at a little-known auditorium, a modest venue just off the Hammersmith Broadway.'

'The Lyric? D'you mean the new Simon Gallway play? The Roman one, um – *Death of a Conqueror's Son*?'

Hugh nearly fell off his chair he was so excited. 'Yes!' he rasped, nearly choking on a rib bone. 'Fuck me, yes! Have you seen it?'

'Certainly I have. It was excellent.'

Hugh's chest expanded until it was fit to explode, his face went purple.

'Well then, surely you recognise me!' he squeaked. 'I'm on stage the whole time!'

Sebastian's eyes widened. 'You are? Blimey, I only saw it a few weeks ago, but . . .' he frowned. 'Oh, hang on. You're the centurion, right?'

Hugh shook his head excitedly. 'No!'

'Er, well. The lead?' he said, somewhat doubtfully. 'Peter the Great?'

'Warmer, getting warmer!' Hugh leapt up and down and hopped about excitedly.

'Er, Peter the Great's son? Michaelias?'

'Hot! Really hot – so close!'

Sebastian frowned. 'Peter the Great's . . . other son? Alexander?'

'That's it!'

'But – isn't he . . . dead?'

'Precisely! From the word go! I'm the corpse!'

'Oh!'

'Front of stage the whole time,' he said proudly, 'lying doggo and deceased. Remember?' Hugh collapsed flat on his back in the daisies to demonstrate, eyes shut.

'Oh, er, well, yes. I do now. You were . . . unforgettable.'

'Wasn't I just?' beamed Hugh, sitting up. 'If I say so myself I was *bloody* unforgettable. Yep, I really got into that part.' He reached for his glass of Pimm's and took a satisfied swig. 'It's all in the breathing, you know,' he informed us importantly, waving his glass about. 'All in the oesophagus control.'

'He made me see it four times,' muttered Molly, leaning back wearily and shutting her eyes in despair. 'I was eight months pregnant, feeling ghastly, and it was like a sauna in there. And he keeps berating me because I won't go again. And he does nothing! He just lies there, for God's sake!'

'Ah, but I *feel* dead, Molly,' he urged. 'I actually feel it, and I convey my deceased state to the audience. Seb here will back me up, won't you, Seb? Oh – and I'll tell you someone else who will, someone else who was sitting at my feet in the front row, looking starry-eyed at my performance, drinking from the muse. Old Imo and Hugo whatsisname, the conductor!'

'Imo came?' said Molly. 'You didn't tell me that. Gosh, that was sweet of her.'

'Sweet!' He gasped. '*Sweet!* Why so? I'm not a *charity*, my darling. They came to marvel, to be enlightened! One doesn't rattle one's tin and give generously to poor old Hugh!'

'So they're still together,' I mused. 'That's nice, and it must be a record for Imo. Have you spoken to her recently, Moll? I haven't seen her since the concert.'

'I asked her to come tonight,' said Molly, sucking the orange from her Pimms, 'but she was frantic in the gallery and couldn't really speak, except to say she had a work thing to go to, so she couldn't come. I did ask how things were going, though, and she said she was besotted.'

'Really! With him?'

'Well, presumably. She didn't say, but I imagine so. I should think Ursula's wetting her pants at the prospect.'

'I saw the pair of them the other night, actually,' said Sebastian. 'The Mitchells asked me to dinner and, having refused two invitations, I thought it only politic to go.'

'Ah,' I grinned. 'So Ursula *is* becoming your benefactress. I knew she would.'

'I must confess I had that same, slightly uncomfortable feeling,' he grimaced.

'And was Hugo there too?' demanded Molly. 'Playing footsie next to Imo and shooting her hot looks over the vichyssoise?'

'He was, although not next to her. I suspect even Ursula's not that obvious. I sat next to Imogen, actually. I thought she was charming. Very easy on the eye and much less intense than her mother.'

'Oh *God*, yes,' I agreed.

'Wouldn't be difficult,' added Molly.

'But scary,' warned Hugh, wagging his finger.

'Imo? No, why?' I said, but I knew what he meant.

'Oh, come on, Livvy, Ursula's overeducated her. Any fool can see that. All those violin lessons at four and cuboid maths at five – you feel you can't open your mouth without her thinking – Christ, what a berk!'

'Entirely valid in your case,' said Molly, getting up. 'More booze, anyone?'

We drank on and on, and I had far more than I should have done, first because I wasn't driving, but also because I felt I might need it. I'd shaved my legs, you see. And my armpits. And as Molly dolled out the strawberries and cream, I gazed at Sebastian as he chatted animatedly with her and wondered just how reckless I was being here. Not very, I decided, taking another swig of Pimm's, and eyeing him carefully, and anyway, he'd won the bet. The one I'd made with myself in the bath, earlier on. It went – why string him along if you're not really interested, Olivia? Then – well, I'm not stringing him along, I really like him. Then – OK, so if you really like him, how about it? You said you wanted to get back to the land of the living. Well, live a little, for Christ's sake! At this point, in the bath, I'd seized the Gillette G2 from the soap dish and depilated furiously. But only, I'd told myself, shaving away like a demon, if I'm totally bowled over by him tonight. Only if he makes me laugh; only if I can look at him without thinking of Johnny; and only if he goes down well with Molly and Hugh – although why this should come into the equation I've no idea since Johnny had never got on particularly well with Hugh, thinking him camp and theatrical – 'dodgy' was how he'd once described him – whilst Hugh, who was as straight as a Roman road, had, in turn, found Johnny just a little too hearty and macho for his artistic taste.

I studied Sebastian now, roaring with laughter at something Hugh had said, head thrown back, wiping tears from his eyes, that narrow, intelligent face creased with mirth. He caught my eye as he shook his head in bemused wonder at Hugh, and I grinned back happily, holding his gaze for just a little longer than was strictly necessary. As I finally looked away it struck me, rather gloriously, that some time later this evening, I was indeed, going to live again. Some time tonight, after all these arid months of mere existence, I was going to uncurl my dry, dusty old roots and drink again, feel the sap of life. I wondered, with a jolt, if I could remember how to do it. Nah, course I could. Just like falling off a bicycle. I frowned, blearily, into my drink. Hang on, wasn't I mixing my metaphors a bit here? And if I *was* going to do it, where the devil was my cap? Gathering dust in my bedside drawer probably, beside an unmade bed and— Hell, when did I last change the sheets? Suddenly I felt my courage begin to slip through my fingers like fine sand. I hastily took another gulp of Pimm's.

Molly came back, armed with a fresh jug, and crouched down between the boys to gather up some strawberry bowls, demanding to know what they were laughing at. Sebastian told her that Hugh had fallen asleep on stage one night and had snored so loudly he'd had to be surreptitiously kicked awake by Peter the Great.

'Not so surreptitiously,' gasped Hugh. 'Apparently I was out for the count. He nearly broke my ribs!'

'You never told me!' Molly shrieked throwing a napkin at him. 'You old fraud – getting into the part, my eye – you never told me that!'

I got up to help her clear away, determining at the same time to tell her of my little seduction plan. I needed encouragement and boy, would she encourage me. 'Go for it, Livvy!' I could hear her saying. 'This man is perfect. This is exactly what you need!'

I followed her into the kitchen, and as she wiped her eyes on a tea towel at the sink, still hooting and dissolving with laughter, I stared at her.

'How are you managing this, Molly?'

'What?' she gasped.

'All this hilarity. You haven't laughed like this for weeks!'

'Oh!' She pulled up her dress. 'Plastic pants! Huge ones, absolutely marvellous, men's ones actually. Bought them in Boots this morning, and padded them out with stacks of those wingy ST things Hugh brought back from the shoot. I was so bloody sick of sitting around po-faced as if I had a cucumber up my bottom, I thought – damn it, I'm going to have a laugh tonight. Honestly, I've practically got a nappy on here, Liv, and I can skip –' she demonstrated across the kitchen – 'I can dance – arabesque – lah-lah-lah!' Her arms flew out and her leg shot up all of two inches behind her. 'Well, almost. And I'm sure I could straddle some gorgeous hunk's shoulders if I really— Shit!' she squeaked, suddenly clutching herself.

'What!' I leapt forward.

She peered down. 'I'm leaking!'

We gazed in frozen horror as torrents of liquid poured down her legs.

'God, that's more than a leak, Moll!'

'My waters! Quick – a bucket!'

'No, no, the loo, hurry – it's closer!' I bundled her towards it.

'No!' she hissed suddenly, digging her heels in. 'I've got to keep some! My midwife told me to, so they can test the amniotic fluid. Get a plastic bag!' She clamped her legs together, bug-eyed with alarm now.

'Where?' I flew wildly round the kitchen.

'Top drawer – there,' she pointed. 'Hurry!'

'They're huge!' I wailed as I pulled a vast John Lewis carrier bag from the dresser.

'Never mind!' she squeaked. 'Just get some of this ruddy stuff!'

I crouched down between her ankles, trying desperately to catch some drops and actually feeling faintly hysterical now. Her legs were no longer dripping, just wet, and the deluge was all over the floor.

'Oh, Moll, I can't!' I gasped hysterically.

'Get a spoon!' she shrieked. 'Look, there's a big puddle. Oh, go away, Digger!' Digger the Border terrier, keen to join the party, looked frightfully excited and all set to clean up. I hurriedly shut him in a cupboard.

'Oh, for God's sake, Molly,' I yelped, bending down again, frantically spooning away, 'you should be at the hospital, not worrying about your amniotic fluid – HUGH!' I flung over my shoulder.

'What?' drifted laconically up from the garden.

'GET IN HERE – NOW!!!'

I reached down deep into my lungs for this, and it did the trick. Hugh and Sebastian arrived at the double, just as Molly, tottering across the floor towards her husband, collapsed stiffly on his neck like a paperhanger's board.

'It's coming,' she moaned. 'Finally, Hugh! Ten bloody days late, but it's actually, finally coming!'

Sebastian, childless, and probably having only ever seen births on episodes of *Casualty*, where it all tends to happen in ten seconds flat on the floor of a phone box, looked horrified. 'What, here? Now?'

'That's it, mate,' said Hugh, grasping his shoulder. 'This is how she wanted it. On all fours on the kitchen floor, that was her birth plan. Glad you could join us. I'd like you down at the works end, if you will. Wash your hands.'

'No no,' I said hurriedly, seeing Sebastian's aghast face. 'He's joking. She's got a while to go yet, and Molly's not into painful home births either. Come on, Moll, let's get you into the car.'

'We're off, we're off!' chortled Hugh joyfully, hopping about from foot to foot. 'God, I wonder what it is. It's just like Christmas, isn't it!'

'Hardly,' snarled Molly.

'Never mind, my love, we'll have you there in a jiffy and it'll soon be over, you'll see. Come on, my sweet.' He helped his huge wife, who seemed to have gone completely rigid now, out of the kitchen, then abruptly lunged back to grab a pewter hip flask from the dresser.

'Hang on, Moll!' He supported her with one hand and filled the flask expertly with whisky with the other. 'Pain relief,' he grinned, slipping it into his pocket. 'In case her agony is too much for me to bear.'

'Oh, the pain,' she moaned, clutching her tummy.

'What – already?' he asked anxiously.

'No, no, I'm just remembering. I want everything, Hugh,' she warned him, staggering out, 'everything that's going, remember that.'

'I will, my love.'

'I want epidurals, pethidine, gas, injections – whatever's going I want it. Unconscious will be just fine. Tell them, Hugh.'

'I'll tell them, my pet, don't you worry.'

'And don't forget to put a ciggy in my mouth as soon as I come round.'

'It'll be my first priority.'

'And your case?' I asked anxiously, following them out of the front door.

'Boot of the car,' she gasped, 'packed and ready. I knew this would happen, knew it would come in a rush, be a bloody emergency. Oh, bye, everyone!'

She turned, halfway down the path, and waved, grinning from ear to ear, suddenly enjoying the moment. Hugh braced up beside her with a huge cheesy grin, never missing a potential audience opportunity.

'Bye, all,' he cried. 'Back soon!'

'Bye!' Sebastian and I yelled back enthusiastically. It was a bit like waving to a royal couple on the balcony.

'And good luck!' added Sebastian as Hugh helped Molly into the car.

'Thanks, mate!'

Moments later they were away, roaring off in Hugh's

ancient MG, roof down, waving frantically, when suddenly – my hand shot up in the air.

'*Stop!*'

Hugh obediently squealed to an emergency halt in the middle of the lane. His head swung back. 'What!'

'You've forgotten Henry!'

Molly and Hugh exchanged horrified looks then – 'Shit!' in unison.

Hugh performed an immaculate three-point turn in the middle of the lane and came roaring back.

'So we have,' he muttered as he raced past me and on up the stairs. 'Well done, Livvy. You're thinking on your feet.'

'But, Hugh, why don't you leave him? Don't wake him up, I'll—'

But he'd gone, and two seconds later was racing back down with a sleeping bundle, wrapped in a duvet, in his arms.

'Hugh, why don't I stay? Or take him back to my house?' I urged. 'He can stay with me.'

'No, no,' he insisted, dashing past me, 'family occasion.' He stopped, turned back. 'In years to come, Livvy, this chap will be able to say that he attended his sibling's birth, and how many boys can say that, eh?' He leant forward confidentially. 'And don't tell Molly,' he whispered, 'but I've got the video camera packed in her case. Thought I'd surprise her, thought we could all be in it, you know, *en famille*, but I'll be down at the sharp end, of course, getting the *moment critique* as she pushes it out, doing a bit of a David Attenborough commentary. Won't she be surprised?' he grinned.

'Oh, Hugh, I'm not so sure she'll—'

'Won't she just love it? And we can play it every year on his birthday!' He turned and ran. 'Bye, all. Just put the dogs out for five minutes, then slam the front door behind you as you leave!'

We watched as he ran off down the path, bundled Henry in the car – no question of strapping him in, of course, or his wife come to that – and then with a throaty old roar of the engine they were away. I saw two cigarettes burning in the night sky as they sped off, shrieking with laughter. Very close. Very happy. Very Molly and Hugh.

Sebastian and I stood and waved until they were out of sight. All was quiet for a moment. Then Sebastian voiced what I was thinking.

'I envy them,' he sighed.

I nodded. 'Me too.'

There was a pause. I shook myself. 'Come on, let's clear up, see to the dogs and get out of here.'

Much of the drive home was spent in companionable silence. I think we were both exhausted by the events of the last few hours and also, pleasantly mellow, and somewhat lost in our thoughts. At length though, Sebastian chuckled.

'What?' I turned, smiling.

He shook his head. 'Just – that pair. What a riot.'

'I know,' I smiled, pleased to have introduced him to a riot. My riotous assembly. I snuggled down happily in my seat.

After a bit, he pulled up in front of my house. 'Here we are, then.'

I turned. Took a deep breath. This was my moment. 'Um, would you like to come in?'

His dark eyes widened with surprise. I hadn't noticed before but they were exactly the colour of expensive chocolates. Belgian browns, they should be called, with black nuts in the middle.

'What, with Maureen there?'

'Well, she could go home,' I said, somewhat brazenly. I felt myself flushing. This was wrong, somehow. I should be having this conversation in his arms, hot with passion, lips a-tremble, unable to control ourselves and needing to prostrate ourselves somewhere horizontally, pronto, not two feet apart as if we were at some executive board meeting.

He scraped back his hair nervously. 'A little, um, awkward, don't you think? Bye-bye, Maureen, see you later, nudge-nudge?'

I licked my lips. 'Well, why don't we go to your house then, have a coffee there?' I offered brightly. What was wrong with this man, and what the hell was I doing in the driving seat?

He regarded me for a long moment. Smiled gently. 'Let's leave it, Livvy, eh? Not tonight.'

I stared. It took me a moment to realise I'd been rejected. Not tonight, Olivia. I felt for the door handle, struggled with it, flushing to my toes.

'You're right, it's late,' I said, rustling up a bright smile, 'and coffee only keeps me awake anyway.'

Suddenly he lunged towards me – yes, he couldn't help himself – and I pitched forward too, kissed his ear as he – opened my door for me.

'It does stick a bit,' he confessed as I retrieved my lips from his hair.

'Oh, right!' I gasped. God, did I get away with that? Did he know I'd tried to snog him? I got out, covered in confusion.

'See you soon then,' I warbled.

He smiled up at me through the open window. 'Definitely. 'Night, Livvy.'

'Good night.' I recovered enough to smile, even challenged him briefly with my eyes. But he didn't seem to notice.

I turned, not waiting to see him drive off the few yards down the road, and walked dazedly up my drive.

When I knew he'd definitely gone, though, I stopped still, turned, and stared back down the empty road. Well. What d'you make of that then? I blinked. Had I got it so wrong? Had I really misread the signs so badly? Had we not, after all, been swimming in a sea of mutual attraction for the best part of the evening? Had he not felt the roaring in his ears, the volts shooting through the old aortas, the throbbing of the pulse points as we'd locked eyes over the buttercups, simultaneously licking strawberry juice sensually from our fingers? I felt – shattered, confused. What was wrong with the man? Was I not right, somehow? Had I said the wrong thing? Offended his artistic sensibilities? I didn't have time to ponder further, however, as Maureen opened the front door.

'Ah, you're back,' she said caustically. 'I thought I heard a car.' Her sharp nose twitched like Hunca Munca's. Probably smelt it too.

'Yes, we're— I'm back.' I sighed. 'Hi, Maureen. All well?' I trudged wearily towards her.

'Fine. Claudia's been asleep for hours. I sent her up at nine, she was so tired, but . . .' she paused.

'Yes?'

'Well, there's a man here.'

'A man? Where?' I peered past her, through the open front door.

'He's sitting out in the garden, on the terrace. Been here for a while, actually.' She swooped forward suddenly and found my ear. 'He says he's your husband!' she hissed.

I stepped back. Stared. 'My . . . Johnny?'

She nodded, wide-eyed, tight-lipped, triumphant. Then she folded her arms importantly and stood aside to let me in. I put my handbag down slowly on the hall table and moved past her dazedly, then realised she was following me down the passage.

I turned. 'Um, thank you, Maureen,' I muttered. 'How much do I owe you?'

'Oh, well, now let me see. I arrived at seven so—'

'Here.' I pressed far too much into her hand, not having time for the mental arithmetic.

She didn't argue and went back towards the door for her coat. 'I'll see myself out,' she called diplomatically, but with a tinge of regret.

I nodded, didn't answer, but all the same waited until the door had shut firmly behind her. Johnny? Here? What on earth for? And why so late? I glanced at my watch. Ten thirty. Not so late, of course, because Molly had abruptly curtailed the evening.

I walked slowly out on to the terrace, tucking my hair carefully behind my ears. My heart was pounding. As I emerged through the French windows, I saw him sitting on the terrace wall, his long, elegant legs dangling. He stood up.

'Hi, Livvy.' His face was strange, taut and pale in the moonlight, yet I knew he had a tan, and he was smoking, for God's sake. Johnny almost never smoked. Then it came to me. In a blinding flash, I knew. Knew what this was. Why he'd come. This was what Nina had come to tell me the other day, what Molly had hinted at.

'Sorry to crash in on you like this.' He cranked up a smile.

'That's OK,' I said carefully.

He took a nervous drag of his cigarette and stared down between his feet. I moved past him and sat, because I needed to, not too close, but just a bit further along the wall from where he'd been sitting. I held on to the balustrade behind in case I needed to clutch something.

'I thought you were in France,' I said lightly.

'I was, we were, but . . .' He bit his lip. 'Well, I needed to talk to you. It wouldn't keep any longer, so I flew back this afternoon.'

I nodded. Blimey. This afternoon, eh? Guilty conscience keeping him awake at night, no doubt. Spoiling his holiday, putting him off his langoustines, keeping him from concentrating on his Jeffrey Archer on the beach. I noticed he was practically wearing beach clothes too – T-shirt, deck shoes, shorts – as if he'd literally just stood up and brushed the sand off himself. Literally just left her, lying supine and bronzed beside him on her raffia mat in her Top Shop bikini, kissed her sun-drenched shoulder a tad regretfully and said, 'It's no good, my love, I must pop back and speak to her indoors. We simply must get this sorted out once and for all. See you back here in the morning for coffee and croissants on the balcony, OK?'

'Right,' I swallowed. 'You couldn't have called?'

'No. I had to see you, Livvy.' His blue eyes were heavy with regret.

I gulped and gripped the balustrade behind me firmly. 'I see. Well, here you are then.' I raised my chin with a brisk, defensive air. 'Fire away.'

He took a quick nervous drag of his cigarette, dropped it and stubbed it out with his toe. His eyes came up to meet mine. Clear as a summer's sky.

'I can't bear it, Liv. I miss you too much. In fact I miss both of you too much. This has been the biggest mistake of my life. I thought I could do it, but I can't, I know that now. I love you so much, Livvy. I want to come back.'

Chapter Twenty-One

I stared at him incredulously. For a moment I couldn't speak. Had neither wind nor words to draw on. My mouth fell open with shock.

'You . . . want to come back?'

He scraped back his hair nervously. 'Look, I know it's a hideous cheek and I should have rung or written – prepared you in some way – but every time I sat down and put pen to paper it sounded so formal, so eighteenth century, I – I just needed to see you.' Suddenly he bounded across to me, took my hands as they lay shocked and lifeless in my lap, and shook them urgently, as if to shake life into me. He gazed desperately into my eyes. 'I needed to plead with you, Livvy, to beg you even, to go down on my knees if necessary, because God knows, I can't do this any more. I'm dying without you. I can't bear it. I just can't bear it any longer!'

I stared into his wide blue eyes, speechless. Then I took my hands away, got up, and walked dazedly round the terrace. I sat down again, my legs feeling very unsteady, and looked down at the moss on the York stone. He wanted to come back? *He* was pleading with *me* to have him back? At length, I unwound my tongue.

'But – you left *me*!'

'I know.'

'For her!'

'I know!'

He shook his head despairingly, scraped frantic hands through his hair again, pulling at the roots as if to punish it. 'And God knows why. Well, no, I *do* know why, exactly why, but that's not important right now. All that matters is that I want to come back, to be a family again, here, with you and Claudia, where I belong.'

'It's important to *me*!' I spluttered. 'Why *did* you leave me, Johnny? And for her! Why her, of all people, and why have her charms suddenly deserted her so dramatically!'

He plunged his hands deep into his pockets and threw back his head. Turned anguished eyes on to the night sky. At length his eyes came down to meet mine.

'Sex,' he blurted out, holding my gaze. 'Pure and simple.'

I nodded. Stared back unflinchingly. Then I took a deep breath. 'Better than with me?'

'No, different.' He shrugged. 'Different person, that's all, so more exciting in the beginning, the thrill of the unknown, that kind of thing. Pathetic.' He gazed down at his shoes, shook his head remorsefully. Then in a low voice: 'I know, Livvy, I know. Sad, clichéd, totally laughable and deeply, deeply, pathetic. A middle-aged man who sees his youth slipping away from him. A man who's always felt young and vital, who can't believe it's all over. Can't believe he's never going to sleep with anyone else, ever in his life again, besides his wife. Puerile, I know. And I'm so, so sorry.' His eyes came up to meet mine, beseechingly.

I nodded, trying to keep calm. 'Well, it's not exactly trail-blazing, is it, Johnny? You're not the first, and you certainly won't be the last, but – God, just for sex! All this – all this pain and heartache, just for sex? Couldn't you have gone off and had an affair? Sneaked off out of hours, seen her in your lunch hour, maybe even had a few old-fashioned dirty weekends, told me you were playing golf with the boys or something, got it all out of your system that way, so no one knew?'

He stared at me, aghast. 'You mean – you'd have *liked* that?'

'Oh, I'd have *loved* it! *No*, Johnny!' I cried. 'I'd have liked it about as much as having a cup of cold sick poured over my head, but I'd have preferred it to – to the cruelty I suffered! Preferred it to the ghastly public humiliation, to the mockery you made of my life, of my marriage, and to the grief and the agony my child went through! *She* wouldn't have known if you'd sneaked off to a grubby motel, half the *county* wouldn't have known, Christ, *I* might not even have known, and since you clearly planned to ditch this woman within a few months anyway, in the long run it would have been tacky but preferable!'

'And deceitful.'

'Oh, Johnny!' I cried, exasperated, banging the palms of my hands on my forehead. 'You and your bloody honour! It's so misplaced, so misguided! You really think you're doing the decent thing by coming clean and walking out on your wife and child and not sneaking around? You really think that's the honourable thing to do, under the circumstances? *Well, I disagree!* The only thing that assuages is your conscience! The only person it helps is you! *You* wanted to feel better, and you couldn't cope with having the guilt hanging round your neck any more! Oh, you could stoop to having the *sex* – that wasn't a problem – but, Johnny, the man of honour, the man with a sense of duty, couldn't stoop to lying, to being deceitful, to not letting me find out. You couldn't stoop to *sparing* me!' My fists were clenched with anger, and for a moment then, I couldn't speak. My voice, when it finally came back, was low, shaky, quivering with rage. 'You destroyed me, Johnny, and you've destroyed our marriage. You've ruined everything! Spoilt it all, and now, months later, as I'm beginning to lick my wounds, beginning to come to terms with the grief, and trying hard to become part of the human race again, you stroll back in here, cool as anything, and declare you'd like to be part of this family again. Lie in your old half of the bed, wash the car, dig the garden, do the washing-up, poke the boring old wife for the rest of your life – well, I'm just not having it, Johnny! I'm just not convinced!' With that I burst into tears. Great racking sobs rent my body and tears poured down my face. I didn't even bother to try to check them, to cover my face in any way. He rushed to put his arms round me.

'*Piss off!*' I shrieked, pushing him away. 'Just piss off!'

He backed off and I sobbed on. Turned my back to him, sat down on the terrace wall and wept. I couldn't stop, actually. It was as if he'd taken a brick out of the dam and it had just burst all over the place, exploded everywhere. He lit a cigarette and perched tentatively a little way along the wall, beside me, but not too close. Eventually my sobs subsided and I got to the catchy breath and shoulder-shaking stage. I threw back my head, wiped my face with the back of my hand and gazed blankly up into the night. I couldn't believe this was happening. Simply couldn't believe it was true. He lit another cigarette and passed it to me. I dragged on it gratefully, right down to my toes, feeling calmer now. Shaky, but calmer.

'You have every right to be furious.'

'Of course I have,' I muttered.

'And every right not to have me back.'

'That goes without saying.'

'And I swear to God this isn't calculated persuasiveness; this isn't me sailing back in here because things aren't working out and I'm wondering if I've been too hasty in abandoning you, abandoning a cosy, settled life. It's much more visceral than that. I'm desperate, Livvy, absolutely desperate without you.'

I couldn't answer.

'Think about it, Liv,' he urged. 'Think about what we had, what we'd be throwing away.'

'I've done nothing *but* think about it!' I replied hotly. Suddenly the rage shot up through my body like a high-speed elevator. I was speechless again, then incensed, incoherent with fury.

'How *dare* you! God, these past few months – what we'd be throwing away – how *dare* you . . . what *you've* thrown away, you bastard!' Suddenly I was on my feet, fists raining down on him, pummelling him as he sat on the wall. He stood up to defend himself, went for my flailing fists, caught my wrists, held them tight, and to my horror, as we struggled I was sobbing again. This time he pulled me close. My strength failed me and I collapsed on to him, wept into his cotton T-shirt. It smelt of fresh air, hay. Of Johnny. He stroked my hair, kissed the top of my head, his arms tight but shaky around me. And it was lovely. Normal. Like coming home. I shuddered into his shoulder. No more chasing rainbows, I thought, peering blearily into his T-shirt through wet lashes and soggy mascara; no more awful dates with Malcolms and Rollos; no more rejections from famous musicians; no more making a fool of myself; no more pity from friends; no more sympathy; no more being strong for Claudia and breaking down when I'd put her to bed and shut my bedroom door; no more empty future; no more living in fear of being like my mother – just Johnny, the love of my life, the ache in my gut, the soulmate I'd had beside me since I was a teenager, my only family, back where he belonged. Who wouldn't be tempted?

'It's just a blip,' muttered Johnny fiercely into my hair. 'Our only blip, in twelve years. Three months of madness, that's all, a madness that gripped me. But it's gone now. Gone for ever.'

I drew my head back from his chest. Found his eyes. 'And her? Why not her?'

He sighed. Loosened his grip on me. Looked away. 'It just didn't work, Livvy. She's so – possessive, so jealous. I couldn't move, couldn't breathe, it was suffocating, stifling.'

I thought back to when I'd seen them together, two blond heads bent over the concert programme. 'You didn't look very stifled at the Abbey.'

'God, that was so awful. Seeing you there, with that guy.'

I frowned. Rollo? Yes, it must have been Rollo. And of course Johnny wasn't to know he spat.

'And then tonight, waiting for you, knowing you were out with someone.' He gazed, hurt clouding his eyes. 'Some guy?'

'It's none of your business, Johnny,' I said quietly.

He nodded, head down. 'No, you're right.'

My God, his penance would be huge, though, wouldn't it? I thought, looking at his blond head, bent low, sorrowful, remorseful. And think of the mileage in that; I could milk it for months, for years. He'd have to toe the line for the rest of his life. I'd have the upper hand entirely, which I wasn't convinced I'd ever had. But would that be healthy? Would that, at the end of the day, help either of us? Surely if this was to work, it had to be with a clean slate. It had to be even-handed, shoulder to shoulder, facing the world together, and with no Sword of Damocles hanging over his head. But how realistic was that? Not very. How often would I be tempted to say as he failed to empty the dishwasher – oh, and I suppose you'd rather be with your bloody whore than tidying up the kitchen! But then again – I gazed up at the night sky and sighed – what was the alternative? To say: no Johnny, sod off, I'm making my own way now, having a great time? Was I? I thought about that one carefully. No, a better time, I decided, but not a great time. And how come I was even weighing it up? I thought, suddenly startled. I pushed an astonished hand through my hair. *Seriously* weighing it up too, genuinely thinking of rejecting him, and not just to play a game, to keep my pride, to make him wait, to have a bit of 'I'll show the bastard' – no, I was seriously thinking of telling him to get lost, and yet this was what I'd longed for, yearned for, all these months!

'Do you still love me, Livvy?' Quietly, it stole out of the night. I took a deep breath. Ah. The trump card.

'Yes.'

Yes I did. Of course I did. How could I not?

'And can you imagine us . . .' he took a deep breath to steady himself, 'not growing old together?'

Sorry, no, *this* was the trump card. The other one was just the knave. Growing old together. Sentimental pictures of white heads and rocking chairs side by side, gnarled hands creeping out from under the knee blankets, and clasping, as we turned wrinkled, faded smiles on each other. I shook my head. My chin wobbled.

'No,' I whispered. 'No, I can't imagine not doing that.'

Don't you dare. Don't you dare play that ace.

'And if not for all that –' he took me in his arms and

squeezed me tight. I could feel his heart racing – 'if not for me, for us, then –' his voice cracked – 'for Claudes? And – and, who knows, Liv?' he said, his heart thumping away now. 'Maybe another child?'

A tiny baby in a crib, with Johnny, Claudia and me all standing round, looking lovingly down, sprang instantly to mind, and for the third time that evening I burst into tears. You wouldn't think there'd be any left, would you, but there were. I soaked his shirt, and he'll forgive me for telling you that he soaked mine, too.

We sat on that wall for a long while on that warm, still, July night, talking softly, clenching and unclenching hands, even crying again – Johnny this time, not me – until eventually, it seemed as natural as anything. To take one another by the hand, to walk through the house, and to mount the stairs to bed. Oh yes, by rights, I should have made him fight, every inch of the way, made it much, much harder, but actually, I wanted him very badly. As we stood up from that wall and hugged each other hard, half a bathful of adrenalin shot up the back of my legs and swept forcefully around my body, and as he tightened his arms around me, I could feel his breath coming in spurts, roaring in my ear. I didn't think – oh yuck, he's been with her; and I didn't think – how frigging dare he? I just thought – yesss. He's mine. And he's come home. And I want him.

We were kissing as we went up the stairs, desperate, tortured kisses, lips trembling, and then again beside the bed, eating the faces off each other as we struggled out of our clothes, falling together, pulling each other down, our naked bodies fitting like parts of a modular jigsaw puzzle, seamlessly entwined. We made love with a frenzy and a passion that I don't think, in all our years of lovemaking, had ever possessed us before, and a greed too. Like a couple of thirsty camels happening finally upon that water hole. Finally we fell apart, flung back away from each other like deflecting magnets, satiated, replete, relieved. We stared up at the ceiling, panting, the duvet in a heap on the floor, the warm night air stealing in across our naked bodies. All was so still, so silent; just the sound of our breathing.

At length I reached down and pulled the duvet back. We curled up and lay together like spoons, Johnny behind me, his arms wrapped around me, both of us gazing out of the open window beside the bed, at the crescent moon.

'Where is she now?' I asked quietly, as reality came seeping stealthily back. So many questions. So many answers I needed. I wanted to sit up and light a cigarette, but that had never been our style.

'She's back at her flat.'

'Oh. Not in France?'

'No, why?'

I shrugged. 'Somehow I thought you'd left her there.'

'France was a disaster. It was a last-ditch attempt of hers to bring us together. She booked a hotel in St-Jean-de-Luz as a surprise. She wasn't to know we'd spent our honeymoon there, of course, but it couldn't have been more fatal. Couldn't have sounded the death knell of our relationship more conclusively. We spent a ghastly few days in a stifling, hundred-degree heat wave, she, in dark glasses in our room to hide her red eyes and me, walking the streets. I walked everywhere, all around those little back lanes we discovered, with tiny painted houses, balconies and terraces spilling over with geraniums and bougainvillaea – remember? Remember how you made friends with all the madames, took cuttings, filling our room with little jam jars, determined to get them home somehow?'

'I remember.'

'I walked for miles. Came back only for silent meals, picking at food in happy, bustling restaurants, with her, still in dark glasses, sitting opposite me, and surrounded by French children on other tables sharing a late supper with their parents, about Claudia's age, younger too, laughing, chattering into the night. Awful.'

I stayed silent.

'After three days of what should have been a three-week holiday, we booked out.'

'She wanted to go too?'

He hesitated. 'Yes. It was a mutual decision.'

I spotted a lie. The first one. I swam towards it – then let it go.

'And now?'

'Now?'

'Well, either she's accepted the fact that the affair's run its course, or she's distraught and in a heap.'

He swallowed. 'Distraught and in a heap.'

For a brief moment I felt a pang of pity for her. Alone in her flat. But not much of a pang.

'Oh well,' I said, reaching for a glass of water, 'I don't suppose it'll take her long to recover. Don't suppose it'll take her long to find another married man to play with.'

He didn't answer. Ah, I thought, sipping my water. He wasn't prepared to rubbish her, then. I wasn't sure if I liked that or not. Yes, I was. 'Isn't that her game?' I demanded hotly.

'She – got caught up in something,' he said, picking his words carefully. 'By accident. I take the blame. For everything. This has all been my fault.'

Suddenly I was furious. He was defending her. As I struggled to contain my temper, he went on.

'But now, because she's desperate to cling on, she's changed. She's doing everything in her power to keep me. She'd go to any lengths: she tells lies, she's manipulative – downright cunning too.'

This was better. I took a deep breath. 'In what way?'

'In extraordinary ways. Recently she's taken to writing letters to herself. Threatening letters.'

I sat up. 'What d'you mean?'

He propped himself on one elbow and struggled to explain. 'It all started when Claudes went missing, remember? God, I was upset – so full of remorse, thought it was all my fault, and I'm sure that's when she felt me slipping away, sensed my first seeds of doubt. First she invented aches and pains, limped about the flat clutching her side and moaning, even made me drive her to the hospital, said she thought her appendix had burst. All spurious, of course. The nurses exchanged knowing glances as they examined her and sent her home within minutes, but I remembered thinking then that in some warped kind of way it was a cry for help. I had –' he hesitated – 'been passionate about her, helplessly so, and I think she was trying to rekindle that passion. Trying to say – look, imagine life without me. Imagine if I were to die, remember how close we were. Does that make any sense?'

I blinked. 'Blimey. Bit extreme.'

'She is,' he insisted. 'She's neurotic and extreme.'

'And the letters?'

'That started quite recently. Threatening letters in childish capitals, Agatha Christie stuff, very naïve.'

'But saying what?'

'Oh, death threats, you know – "Dear Nina, you'd better

watch out, we're after you" – all designed to make me hugely protective, to make me hole up with her in that flat for ever, barricade the door, put bars on the windows, shut out the world, never let her out of my sight.'

'Good God!' I gazed at him.

'I told you, Livvy, she's nutty. She'd do anything.'

Naturally that frightened me for a second. I thought of Claudes, of *Fatal Attraction*, of boiling bunnies. 'She'd bloody better *not* do anything,' I said hotly.

But I felt stronger, too, because of it. United against her. If she was nuts, it helped enormously. But once again, ridiculously, a pang of sympathy. Because for a while there, I'd been nuts too. I remembered trying to make a friend of her, practically offering to iron her underwear, much to Molly's horror. I shuddered. Lay down beside Johnny.

He turned from his side on to his back and I gazed at his profile. Gazed at this husband of mine, square-jawed and bronzed, lying beside me in the moonlight. His hand, curled in mine, gradually loosened its hold as his eyes shut and Morpheus welcomed him back, down the dark lanes of sleep. And as I stared and stared until my eyes began to hurt, I thought – how weird. How strange. How . . . very curious. Four hours ago I'd been in Molly's garden flirting with another man. Two hours ago, I'd been in aforementioned man's car, as near as damn it propositioning him. And now, here I was, in bed with Johnny. If your probing, investigative, fly-on-the-wall reporter had slunk through my bedroom door right now, crept up to the bed, stuck a microphone under my nose and hissed urgently, 'So how d'you feel, Mrs McFarllen? Our viewers are keen to know?' I'd have had to have answered, in the words of the tabloid press – gobsmacked. If he'd persisted, pursued his tack with, 'But happy? Happy, surely, Mrs McFarllen?' I'd have replied – yes. Very. But, I decided, turning over to face the wall, I'd qualify that with 'unsettled'. Happy, but unsettled. Those, I decided as I too, finally shut my eyes, were definitely my overriding emotions of the moment.

Chapter Twenty-Two

Of course, that's not the way it should have been. As any good counsellor, psychologist or best friend worth their salt would tell you, what I should have done was turf him out. Given him the never-darken-my-door routine, the how-dare-you-come-grovelling-back-after-all-you've-done-to-me malarkey. Sent him away with a flea in his ear. Then, naturally, he'd have wanted me even more. And at some point, weeks – no, maybe even months – later, I might have agreed to meet him for dinner. In an incredibly expensive, swanky London restaurant, looking gorgeous. (Me, not him, hell no, he'd be pale and gaunt, a shadow of his former self.) Oh, I'd *agree* to meet him, but I wouldn't turn up. So there he'd be, at this impossible to come by corner table, chewing his napkin nervously, drinking heavily, trying to avoid the disdainful eyes of the waiters as they scornfully observed his solitary, stood-up status, before emerging hours later, seriously drunk, reeling down Knightsbridge, and stopping every passer-by with the requisite number of ears to inform them jusht how mush he was in love wish his wife, and how he'd alwaysh been in love with hish lovely wife, before being discovered in the gutter by a passing policeman and taken to the cells for the night.

And meanwhile, of course, I'd be out with my boys. My

Malcolms, my Rollos, my Sebastians – the former in a hat and dark glasses and the second under strict instructions not to open his mouth – parading them up and down in front of his nose until it turned green and fell off. Then maybe, *maybe*, I'd agree to meet him again. For, hmm, let me see now – coffee. And on the understanding that he had precisely half an hour to present his case because I was a very busy woman. (By this stage I'd naturally have that aforementioned, much discussed, high-powered job at the Chelsea Physic.) In I'd click in my designer mules – I'd be on the management side, rather than the soil-tilling, gumbooted side – and there he'd be, cowering at a corner table again, sweaty-palmed, getting eagerly to his feet, knocking his chair flying in his haste. Oh yes, it could have gone on and on like that. I could have milked it for months, brought him to his knees, given him to understand that only under very exceptional circumstances would he ever get so much as a toe in my door again. Instead of which, with a belly full of Pimms inside me as Dutch courage to take another man to bed, I'd taken Johnny instead. Just like that.

More kindly critics might argue that if getting Johnny home was indeed the endgame, the *raison d'être*, why shillyshally about? Why play the fish, dangle him at length for no apparent reason, when actually, it was the landing of him that was so important? We weren't seventeen, after all; this wasn't an extended flirt, this was serious stuff, this was a marriage.

I suspect there may have been some middle ground, but I didn't find it. I simply saw the green light, put my foot down and went for it. Marriage, it seemed to me, was rather like one of those great big shiny Jeeps, driven by mothers with expensive highlights and crammed full with children at private schools; the whole family perched up high, roaring around bends, confident, loved, cruising into the future, pushing the odd bicycle into the verge, which to me, felt like the single life. Pedalling hard, alone, feeling every bump, every rut in the road, never quite knowing what was around the next corner. I'd been in the Jeep for ten years and then I'd got on the bicycle and I knew which I preferred, which was harder work, and which was more terrifying. Not seeing round corners frightened the life out of me, but now, the future was simply a scene I could cruise back into. What a relief to let go of those handlebars. Weak? Possibly, but on the other hand, who on earth was I supposed to be brave for? Surely this was about me? About what I wanted?

As I lay there the following morning, feeling I really should pinch myself extremely hard, I took in the surreal scene around me. Johnny was still asleep beside me, his clothes in a familiar heap on the floor, his brown arm flung over me in its habitual fashion, one leg sticking out of bed, his eyelids just beginning to flicker. They opened, and as he saw me, a huge smile spread instantly across his face. It was so instinctive, so very much the moment he'd opened his eyes, so free of any ghastly doubt, any 'holy shit, what have I done?' that I beamed back, delighted. And it was at that, highly seminal moment, that the door opened and Claudia appeared in her nightie. She stopped dead in her tracks, her hand frozen on the handle. Her jaw dropped.

'Daddy!'

He turned quickly towards her. She stared in astonishment, her grey eyes huge, first focused on him, then on me.

'It's Daddy!' She gaped incredulously at me, as if perhaps I didn't know. I smiled, waiting.

Johnny sat up and stretched out an arm to draw her close.

She came, but slowly, looking to me first for reassurance. I nodded, still smiling.

'Daddy, what are you *doing* here!' she squealed suddenly, leaping forward excitedly, jumping high in the air, and coming crashing down on top of him with her knees bent, catching him neatly in the groin.

'Oooomph . . .!' he groaned, bringing his knees up in pain. 'Aaarrgh! What am I doing? I'm being beaten up by a ten-year-old,' he gasped, 'that's what I'm doing, and on the day of my homecoming too. What sort of a welcome is that?'

'Home . . .?' Again, wide grey eyes shot across to me.

'Daddy's coming back, darling.'

'Really?' Her mouth dropped.

'Really,' said Johnny firmly.

There was a silence. She didn't whoop, and she didn't shriek, and for a moment there, I was nervous. But then a slow smile spread over her face. She reddened a bit too.

'Well, about time too,' she said hotly, giving him a playful clip round the ear. She folded her arms and pursed her lips, affecting a rolling-pin-wielding, northern harridan style. 'Moother and I 'ave bin worried sick, 'aven't we, moother? All this time without a word, you never call, you never write, we've been that fussed!'

He laughed, catching her wrists as she made to beat him up with her rolling pin and then they rolled about on the bed, wrestling and fighting amid shrieks of giggles.

I watched them for a moment, tussling away beside me. Just like old times. Extraordinary. Like he'd never been away. How could that be then? Because he had been away. I blinked, shook my head in wonder, then grabbed my dressing gown, rolled neatly out of bed and slipped into it. I smiled down as they rolled about, Johnny pinning Claudes to the bed now, telling her that 'if she gave 'im any more lip e'd come down from mill or oop from pit and give 'er a right good thrashin',' and Claudia shrieking that if he did that she'd 'put on clogs and shawl and get a job oop big house as servin' wench!'

I tied my silk dressing gown around me and gazed out of the window. A hazy mist was hovering over a dewy lawn, full of the promise of sun. The caravan was still in situ on the other side of the river (despite Mac's assertions that they'd be gone soon, predictably, they were still here), and I saw the door open and Lance appear. As I watched him yawn, stretch, gaze up at the blue sky then make his way over the bridge and up the dewy lawn, I realised, in a sudden rush, the enormity of what I'd done. Realised what a huge leap of faith I'd taken. I also realised, with something approaching panic, that having taken that leap, it simply had to work. Shrieks of glee rang out behind me. It had to. If not for me, then for Claudia. We couldn't do this to her only for Johnny to disappear again, could we? But of course that wasn't going to happen, was it? I thought hastily. He was back for good now and we were a family again. As I watched Lance potter off round to his workbench in the garage, I leant forward and rested my forehead on the glass. Was it really that simple? Did we just erase the last few months and start again? Carry on from where we left off without even skipping a beat? I gave myself a little inward shake. Why, yes of course we did, why not? As I turned, I saw Johnny's eyes on me as he tussled with Claudia. They seemed anxious.

I straightened up. 'Right, you lot!' I said with a bright smile. 'Scrambled eggs and bacon in the kitchen in ten minutes, and the last one down washes up the scrambled egg pan!'

I swept out joyfully and clattered downstairs. Well, if they were looking to me for guidance, that was fine. I could do that, I could be the leader. In fact, it would make an extremely pleasant change.

It was a beautiful morning. I threw open the back door and humming happily, gathered some eggs from the fridge. Yes, breakfast in our new kitchen, cooked on my shiny blue Aga, with the sun streaming in on the pale yellow walls, hung now with blue and white plates, casting shadows on the smooth, mellow wooden floor, and all of us here, together, back where we belonged.

As I fried the bacon at the stove, simultaneously laying the table with orange juice, toast, cereal, quickly flicking on the radio as I went past, Johnny and Claudia came bounding in. They flopped happily down at the table, still chattering away, and occasionally, Johnny would catch my eye as in, 'Isn't it great? She's delighted!' And I'd respond with a smile which agreed.

Meanwhile, the laughter and the jokes continued apace. But it seemed to me, as I listened, my hand pausing for a moment as I went to break an egg in the pan, that somehow, he was hiding behind Claudia. Something, and I couldn't quite put my finger on it, was wrong. His larking was extravagant, and OK, it always had been, but somehow . . . No. I cracked the egg. No, you're wrong, Olivia. It's just that he's bound to be slightly nervous. Why d'you think you flicked that radio on so quickly if not for some background hum, and aren't you secretly glad that Claudia's here and not round at Lucy's? And after all, I thought, reaching for the milk and sloshing it in, why shouldn't he be in glorious, over-the-top high spirits on this supremely, glorious, heady day?

That day, and the next few, proceeded in much the same

pattern. I seemed to vacillate between strange extremes of emotions. I'd notice every nuance, every flicker of Johnny's eye, every intonation in his voice, but as the days progressed, my reactions to these nuances became more pronounced. One moment I'd be almost incandescent with happiness, hugging him to bits, showering him with kisses, and the next, tears of doubt and rage would spring and I'd be stomping round the house in fury, practically spitting in his coffee as I handed it to him. Johnny indulged these moods, knowing, I'm sure, that they were entirely natural and that it was better for me to get it all out rather than bottle it up. He did his best to ride the waves. He also indulged my rather erratic desire for information, as one minute I decided I wanted to know absolutely everything about Nina, and the next, nothing. Sometimes, the minute Claudia had gone out to play, I'd seize his wrist, drag him to the kitchen table, sit him down, and with frenzied, burning eyes demand, 'Where? How? How exactly did it happen – how did you meet her? I want to know precisely – tell me again!'

And he'd light a cigarette and patiently explain, yet again, that the day we'd been to look around Claudia's new school, a year or so ago, on the open day, Nina had been there too. As a new teacher, available to meet new parents.

'You picked her up at an open day!' I screeched, fumbling for a cigarette.

'No, I just talked to her, but for quite a while because you were off touring the school. You wanted to see the new science block again, remember? The headmaster took you, and while you were gone, we chatted, that's all.'

My mind scuttled back. Was that right? Had I gone off? Maybe I had.

'And then?' I demanded. 'How the hell did you progress

from there? Listen, Miss Harrison, we seem to have a few minutes, fancy a quick one behind the bike sheds while my wife's examining the Bunsen burners?'

'No,' he said levelly, ignoring my sarcasm, 'it happened quite by chance, actually. A couple of months later the gears were playing up on the Lagonda, so I took it into the Classic Car garage in Finchley – you know, the one Dad used to go to, and the one I still use. Well, it was quite extraordinary, because there she was, just coming out of the front door to the flat next door. She recognised me and smiled, and at first I couldn't think who the hell she was, but then I remembered I'd met her at the school. We got chatting and it turned out that her father owns the garage, which is extraordinary really because I've known Bob Harrison for years, and – well, I suppose we laughed about the coincidence, said what a small world it was, talked for a bit.' He shrugged. 'It just went from there.'

'How?' I yelled. 'How did it "just go from there"!'

He sighed, frowned and picked at an eggy stain on the kitchen table. 'I suppose . . . I asked her if she fancied a drink.'

'What – just like that? Oh golly, Nina, what a coincidence, your Dad mends my cars, fancy a lager and lime?'

'Well, it was a hot day, the pub was opposite . . . I don't know. It seemed natural at the time, somehow.'

'Natural?' I sneered. 'But you're married, Johnny. A married man.'

'I know.'

I dragged hard and deep on my cigarette, eyes a trifle wild. 'And then?'

'Well,' he shifted uncomfortably, 'then I suppose we arranged to meet again, only this time it was for dinner, and then—'

'*Stop, Stop!*' I cried, clapping my hands over my ears. 'Stop this minute! I don't want to hear another word!'

And so it went on, with me oscillating wildly between a greed to be informed and a revulsion at the details, between hate and happiness, and in the midst of all this, many bouts of desperate, frenzied lovemaking. Oh yes, there was a definite desperation about it, as if sex was the filling in the sandwich, something which would glue us together, and which we had to have, as much as possible, at any conceivable opportunity, to stop us falling apart. In some ways I was more worried about me than I was about Johnny. He seemed so sure, so strong, so ready to go along with anything I wanted, and I began to wonder if it was me who was the neurotic here, me who was having the mid-life crisis.

I seemed to veer from an insatiable desire to run down the street shouting, 'He's back! My husband's back!' to not wanting to answer the telephone in case it was Someone Who Should Know. My mother, for instance, or Angie, maybe Molly, or Imogen. Of course we did tell these people, we told them all in time, but gradually, letting it leak out over a period of days. Looking back, their reactions fell neatly into two camps: modified rapture from my mother, Molly and Hugh, and unmitigated delight from Angie and Imogen.

My mother's subdued reaction – 'Well, darling, I'm pleased for you, of course I'm pleased, it's what you wanted, isn't it?' – together with a promise, when pressed, to come over soon with Howard, was, in light of her new incarnation as a born-again romantic, a no-longer-passed-over, shat-upon woman, I suppose somewhat predictable. But Molly surprised me.

'And you've taken him back?' she demanded from her

hospital bed, newly delivered of a nine-pound baby girl named Flora, after the cottage garden she was very nearly born into, and who, her mother declared, was even more stunning than Helen of Troy, fed beautifully, didn't crack her nipples, and had yet to be sick all over her.

'Well – yes. I have.'

'No questions asked?'

'Of course, Molly, many.'

'Good. Well, I just hope he's got some answers.' A pause. 'Sorry, Livvy, I'm delighted for you, of course I'm delighted. God, ignore me, I'm just hormone soup at the moment. This morning I was in floods of tears because I was convinced Flora was going to grow up to be a lesbian. One of the nurses missed her pink wrist tag and called her a great big bruiser of a boy, and I could suddenly see her in dungarees, with a number-one haircut and a lover called Brenda. I cried for half an hour. Added to which I feel like my undercarriage has been sown up by some malicious, sharp-eyed seamstress from the WI, while at the back I've got a bag full of jelly beans swinging jauntily out of my bottom. Just ignore me, I'm a mess. Hugh's here and he's thrilled for you, aren't you, Hugh?' She held the phone out to Hugh for confirmation.

'Am I?'

There was some muffled confusion as her hand clamped over the mouthpiece, a fair amount of hissing, then – 'Thrilled!' came back a chipper male voice. 'But tell her I thought she was doing pretty well under her own steam, too.'

Angie cried on the phone, so relieved was she, and promised to come round soon, wondering also if Claudia would like to come and stay a while and give us some space? I turned, the receiver at my ear, to ask Johnny and we both instinctively shook our heads and said – no! Then we stared, anxiously at each other. Why didn't we want space? Why didn't we want to be alone? Because we wanted to be a unit, a family, I decided firmly.

Imogen, though, surprised me most. I left a message on her answer machine at work – she was out at Sotheby's – and that evening she appeared on my doorstep, loaded with flowers, hugging us through her tears and her orchids, hugely overcome and emotional.

'Oh God, guys,' she gasped, 'this is so much what I'd hoped for! It's just the answer to everyone's prayers! I just can't believe it – I'm so, so happy for you!'

'Imo,' I said, touched as she hugged me tight, 'you're so sweet to come.'

She sat in the garden with us a while, shared a bottle of wine with us, but when she left, I closed the front door thoughtfully and went, biting my thumbnail, back to Johnny on the terrace. He was hidden now, behind the *Telegraph*.

'I can't believe she came all that way just to give us some flowers,' I said in astonishment. 'And she's so busy. She's got a private view to organise tonight.'

Johnny didn't answer, immersed as he was in his broadsheet, and suddenly I felt a bit guilty. I adored Imo, always had done, but always from a slightly respectful distance, always from afar, and yet here she was, on my doorstep the moment she'd heard, brimming over with tears for me. I had no idea she'd felt my loss so keenly.

Claudia was skippy and happy most of the time, but cautious too, I noticed. Johnny would pull her on to his lap, maybe after Sunday lunch, and she'd laugh, fool about with him a bit, but be quick to slip away, too. If he noticed, he didn't say.

Once, when she and I were picking strawberries together

in the vegetable patch, she suddenly paused, face down in the fragrant, star-shaped leaves. Crouched on her haunches, she said abruptly, 'Is Daddy back for good, then?'

I straightened up. 'Yes, of course, darling. This is for ever. We're a family again!'

She didn't reply.

I frowned. 'Claudes?'

'It's just . . . well, Granny says, "Never say never, and you can't say forever." '

'Oh, Granny and her little homilies!' I said, exasperated. 'When did she say that?'

She shrugged. 'The other day.'

'You saw her?'

'No, I rang her.'

'Oh!' Again, panic. She rang her? Why couldn't she talk to me? 'But – but you wanted Daddy to come back, surely?'

'Of course. I'm just asking, that's all. I can ask, can't I?' She straightened up and stared defiantly at me in her blue shorts and ancient Mickey Mouse T-shirt, her cheeks glowing. Yes, of course she could ask, I thought slowly as she threw down her basket, brushed past me and stomped off. Why not? Children have every right to assume their parents will be together for ever, so if one disappears, then comes back to the fold, surely they have every right to question that reappearance, too?

And then of course there was Sebastian. Initially I'd almost gone down on my knees and thanked God that I hadn't seduced Sebastian that night. Thanked God that I hadn't forced him, protesting, back to his towering town house, drugged his wine before dragging him by the hair up all those zillions of stone steps to his bedroom, slammed the door shut, refused to take no for an answer, cracked my whip, thrown him on the bed and given him a damn good seeing to, because look what I'd have been missing in my own back yard? Look who was waiting for me, under the stars, on my very own terrace?

Then again, I thought, running the tap over a lettuce I'd just picked for lunch and gazing out at Johnny through the kitchen window, snoozing in a deck chair with a Panama hat over his eyes, then again, as every how-to-get-your-man manual would tell you, that probably couldn't have been better. What – to have the errant husband sitting waiting on the matrimonial doorstep until two in the morning, wondering where the hell the abandoned wife was, and then for me to arrive back, panting and dishevelled, knickers in my handbag, very definitely post-coital, very definitely deflowered? Oh perfect, the revengeful would breathe ecstatically, perfect! But I knew better. Johnny, with his code of honour, would have been horrified. He wouldn't have spoken to me, let alone touched me; would have brushed straight past me, stony-faced, got back in his car and roared off, because whilst it was OK for him to be promiscuous, for his *wife* – oh, heavens no. Hadn't he already quizzed me – gently but searchingly – about the possibility of my having seen some action these past few months? Eyes trawling my face for lies? Suddenly I flung down the lettuce and threw open the window in rage.

'Double standards!' I shrieked. 'DOUBLE FUCKING STANDARDS!'

Johnny awoke from his deck chair with a jolt and swung round, astonished, his Panama dropping on to the grass. In the bathroom above, Mac and the boys laid down their tools. It wasn't the first time they'd halted their hammering to listen to the 'domestic' below. By the time Johnny had run in and reached me in the kitchen I was hanging on to the sink, sobbing uncontrollably into the lettuce water. As he rushed up I seized the wet lettuce and slapped it in his face, hitting him again and again with it. He stood there, taking it, soaking wet, eyes shut, bits of green slime all over him, until finally I dropped it and sank down into a chair. Johnny crouched, took me in his arms and held me as I sobbed. You see, this was nothing new. Our days were full of interesting little episodes like this. He never argued his corner – well, let's face it, he didn't exactly have one – just let me get it all out of my system, and then when it was over, went slowly back to his deck chair, his garage, his toolshed, or whatever it was he'd been doing before. Occasionally, though, after one of these outbursts, I'd catch him later in an unguarded moment, and see his eyes, full of sorrow and regret, so profound it shocked me. I hoped it was for me, for what he'd done to me, for the time we'd lost together, but I couldn't be sure. And, feeling my eyes on him, he'd quickly respond with a bright smile and then we'd be back on track again, but often, they were tracks I didn't recognise – polite, dissembling tracks. Where the hell were they going?

And so, as I said, Sebastian had to be dealt with. Had to be visited. Well yes, of course he did, didn't he? I mean, we'd never been lovers, but I was pretty sure we'd been more than friends, and I couldn't exactly have him popping round wondering if I fancied dinner; couldn't just leave it hanging in the air like that, could I? And so I went one afternoon without warning, simply because I saw his car outside and I knew he'd be in. Maureen opened the door.

'He's in the study,' she said with a brisk jerk of her head upstairs. 'Will I tell him you're here?'

'Could I just go up?' I asked tentatively. 'I'll knock, I won't just barge in.'

She gave a hint of a smile. 'Since it's you.'

And so I crept up the millions of stone stairs, knocked gently on the study door, and on hearing a curt 'Come!', entered.

Sebastian was standing at the tall, floor-to-ceiling Georgian window, facing the street, fingertips pressed to temples, eyes shut.

'You old poser,' I muttered brightly as I went in. He opened his eyes and swung round, and for a moment, my heart stopped. I instantly wished I hadn't said it. His eyes were distant and preoccupied, about to be annoyed, but then remarkably, his face cleared, in the way I remembered, but had recently forgotten.

'Olivia!' He was across the room in seconds. 'How extraordinary, sixteen more bars of this wretched piece and I was coming over to see you! Did you get my postcard?'

I nodded and sat down quickly on a button-backed chair, eschewing the sofa on the grounds that I didn't want him too close. 'From Paris, I did. How did it go?'

'Marvellous,' he beamed, dragging up a chair, eyes shining. 'To my utter relief they absolutely loved it, thank goodness, and let me tell you those Parisians are harsh taskmasters. Not so much the audience, who adore anything so long as it lets them get dressed up in their Chanel and pearls and go swanking about town, but the music critics. God, they're sharks. And there they all were, in the front row – where stupidly I'd parked myself too – and I kept glancing along the row, watching their impassive poker faces. My heart was sinking fast, I can tell you, and then at the end there was this horrible hush, and then – thunderous applause! They even got to their feet, for God's sake, and old Claude Pastiche from the *Figaro* doesn't stand up for his grandmother!'

I laughed. 'Oh, Sebastian, I'm so pleased. You were so nervous about Paris. And Hugo conducted?'

'Quite magnificently. Best yet, actually.'

I smiled. 'Missing Imo, no doubt. Her memory must have stirred him to passion.'

'Oh no, not the memory, no, no, she came out.'

'To Paris? Did she!'

'Oh yes, for four or five days. God, we had some fun, though, the three of us – lots of laughs, lots of gastronomic delights and a huge amount of drinking – too much, actually, bearing in mind that at least two of us were supposed to be working.' He glanced down. 'Oh Christ, Olivia, excuse my clothes. I'm in the old working pyjamas again, my nutter outfit.'

'But how odd,' I mused, gazing past him, ignoring this. 'I mean – I saw Imogen the other day, and she never said. Never even mentioned it.' I glanced back and felt his dark eyes upon me. Abruptly I remembered why I was here. I took a deep breath. 'Look, Sebastian, the reason I've come—'

'If it's about the other night,' he interrupted anxiously, 'after Molly and Hugh's, maybe I should explain—'

'No, no,' I stopped him hurriedly. 'No, it's not about the other night. No, what I came to tell you was –' I went on in a rush – 'well, Johnny's home.'

'Johnny?' He frowned.

'My husband.'

'Oh – oh yes, of course.' There was just a flicker of surprise, as if he'd momentarily forgotten who Johnny was, then his eyes widened in recognition. Slowly, a lovely, warm smile spread across his face.

'But this is wonderful news, Olivia, and just exactly what you'd been hoping for, isn't it?'

'Yes, yes it is.'

'How amazing! And a complete surprise? I mean, did he give you any warning or—'

'Complete,' I breathed, relieved he was taking it like this. 'So unexpected, Sebastian, totally out of the blue. And you know, if I'd known he was coming back, well, I would never have – well, you know, in the car the other night. I hope you don't think . . .' I panicked. What? What was I trying to say? I hope you don't think I was stringing you along? But no, I hadn't been stringing him along. I'd liked him, and, anyway, why was I sitting here explaining myself? Surely he'd rejected me? God, he was probably *genuinely* delighted.

'I'm delighted,' he beamed. 'You're back together again, a family, and it's how it should be. Claudia must be thrilled!'

'She . . . is,' I said, confused. Confused about how I felt, as much as how he felt. I studied his face, lean and elegant with those high cheekbones and dark brown eyes, which gave no clues, but which regarded me kindly now, rather as one would a small child.

'D'you know,' he said thoughtfully. 'I thought I saw her cavorting rather skittishly yesterday.'

'Who?' I said, muddled.

'Claudia. She pogo-sticked down practically the entire length of the road!'

The phone rang and he got up and went to the piano to pick it up. His back was to me. I gazed. I'd forgotten how tall he was. How dark his hair was. He half turned and his face clouded as he listened.

'Yes, yes, I know,' he said, scratching his forehead, 'but, God, Louis, their timing is absolutely lousy. I can't just churn these things out at a drop of a hat. I know they think I can but . . . Yes, yes I know . . . Yes, I said I would so I will, of course I will, but . . . OK, OK, keep your hair on. Yes, they'll get it. Relax . . . You too . . . Bye.'

He replaced the received and grimaced. 'My agent, Louis. Apparently some film director is screaming for this score I'm supposed to be writing, although why I ever agreed to do it in the first place I'll never know.' He rubbed his forehead sheepishly. 'Well, yes, I do know actually, money, together with the promise of popular recognition, but remind me, Olivia,' he wagged a finger, 'never again. There's a joke in the music world that goes – when someone asks you to write a film score you reply, "D'you want it good, or d'you want it on Thursday?" Couldn't be more apposite in this case.'

He glanced surreptitiously at his watch and moved imperceptibly towards the door. Suddenly I realised the interview was over and I was being shown out. I got up hurriedly. God, perhaps I shouldn't have come at all? Perhaps I was overstating my position here. Maybe we hadn't even remotely been 'an item' as Claudes would put it, but surely . . . Oh well. I grabbed my bag and scuttled doorwards.

'There's still your London premiere, isn't there?' I said nervously as he held it open for me.

'At the Wigmore Hall, that's right.'

I wondered for a minute if he was going to offer me a ticket but he seemed miles away.

'Well, good luck,' I faltered.

He smiled. 'Thanks, I'll need it. I'll be a nervous wreck that night. I could really do without this can of worms on my plate, too.' He scratched his cheek anxiously and glanced across to the piano. 'I usually like to be completely free of any work at a premiere, so I can empty my mind.' He continued to gaze past me, then abruptly came to, shrugged. 'Oh well, can't be helped.'

'I should just bung any old thing down and tell them it's a masterpiece,' I joked, in an effort at levity.

He laughed. 'Nice idea, Livvy, but I'm afraid I'm far too analytical and self-obsessed to "bung". No, I won't be happy until these final closing bars lie down and behave.'

'You'll knock them into shape.'

'Let's hope so, otherwise the London music mafia will knock me into shape!'

I went past him and out towards the stairs. 'Oh, you don't have to come down—' I glanced back as he made to follow.

'It's OK,' he said easily, 'I need another pot of coffee and I feel horribly guilty if Maureen has to puff all the way up here. By the time she arrives at the door she has steam coming out of practically every orifice, except the coffee pot, of course, which is stone cold.'

I smiled, but couldn't think of anything to say in reply. I was drained of all wit and words suddenly, and talking to him had always been so easy. Finally we were at the bottom.

'Well, goodbye,' I turned.

'Goodbye, Olivia.'

He smiled, held the front door open for me, lightly touched my shoulder and kissed me warmly on both cheeks. Out I went.

The red front door shut fast behind me, and the sultry, heavy, mid-afternoon air wrapped itself around me like an electric blanket, hot and oppressive. I walked down the steps and wiped my forehead. God, why the hell did it have to be so hot all the time? This was supposed to be England, for crying out loud, not Madagascar. And talking of crying, I realised with alarm, there seemed to be a bit of a lump in my throat. As I walked up the cobbled street, I appeared to be gulping down a fresh supply of tears. God Almighty, I dragged a hanky from my pocket and blew my nose loudly, where was all this water coming from? Was I compensating for the drought? Doing my bit for the national crisis? I was so flaming overemotional at the moment, so permanently on the point of bursting into floods or punching a wall, and – well, I was supposed to be the happiest girl alive! What the hell was the matter with me?

Chapter Twenty-Three

Various factors combined to convince me to pay Nina Harrison a visit. Outright curiosity, for a start, together with a desire to tie up all the loose ends and to see that all the stories did indeed tally, but I could have resisted both of these impulses, were it not for the fact that Johnny's mood swings were beginning to rival mine. Now, I was allowed to be volatile – I was the wronged wife, for heaven's sake – but over the last few days, Johnny, from a standing start, was whipping up a performance that was positively Wagnerian in style. It certainly knocked my lettuce slapping into a cocked hat. He'd suddenly taken to getting up at dawn, wandering around the garden smoking furiously, and then at about nine o'clock, coming inside to pace the house. From that moment on, the telephone was rarely out of his hand and he'd negotiate urgently all morning, before slamming the receiver back in its cradle, punching the air, and giving an elated cry of, 'Yes!'

'Yes what?'

Yes, it transpired, we simply had to fly to Geneva to stay with some people we hardly knew but who he'd managed to track down, and if he got enough of a party together he'd even hire a private plane to get us there! I'd watch, sweaty-palmed and with a horrible sense of *déjà vu* and memories of Normandy ballooning trips, as more and more of these plans unfurled. I wondered in bewilderment where on earth the rocklike, calming influence of a few days ago had gone. The following morning I'd take him up a cup of tea in bed, only to find that Geneva was off and he didn't even want to get up. At all. Later that morning, though, I'd glance out of the kitchen window to see him still in his pyjamas, but careering around the garden with a squealing Claudia on his shoulders, shrieking with glee and terror as he threatened to throw her in the river. An hour or so later would find us at lunch, Claudia beaming up at her jocular Daddy, who for no apparent reason, would suddenly turn on her, yelling at her with such ferocity about the atrocity of her table manners that the poor child was forced to shrink down in her chair and peer at him from under her fringe, so strong was the stream of his invective.

At this yo-yoing continued I began to wish he'd go back to work, just to give myself time to think, to regroup, to consolidate, but as far as the office was concerned, he was still ostensibly in St-Jean-de-Luz and had time on his hands. Time to dig enthusiastically beside me in the flowerbeds, time to accompany me to Sainsbury's and commandeer my trolley, questioning loudly my need for quilted loo paper and other luxuries, just when I wanted to cruise those aisles in peace and give myself time to think.

But it was Mac and the boys who really took the full force of his boomerang style. Since Johnny had been back he'd been wont, at the end of a very warm day, to take a six-pack from the fridge and wander upstairs to the bathroom, where they'd all be sweltering away amongst the archaic plumbing. There he'd open a can or two with them, take a debrief on the day's work, and perching on the side of the bath, recall his own days as a student, when he too had worked on a building site, joking laddishly with them the while. Now, suddenly, puce in the face with rage, he was telling them their work was shoddy, that they had to redo the entire bathroom, strip the plaster work off, repin the boards underneath and start again.

'You can see great lumps and bumps in the wall, Livvy,' he stormed as he dragged me upstairs one evening to see. 'Look, even *you* can see that's hopeless, surely!'

I ignored the implicit insult. 'But we're going to tile it,' I soothed. 'They'll plaster it over and then the tiles will cover it. You won't even see it.'

'But I'll know it's there,' he hissed. 'And I want it all off!'

My builders were subdued. Johnny's return had been greeted with polite congratulations and a searching look from Lance which I'd ignored, followed by studied concentration, heads down, and a deep desire to finish the job and get the hell out as soon as possible. Any hopes of finishing that imminently, though, were dispelled by Johnny, who made it quite clear – politely or forcibly, depending on which way the wind took him – that much of the work done in his absence had been second rate. Clearly, he seethed, they'd hoped to get away with it, but that now that he was back and was once more 'the guv'nor', they wouldn't. Spiro whimpered and twisted his hat in his hands, Alf cowered, Lance looked angry and defiant and Mac was mutinous but tight-lipped, because he'd been a builder long enough to know that keeping shtumm was the only way to get paid.

As Claudia and I sat in the kitchen at breakfast one morning, listening to him berating them upstairs, I felt sad. On the whole I believed their work to be good and professional, but aside from this, I'd been close to these people. They were my friends. They'd helped me when Johnny hadn't been there and seen me through some very dark days. I clenched my hands under the table and felt a sense of betrayal as Johnny's irate voice resounded through the rafters.

'It's just incompetent!' he was saying. 'Just downright incompetent!'

Claudia was wide-eyed over her Coco Pops. 'Why is Daddy so cross?' she breathed.

'I don't know,' I replied. I pushed my chair back and got up. 'But I intend to find out.'

I may have sounded determined as I snatched my car keys from the dresser and grabbed my bag, but as I went into the sitting room to find the A to Z, it was with a thudding heart. I knew Nina Harrison's address off by heart, but as I flipped through the pages to find the route, my hands were shaking. You see, for the first time since Johnny's return, it occurred to me to wonder if the object of his affections had rejected him.

Clarendon Road wasn't hard to find. Plenty of my friends had lived in the Finchley, Highgate area, premarriage, and as I drove around the quaint little back streets, I thought what happy times I'd had here in my single days, tipsy and shrieking with laughter in a girl-friend's basement kitchen, a crowd of us cooking spaghetti bolognese and talking long into the night. In fact, if I remembered rightly, Imogen used to have a flat right – here. I went past her old flat, peering into the familiar windows, then turned down another familiar side street, and left into a mews. I purred along, and drew up slowly, right opposite number 32. I checked my scrap of paper. Yes, 32, next door to a garage Johnny had said. I gazed out of the window. And yes, there it was. Not a tacky, filling-station-type of garage, though, more of a discreet workshop affair, with double barn doors painted bottle green, and opening on to a small forecourt with a couple of classy vintage cars parked outside.

A silver-haired, narrow-faced man with glasses looked up from polishing a hubcap as I got out of my car. He straightened up and wiped his hands on a rag. It was a quiet, dead-end street so I imagined any visitor was something of a diversion. As I locked my door I felt his eyes on me and I wondered if he was just a mechanic or indeed Bob, the father. Either way I ignored him as I walked confidently across the street, glancing up at a rather dear little mews house, painted pink with a green door to match the garage beside it, with window boxes and pots spilling over with bright red geraniums. I reached the door and stared nervously at the bell. 32A or 32B. Oh help, which one was she? I couldn't remember. Suddenly I realised the silver-haired man was behind me.

'Can I help?' in a friendly voice.

I turned. I knew at once it was her father. I managed a smile. 'Oh, well, I was looking for Nina actually.'

'Ah, you want the top flat then. We're down below in the servants quarters where we belong.' He chuckled. 'Hang about, I'll see if she's around. Sheila!' He rapped his oily knuckles on a downstairs window.

A net curtain parted and a middle-aged woman appeared between the Fairy Liquid bottle and a spider plant. She was attractive in a faded blonde sort of way, with good bones and pale hair coiled neatly round her scalp, secured with gold hairpins.

'What?'

'Is Nina about?' he yelled.

She shook her head and smiled, indicating by a wave of dithering hands in the air that she couldn't hear a thing. 'Hang on,' she called. 'I'll come out.'

'Deaf as a post,' he grinned. 'Although I always maintain it's selective. She can hear the postman arriving with her new Freemans catalogue halfway down the street!'

I groaned inwardly. Oh God, did we have to get the whole family involved here? Why on earth had I come? In fact, why didn't I just slip away now and forget all about it?

The green door opened and the woman peered around. She was wearing a housecoat and Dr Scholl sandals, and I spotted a wheelchair behind her in the hall.

'This lass has come to see Nina,' explained Bob with a sideways nod at me.

'Oooh, has she now?' she said with evident interest, coming more squarely into the doorway. 'Well, she should be up there, luv. Is she expecting you?'

'Um, well not exactly.' I hesitated. They gazed expectantly at me. 'I'm – I'm a parent, from school. From – her school.'

She beamed. 'Oh well, she'll be pleased to see you, I know she will. She's always keen to get involved with the kiddies, isn't she, Bob? Have you tried the bell?'

'No, I—' haven't had a chance, I wanted to say through gritted teeth, but stopped short of saying anything at all as I heard a clattering down the stairs behind her. Pink, fluffy slippers appeared, then nylon encased legs, a floral skirt, and then Nina was beside her mother in the communal hall. She looked tired, dishevelled and unmade up. Her face was very pale. As she stared at me, her right hand slowly reached out and gripped the banister rail tight.

'What d'you want?'

Her parents caught the tone of her voice and turned quickly. They glanced at her, then back at me. As they did, I could see the penny making its slippery way down and, as it dropped, so did their smiles. Her mother's face sagged.

'Well, I – I wanted to talk to you,' I faltered nervously. I flushed, from nerves, sure, but actually, from anger too. Jesus, who was the wronged party around here? Why should I be feeling guilty? Surely the aggressive, defensive tone should be mine, not hers? Who exactly was the floozie here, hmm? Nina's eyes dropped to the lino floor, almost, I thought, in recognition of this. She nodded.

'You'd better come up.'

'Nina, d'you want me to—' her mother shot out an anxious hand. Nina shook it off her arm.

'No, Mum, I'll be fine.'

They both watched silently as I followed their daughter upstairs, and as I turned at the top, I saw the man put an arm around his wife's shoulders.

A separate front door opened on to a tiny hallway with a night storage heater and not much else, which in turn issued on to a light, airy sitting room. I followed Nina through and realised it stretched the length of the flat – which wasn't large – with two sash windows on to the street. Coir matting covered the floor and a pair of identical white sofas with rather worn, washable damask covers stood either side of a wooden fireplace. Oatmeal hessian curtains hung at the windows from black, wrought-iron poles and on the white walls or on shelves, driftwood collages, twiggy sculptures and large church candles perched. All was cream, all was neutral, all was very safe and very Habitat. And how unlike my own eclectic, cluttered chintzy home, I thought, glancing around, full of clashing colours and mistakes, but at least they were my mistakes and not Terence Conran's. I tried to imagine Johnny here, full length on one of those creamy sofas, reading the Sunday papers, picking his nose, swigging a beer. Suddenly, I realised I could. Yes, why not? Totally at home, no doubt, his feet on that ethnic wooden coffee table. Fury rose and it strengthened my resolve.

'So this is it,' I sneered. 'The love nest.'

'Would you like a cup of coffee?' she asked, wrong-footing me.

I stared. 'Um, yes, all right,' I muttered. I'd rather expected a defiant stare back.

I followed her into a little white galley kitchen, the paint peeling slightly on the walls, and watched as she fiddled about making real percolated coffee, something we never bothered with at home. I didn't think Johnny liked it. I glanced at the efficient, stainless-steel kitchen. Clearly his tastes had changed. Then I studied her in the silence. Her hair was mussed and flat on one side and there were pillow marks on her cheek. I realised she'd probably been lying on the bed. I used to do a lot of that, too.

'I don't know why I'm surprised,' she said suddenly, snipping the top off a gold foil coffee bag. 'I half expected you to come every day.'

I startled. 'Really? Why?'

She shrugged. 'To fit the jigsaw together, I suppose. Find out about the other side of the story. After all, I came to see you.'

'You did,' I said, remembering how Mac had described her sitting on my terrace. 'And I never found out why.'

She shrugged again. 'An impulse, which I didn't have the nerve to repeat. I wanted to present my case, I think.'

'Which is?'

She turned and handed me a mug. Her eyes were very blue, but pale, like a duck's egg, fringed with blonde lashes. 'Look, why don't you tell me why you've come here, first? Something clearly brought you, and then we can take it from there, eh?'

It was said gently, but I found the 'eh?' patronising. None

the less I nodded and followed her back into the sitting room, thinking that even if I looked compliant, I wasn't bloody feeling it. Oh no, I was thinking fast. In the first place I wasn't going to tell her what a mess Johnny was and how worried I was about him, and I wasn't going to enquire as to whether she knew what was driving his erratic behaviour either, and whether it stemmed from her. No no, I could box a bit cleverer than that. I perched on the edge of a sofa as she bustled about getting mats for the mugs. She still had her ghastly fluffy slippers on and I just knew I'd have kicked those off the moment I'd heard the door. Well, actually I wouldn't have bought them in the first place; how could Johnny bear to look at them? Did she slop around in them all day? They closed neatly together on the coir matting as she perched opposite me. Her face was expectant. I took a deep breath.

'Johnny says – well, he says he left you because he missed me too much. He says he made a mistake and that he should never have gone in the first place, that it was a madness that should never have happened. He's adamant he loves me more than ever now, but I need to know that for sure. I need to know you're out of our lives for good.'

The pain this gave her made her catch her breath, but I didn't care. I'd caught my breath a few times recently too. She gripped her cup, glanced down at the carpet. Presently she nodded.

'Yes, he left me because he missed you.' She raised her eyes. 'And I dare say he loves you above me. There now.' She smiled. 'Is that what you wanted to hear?'

She gazed at me with her steady baby blues, and it seemed to me she was mocking me. I hesitated. Somehow I'd expected her to deny it, say that he'd only returned to me through feelings of guilt, of marital duty.

413

'Well, obviously I came to get the truth.'

'The truth.' She smiled again, eyes still on mine. She shook her head slowly. 'Well, I'll answer any questions you care to ask truthfully, but what about the ones you don't know how to ask? What about them?'

I stared. 'I . . . don't know what you mean.'

'No. You don't. How could you? And actually, it doesn't matter. You're right, all that matters is that he left me to go back to you.' She picked up a glass ashtray from the table beside her, turned it around in her hands thoughtfully. 'Nothing else matters now.'

I licked my lips, confused. Tried a different tack. 'OK – so, if that's all that matters, why did you come and see me that night?'

She sighed and put the ashtray down. 'Because I could feel him going. I could feel him slipping away. I wanted to explain to you – to appeal to you, really – try to make you understand why I needed him so much. It was a last, desperate attempt to hold on, I suppose.'

'To appeal to *me*? But why me, for Christ's sake. God, I – I probably would have socked you in the teeth!'

Not for the first time her eyes flitted back to the little table where she'd replaced the ashtray, darting, involuntarily almost, to a large black and white portrait photograph in a silver frame. I realised with a start that it was a picture of Johnny as a baby, dressed in a sailor suit. It was very similar to one that Angie had given me. Had Angie given it to her? Was it some sort of warped, setting-up-home present? I reached across.

'Where on earth did you . . .?' I studied it. 'It's Johnny, isn't it?'

'No, it's not Johnny. Everyone says that, but it's not.'

As I stared I felt the blood drain from my face. Suddenly

I dropped it. It clattered down on to the carpet, still face up. I gazed down. No, it wasn't Johnny. It was too modern a pose. It was very like him, but – it was his son. I put my hand to my eyes. Covered them so as not to see.

'Oh God.'

'That's what I came to tell you,' she said quietly, reaching forward and picking it up. 'Johnny wouldn't, couldn't, but I felt you should know.'

I had a moment of complete light-headed nausea. For a second, I thought I was going to pass out. They had a son. Johnny had a son.

'I wanted you to know I wasn't just some two-bit tart he'd picked up, that I was the mother of his child too.'

Doesn't stop you being a tart, I thought fiercely. Plenty of mistresses have illegitimate children. But my head was spinning now, full of unanswered questions. The mother of his child. Jesus.

'How – how old is he?' I whispered, staring blankly at the photo again that she'd set back on the table. God, so like Johnny – that nose, those eyes. The smile. The smile destroyed me.

'Nine months.'

'Nine—' My eyes shot back to her. 'But he's only been with you for—'

'Six years.'

My mouth dried. 'Six years!'

She nodded. 'But I've known him a lot longer than that.'

'But how! How can you have!' I blurted out, clenching my fists and realising my voice was shrill and uncontrolled and not at all as I'd intended, but I was shaken to the core.

'Because every Saturday for years, he used to come here with his father, tinkering with cars with Dad. I've known him since I was about twelve, when Oliver gave him his first car, in fact. He must have been – ooh, about seventeen.'

'Seventeen!' I gasped. 'You knew him – shit!' I got up and walked quickly over to the window, gripping the sill hard.

'My parents knew Oliver very well. He brought all his cars here to be serviced, you see, took Dad's advice whenever he bought a new one too. They used to travel all over the country together, to view them.'

'But – but Johnny told me –' I swung round – 'he told me he met you at an open day. At the school, he said—'

'Yes, well, he would, wouldn't he?' she interrupted without a hint of irony. 'Of course he would. He didn't want you to know, did he? Didn't want you to discover he'd been living a secret life for years, had a mistress. What husband would? You might have been a mite upset had you known he came here most Wednesdays, had a chat with Dad and a cup of tea with Mum, before nipping up here and making love to me. I dare say he also didn't mention the fact that last year I gave birth to a son. Of course he didn't!'

My heart was hammering; I couldn't think straight. My God, where did this leave me? And Claudia too, with a brother? I felt sick.

'Where is he?' I whispered, glancing nervously about, half expecting a small blond head to pop up behind a sofa. I didn't want to see him. Ever.

'Peter? He's downstairs with Mum. She has him every morning. Usually I'm teaching, but she still has him for me in the holidays. It gives me a bit of a break.'

'Convenient,' I muttered drily.

'Well, yes, I suppose so, but it's also fairly essential. We all need a break from him now and again. Peter's got cerebral palsy.'

I stared, shocked. 'Oh! God, isn't that – serious?'

'Very. Although some kids are not too badly affected. But Peter's very ill. Very – severe.' She swallowed and her eyes filled.

I gazed. 'I'm . . . sorry.' I was. Confused and angry and shocked as I was, I could still feel sorrow for a handicapped child.

'My God – Johnny!' My hand clutched my mouth. 'How did he—'

She nodded. 'Devastated. Totally devastated. We only found out when Peter was six months old. It wasn't diagnosed until then. That's when he moved in with me.'

I gazed at her incredulously. 'You mean – that's when he decided to leave me? When he heard the child was sick?'

'Yes, he said he couldn't leave me alone with him then. We'd never intended to live together, you see. I'd always known he loved you much more, and I'd always known I was just a harmless diversion, a mistress, and for a while, it suited me. I wasn't unhappy with that. He was great fun and we always had a lark, a good roll in the sack, but I'd always known he was beyond me, totally out of my reach. I thought I was lucky to have him as a lover, but I never thought long term. I'd always assumed that in time I'd marry someone else, someone from my own sort of background. But then Peter came along.'

'But couldn't you have had an abortion?'

'I could, but I didn't want one. Johnny wanted me to, of course. He was horrified when I told him I was pregnant, but I assured him I'd be no bother. I wasn't trying to trap him or anything. I promised I'd have absolutely no contact with him ever again, and I didn't want any money either, said I'd never intrude on his life in any way, that once the baby was born he wouldn't see me for dust. Well, he wasn't happy about it, of course he wasn't, but what could he do? I was absolutely determined to keep it.' She sipped her coffee, two hands cradling the mug. They were trembling.

'Well,' she whispered, gazing at the carpet, 'Peter was born, and Johnny sent some flowers to the hospital, he didn't come to see us, but that was fine, I didn't expect him to. Then a few months later I had this awful shock. Peter had been having all sorts of tests, routine they said, and only because he didn't seem quite as advanced as other babies of that age, but then the paediatrician at the hospital called me in and gave me this terrible diagnosis. Mum was with me, and when we got home, sobbing our eyes out, she persuaded me to tell Johnny, said it was only right; that it was unfair to keep it from him. Well, I didn't want to, but she insisted, and I was in a hell of a state, so I rang him at work.' She gulped. Brought her eyes up from the carpet to meet mine. 'I couldn't believe it. Twenty minutes later a black cab drew up and he was on my doorstep, his face as white as a sheet, and when Dad let him in, he cried. I'll never forget it. I came downstairs and he just stood there in the hall, leaning against the wall, the tears streaming down his face. We all cried then. We came up here, Mum, Dad, Johnny and me, and we sobbed. Then after a bit Johnny got all forceful and said he wanted to live with me, said he couldn't possibly leave me with a disabled child, that he wanted to share the responsibility. He said it was all his fault and we'd get through this together, bring him up together. We were all astounded, of course, and Mum and I both said don't be ridiculous, what about you and Claudia, and Dad said it was an outstanding offer but one he'd regret later so totally out of the question. We were all astonished. But Johnny kept on, he wouldn't drop it, kept insisting he was moving in. Well, Dad got cross in the end and said, "No – listen, lad, it's just not practical." I can hear him now. "You've already got a family," he said. "You can't just leave one for another, and our Nina here's a grown woman. She knew what she was getting into when she had the baby." Then he held out his hand to Johnny and said that most men would run a mile from an illegitimate baby, let alone a disabled one, and he appreciated the gesture.' She gulped. 'But Johnny wouldn't shake his hand. He said it wasn't a gesture. He was adamant. Said he wanted to be involved, fully involved, and swore he'd devote his life to Peter and me. We were staggered, of course, but all so grief-stricken and confused, especially coming on top of Martin.'

'Hang on,' I said, bewildered. 'Who's Martin?'

'My brother. He's fourteen now, but he's been in a wheelchair all his life, so it seemed like history repeating itself. Anyway, we let Johnny have his say and thought that in the cold light of day he'd probably change his mind, but later that night he arrived, with all his bags, ready to move in, but still as white as a sheet, as if he'd seen a ghost.'

In a flash that night came back to me. The night he'd left me. Is it serious? I'd asked, crouched down amongst my paint pots by the front door in the hall. 'It wasn't,' he'd replied, ashen-faced and sweeping past me with his suit-case, 'was never meant to be . . . but now . . . yes.'

'Anyway,' Nina went on, 'I said, "Oh, don't be a fool, Johnny. Go home, go back to Olivia, I'm going to give up teaching and look after Peter full time. You don't need to worry about me," but he wouldn't have it. He persuaded me to take the job at St Luke's—'

'Yes – How the hell did you end up there? At Claudia's school!'

'That was Johnny. He got me the job. The Montessori I'd been teaching at closed down and reasonably-paid private

419

nursery jobs are like gold dust in London. He made a few discreet inquiries and found out that they were looking for someone in the nursery. At first he didn't tell me Claudia was there and I felt really terrible when I found out, but Johnny said it was fine. You know how he does, with that winning smile of his – "It's fine, Nina, don't worry about it! Claudia's going up to the senior school soon, and anyway, no one will make the connection. No one will ever know who you are." ' She grimaced. 'Naïve, of course.'

'Just a bit!' I exploded. 'I found out on bloody day one! Along with the rest of the world!'

'I know, and I knew you would, but you know Johnny. Likes to think he's Mr Fixit, Mr Control Freak.'

I knew Johnny. Did I know Johnny? No I didn't recognise this man. This wasn't the man I married.

'Second rate,' I muttered, moving unsteadily back to the sofa and perching shakily on the edge. 'This is second-rate stuff. Sneaking around, betraying his wife – go on, do it, Nina, take the job. Olivia will never find out.' I felt sick.

She leant forward. 'Ah, but Johnny would say he was being honourable. He'd say he was honouring his commitment to us.'

'But what about his commitment to me!' I shrieked.

'I know, I know.' She gazed down.

The blood rushed to my head. 'And you didn't even bloody want him!'

'Oh yes I did!' she said sharply, jerking her head up. 'I just never thought I'd have him, that's the difference. I'd told myself for years it was unthinkable. Unimaginable. What – Johnny McFarllen? *The* Johnny McFarllen? The one I'd gaped at and admired for years, run to the window to catch a glimpse of since I was a child, breathing on to the glass to see him draw up beside his father in the convertible

Lagonda? Blond, gorgeous, languid, laughing Johnny, with his lovely lazy, sexy smile, Johnny from the huge house, from that big, powerful family, with all that wealth, that opulence, that joy? Oh no,' she shook her head vehemently, 'it wouldn't be true to say I didn't *want* him, I just never believed it possible before.'

'Until you trapped him with a disabled child,' I snapped.

'I told you,' she said patiently, 'I didn't want him to stay. I told him to go home, we all did. Then when he wouldn't, when he moved in – well, I told myself not to fall in love with him. Told myself it wouldn't last, that he'd be gone, but how could I help myself?' Her eyes appealed to me. They were very round, the blue exactly in the centre. 'You know how he is, how he lights up even the most dismal, the most mediocre of lives – well, think what he did to mine!' She swung her arm around. 'Look at me, look at this place! I thought I'd died and gone to heaven, thought I was walking on air!' Her pale eyes were bright with emotion now, sparkling. She lowered them to her mug.

'But then, as the weeks went by, and living together in this cramped flat with Peter screaming all hours of the night, needing constant attention and massaging, and my parents running up and down the stairs to help – well.' She grimaced. 'You can imagine. He'd sacrificed himself at the altar of "care" and hadn't realised he wasn't sacrificial material. He thought he'd been "called", thought it was his duty or something equally crappy – God's will if you like – but he couldn't do it. And if anything,' she said sadly, 'he'd made it worse. His fine gesture had worsened the situation.'

'Why?'

'Because I became infatuated with him, and previously I'd never allowed myself to do that. But he was with me every moment of the day now, you see, every night. I couldn't help it. He could see it too – my obsession. I couldn't hide it.' She gulped and picked at some ancient pink nail varnish on her fingernail. 'About a month ago, after Claudia went missing, and after he'd seen you at the concert with someone else, I felt him slipping away. Like sand through my fingers.' She stopped picking and clasped her hands tight. 'I panicked. And the more I tried not to, the worse it became. I've always had a nervous, respiratory thing, a bit like asthma, and when I'm worked up I can hardly breathe. It's all psychosomatic, of course – panic attacks they're sometimes called – but I had to admit myself to hospital to be put on breathing apparatus. Well, what with Peter being so ill, Johnny thought it was outrageous, total histrionics, especially when I strolled out a couple of hours later, right as rain. He thought it was a ruse, thought I was attention-seeking.' She shook her head sadly. 'But I wasn't, that's how it's always been with me. How anxiety takes me. And then there were the notes.'

'Yes, he said . . .'

She reached under the coffee table to a magazine shelf below and took out an old *Cosmopolitan*. She opened it and handed me two pieces of scruffy paper. They'd been torn out of a cheap, ring-bound notebook, and on the top one, in scrawled, capital letters was written: 'KEEP YOUR MOUTH SHUT OR THE KID GETS IT.' The second one read, 'GOOD GIRL. YOU KEEP QUIET.'

I read them again, frowned, then raised my eyebrows at her. She shrugged.

'I have no idea. Dad's convinced it's one of his mechanics. We found out he'd been involved in passing on some cannabis to teenagers and Dad had to sack him. I occasionally work downstairs in the office, and Dad thinks this guy may have thought I overheard him doing a deal one day on his mobile phone.' She gave a wry smile. 'Johnny's convinced I wrote them to myself, though; thinks it was some kind of neurotic attempt to keep him. You know – oh gosh, I've got a disabled son and his life's being threatened. Johnny you'll *have* to stay now.'

'But you didn't.'

She shook her head sadly. 'No. I didn't.'

'And was this what you came to tell me? That night when you sat on my terrace?'

'No, this hadn't happened then. I came to tell you about Peter, and about how long the affair had been going on. I wanted you to understand where I was coming from. Why I needed Johnny so badly. That I wasn't just some scheming opportunist who'd briefly got her claws into someone else's man, some ghastly husband-snatcher.'

I regarded her for a moment clutching her mug, in her pink slippers, with her pale, unmade-up face and her round blue eyes. I cleared my throat.

'But you are, Nina. That's exactly what you are. Because in the beginning that's precisely how it was. Just a bit of fun, a roll in the sack, with someone else's husband. Oh, you'd never met her, the wife, but sod it, who cares? Some up-tight rich bitch who was probably as frigid as hell and deserved all she got, and anyway, you'd known *him* all your life, hankered after him for years, so somehow, it seemed all right. Somehow, it seemed justifiable. But when the shit began to hit the fan, when the "fun" had some terrible repercussions and you gave birth to a disabled child, you began to think you were entitled to some dignity. Well, I don't think so. You're still the same person, Nina, all that's changed is your situation. You've gone from being a fun-loving mistress to a single mother, only your task as a mother is harder than most. I do pity you, Nina, if pity's

423

what you're after, but funnily enough,' I gave a shaky little smile and reached down for my bag, 'I pity me and my daughter more.' I swung the strap over my shoulder and gripped it hard. I made myself look at her, stared at her coldly, but her eyes couldn't meet mine. They fled to the floor. After a bit, I stood up, turned, and made my way to the door.

'Are you going to tell him we've had this conversation?' she said in a small voice.

I paused, leant against the door frame for a moment. For support. 'I don't know,' I replied without turning round. 'To be honest, Nina, I don't know what I'm going to do.'

And with that I left the flat.

Chapter Twenty-Four

I drove home in turmoil, my mind racing. The heavy, oppressive weather had finally broken while I'd been in the flat, and a fierce storm had erupted overhead. The windscreen wipers danced at top speed in a manic fashion as my brain cells, at an equally accelerated rate, attempted to clear the chaos in my mind. As I tore perilously around the Finchley back streets, heading blindly for the M1, my insides heaved with revulsion. A love child. A six-year relationship. Not a quick fling with a local girl he'd picked up on a whim since we'd moved house, but a long-running affair with someone he'd known since he was a child. Someone he'd been seeing when we lived in London, sneaking out to sleep with from the office. A mistress – yes, that was the word, that was her job description – who'd been a huge part of his life, had had a role in his life, almost as large as mine, for God's sake, and for a hell of a long time.

Gripping the wheel tightly and totally ambushed by tears, I swerved violently to avoid a lorry as I careered on to the motorway. But how much did this really change things? I thought wildly, wiping the tears desperately with the back of my hand. How much did it actually matter? A lot, my head suggested grimly, but my heart was set on damage limitation. Not necessarily all that much, it declared, defiantly. After all, there was no rule book to consult here, no scale at which one's emotions were deemed to be stretched to the limit and must legitimately snap. This was a purely personal thing. How much could I take? How much could I, Olivia McFarllen, put up with? Or, to put it another way – I squared my shoulders – yes, how strong was I, surely?

Now some women, I was sure, couldn't take adultery in any denomination. One whiff of Chanel on the pinstriped suit and they'd be off, a child under each arm, divorce petition clenched between the teeth, Harvey Nichols account right up to the limit, heading for those wide open spaces. Some, on the other hand, having suspected for years, might quietly have got used to the idea. Got used to all those late meetings and seemingly needless overnight stays in provincial hotels, but having taken a long hard look at their children, at the roof over their heads, at the clothes in the cupboards, the food in the fridge, had decided – Christ, he's only a man, for heaven's sake. What d'you expect? At least he can fix the boiler; at least his armpits don't gush too much; at least he makes good money and, let's face it, if it wasn't him it would be some other bugger, so let's hammer out some sort of *modus vivendi* here, shall we? Let's be a big girl and take it in our stride. I gripped the wheel tight, sniffed hard and let out a long, shaky breath. It all came down to personal choice really: how humiliated and betrayed was one prepared to be to preserve one's world, and how much extracurricular sex was one prepared, metaphorically, to swallow?

Now Nina, no doubt, was hoping I couldn't swallow this at all. She was hoping I'd gag on this latest sensational dollop, spit it out – and Johnny with it – right back on to her plate, where quick as a flash, she'd pick it up and run with it. She was no doubt hoping our conversation had persuaded me he was a cad of the highest order and was, even now, kicking off her fluffy slippers, rolling on her nylons and preparing to glide seamlessly back into his life to pick up the pieces. I gripped the wheel fiercely. Well, we'd see about that.

I realised, though, still gulping down the tears, that on a less emotional level, if I was going to take this on the chin, I needed to deal with the practicalities. Peter, for instance, I caught my breath. Christ, Peter. How much of an impact would he make on mine and Claudia's lives? Well – no more than he had up to now, surely? I thought desperately. I mean, I'd *know* about him, be aware of his existence, but I'd never have to see him, and Nina was clearly determined to be totally self-sufficient. She didn't seem the type to arrive in her clogs on our doorstep, with Peter wrapped in a shawl, demanding ten thousand a year and the right to the McFarllen surname, so in actual fact, what difference did this new revelation make? Oh, it made me hysterical and upset, I knew that from the amount of tissues I was getting through, and the number of stares I was getting from lorry drivers who peered curiously down from their cabs at this pitiful woman dissolving behind her wheel, chucking lighted cigarette butts out of the window every few minutes, but temporary hysteria aside, precisely how torn apart was I going to be on a long-term basis? Just how traumatised was I?

I slowed down a bit and sank back in my seat. The rain was abating and I turned the windscreen wipers down from manic to relatively sober. As I wiped the mascara from under my eyes with a shaky finger I noticed that the tears were drying up slightly too. Yes, now that the storm was over, I could surely assess this in a rational manner. Assess whether or not I'd actually taken so much already that this was just another well-aimed blow that had stunned, but not entirely knocked me for six. A body blow, but nothing critical.

Ten minutes later, with thoughts still jostling furiously for position in my mind, I pulled up in my drive and instantly realised my mistake. God, how stupid! Why on earth had I come straight home? Why on earth had I raced, instinctively, back here when what I really needed was time to think, hours – days in fact – to let this sink in? Now I literally had minutes before I had to confront it all, confront Johnny.

Feeling hot and panicky I fumbled for the ignition, quickly started the car again, and was about to plunge it into reverse and charge out backwards – when I realised it was too late. I'd been seen. Johnny was actually in the drive and was, even now, walking towards my car at the same time as yelling something furiously over his shoulder to Claudia, who was running after him in floods of tears. As I turned off the ignition and slowly opened my door, I spotted my mother and Howard in the porch, looking distinctly shaken, and slinking, heads down, towards their car.

I got out. 'What's going on?'

Howard and my mother stopped, mid-slink, and Mum came scuttling towards me.

'Oh darling, this is all my fault,' she breathed, putting an anxious hand on my arm. 'We just popped round, you see, on an impulse, to see you all together again, and we had a lovely cup of tea in the new kitchen with Johnny and Claudia, but then stupidly, well, I went and put my foot in it, just as we were leaving.'

'What d'you mean?'

'Well, I brought up the business of the schools,' she

hissed, wide-eyed. 'You know, the boarding business. I gather Johnny didn't know.'

Her face betrayed nothing, but one never knew with Mum. Never quite knew if she'd been deliberately meddling.

'No, it's out of the question!' Johnny was saying, shaking Claudia's pleading hand off his arm as he strode towards me. 'God, this is ridiculous, Livvy. I don't know why you said you'd even consider it! There's no question of her going away, especially now I'm back!'

'Why, especially now you're back?' I asked calmly.

He stopped in front of me. 'Well, I can see that the two of you here on your own might have seemed a bit quiet, a bit lacking in colour, but now that I'm back, well, we're a family again!'

'Ah. So you make all the difference?'

'I didn't mean it to sound as arrogant as that,' he spluttered, 'but I certainly make *some* difference to home life, surely?'

'It's got nothing to do with that!' sobbed Claudia hysterically. 'I wanted to go away before, I've always wanted to go, even when you were here, before you went! And Mum said I could, didn't you, Mum?'

'I said we'd discuss it,' I said quietly. 'And that's what we will do, but not here, not now, not screaming like banshees in the middle of the drive in front of Granny and Howard.'

I turned to Howard, who was looking distinctly embarrassed. I managed a smile. 'Howard, what must you think of us?'

'I think you have a mighty characterful daughter who knows her own mind,' he said, scratching his chin. 'But I also think it's not our place to get involved. Come now, Sylvia, we'll be on our way.' He held out his arm to Mum, who took it hastily. I walked them to their car.

'Absolutely right,' muttered Johnny in a low voice, coming up behind me. 'Mind your own bloody business.'

Mum and Howard were very definitely in their seats at this point, so didn't hear, but I did. I waved them off, then turned slowly. My hands were clenched by my sides.

'Johnny, he might have heard you.'

He shrugged. 'So what? It isn't any of his bloody business, just as it isn't any of his bloody business how "characterful" my daughter is, either. God – some jumped-up, overweight, ee-by-gum widower from Yorkshire who specialises in bladder problems telling me how I should educate my child? Jesus! And your mother! Honestly, Liv, what a joke!'

'What?'

'Well, I mean those clothes! Mutton dressed as lamb, or what? I hardly recognised her! I mean, turquoise trousers, for heaven's sake, and beads, and her hair!'

'I think she looks lovely!' blurted Claudia, her voice cracking, her pale face stained with tears. 'And we like Howard too, don't we, Mum?'

I turned to her and took her shoulders. 'Darling, go upstairs, wash your face and have a lie-down on your bed. I'll be up in a minute.'

'But—'

'Now, Claudia.' I gazed down at her and she caught my eye and the tone of my voice. With a last defiant glare at her father she brushed past us, marched in, and slammed the front door behind her.

'You must admit, my love,' laughed Johnny, moving to put an arm round my shoulders, 'they don't exactly wear their new arrangement well, do they? I mean, with the best will in the world it's hardly love's young dream, is it? Christ, I found the whole thing positively embarrassing, and

I wished to God you'd been here. When they were billing and cooing and holding hands at the kitchen table, I didn't know where to look!' He chuckled and made to lead me back to the house. 'Ah well, you know what they say, there's no fool like an old fool, but I mean – what exactly is the setup there? I think we should know, shouldn't we, if only for Claudia's sake? Are they living together or something crass?'

I shook his arm off and backed away.

'Johnny, why didn't you tell me you had a son?'

He turned, stared at me. Then he took a step back. I watched him visibly pale. 'You know.'

'Yes, I went to see Nina. She told me.'

His arms came up from his sides, then flopped down limply in a gesture of defeat. His knees apparently wouldn't hold him any longer, because he slumped back on the bonnet of my car. He rubbed his eyes with a shaky hand.

'Livvy, I'd have done anything to have spared you this.'

'So it appears. Like lying through your teeth for years.' I knew I was trembling, but I felt a terrible clenched calmness too.

'Look, it's not that I was never going to tell you,' he said desperately. 'I was, honestly I was, and I've been building up to it. I knew if I came back you had to know, and I was going to tell you – this week, in fact. That's why I've been so upset these past few days. I keep trying to tell you, I've been on the point of it so many times, but it's so hard – *so* hard!'

'Not as hard as it is for me, though, surely, Johnny? Please don't ask me to pity you too. As I told your girlfriend earlier, I'm afraid I'm claiming the monopoly in that department, because nobody, Johnny, not you, not your mistress, not anyone, has taken quite as much shit as I have.'

'Except . . . perhaps my sick son.'

'That's out of my jurisdiction. And Godlike and all-controlling though you most surely think you are, for once, it's out of yours too.'

'Divine retribution,' he muttered, 'for all my mistakes.'

'I doubt it. I doubt if He's that interested in you, particularly since you can't even call them sins. No, Peter's affliction was caused by casual, careless, unprotected sex, together with the law of averages governing the amount of oxygen reaching babies at birth. It was bad luck.'

His face contorted with pain at this. He clenched his fists, rapped his knuckles on his forehead. 'I've tried so hard to make it up to him, to do the honourable thing! I went back, and it was only for the child! I went back! I was prepared to sacrifice everything, I—'

'Oh, don't give me all that honour-and-duty crap, Johnny,' I snapped furiously. 'Was it honourable to poke the garage owner's daughter in the first place? Was it honourable to get her up the duff when you had a wife and child of your own at home? Hmm?'

He gazed at the gravel, couldn't look at me. I stared at that troubled blond head that I'd loved so much, stroked so often, and my heart heaved. Finally he looked up piteously.

'I'll make it up to you, Livvy.'

'Oh really? In what way?'

'I'll never see her again, never see either of them again.'

'That seems a little harsh, particularly in Peter's case. It's all or nothing with you, isn't it, Johnny?'

His blue eyes widened, and the first truth for a long while fell from his lips.

'I don't know how else to be.'

I nodded. 'I know.' I regarded him silently. 'Pack a bag, Johnny.'

'What?' he said, startled.

'You heard me. Pack a bag. I really don't think I can live with you any more. I can't live with your wholeheartedness, your honour, your sense of duty, nor your integrity. I just can't do it.'

With that I turned on my heel, and left him standing, staring after me as I walked into the house.

I went on through the hall, up the stairs and across the landing to Claudia's bedroom. I peeped around the door. She was lying on her side on her bed, fast asleep, as I knew she would be. Sleep had always been her defence mechanism for any sort of upset or trauma. I closed the door softly and went downstairs, turning smartly right at the bottom and going out of the back door so as not to encounter Johnny, then on down to the potting shed.

As I let myself into the cool, dark space, shutting the door behind me, I leant back on it and let out a long shaky, breath. My God. What had I done? I blinked into the woody gloom. Well, I'd sent him packing, that's what I'd done. I'd known instinctively, in those few moments as I stood there facing him, that I simply couldn't take any more. Didn't want to either. Didn't want him in my life. My eyes widened in the darkness, boggling at this revelation. God, had I really admitted that? I was so startled my hand went to my mouth. Surely in the car just now, I'd been so convinced I could overcome it all, could overlook everything . . . I lowered my hand. But I couldn't. I shook my head in bewilderment. Extraordinary. All this time, all that anguish and heartache and now, suddenly, right in the middle of swallowing the crap just as fast as he could shovel it in – I'd gagged.

After a moment I sat down shakily at the potting bench. Peered into my seed trays. Yes, those antirrhinums were getting a bit leggy. Could do with pricking out. I noticed my hands were trembling as I went about my business, but I also knew that I was quite clear about what I'd done. That I felt lucid and calm. And it was comforting to know that I could quite easily spend the next couple of hours in here and not have to witness his departure.

When I did emerge, a while later, he had indeed gone. To her, I wondered, as I crept around the house? Who cares? At that moment I really didn't; I just wanted to be on my own. Alone with Claudia. As I went upstairs to find her, it occurred to me that I might sell this house. I paused for a moment on the stairs. Stroked the banister, but not regretfully. Oh, I'd loved it in the beginning, we'd both loved it, thought of it as a forever place, but he'd been living a lie in it even then. That soured everything, and I wasn't sure I wanted it any more. On an emotional level too much had gone on under its roof, too many unhappy memories, but on a practical level too, it was too big for us. We'd need something smaller now, the two of us. A cottage maybe, near that school that I knew Claudia was really keen on, but hadn't mentioned because she thought it was too far away. The one on the cliffs in Dorset, with the sea beating against the rocks below, and the ponies in the paddocks above. I'd found the prospectus hidden under her bed, well thumbed and with 'Cool!' scrawled all over it. She'd thrive there, of course, in a place like that, and I could be close by in – yes, I thought wildly – a little whitewashed cottage, with a fabulous cottage garden full of poppies and lupins that she and her friends could come back to at weekends. Oh really, said a wry little voice in my head, and what about you? Would you give up on your own life altogether? Make jam, pickles, grow your own turnips, grow your own underarm hair, become a hermit or something? I sighed and trudged on up the stairs. Maybe, maybe. Because frankly, after all I'd been through, jam, pickles and hairy armpits sounded remarkably alluring.

Claudia was still fast asleep, spreadeagled on her back now, her mouth wide open. I took off her shoes and brushed the hair back from her face. Her forehead was hot and damp and I moved to the window to open it, to let a breeze in. As I flung it open, I hung out for a moment, feeling the wind on my own face, marvelling at what I'd done, at the empty drive below where his car should be. Just to the left of the drive, a stunning white, Himalayan rambling rose was taking over a tiny apple tree, killing it probably. I must chop that out, I thought suddenly. Why hadn't I done so before? Yes, a beautiful, charming killer that, up to now, I'd just watched, transfixed, in a powerless state of fascination. But not any more. Nothing, and no one, was going to get away with that sort of bullying behaviour any more. As I gazed into the hazy sunshine, marvelling at the turn my life was taking, I suddenly spotted Imogen's car. It was coming round the corner. Yes, that was surely her distinctive red Mercedes, indicating right now, and cruising slowly down our road.

I raised my hand in welcome and was about to call out, rush downstairs, throw open the door and drag her in for a much-needed gin and tonic on the lawn, when abruptly, she stopped short. Not outside my house, but Sebastian's. Oh, of course, I realised, she was probably with Hugo. Sebastian's concert was about to be premiered at the Wigmore Hall and he was no doubt having last-minute consultations with his conductor. I watched, disappointed, as she got out, looking stunning in a sleeveless cream dress, her blonde hair swinging and shining like a girl in a shampoo advert, and waited for Hugo to get out the other side. But Imogen was on her own. Oh, so Hugo was clearly inside already. Either that or he was coming along later, under his own steam. As I watched Maureen let her in, I thought what fun they must have all had in Paris. Imo and Hugo, happy and in love; Sebastian, carefree, delighted his piece had been such a hit, high on success. God, if only I'd played my cards right I might have been there with them – made up a jolly foursome, guzzled champagne into the night, trawled the bars and cafés with the best of them, instead of which I'd welcomed my errant husband back with open arms. Fool.

As I crept out of Claudia's room, though, I decided that foolish though I'd most surely been, I was now getting stronger by the minute, and surer than ever that I'd done the right thing. I knew what Claudia would ask in the morning: 'For ever? Has he gone for ever, Mummy?' My insides twisted briefly. My gut feeling was yes, for ever, but I'd say I didn't know. Let it sink in. Say, 'Well, as Granny says, Claudes, never say never and you can't say forever, but what I do know, darling, is that I'm in the driving seat. For the first time in a long while, your mother, Olivia McFarllen, is calling the shots.' She'd like that. She'd be sad too, of course, and yet . . . and yet . . .

As I made my way slowly downstairs, biting my thumbnail and lost in thought, I suddenly spotted Spiro, hovering on the front step behind the glazed front door. He was twisting his hat in his hands and peering through the glass, clearly looking for me. I stopped, sighed. And so life goes on, I thought wryly. I might, just this minute, have discovered my husband's love child lurking in a North London bedsit, I might, tomorrow morning, have to tell my sensitive ten-year-old that her family unit had once more collapsed, but no matter. Come what may, one still had to deal with the day-to-day. One still had to deal with the builders.

'Spiro, come in,' I said, throwing back the door. 'Do just walk in and yell if you can't find me. You don't have to loiter outside. Good heavens, you look very smart. Where are you off to?'

His normally unruly black curls were brushed neatly to one side and slicked down with water, his jeans were pressed, he had a clean white T-shirt on, and he was carrying his tea-cosy hat, rather than wearing it.

'Out,' he said, puffing up his chest and beaming proudly. 'But first, Mac, he say to me – can I please bring Meeses McFarllen the latest bill and ask her, very, very kindly, and thank you so much, for an advance on the readies?'

'Oh, he did, did he?' I took the bill he proffered and looked at it. Looked again. Blinked. 'Blimey, as much as that, Spiro? Bit steep, isn't it? How many weeks in advance is this for?'

'Only one, but he say we need so many building supplies, breeks, copper piping, cement and things, and so he order it, but he no pay for it yet. It all here, see?'

He pointed to a shopping list of masonic items in Mac's hand.

I sighed and tucked it in my pocket. 'Yes, I see. Well, I'll go down and talk to him about it. I'll certainly give him some of it, but I'm not sure I can ante up the whole lot right now.'

Spiro looked anxious. 'But he say to be sure to bring it back and—'

'Look, I'll talk to him, Spiro, OK? Now don't you worry, no one's going to shoot the messenger,' I smiled. 'So, where exactly are you off to in your Sunday best, then?'

'Ah yes, well, that also why I want to speak to you.' He twisted his hat nervously. 'You see, I got a leetle job, a very tiny one,' he held his forefinger and thumb apart a fraction, 'and it only take a jiffy, but I don't want to step on your feet, so first, I come here, to ask your permission and see if you don't mind.'

I folded my arms in mock horror. 'Good heavens, another job? Don't tell me one of my staff is moonlighting? Where exactly is it, Spiro?'

'Ees only down the road, at number 42. You know, at your dear friend, Meesis Nanette's.'

I frowned. 'Really? And what exactly are you doing for dear Meesis Nanette?'

'Ah,' he rolled his eyes. 'Poor lady. She have beeg, beeg problems with her bed.'

'Her bed?'

'Yes,' he sighed, 'an antique bed, you see, so very beautiful, but very old, and some of the springs, they go flippy floppy on her. They shoot through,' he demonstrated with a sharp upward thrust of his fist, 'and hurt her something chronic she say. She want me to come with my spanner, you see, adjust them, and she say, "Spiro, you wear clean clothes now, please, because I have a cream carpet, and also, I may need you to lie on my bed to test it." '

'Did she now?' I said grimly.

'Yes, and you know what, *she* may have to lie on *other* side of bed because sometimes,' his eyes widened, 'the springs, they go plippy-ploppy all over! So we do a practical demonstration.' He nodded sagely.

'Ah. And I take it Roger isn't around to help with this practical? He's not hovering about helpfully with *his* spanner?'

'No, no, so sad. You see Meesis Nanette, she say, "I'm Rogerless, Spiro! And he such a handy man, my Rog, but he not here to do the business!" '

'Is he not. I see.' I nodded. Pursed my lips. 'Spiro, have you ever heard of a nymphomaniac?'

He frowned. 'Nymph? Ah yes, ees Greek, you know, for youth, and beauty.'

'Possibly, and in her dreams, but in England, together with the maniac bit, it means mad about sex.'

He frowned. 'Ti?'

'Sex, Spiro – she loves it. Lots of it, and with dewy young men like yourself and Lance, see? Oh, there's nothing too terrible about it. It's a harmless enough hobby, a frivolous diversion from the ironing and the dusting, something to do between *Neighbours* and *Countdown*, and I dare say it's a marvellous tonic too, but just so long as you know the score. Just so long as you know what you're getting into here. Because tomorrow morning, I really don't want to find you weeping in the back garden, sobbing into your hat about what you've done to your poor Atalanta, when I'd really rather you were rodding my drains.'

'Sex!' he gasped. 'No bad springs?'

'Oh, I should think they're fairly bad, pretty rotten and worn out by now, but I'm sure they're up to just one more hammering.'

'Never!' he spluttered, backing away in horror. 'Never would I cheat on my Atalanta to hammer this woman!'

I patted his outraged shoulder. 'Attaboy, Spiro, that's the spirit. Now you hold on tight to that righteous indignation and pop down the road and put her straight. Tell her you won't be making an appearance in her boudoir this afternoon. Oh, and while you're there, you might tell her from me that she's a terrible old slapper and to keep her thieving hands off my workforce. Tell her that if she's that desperate for company, she can come and have a gin and tonic on the lawn with me instead. I'll be getting the ice out right now.'

Opening and shutting his mouth he backed away. 'Yes, I go, I go. And I tell her!' Suddenly he stopped, frowned. 'Slapper?'

I grinned. 'That's it.'

He nodded. 'OK.'

He squared his shoulders, turned and marched out of the drive, for all the world like some proud Cretan soldier off to rout a young Turk. Head high and bristling with indignation, he swept the tea-cosy hat out of his pocket and plonked it firmly on his head again.

I watched him go, smiling, imagining Nanette's stunned face. I also felt sure she'd have the nous to see the funny side, though. I could see her, listening incredulously to his indignant, disjointed spiel, then as she shut the door, throwing back her head and roaring with laughter, before charging upstairs, ripping off her black camisole, throwing on her old sequinned jeans and coming over to have a drink with me. I'd tease her mercilessly, of course, and no doubt she'd stay a while, help me see the bottle off, and we'd roar drunkenly into the night. Yes, two single, frustrated women, knocking it back. 'Ha!' I laughed out loud. Because for the first time for ages, that didn't make me feel either sad or lonely. It simply amused me.

I was still smiling as I went down to the cellar, en route to the safe to get some money out for Mac. As I crouched down and punched in the combination number, I looked at the scrappy piece of paper Spiro had given me. I'd give Mac half, I decided, slowly opening the safe door. Two thousand pounds really was too much all in one go. I counted out the cash, popped it in an envelope, put the rest away, and then shut the safe again. God, no wonder he'd sent Spiro, I thought wryly as I mounted the cellar steps. For a start I generally paid him on a Friday, so this was earlier than usual, and also, I wanted to ask him about all these so-called building supplies. I could have sworn I'd paid for a whole lorryload only last week.

I put the envelope in my skirt pocket and wandered down the garden to the caravan. I could hear voices and a light was on. I glanced at my watch. Four o'clock. Well, they'd knocked off slightly earlier than usual, but I wasn't going to quibble about that. They worked jolly hard during the day. I knocked on the door and Alf answered.

'Oh, Alf, look, Spiro gave me this bill, but I have to say it's rather hefty and I'm minded to give you only half at the moment. I'll speak to Mac about having the rest later. Is he about?'

Alf looked worried. 'It's all kosher, luv, all straight-up stuff.'

'I'm sure it is,' I soothed, 'but if I could just have a word . . .'

'E's in the karzy, luv, d'you wanna wait? He won't be long.'

'Er, well, no I won't, if you don't mind,' I said nervously, eyeing the Portaloo door, not convinced I wanted to encounter Mac before he'd washed his hands. 'Just ask him to pop up and see me, would you?'

Alf took the bill. 'Swear to God it's all stuff we need, on my life. Copper piping an' that for the bathroom, skirting and architrave for round the doors, and—'

'I don't doubt it, Alf,' I interrupted patiently, 'I just want to go through it, that's all, sitting down at the kitchen table. Tell Mac I'll speak to him later.'

'Yeah, orright.' He scratched his head, looked anxious. He glanced at the envelope in my hand. 'I'll take that little lot then, shall I? Just for the minute?'

'Oh – sure.' I handed it over. 'Oh, and could I have a receipt please, Alf?'

'A receipt?'

'Yes, you know, just to say I've given it to you.'

'Oh! Right.' He turned, went inside, and came lumbering back a moment later with a pencil and paper. 'What does Mac do then?'

'Oh, just your name and then write received, from me. You know, Mrs McFarllen,' I said, just in case he didn't.

'Right.' He licked the end of the pencil. It hovered doubtfully over the paper. For an awful moment I thought perhaps he couldn't write, but then slowly he began to etch away and I realised his eye probably gave him trouble. Finally he handed it to me.

'There.'

'Thanks, Alf.' I took it and glanced down.

'FROM MRS O. MCFARLLEN. THE SUM OF £1,000, RECEIVED BY MR A. J. TURNER.'

I was about to stuff it in my pocket, when suddenly I stopped. Pulled it out. I read it again. Stared. I knew this writing. Childish capitals, scrawled on cheap, lined paper, torn out of a spiral-bound notebook. Slowly I looked up and met Alf's eye. I knew in an instant where I'd seen this handwriting before.

Chapter Twenty-Five

I gazed into his eyes, one brown and watery, the other, unfocused and veering off to the right somewhere.

'Orright, luv? That the sort of fing?' Alf nodded down at the receipt, shuffling nervously from foot to foot, clearly keen to shut the door.

'Yes. Yes . . . that's fine, Alf.'

'Right. See you later, then.'

I didn't respond, so with a curt nod of his head, he shut the door anyway.

I stared down at the piece of paper again. After a moment I turned and walked slowly back up the lawn. Then I stopped. Turned back, and looked at the caravan door. For a moment there I was tempted to run back, bang on it, and demand an explanation, but then in another moment I'd changed my mind. I stuffed the bit of paper in my pocket and walked quickly back to the house. I marched through the French windows, made straight for the telephone in the hall, and started riffling furiously around on the chaotic hall table, searching for that scrap of paper with the number scrawled on it that had *still* not made it into the address— Ah! There it was. I pounced on it and punched out the number. Nina answered more or less immediately.

'Oh God, I'm so glad you've rung. I've been really worried about you.'

I was momentarily taken aback. 'Really? Why?'

'Well, telling you all that stuff about Johnny and then letting you get in the car and drive home in that dreadful storm. Mum said it was an awful thing to do, said you must have been in a terrible state. I kept imagining you, blinded by tears, tearing down the motorway and ploughing into the middle of some ghastly pile-up or something!'

I paused. Sat down and crossed my legs. 'No, not at all,' I said slowly. 'In fact, quite the reverse. I'm delighted you gave me the missing pieces to the puzzle. You see it merely confirmed some suspicions I'd had all along, made me realise I'm definitely doing the right thing. But I wasn't ringing about my husband, Nina. I wanted to ask you something else.'

'Oh! Right.' Her turn to be wrong-footed.

'That night you came to see me, the evening you sat on my terrace. Did you see anyone else in the garden?'

'Well, one or two of your builders were about, yes.'

'Which ones – Mac? The small one, quite thin and wiry?'

'Um, yes, I think so. Skinny with bristly hair.'

'That's it. He said he was having a pee in the bushes and turned round and saw you there, is that right?'

'Oh no, he certainly wasn't having a pee. I'd have remembered that. No, he was sitting on that little brick wall round the corner, on the other side of your patio, the main bit. He had his back to me, he was talking to the big one.'

'The big one?'

'You know, huge, funny eye. I couldn't see much because it was dark, but I remember him.'

'Alf,' I breathed, and Mac had told me he was alone. Said

444

that Alf had been monopolising the bathroom, getting spruced up for their night out in the curry house.

'What were they talking about? Did you hear?'

'Not really. It was all in whispers. You know, very hushed and urgent. They seemed to be arguing a bit about something, though, and that pushed the volume up occasionally.'

'But you don't know? Not a word?'

She paused. 'No, except . . .'

'Yes?'

'Well, something about – how to get rid of it. But I don't know what. That was all, really. Why, is it important?'

'I don't know,' I said slowly. 'So what happened next? They saw you?'

'Yes, well, I coughed actually, on purpose. I didn't want them thinking I was spying on them or anything, and the small one swung round and saw me. I heard him say "Shit" under his breath, and then the big one scuttled away, back to the caravan, I think.'

'And Mac came over?'

'Oh yeah, he came storming over, wanted to know what the hell I thought I was doing there and I sort of stuttered something about waiting for you. I'd seen the foreign one in the front drive, you see, and he'd said it was OK to wait. This one was pretty mad, though.'

'Was he?' I murmured. Yes, not at all how Mac had related this encounter. A polite conversation, he'd said, about when I might be expected back.

'Um, how is he?' she faltered nervously.

'Who, Mac?'

'No! Johnny.'

'Oh. Oh, fine, I expect. He's not here, though. I rather thought he might be with you. Still, the traffic could be bad on the M1. I'd expect him any time, Nina.'

I heard her catch her breath. 'You mean – he's left?'

'No, no,' I smiled. 'I threw him out.' I found a nail file and picked it up, pushing back a cuticle or two. 'There's only so much crap a person can take, you know, and frankly, I'm grateful to you for showing me just how much was being dumped my way. Goodbye, Nina. Oh, and incidentally, don't throw away any of those little notes you've got tucked away in that magazine. They may turn out to be what I believe is known as admissible evidence.'

I replaced the receiver before she could utter a response. Right. That, I thought with some satisfaction, had surely killed two little birds quite neatly with one stone, hadn't it? In the first place I'd let her know that I wasn't exactly breaking my heart over her liaison with my husband, and in the second place, I'd got her to reveal just a *soupçon* more about what was going on here. I frowned. Twisted round in my chair to face the garden. But only a *soupçon*. Because what exactly *was* going on in my back yard that I didn't know about? What sort of scam was Mac operating here, and was it being conducted from my house? Right under my nose? I took Alf's receipt out of my pocket again. Should I ring the police? Get them involved? I instantly decided against it. God – no, what was I thinking of? What, shop these guys; my friends, who'd helped me through some tricky times, just because my husband's mistress had been threatened by them? No no, I ought to be grateful to them! Pat them on the backs, buy them all a pint, tell them how delighted I was that they'd put the wind up her adulterous knickers, sparked off her neurosis, which, let's face it, had been the catalyst for Johnny leaving her. Only a few weeks ago I'd have been thrilled to bits about that. I smiled. Yes, strange to think, I mused, that in an ironic sort of way, they might have saved my marriage. Only they weren't to know, as I did now, that there was nothing to save.

No, I decided, getting briskly to my feet, no, I wouldn't talk to the police, I'd talk to Mac. He was a shrewd, intelligent man and we'd always got on well, always talked frankly to one another. There was bound to be some terribly simple, innocent explanation to all this. I'd go and see him now, right this minute while I was still feeling bullish and elated about throwing Johnny out, go and have it out with him. Right, absolutely, go for it Olivia. Go call those shots.

I sailed off back through the house, through the French windows and marched back down to the caravan. Smiling and holding my head up high I felt that in my present mood, there was very little I couldn't accomplish right now, very little I couldn't achieve. I rapped smartly on the caravan door. There was a sound of scuffling inside, then Mac stuck his head out.

'Yes?' he barked in my face.

'Oh!' I stepped back in surprise. 'Um, Mac, I'd like a word, if – if I may.' I faltered.

'Oh, sorry, Livvy,' he recovered with a smile. 'I, um, fought it was someone else.'

'Ah.' I blinked. Who? I wondered. In my garden? 'Well – is it convenient?'

He hesitated. 'Yeah. Yeah – hang about.' He pulled the door to for a second and shot back inside. I heard muffled whispers, urgent instructions, but to whom, I didn't know. I crept forward and peered through the crack he'd left. I could just about make out the side of Lance's head, sitting at the table. Ah, so he was in on this too, whatever it was. I stepped back smartly as Mac reappeared. He came right out this time, and shut the door firmly behind him.

'Yes, luv, what can I do for you?' He rubbed his hands together briskly, grinning.

'Mac, I'm a little concerned.'

'Oh yeah?'

'Yes, only I went to see Nina Harrison today. D'you know who I mean by that?'

He scratched the top of his head, looked puzzled. 'Can't say I do, luv.'

'Well, she's my husband's mistress, Mac. She's the one you treated to a grandstand view of an al fresco pee one evening not so long ago, remember?'

He looked startled, but recovered quickly. 'Oh yeah, yeah, it's all coming back to me. I didn't know her name, see.'

'Didn't you? Or her address in Finchley, I suppose?'

He scratched some more. 'Her address?'

'Yes, Mac. You see, today, when I went to see her, she showed me some letters. Two, actually, both anonymous, both threatening, and both written in this hand.'

I got out Alf's receipt and handed it to him. He looked at it. Pursed his lips, but otherwise his face betrayed little.

'She also,' I went on, 'has a very different account of that evening in the garden. You see, you told me that Alf was in the bathroom, but she maintains you were having a whispered discussion with him on the other side of the terrace.'

'What did she say?' he said quickly.

I folded my arms, smiled. 'Ah, Mac, you surely don't expect me to divulge what she overheard, do you? I mean, yes, you're right, she *did* hear quite a lot, but snatches, naturally. Snippets of conversation. She couldn't piece it all together herself, but I dare say if she related it to the police they'd have no problems.'

He looked at me for a long moment. His blue eyes were sharp and hard and I felt a small frisson of fear. It occurred to me that Mac was quite capable of being the affable brickie one minute and the hard-as-nails-East-End-boy the next. As quickly as the look had come into his eye, though, it vanished, and a second later he'd taken me by the elbow and was leading me gently away from the caravan door.

'Orright, luv, I shouldn't tell you,' he glanced about him cautiously, 'but I'm gonna now, 'cos you know too much already. Alf's in trouble.'

'Well, I rather gathered that.'

'Big time, like. It's the gee-gees.'

'Gee-gees?'

'Horses, luv. You know, gambling an' that.' He glanced nervously over his shoulder, then round the side of the house. 'Well, you know how he loves the racing, always sneaking in to watch the two-thirty from Kempton when he should be mixin' cement an' that, and that's 'cos he's always got a bet on, see? He's always gambled – well, we all have, to be fair, all like a flutter – but Alf's got it bad, and he's got himself in a right pickle now. He had a couple of big losers see, big-cheese debts to pay off, so to cover it, the stupid sod went and put all he had in the world on the appropriately named Fool's Gold, which managed to limp home last in the three fifteen Novice's Cup from Newmarket a few weeks back.'

'Oh! Oh dear. So – how much does he owe now?'

Mac rolled his eyes. 'Don't ask. Just don't ask. Thousands, luv. Can't be more pacific. And they're after him for it, an' all.'

'Who, the police?'

'Nah, not the police, the bookies. Gaming debts aren't enforceable by law see, so what the bookies do is they get some heavies on the case. A couple of big leery bastards in jangling jewellery generally turn up in a Ford Capri and ask you ever so nicely if you'd mind coughing up or they'll shorten yer legs for you, that sort of thing.'

'Heavens!'

'That night your friend was 'ere, we was in conference, see, discussing where Alf should go. To hide, right, a safe place, like. Well, when we swung round and saw that tart, Alf got windy. He was petrified she'd overheard and so the stupid git found her number by your phone and rang her to warn her off. Well, he got the muvver instead, didn't he, who says she's taken the baby out.' Mac gave me a sideways glance at this but I didn't even flinch. 'So instead, right, the pillock thinks – ah-hah, a kid! Maybe I'll write her a note instead, put the wind up her a bit, rattle her cage an' that, so he finds her address by the phone and goes for it. Well, I went ape-shit when I found out, but by then it was too late. He'd sent them.' He shook his head sadly, tapped his temple. 'He's never had much up there, our Alf.'

'Evidently. I mean – as if she'd get involved anyway! It wouldn't mean a thing to her.'

'Yeah,' Mac sighed, 'but like I said before, he's not a bright lad, our Alf. He don't fink fings frough, he just panics and gets in a state, don't he?'

'But if Alf's in such danger, why is he still here? I mean, that was a while ago, wasn't it?'

'Yeah, but then again, this is as good a hiding place as any, innit? I mean, who'd fink of looking for Alf here, deep in leafy suburbia? But it won't do for much longer,' he pursed his lips. 'We just got word from some mates down Hackney way that Trinidad and Tobago is on their way, so Alf's out of 'ere first fing tomorrow. We've only got your bathroom to go now, luv, and me an' Lance an' Spiro can handle that.'

'Trinidad and Tobago?'

'The heavies, luv. Big black bastards whose ancestors hail from sunnier climes.'

'Oh! Good grief. Yes, well, I'm delighted in that case that Alf's going. I certainly don't want any broken legs decorating my back yard, thank you very much, and what am I supposed to do if they come to the door?' I asked a trifle nervously.

'Send them straight down to me, luv. I'll sort them out.'

Really? I looked dubiously at Mac's tiny frame. 'Well, I sincerely hope you're right.'

'Oh, they wouldn't touch me. I know too many influential people, see,' he tapped the side of his nose. 'Too many people wiv more subtler, but probably more interesting, mefods of persuasion.'

'Oh! Right.' Bloody hell. Yes, I imagined he did. It occurred to me that Mac had probably led quite an exotic life – this tiny little man who'd protected his big, lumbering, younger brother from a vile stepfather, been through Barnardo's and then out the other side into the turbulent East End. I expect Mac knew quite a few colourful characters.

'So don't you worry, luv,' he said, taking my elbow again, only this time, subtly propelling me housewards. 'We can handle it. Only I'd be ever so grateful if – you know.' He tapped his nose again. 'Mum's the word.'

'Oh – yes, of course. I mean, I don't know anyone to tell, Mac.'

Don't actually know anyone in gangland Hackney who'd be interested in his brother's whereabouts, I thought as I made my way slowly back to the house. It struck me, though, that there were clearly some lawless places out there. Not exactly Al Capone land, but a shady, grey, wheeling-and-dealing area where people still got their legs broken, a place that most ordinary people didn't even know existed. I pulled my cardigan around me with a little shiver. Well, I for one was far happier being blissfully ignorant.

As I wandered back through the French windows I closed them behind me, shooting the bolts up firmly. Now that the weather had broken there was a chill in the air and the wind was getting up. In fact, it occurred to me that the reason it was gushing through here like a raging monsoon was because the front door was wide open. God, no wonder there was such a gale. As I crossed the room to the hall and went to shut it, someone coughed behind me. I froze. Stood there, paralysed with fear, one hand on the doorknob. Then I swung around. Over the back of the sofa, the top of a man's head was clearly visible. A dark head.

'Who is it!' I yelped, swinging the front door open again. 'Christ! What d'you want!'

'Peace and quiet and a large gin, since you ask.' Hugh's head popped up over the sofa.

'Omigod!' I clutched my thumping chest. 'Oh my *God*, Hugh, don't *do* that! I thought you were Trinidad and Tobago!'

'Who?'

'Trinidad and Tobago, the heavies, well versed in the art of subtle persuasion!'

He frowned. 'What the hell are you talking about, Livvy?'

Still hanging on to the furniture, I told him all about Alf and his debts. He chuckled.

'Blimey, I should think he's scared witless. I'd rather be hounded by the police than those hoods. Can't he raise the money?'

'I think,' I said, collapsing into a convenient armchair, still suffering from shock, 'that if that had been an option he'd have explored it by now, don't you?' Suddenly I sat bolt upright. 'Oh help – I'm not supposed to tell anyone!' I clutched my mouth. 'Oh God, Hugh, I swore I wouldn't breathe a word to a living soul and I've just told you the whole story!'

'Oh, don't worry, my love, I'm not a living soul, just a grey, shambling wreck inhabiting a living soul's body. Your secret's safe with me. My lips are sealed.'

'Well, they bloody better be or I'm in deep shit,' I said reverting to gangland parlance. 'And anyway, what the hell are you doing here, Hugh, frightening the life out of me? Why aren't you at home changing nappies and rubbing cream into cracked nipples?'

'Because – something terrible's happened.' I realised with a start his face was very grim.

I gasped. 'Oh God, not the baby!' I shot out of my chair.

'No, no, not the baby,' he said hastily. 'Sorry, Livvy, didn't mean to frighten you. No, Flora's fine, that would be tragic, this is merely terrible. No, Millicent's arrived,' he informed me darkly.

'Ah!' I sank back down again. 'God, don't *do* that to me, Hugh. I've had more than enough shocks for one day!'

'Sorry. Still, you must admit it's fairly appalling. She breezed in this morning, totally unannounced, of course. She knows full well we'd go into hiding with Alf if she'd given us prior warning.'

'Oh dear, poor you!' I giggled. Millicent was Molly's huge and formidable mother, truly a woman of substance, about fourteen stone in all, and still firmly entrenched somewhere in the 1950s, when being a housewife really stood for something. She couldn't understand why Molly didn't darn her husband's socks, boil giblets for gravy and knit her children's vests.

'There I was, upstairs,' Hugh went on tragically, 'casting a dreamy, casual eye out of the bedroom window, minding my own business, quietly picking my nose and idly wondering whether Molly would like to be eased gently back into the sexual saddle tonight – albeit a few weeks before she goes up on the ramps for her six week checkup – when suddenly, a horribly familiar white Fiesta draws up. The door opens, there's a ghastly hiatus . . . and then Millicent's unmistakable bulk is disgorged, a carrier bag in each hand – one, no doubt full of nourishing food (bits of dead sheep to you and me) and the other full of Pingouin knitting patterns – and all I could do was watch, petrified, as she cruised menacingly up the garden path like a battleship under full steam.'

'Oh God! What did you do?'

'Well, first I dropped my bogey—'

'Hugh!'

'Then my fantasy, and then I legged it downstairs and out of the back door, just as her humongous fist was hammering at the front. I tell you, Livvy, it was a close-run thing. I mean, normally I can spot her heaving into view at twenty paces and divert at nineteen, but this time she caught me on the hop.' He shuddered. 'Frankly I'd rather meet your brace of black boys in a dark alley than Millicent in the front hall. Now where's that drink I ordered?'

'Poor Molly,' I sighed, getting up to pour it.

'Ah yes, alas, poor Moll,' he intoned sadly. 'Trapped for hours, nay, days even, being permanently scolded about how she's not looking after the baby properly, and being told how Alison – married to Moll's brother, remember? Mousy little wifey thing? Wears an apron? Probably wears it in bed.'

'Oh yes,' I giggled.

'How Alison— God, quite sexy actually. Naked but for an apron.'

'Get on with it!'

'Oh yes, well how Alison never gave baby Hannah the breast unless it was absolutely bang on four hours since she'd been offered it the last time, whilst my poor Moll sits there, being constantly milked by our demanding daughter and looking like some mad cow, all wild about the eyes, and now about to be driven even madder as Millicent subjects her to reams of photos of young Hannah – who looks like a cross between Boris Yeltsin and a Vietnamese pot-bellied pig incidentally – dressed in cutesy little smocky things, *all* of which the sainted Alison has made *by hand*, whilst the only thing poor Moll has ever made by hand is a mess.'

I giggled and passed him a large gin, sipping my own and sitting down beside him on the sofa, pulling my legs up under me. 'Which is precisely why you should get back,' I said, wagging a finger sternly. 'It's unfair to leave her on her own.'

'I thought we'd do it in shifts,' he said, resting his head back and gazing at the ceiling. 'I thought I'd creep back when it's dark, smuggle her and Flora out, and tell her that your front door is always open – which it was, by the way – and that even better, Johnny's car isn't even in the front drive.' He turned his head, eyed me beadily.

I swirled the ice in my glass. 'Well spotted,' I said levelly. 'I'd noticed that too. But I had no idea,' I went on brightly, 'that you and Molly disliked him so much, Hugh.'

'Oh, I wouldn't say that,' he said lightly, 'nothing so strong as dislike. No, no, we just thought he treated you like dog poo, that's all. And I'm not just talking about the last six months, either.'

'Ah, I see. So, therefore you thought I was pathetic, cringing and downtrodden?'

'You can only be downtrodden, Liv, if someone bigger is doing the treading, but I'll say no more, because I've learnt from past experience that it's a mistake. Only the other day a mate of mine, Tom, confided to me that he'd left his wife and I yelled, "Terrific! I always thought Geraldine was a dog, and you wouldn't *believe* the number of times I've had to wrestle her hand out of the front of my trousers!" Well, bugger me if two weeks later I'm not sitting next to "the dog" at a dinner party, and Tom's shooting me homicidal looks over the salmon mousse. I think Johnny's a wonderful, caring human being, Livvy, and I love him to bits. Now, moving smartly on, the *other* reason I came, aside from not meddling in your domestic setup and *aside* from escaping Millicent, was to give you these.' He lifted his bottom off the sofa, reached into his jeans pocket and flicked some pieces of paper at me.

'What are they?'

'Tickets for Sebastian's concert tomorrow night. He very kindly sent them, together with some flowers – which was totally uncalled for – as a thank you for supper the other week.' He sighed, wistfully. 'Believe it or not we were actually thinking of going. Moll's got terrible cabin fever – you know, four-walls-and-a-baby-not-to-mention-sodding-Henry – and she thought she could easily feed during the performance and meanwhile we could greedily observe other life forms, be reminded that there *is* a world out there.' He sighed. 'But now that HMS *Splendid's* arrived our plans lie in tatters. We shall no doubt be sitting down to supper and sampling some of her famous desiccated lamb's heart stew instead.' He shuddered. 'She brings the bits of sheep with her, you know. They're the oldest ewes in Wales. I'm sure she sits on the hillside watching them, waiting for them to die – which they gladly do under her gaze – before smuggling them home and hanging them for six months prior to foisting them on to us.'

I smiled, but I wasn't really listening to his habitual patter, I was gazing at the tickets, turning them over in my hand. 'But – how very kind of him,' I said slowly, as it also occurred to me that – God, he hadn't sent *me* one, had he?

'Wasn't it?' Hugh agreed. 'I popped in to thank him just now, actually, en route here. Didn't stay, though. He was having a bit of a pre-concert drinks do with the musical élite, and they all looked a bit scary and sophisticated to me.'

'Oh yes,' I sat up eagerly, 'I saw Imo's car. She and Hugo are over there, did you see them?'

'I saw Imogen,' he said carefully.

'I wonder if she'll pop over later,' I mused, gazing somewhat wistfully in that direction.

'I doubt it somehow,' he said quietly.

I glanced back. 'Why?'

'Oh – just that it looked like it was going to go on a bit,' he said quickly. 'You know.'

'Oh, right.' I felt a brief pang of jealousy. A roaring pre-concert drinks party, eh, and if I'd played my cards right I could have been there too. Christ, been there – I might even have been the hostess. I chewed my lip ruefully for a moment, then smiled.

'God, I'm *so* pleased about Imo, though, aren't you, Hugh? She's absolutely ecstatic about this guy. Honestly, you should hear her eulogising about him. Molly said she left a message on the answer machine the other day saying she was absolutely besotted, and that's so unlike her, isn't it? She's keeping a hell of a low profile, though,' I said, frowning. 'She popped in briefly when Johnny came back, but I was just thinking, I haven't really had a proper evening or lunch with her since that terrible concert in the Abbey. Does Moll see much of her?'

Hugh took a deep breath. 'Um, Livvy, look. I wasn't going to tell you this, but I think there's something you should— Shit!'

We both jumped and I spilt my drink as a tremendous banging came at the front door.

'Bloody hell!' I squeaked, jumping up. 'I do have a bell!'

The banging came again, only more of a hammering now. Hugh and I gazed at each other, stunned.

'God, who the hell would do that?' whispered Hugh, getting up and moving behind the sofa.

I went to answer it. 'Well, I don't know, but I'm bloody well going to—' I stopped. Swung round. My hand flew to my mouth. 'Trinidad and Tobago!' I breathed.

'Oh, good point,' he muttered with relief. 'For an awful moment I thought it might be Millicent.'

'Quick, in here!' I grabbed his arm and pulled him through into the study, which looked out on to the front drive. We scuttled to the window together and peered out round the red velvet curtain. A small, bald-headed man in a beige, belted raincoat was standing on the step, beside a middle-aged, peroxide-blonde woman in a well-worn, shiny C&A suit.

'Oh. How very disappointing,' observed Hugh flatly. 'They look like insurance salesmen. Either that or Jehovah's Witnesses.'

'Well, thank goodness for that,' I said with relief, going to answer the door. 'They certainly don't look like knuckle breakers, anyway.'

I opened it.

'Mithith McFarllen?' the man enquired softly. He had a lisp.

'Yes?'

'I believe a gentleman named Mithter Alfred Turner ith currently in your employ. May we thpeak with him, pleathe?'

My heart skipped. God, yes, of course, far more sinister. The quietly spoken gunman and his female accomplice, his moll, his *femme fatale*, brought along for cover. Nothing brutal and thuggish, mind, just a single bullet to the head, while the girl wiped the revolver clean with a white silk handkerchief.

'Oh! Well, yes I—'

'Police,' the moll informed me helpfully, flicking out her ID card.

'Oh!' I gasped with relief. 'Good, heavens, I thought you were—'

'Yes?'

'No, no, nothing. Um, yes, well do come in. In fact – no, no, don't come in, there's no point. We'll go round the back. They're down in a caravan, you see, in the garden. Such fun, you'll see!' I breezed nervously. I stepped outside and began to lead the way, when abruptly I stopped. 'Oh – except I have to tell you, I have a feeling Alf won't be there.'

'Really? Why so?' asked Raincoat.

'Well, because they always go to the pub at about this time,' I glanced at my watch. 'Yes, they'll be having a pint.'

'Ah.' He gave a thin smile. 'Well, shall we go and thee,

anyway, Mrs McFarllen? Jutht in case? Shall we go and find out?' he gestured with his arm that I should lead on again.

'Oh, yes, OK.' God, he was a bit creepy, wasn't he? A bit – you know – unnecessary? 'Um, coming, Hugh?' I glanced back over my shoulder.

But Hugh was recovering from shock and cowering in the porch, desperately trying to light a cigarette with an empty lighter. 'No, no,' he muttered faintly, 'don't worry about me. I'll be off now. Might even go to the pub myself, have a large Scotch. Toodle-oo, my love, and thanks for the drink.'

'Love to Molly,' I called as he shuffled off down the drive.

Gosh, the police, I thought, my head spinning as I led them away down the garden. Now, that was an interesting development. Hadn't Mac said that gambling debts weren't enforceable by law? But then, perhaps they were here to protect Alf? Yes, that must be it, I decided. They'd probably heard that some unsavoury characters were after him and were here to warn him, offer him some protection, perhaps. Well, thank goodness for that. I wasn't unhappy about a bit of police presence if there were going to be some undesirables knocking about. I banged on the caravan door.

'Mac! Alf!'

Spiro answered. 'Yes, Meesis McFarllen?' with studied politeness.

'Oh, Spiro, are the others in?'

'No, Meesis McFarllen, they have gone out. They have gone to the public house.'

It was quite obvious Spiro had been well briefed. He was talking in an even more unnatural and stilted manner than usual, as if he'd rehearsed, and was now regurgitating the words.

'Do you happen to know which public houthe?' whispered the man in the raincoat.

Spiro smiled ruefully. 'I am so very sorry. I am so very afraid that I do not know wheech public house.'

God, he sounded brain dead. Raincoat turned to me. 'What's the nearest local then, Mrs McFarllen, the Fighting Cocks?' He paused. 'Mrs McFarllen?'

'Oh, I'm sorry,' Just behind Raincoat, I'd suddenly caught sight of Mac, hiding in the rhododendron bushes. I'd also spotted Lance, tucked away behind him. Lance put a finger to his lips. I turned wide eyes on Raincoat. 'What . . . did you say?'

'I thaid, is the Fighting Cocks the nearest?'

'Yes, yes, that's it.'

'But they go on a creep, I theenk,' added Spiro, imaginatively. 'They go creepy crawly.'

The policeman stared.

'A pub crawl, he means,' I put in quickly.

'Ah.' Raincoat nodded, then squinted at Spiro as if he'd never seen anything quite like him before. He pursed his lips. 'Well, how very inconvenient, but I don't believe I shall trouble to "creep" around the local hostelries after them. Would you thimply inform Mr Turner that I would like a word with him on a matter of great importance, and will be returning forthwith, in other words, tomorrow morning, Mrs McFarllen?'

'Of course!'

'And meanwhile, thank you for your time.' He inclined his head slightly, then with a sharp 'Come!' to his accomplice, they turned to go.

Spiro and I watched as they made their way up the garden, not quite goose-stepping but almost, up the lavender walk, and under the rose arbour. My eyes darted briefly

461

to the rhododendron bushes, but then suddenly, on an impulse, I ran after them.

'Um, excuse me,' I called, 'can I just ask,' I said, breathlessly, catching them up, 'since this is my home, and Alf Turner is staying on my premises – can I just ask what this is all about?'

He turned. 'Yeth of course. It's about his wife.'

'Whose wife – Alf's?'

'Yeth. She appears to be missing.'

'Missing! Oh, oh no, now you see I can help you with that, officer,' I said eagerly. 'If you mean Vi, she's gone to Spain!'

He gazed witheringly at me. 'No, Mrs McFarllen, she hasn't gone to Spain. For one thing she has never in her life possessed a pathport and she certainly hasn't forged one and sneaked her way out of the country. She's missing, believe me. In fact we're very much afraid she may be dead.'

I stared. 'Dead!' My hand shot to my mouth. 'Oh!' I gasped.

'Exactly. Oh,' he repeated quietly. His pale grey eyes bored deep into mine. 'Bear that in mind, Mrs McFarllen, when you answer any more of my questions, hmm?'

And with that he turned and left.

Chapter Twenty-Six

'Dead!' I stared after his retreating back. Spiro came up behind me.

'Spiro, she's dead!' I gasped.

'Who dead?'

'Vi, Alf's wife!'

He gazed at me, open-mouthed. Slowly it dawned. 'Oh! Oh no, so poor Alf! He be so sad, Meesis McFarllen! He have his heart broken in a million tiny pieces, he—'

Mac and Lance materialised from the bushes and came over the bridge, just as Spiro was filling up and reaching for his hat. Mac jerked his head. 'Vamoose, Spiro.'

'*Ti?*'

'You heard, Zorba, beat it,' he snarled. 'Go find a kebab house to loiter in and bring us back a donna while yer at it. Go on, get out of here.'

Spiro's eyes widened. 'Ah yes, yes.' He looked suddenly nervous. 'Good idea, I go for donna.' He backed away.

'Excellent. Now.' Mac's steely-blue eyes met mine. 'We need to talk.'

'We certainly do,' I muttered.

'Over here.'

He led the way back across the bridge, pausing only at the caravan to reach in and grab a six-pack from inside the door. Then the three of us, under his guidance, moved further along the river and sat down on the grassy bank. Lance was silent.

'She's dead, Mac,' I breathed, staring into the water.

'I know.'

'Does Alf know?'

He turned his head, looked at me for a long moment.

'He killed her?' I gasped.

'Didn't think it would take you long. But he didn't kill her, as in murder her, right? It was an accident.'

'Jesus!' I got to my feet, knocking his Pils over. 'He killed her, Alf killed his wife – *Jesus*!'

'Sit down,' hissed Mac, reaching up and taking my arm roughly, dragging me down. 'An' keep yer voice down!'

I glanced around. There was no one about, but I appeared to be trembling. I sat down again.

'Now listen,' he breathed hoarsely in my ear. 'It was an accident, right? A terrible, tragic accident, like a kiddie drowning in a pond while his mum's not watchin', or like knockin' an old lady down 'cos you didn't see her suddenly step off the kerb, and that's not murder, is it? That's manslaughter, innit? See the difference? He's not a bad man, our Alf, orright?' His blue eyes bored into mine.

I gulped and inched back slightly on the grass. 'All – all right.' I nodded. 'What happened?' I whispered.

Mac took a slug of beer, narrowed his eyes across the river.

'That weekend, a while back, when we went home, and Lance stayed here, remember? Real scorcher?'

I thought back desperately. My mind whirled for a moment, then memories of Malcolm standing me up and Lance sitting me down and me slapping the Ambre Solaire all over him in the garden and Claudia going missing jostled for position so – yes, that weekend, it must have been . . . 'Yes, yes, I remember,' I muttered.

'Well, previous to that, she'd bin ringin', right?'

'Who had?'

'Vi, on his mobile, ringing and ringing, all week, and always givin' him earache – remember that? 'Member how his phone never stopped goin'? An' we all kept groanin' and sayin', "Bloody hell, it's bleedin' Vi again," an' laughing about it – yeah?'

'Oh yes, yes, I do remember.'

'Well, what it was, right, what she was on about, was some kitchen cupboard she wanted puttin' up. On an' on she went, an' she wouldn't let it go. Right bleedin' nag, she was, always giving it verbal, but old Alf, he don't mind, see, he never minded, 'cos he loved her, right, and he was used to it, wasn't he? So anyway, he went home that Friday night and said – yeah yeah, orright luv, stop givin' me grief, I'll do it, orright? I'll put it up.

' "Now," she says firmly.

' "Aw, come on," says Alf. "I've had a hard week, I've just got in, luv. It's bin a long drive, I need me tea. Tomorrow morning, like."

' "No, I want it tonight," she says. "You never do sod all round this place for me, Alfred Turner, always fixin' up someone else's place. Well, bleedin' well fix mine up for a change!" '

Mac sucked his teeth. 'That's what she was like, see,' he muttered. 'Never mind that he was bringin' home the dosh "from fixin' someone else's place up", never mind that he was handin' the whole lot straight over to *her* every bleedin' Friday night. Oh no, never mind all that.' He took a deep breath. 'So anyways, old Alf, he hauls himself out of his chair, even though he's knackered and he ain't even had his tea or anyfing, and goes to the shed and gets this cupboard, right? He's made it already, see, made it the weekend previous – and then he gets the step ladder out too, an' he starts fixin' it up, an' all the time she's standing there giving' him earache below about how he's never home and what a useless lump of lard he is. Well, finally, right, he gets this cupboard up on the wall, hammers it home, and he's wobbling about on top of the ladder and he calls down, "About there orright, luv?"

'And she stands back and says – "Bleedin' heck! It's not even bleedin' straight, you useless lump of shit!"

'Well, Alf, he loses it then. He's tired and he's hungry and he's up this ladder, and he slams his hammer down on the floor – chucks it away in disgust. Only what he don't realise is, she's moved forward, hasn't she, and she's standin' right underneath him now. Well, it gets her – WALLOP! – right on the side of the head, right on the temple, and she falls to the floor in a heap, crumples like a pack of cards. Well, the next thing Alf knows, he's tearing down that ladder, and then he's crouched down beside her in a pool of blood, feeling for her pulse, which she ain't got.'

'Oh God,' I breathed.

'So anyways, trembling and sobbin' like, he gets straight on the blower to me. Really cryin' he is, and I can hardly make out a word he's sayin', but I get the gist orright when I hear him say, "I've killed her, I've bloody killed her, Mac!" So I'm shitting myself, right, but I tell him to calm down an' I get round there sharpish and I don't tell no one where I'm going, not even the missus or nofing. Well, when I get there, burst through the door, there he is. Sat there, poor sod, sobbin' his eyes out on the kitchen floor, covered in blood 'cos he's tried to revive her, tried to give her mouf to mouf, the daft sod, and the poor bitch is in his arms, head back, mouth open, bleedin' like a stuck pig, cradled like a baby.'

'Oh Christ.' My hand flew to my mouth. I glanced at Lance. He was hugging his knees tight, staring at the grass. He'd gone very pale.

'Well, I'm in a right state now, aren't I? On the one hand I'm all for ringin' the police an' tellin' it straight, leavin' the steps right where they are, hammer an' everything, all just as it is, but on the other, I've got Alf, see, cryin' his eyes out, huggin' an' kissin' her an' that, and strokin' her hair which is covered in blood and moanin' about how he didn't mean to do nofing, and in that split second I fought – well, who the hell are they goin' to believe? Not my little brother, that's for sure. What, married to some naggin' old witch that everyone knows is a right pain in the arse and would testify to that effect? A right old cow who finally gets her comeuppance in a well-deserved hammer blow to the head? Just slipped out of my hand, your honour, didn't mean to chuck it, honest? Do me a favour,' he scoffed. 'And old Alf – he'd be useless in the dock, under fire from some poncy brief – "Er, now tell me, Mr Turner," Mac puffed out his chest and popped his thumbs into an imaginary barrister's gown, "would you concur that you were actually involved in an argument with your wife at the time of the assault?"

' "Well," ' Mac shuffled sheepishly on his bottom, aping Alf, "yeah, she was windin' me up a bit, yer honour, yeah."

' "She was . . . Winding You Up. Hmm. I see. And did you therefore lose your temper?"

' "Yeah, well, I was cross an' that but I—"

' "Did you, in fact, slam that hammer down with some considerable force?"

' "Well, I didn't mean to, like, but I suppose—"

' "*Aha!* So you *did* slam the hammer down with—"
Nah.' Mac broke off in disgust, spat in the bulrushes. 'He
don't stand a cat's chance in hell. He'd be in that slammer
before you can say hot porridge, and that's unnecessary.'
Mac wagged a finger. 'He's never hurt a fly in his life, old
Alf. He's as gentle as anyfing, we all know that, and he
don't deserve that, not life imprisonment. No, he don't
deserve that.' He reached for his Pils and threw his head
back, sucking on his can with a vengeance. As his head
came back down, I realised there were tears in his eyes. I
remembered the story about Alf's eye – what horrors they'd
been through together.

'So . . . what did you do?' I asked tentatively.

Mac swallowed hard and I realised he was in trouble. He
shook his head to indicate he couldn't speak. Lance cleared
his throat.

'He got her out of his arms – prised her, apparently, Alf
was clinging on to her for dear life – stripped off all of Alf's
clothes and burnt them, then he took him upstairs and gave
him a shower. Dad said it was like washing a baby, said he
just stood there, dumb, not resisting or anything. Then of
course he had to scrub the kitchen, and the shower, and
then . . .' Lance swallowed.

'Then I realised there was no goin' back,' Mac continued
gruffly. 'I'd done it, then, see? Burnt the clothes, scrubbed
away the blood, got rid of the evidence. All in a matter of
minutes. It dawned on me then that there was no way I
could go to the police. I had to carry on.'

'And the body?'

Lance shook his head. 'Dad won't tell me.'

'Alf and I dealt wiv that,' said Mac gruffly. 'It's not for
the lad to know. He's got enough on his conscience already

through no fault of his own, an' it's not for you to know neiver.'

'No! No absolutely not, don't tell me, Mac!' I got up hurriedly, suddenly realising I knew far too much already. I moved along the river bank, hugging myself. I felt so cold, freezing actually. I clutched my upper arms tightly. My mind was spinning. God, I – I was an accomplice now or something wasn't I? In it up to my neck! Christ, how on earth had I managed to get involved in this? I had to extricate myself forthwith! I had to – well what did I have to do? I swung around. Mac was watching me closely.

'But – but surely, Mac, now that the police have got a whiff of this, now that they think she might be dead, surely you'll have to come clean? I mean, they definitely suspect Alf. You heard what that guy said, so Alf will have to talk to them now, won't he? Tell them what happened? You could persuade him to, and you could help him, too. I mean I know Alf's likely to get in a muddle and say the wrong thing, but between you, you could both tell them what you've just told me! I mean, I believe you, so why shouldn't they? It looks far more guilty *not* to say anything, *not* to go in and answer their questions!'

'Don't be soft,' he scoffed. 'The only reason you believe us is 'cos you know us, and trust us. They'd take one look at us, root around in our backgrounds – which are tidy, but not immaculate – see how we've tampered with the evidence, and then they'd be rubbing their hands wiv glee! Oh yes, yet another conviction to pop under the DI's nose, yet another murdering bastard nailed, and a right feaver in their caps, too! Nah, do me a favour. That's right out. There's no question of that, not now, it's too late. Alf's got to get away, that's the only answer. He's gone, anyway, see. Gone to a safe place.' He checked his watch. 'In a couple of hours he'll be out of the country, heading for the Spanish—'

'OH, MAC, DON'T TELL ME!' I shrieked. 'I – I don't want to know!' I swung round, turning my back on him, biting my thumbnail frantically, and staring, horrified, into the gathering gloom of the middle distance. My God, what was I doing even *listening* to this? This was like – well, like getting involved with the great train robbers or something! A nice bunch of cockney lads, kind to animals and old ladies, always sending flowers to their mums, and who'd only meant to rob a train like Butch and Sundance did, who hadn't meant to blow the guard to bits and skip off to Puerto— I swung back. 'And has *he* got a passport?' I demanded. 'Alf?'

'He has now.'

I groaned, clutching my head. Oh God, why did I *ask* that? Now I *knew*! A false passport probably, and – oh crikey, yes, of course, a thousand pounds in folding readies stashed in his pocket. I gulped. Kindly donated by yours truly, not two hours ago. No wonder he'd wanted more.

'And you? You and Lance? They'll be back to question you in the morning, surely?'

Mac lit a cigarette and sucked hard. 'I'm sure they will, and we know nofing. All we know is what Alf told us, that Vi left him. Packed her bags 'cos she'd had enough of 'im and went to Spain to stay with a friend, and as far as we know, that's where she still is. Right, Lance?'

Lance was still staring miserably at his shoes. 'Right,' he muttered bleakly.

'And Alf? Where's Alf, they'll ask.'

Mac shrugged, expressionless, just as he no doubt would in the police station. 'Alf? Dunno. Really, dunno, guv. Christ, I'm not my brother's keeper, am I?' His blue eyes widened innocently at me.

470

Oh, but he was, he most definitely was, and always had been. And I had no doubt that in the not-too-distant future, Mac would be joining his brother in Puerto wherever-it-was, taking the whole family with him, upping sticks, buying a little villa, running up a few haciendas with the help of his masonic brothers and sons, before going on to buy a bigger villa, with luxury pool and then retiring to run a beach bar. Mac had neatly averted disaster all his life, slipping and sliding, ducking and weaving, just one step ahead of his clumsy, not-so-sure-footed brother, but always there to stretch back a hand to catch Alf, should he need one, should he fall. I crouched down beside him.

'So why tell me?' I breathed. 'Why not just tell me what you'll tell the police? That you're not your brother's keeper and you haven't a clue where he is?'

'Because you know us too well and you know about Alf's stupid letters and you're too bleedin' smart into the bargain. I had you fooled wiv the Trinidad and Tobago stuff, which, incidentally, happens all the time round our neck of the woods, but I knew I'd have to tell you if the old bill came snoopin'. They just came a bit sooner than I'd hoped, that's all. We should have 'ad Alf away days ago, but these fings take time to arrange, if you know wha' I mean.'

'No,' I said firmly. 'I don't.'

And I didn't want to know either. Didn't want to know about false passports, false identities, someone to meet him on the other side, no doubt. Let's face it, there'd have to be. I couldn't see Alf getting to Tooting on his own, let alone Marbella. No wonder it had taken time to arrange – and then a safe house somewhere, with someone to look after him until Mac could get out there. And of course extradition was still lax in some areas on the continent. For all the Spanish protestations that they did their best, if you knew the right people, it was still possible to lie low, and if the heat was turned up, why, you could always get on a boat and hop across to Marrakesh until things cooled down. And meanwhile, yes, meanwhile, poor old Vi lay a-mouldering in a shallow grave somewhere. Mac caught my eye.

'An accident, remember?' he said sharply. 'He loved her, orright? Really loved her. You saw 'ow he was for weeks afterwards, beside 'imself he was, weren't he?'

I nodded. That much was true. I remembered them all coming back that weekend: Alf in tears; Spiro, with presumably not a clue what was going on but joining in on the waterworks front anyway out of sheer solidarity; Mac, pale and tense, hustling them all to work like demons that morning, taking their minds off the horrors of the past couple of days with some hard graft; and Lance – no. No, of course, Lance had been here that weekend. It was the weekend that Claudia had gone missing. I suddenly remembered rushing to the pub to look for her, but finding him on his mobile phone instead, talking to his father, looking deadly serious, grim. And then I remembered his strange reluctance to call the police to find Claudes . . .

I turned. 'You knew? When I found you in the pub?'

'Only that Vi was dead,' he said quietly, 'and that it was an accident. I didn't know what Dad was planning to do, but I knew enough not to get the police round here if I could possibly help it.' He regarded me squarely. 'Although I would have done, Livvy. Had we needed to.'

I nodded. I believed him too. Believed both of them, knew instinctively they were both telling the truth, and knew instinctively that the police wouldn't believe them and would nail Alf, and that life was so unfair. But where did that leave me?

'I'm counting on you to stay shtumm, luv,' said Mac

quietly. 'Not to lie or anyfing, not to tell any porkies, right, but just to say nofing. Say you don't know, orright?'

I looked at him, then glanced away. Across the river, the fireflies were dancing in the beams of the low evening sun. It sounded so easy, didn't it? Just don't say anything. Say you don't know. I swallowed.

'You need to know, Mac, that I can't do that,' I said quietly. 'I won't go to the police, won't actually seek them out, tell my story, spill the beans, but if they come here asking me questions, I won't stay "shtumm," either, as you call it. I have to tell them all I know. The letters, everything. You need to know that.'

I held his eye firmly as he looked at me long and hard. Finally he nodded.

'Yeah, well, I rather thought you'd say that. Rather expected it. Two different walks of life, eh, luv? Two codes of practice, somefing to do with morals and duty – rules, too, I expect.'

'Something like that.'

'Yeah, well, when the chips are down, I make me own rules.' He eyed me beadily.

I eyed him nervously back. There was a pause. 'So what are you going to do then, Mac? Boff me on the head to keep me quiet?'

Suddenly he flared up. 'I fought I'd make it clear we ain't like that!'

'Sorry, sorry,' I muttered quickly. 'That was cheap.'

Cheap, but quite a relief to know he *wasn't* going to, actually, I thought nervously.

'No,' he said thoughtfully, scratching his chin, 'but what it does mean, though, is I might have to make tracks sooner than I thought. Might have to—'

'Mac, enough!' I gasped, jumping up. 'Just do what you

have to do, but don't tell *me* about it, all right? Don't tell me any more!' I folded my arms and marched off a few paces, then spun round and came back again. I glared down at him. 'Just – keep it to yourself, OK!'

He gazed up at me for a moment, pursed his lips, then sprang athletically to his feet. 'Yeah, yer right,' he agreed. 'The less you know the better.' He jerked his head. 'Come on, Lance, my boy, we've got work to do.'

Lance got miserably to his feet and then they both made to go, but then suddenly Mac turned back, regarded me squarely. 'Lance and Spiro will finish up here, luv. There's precious little to be done in that bathroom, but they'll do it, and you can settle up wiv them later, orright?'

'Orright,' I growled. 'I – mean, right.'

He held out his hand. 'Goodbye then, Olivia. Nice doin' business wiv you. Only do us a favour, eh? Give us a day's grace before you go an' spill the beans?'

I stared at him. 'Well now, how on earth am I supposed to do that,' I said slowly, looking at his outstretched hand. 'They'll be back here tomorrow morning, Mac, first thing. You heard him say so yourself.'

'Ah, but not to speak to you, luv, to us. You could make yourself scarce for the day, couldn't you? Not be there when they bang at the door? Have a pressin' engagement?'

I could feel Lance's eyes on me too now. I licked my lips. Could feel myself wavering for a moment. 'Well, I sup- pose . . . I could try, but—'

'Good girl,' he beamed. 'You're all right, Olivia. You're straight and you mean what you say. I like that.' He offered his hand again and this time I shook it, albeit gingerly.

'Yes, but listen, Mac,' I said nervously, 'I said I'll try, that's all. I'm not promising anything. I mean – I might not be able to get away, it may not be poss—'

'Oooh, you'll do just fine, luv, believe me. I knew I could count on you. Knew you wouldn't let us down.'

'Well I—'

'*Arrivederci* then,' he said briskly, giving a mock tug of his forelock and turning smartly on his heels. Lance fell in quickly behind him.

I watched, somewhat slack-jawed, as they went quickly back to the caravan, disappeared inside, and then I saw the door slam behind them. I stood for a moment, my mind racing, but with a nasty sickly feeling in my stomach, too. Finally I turned myself, walked slowly over the bridge, and on up the lawn to the house.

Dusk was falling fast now, and the fireflies were doing a last frantic dance in the low, flickering light. My own head was dancing fairly frantically too, and as I ducked under the blossoms of Madame Hardy covering the arbour, I realised, with a sudden start of horror, that Mac had very subtly turned the tables on me there. With his steely blue eyes upon me I'd promised— What exactly had I promised? I stopped still. To disappear for twelve hours so as not to blow their cover while Mac slipped the country? Good God! My hand shot out and clutched the wooden arbour, crushing petals, feeling thorns. Oh Lord, Olivia, that's – that's tantamount to harbouring criminals, isn't it? Or at least aiding and abetting them? Well, it was certainly something dodgy, I wasn't sure what, but on the other hand what else was I to do? I turned, gazed back at the caravan door. I'd more or less given my word, shaken hands even, and I'd feel such a heel shopping them first thing tomorrow, I'd – Well, I'd be a *grass* or something terrible, wouldn't I?

I chewed my lower lip nervously. Should I go back and tell Mac I couldn't do it? Couldn't go through with it? I wasn't altogether sure I could face those piercing blue eyes upon me again, though. Oh God, I thought, raking a hand through my hair, if only I wasn't so thoroughly on my own here! I just longed to *talk* to someone about this, longed not to be so flaming independent, so very solitary, longed to wail, '*Help!* I'm caught up in a murder inquiry here. What the hell should I do? What would *you* do? It struck me, in a flash, that Imo was literally only over the road; dear, smart, sensible Imo. Should I dash over and bend her ear? I blinked. What, in the middle of a smart cocktail party, Olivia? Muscle your way through the rattling jewellery and the clinking champagne glasses to tug at her sleeve, hiss in her ear? And what would she say? Well, you know damn well what she'd say: she'd say go to the police right now, of course she would! And Sebastian? I took a deep breath. No. No, I mustn't even think about Sebastian. That way madness lay, and I certainly mustn't involve him in this. Molly and Hugh I'd love to speak to, but they were both caught up with Millicent and the baby, and although they were both woolly-minded liberals I had a nasty feeling that even *they* might point me in the direction of the police station. In fact, anyone who didn't know these boys, who hadn't heard their story, who hadn't seen Mac's eyes fill up with tears just now, and who hadn't seen Lance's white, scared face, would say just the same. But I had. I had heard them, and I had seen them, and I knew Alf and I knew he wouldn't hurt a fly, and d'you know, I just . . . couldn't do it.

I turned back and walked quickly inside, perching on the first convenient chair that came to hand, just inside the French windows. I bit my thumbnail furiously for a moment, then got up and lit a cigarette. More thumb gnawing as I paced about the room, then – a thought. I stubbed my cigarette and hastened to the calendar in the kitchen. Maybe, just maybe, I *had* got a pressing engagement tomorrow? I mean, you never know, I might be incommoded at the dentist's, be flat on my back at the gynaecologist's or – ah, here, the 22nd, anything doing? . . . I gazed. Blank. Damn. Except – what was this, at the bottom, in pencil? I peered. 'Claudia to Lucy's for night.'

Ah yes, of course, I remembered now. Amanda, Lucy's mother, of the disappearing child episode, was desperate to have Claudes back and prove her worth as a competent mother, so if Claudia was away all day and all night, I reasoned rationally, what would I normally do? What would *any* normal, right-minded mother do on a child-free day in the middle of the school holidays? Well, she'd go to London, of course, that's what! Yes, I thought with a surge of joy, she'd spend the entire morning – nay, the entire *day*, in Harvey Nichols, of course she would! She'd have lunch, maybe take in an art gallery or two, have a leg wax, get her hair done – perfect! Oh golly, yes, *per*fect. My day was really taking shape! And it wasn't even a ruse, I thought happily. I really, honest to God, might well have done just that had I glanced at my calendar in the morning and seen Claudes bolting down her cereal all set with her overnight bag. And if I could set off bright and early, I thought furtively, really bright and early, before Raincoat and C&A Suit had even got a toe on the doorstep, well so much the better.

I quickly lunged for the telephone and rang Amanda, who instantly thought I was cancelling.

'Oh God, Livvy, I'll look after her,' she wailed. 'I swear to God I won't lose her!'

'Don't be silly, Amanda,' I scolded. 'I'm simply ringing to say could you possibly have her slightly earlier than we said? Like – ooh, I don't know, sort of, breakfast time?'

'Of course,' she agreed happily. 'Really, *any* time, Livvy.

Drop her off in the middle of the night if you like.'

'Don't tempt me,' I said grimly. 'But rest assured, Amanda, you'll be seeing me pretty bright and early tomorrow morning.'

I put the receiver down and noticed my hand was trembling. I stared. Well, it would, wouldn't it? I thought, regarding it with interest. After all, here I was, an ordinary middle-class housewife, pillar of the local community, erstwhile member of the PTA, coolly, coldly and calculatingly working out the perfect strategy to give the police the slip.

Chapter Twenty-Seven

The following morning the alarm went off at ten to six. I sat bolt upright, felt a bit sick, couldn't think why – then remembered, and felt even sicker. Hand to mouth I leapt out of bed, showered quickly, got dressed, and went to wake Claudia, who was kipping deadly.

'Claudia. Claudes, wake up!' I shook her shoulder.

She moaned and rolled over on to her face. I pulled back the covers mercilessly.

'Claudia, get up! We'll be late!'

'Geddoff!' She tried to wrench the covers back but I had them in an iron grip somewhere down by her feet.

'Up now, darling, with the lark! Be quick!' I trilled brightly.

She turned bleary eyes on her clock. 'But it's only six o'clock!'

'Yes, but you're going to Lucy's, and I have to go to London today, remember? Remember I told you I was going, darling?'

'No,' she muttered, dragging her legs around and stumbling out to the loo. 'I don't.'

I left her to it and dashed downstairs to the kitchen. Seizing the calendar from the larder door I wrote in bold felt pen 'Shopping in London!' Then I smudged it a bit with my finger. There. I stood back and admired my handiwork with narrowed eyes. Looked like it had been there for ever, decades even. Plunging my bare feet into wellies, I then flew out of the back door and raced down the garden, leaping a flowerbed brimming over with dew-soaked *Alchemilla mollis*, dashing down the lavender path, across the lawn, under the cedar tree, and across the bridge to the caravan. I rapped on the door, holding my side and panting. No answer. I rapped again, harder. The door finally opened and Lance stuck out a very tousled, blond head. He yawned and rubbed his eyes.

'Olivia,' he muttered. 'What's happened?'

'Lance, I'm going to London,' I hissed. 'I want you to know that, it's very important.'

'Fine.' He nodded.

'So if the police come,' I urged, 'it's been arranged for ages, OK? I've been excited about this for weeks, OK, Lance?'

'OK, OK.'

'Mac's gone, hasn't he?' I peered past him to the sleeping form of Spiro on a lower bunk. 'I heard his van go last night.'

'Yes, he's—'

'*Don't tell me!*' I shrieked, clapping my hands over my ears and shutting my eyes. When I opened them again, his steady blue eyes were trained anxiously on me.

'Olivia, listen to me. Don't worry about this, all right? Don't panic. This has absolutely nothing to do with you. This is our own personal tragedy and you'll be kept well out of it, OK?'

'OK? OK? Of course it's OK,' I spluttered, 'and of *course* I'm nothing to do with it. Jesus, I – I never imagined for one moment I was!'

I gave him what I hoped was a look of withering magnitude, but probably had more than a hint of frightened rabbit about it, then turned and bolted back up the garden, veering off left in a sudden tangent to glance round the side of the house and just make sure that a flashing blue light wasn't cruising menacingly my way.

Ten minutes later I was hustling a sleepy and protesting Claudia out of the front door, down the drive and into the car. I was just running furtively round to the driver's side, when abruptly – I heard a roar behind me.

'Hang on – I want a word with you, young lady!'

My blood froze. I shut my eyes and stood, sledge-hammered to the spot, awaiting the first stone, the first clink of handcuffs. Then I opened my eyes, and forced myself to turn, slowly, to see – Mr Jones, tearing down his path towards me, dressing gown flying, slippers flapping. Oh, thank you, God, thank you! Thou art a real brick!

'Mr Jones!' I cried.

'I'm soa, soa glad I've caught yew, like,' he panted. 'Tried to get hoald of yew yesterday, but yew didn't seem to be abowt. You see – I've heard all about your pickle!'

My heart stopped again. How the hell . . .? 'But I'm not in a pickle, Mr Jones!' I gasped.

'Oh noa, noa, your chutney! Gwyneth told me, see. Says yew always swear by those Unwin's green tomatoes yew grow, but I'll bet you've never tried making it with one of these boyos, eh?' He held up a whopping great pair of plum tomatoes, hanging pendulously together, side by side.

'Gordon's Bliss!' he hissed dramatically. 'Bet yew've never even seen the like, 'ave you now?'

I blinked. 'N-no, you're right, Mr Jones, never! How splendid, and – how kind. I'll pickle them this evening, shall I?'

I made to reach out for the voluptuous orbs, chuck them in the back of my car and be on my way, but he was too quick for me.

'Oa, steady on now!' he twinkled, holding them aloft, 'thought yew'd be interested, like! John Innes No. 2 and plenty of bone meal is the secret, but not soa fast!' He lowered his pink, excited face to mine. 'Fair dos, eh, girl? I've had my eye on that flat-leafed parsley of yours for some time now; wouldn't mind getting me 'ands on a sprig or two of that before yew pop these boyos in your chutney locker!'

'My . . .' I gazed. 'Oh! Right! Yes, well, be my guest, Mr Jones. Heavens, take the lot, do, only I really must fly. I'm off to London for the day, don't want to be late.' I jumped in the car. 'Really, take the lot!'

He frowned. 'Oooh, noa, noa, I wouldn't do a thing like that. Wouldn't dream of it, girl. I only meant—'

But I didn't hear the rest, I was away, leaving him standing in his dressing gown in a cloud of dust, clutching his vast tomatoes, whilst I roared off at breakneck speed to do business on the other side of town.

Ten minutes later, I was banging on Amanda Harper's mock-Georgian, twin-pillared front door in an immaculate, sleepy little cul-de-sac full of frothy Austrian blinds which were still very firmly down. Claudia was beside me, yawning her head off and looking like a bag lady as she clutched her possessions in a Tesco's carrier she'd had to grab hastily as I'd hustled her out. Finally Amanda appeared in her dressing gown, hair on end, mascara down her cheeks.

'Oh! Livvy. Gosh, I didn't realise you meant sparrow's fart.'

'Amanda, I'm so sorry. I know it's terribly early,' I

breathed, 'but I'm off to London today, been looking forward to it for ages. Shopping trip, you know.'

She rubbed her eyes. 'Blimey, at this hour? God, you'll be there in half an hour, there'll be so little traffic. I'm not sure the shops open at seven thirty, do they?'

'Ah, but I'll get a good parking place,' I beamed. 'So exciting. I've been—'

'Looking forward to it for months,' said Claudia wearily, pushing past me with her arms full. 'You've told us that about twenty times. She's lost it,' she informed Amanda as she went on past her and trudged upstairs to find Lucy, whom she'd no doubt crash out next to on her bed. 'She's really lost it this time. We're talking beyond Prozac.'

Oh God, was I overdoing it? I wondered, as I fled back down the path. Making too much of a meal of it? That would look even more peculiar. I must calm down. As Lance had said, this was absolutely nothing to do with me. Don't panic. Nevertheless, as I roared up the M1, every so often an image of Alf, kneeling, and holding a blood-soaked Vi in his arms, like Lear, sobbing over a lifeless Cordelia, would spring to mind and make me clutch my mouth with horror, and simultaneously put my foot down in an attempt to distance myself.

As a result, the speedometer hit 90, and I found myself in central London by seven forty-five along with all the early bird commuters. I parked in a Knightsbridge NCP, bought a paper, then had tea and toast in the Brompton Arcade, feeling I really should have a hat and dark glasses on in case someone recognised me and asked me why the devil I wasn't at home, where I belonged. The minutes ticked by. As I sat at the little café table I peered over my paper, gazed around a bit, a little more adventurously now perhaps for a wanted woman, and looked at my watch. Eight fifteen.

Good grief, only eight fifteen! What the hell was I supposed to do now?

'Um, what time do the shops open?' I bravely asked my Italian waiter, breaking my cover as he sauntered languidly up with my third cup of tea.

He shrugged, shoulders up around his ears somewhere. 'Ees supposed to be ten, but you know, ees summer time, so . . .'

So – what, the shopkeepers have a lie in? I sighed. Excellent news. Well, the plan was to stay for late-night shopping and go home at about ten o'clock. At this rate I'd have to shop till I was vomiting. More tea was required. I ordered it and read the *Daily Mail* more minutely – from cover to cover, in fact – until I noticed that according to Patrick Walker's replacement, Saturn was dominating my sphere and would undoubtedly be my downfall today. 'Don't expect to come up smelling of roses if you've deliberately deceived someone,' it warned grimly. I put the paper down with quivering hands, wondering if the deceived detective was even now banging on my front door, demanding to see the lady of the house, sniffing around to see which criminals I was harbouring today. Heavens, how brave those Resistance people must have been, with fighter pilots in the attic, whilst here was I, quivering with nerves at the thought of a brace of brickies in a caravan. Calm down, Olivia, just calm down. In an effort to do so, I emptied the entire contents of my handbag on to the table and sorted it out methodically. This, in the event, was just as well, because it was during this little operation, that a plan was hatched. You see, as I sorted around amongst the ancient cough lozenges, the parking tickets, the sweetie wrappers and a very tired-looking tampon, there, nestling at the bottom of my handbag, I spotted two tickets. Two tickets to a concert at the Wigmore Hall.

I sat back and stared at them. Of course, Hugh had given them to me, hadn't he, and I must have stuffed them in my bag. I took a sip of tea, turning them over in my hand. Yes, why not? Why not, in fact, spend the entire day preparing for this very event? Why not go to the hairdresser's, buy a new dress to wear, maybe even have my nails done for the first time in my life, and then, looking drop-dead gorgeous – well, as near as damn it, anyway – swan off to the concert in the evening? Imogen would be there, of course, and we could probably sit together since Hugo would be conducting, and naturally Sebastian would be there too . . .

I took another sip of tea. It was colder than one would wish. I hadn't allowed myself to think about Sebastian yet, you see. Since Johnny had gone, I realised I'd mentally put him up on a high shelf so I couldn't reach him. Not out of my mind, because that was impossible, but out of reach, because that was where I knew him to be. But I missed him – yes, of course I did. I missed the easy friendship we'd had and his downright niceness but, more than that, something deeper, more visceral, something in my heart ached for him too. If I allowed it. Mostly I didn't, but just occasionally I'd let it out of its cage, give myself a glimpse of him, at Hugh and Molly's maybe, his face creasing up with sudden mirth as he chewed gamely on a burnt sausage, or hauling a dripping Claudia out of the river, or just the two of us together, cooking in his basement kitchen, giggling as we threw Maureen's putrid casserole in the bin . . .

I traced the gingham pattern on the café tablecloth sadly. I knew I'd blown it, you see. I realised that. I knew I'd always thought of Sebastian as a first reserve, a sort of – well, if Johnny doesn't come back then who knows? Better than Malcolm and Rollo and Lance but not as good as

Johnny. And I'd more or less said as much, hadn't I? Said, sorry Seb, old boy, Johnny's back now, I'm afraid, so it's bye-bye and on yer bike, OK? Well, I could hardly turn round now and say – hey, guess what, great news! He's gone, so you're on again! Except that Johnny hadn't gone. I'd thrown him out. Surely that was different? Surely that changed the whole complexion of the situation somewhat? And maybe if I explained that to Sebastian, maybe if I didn't ask for too much, no more than our familiar old friendship back, then perhaps – perhaps something deeper could develop? Into what it should have been?

I lit a cigarette and watched a couple go by, arm in arm, the boy turning to drop a kiss on the girl's head. I glanced dreamily down at the tickets and for one giddy moment, saw Sebastian with his arm through mine, turning to drop a— Christ! My eyes suddenly snagged on a headline in the *Daily Mail*. 'British girl arrested for her part in cover-up.' I gasped, horrified, and read on. Oh – drugs, oh no, no, I wasn't involved in that, thank heavens, but what was I *thinking* of? Sitting here, mooning about Sebastian, when all the time . . . didn't I have enough on my plate? I mean, I had the murder squad on my doorstep, the boys in blue snooping round my house, what I needed was advice, not frigging romance! I took a deep, deep drag on my cigarette. OK, I reasoned calmly, so forget the romance bit, but – how about if I just talked to him? To Sebastian? About my present pickle? About the almighty Horlicks I seemed to have got myself into? See if he could give me some words of wisdom, some words of advice, because actually, I realised with a jolt, his were the only words I'd care to listen to. If he told me to go straight to the police, do not pass Go, do not collect £200 then I would, unreservedly, and conversely, if he said I was under no compulsion to do anything of the kind, well then, I'd go along with that, too.

Of course, I reasoned, packing up my bag again, it would be nigh on impossible tonight. I could hardly sneak up to him in the interval, tug at his sleeve and hiss, 'Listen, Seb, down at the bottom of the garden where most people have fairies, I've got these self-confessed killers who are frightfully sorry but would like me to cover up for them, what d'you think? Loved the violins in the first half, by the way.' No, no, that would never do. But perhaps afterwards, if I crept backstage and caught his eye, then maybe I could pass him a note? Ask him, if he wasn't too busy, if he could possibly spare a moment tomorrow? At about six in the morning, before the police popped round again?

I gulped and took another terrified drag of my cigarette, but felt relieved at least, to have something of a plan. Something to cling to. Resolving to stick to it, I heaved my by now groaning bladder from the chair, tottered to the counter to pay for four cups of tea, then embarked on my exhausting day.

As I trailed between Harvey Nichols and Harrods, filling in cancelled manicures here, and leg wax appointments there, it occurred to me to wonder how on earth French women managed it? All this beautifying? On a weekly basis? What, face, nails, toes, the lot? How very tiring, and how on earth did they find time to prick out their dahlias? As I emerged from yet another salon, having gamely entrusted myself to a student who'd never plucked an eyebrow in her life but was keen to try, I finally ended up, sans eyebrows, at the hairdresser's, with Marco, a drop-dead gorgeous blond, standing behind me.

I could tell at a glance that Marco was more used to positioning himself behind members of his own sex, and was standing now as though he was slightly uncomfortable, as though there might even have been someone standing behind him last night. Gosh, it could go on for ever, couldn't it, I thought, lines of them, my mind boggling at the possibilities. Marco gave a little sigh.

'So what are we doing today then?' he enquired in a bored little voice, gazing distractedly across the salon to where a fresh-faced young lad was sweeping the floor.

'We're doing sex and glamour,' I informed him firmly.

His peroxide head spun back like a machine gun, and his eyes met mine in the mirror. 'Ambitious,' he murmured doubtfully. Then arching his eyebrows in pained disdain he began plucking sniffily at my split ends. 'But then again,' he murmured, 'I always like a challenge.' Pausing only to shriek imperiously, 'Cindy, a coffee for my lady, please!' he pursed his lips, clenched his tight little buttocks, flexed his scissors, and went to work with alacrity.

Well, I have to say that half an hour later, albeit with a frightening amount of hair on the floor and an exhausted Marco behind me, the end result wasn't half bad. He'd cut it short, shorter than I'd normally have it, but had given me a long and sexy fringe which flopped right down over one eye, and which I had to flick back if I wanted to see daylight.

'What am I supposed to do with this then?' I said, lifting it doubtfully.

He sighed. 'You're supposed to smoulder through it, darling, but if that's a problem I'll cut it off.'

'Oh!' I dropped it. 'No, that's not a problem at all, watch.' I pouted kittenishly at him in the mirror.

He shuddered and reached for the scissors. 'Off, then.'

'No no!' I laughed, stopping his hand, 'I'll practise. Trust me, Marco, in a couple of hours I'll be smouldering so hard

I'll have half the men in London spontaneously combusting.'

'Scary,' he muttered drily, tossing his pretty little head and tucking his scissors in his tight back pocket. 'Well, be sure to leave a nice red-hot one for me.'

I assured him that I would and as he minced away I sailed out, feeling really rather sassy and pleased with myself. I kept catching glimpses of myself in the mirrors as I rode the Harvey Nicks escalators, and the effect was so gratifying, it gave me the confidence to sail straight into the hushed portals of the Donna Karan franchise and try on the first little black dress I came across. Yes, OK, it was a bit tight across the bottom and perhaps a bit short – sleeveless and backless too – but, boy, did it look terrific. I bounced out of the changing room delightedly and saw the young, male sales assistant glance admiringly.

'You don't think it's a bit young for me?' I asked with a confident smile.

'You're right,' he nodded, 'it is. How about this?'

Thunderstruck, I watched as he minced to a rail and plucked out a vast black tent. He dangled the hangar from his manicured little pinky and raised his eyebrows quizzically. Bastard. This was clearly Marco's boyfriend and there was obviously some homosexual conspiracy afoot here to put thirty-something women in their place. Well I, for one, wasn't going.

'I'll take it,' I said, smiling sweetly, 'and what's more, I'll be wearing it this evening!'

'Certainly, madam,' he murmured demurely, gliding seamlessly to the cash desk, 'but if you don't mind my saying, madam might want to pop to the beauty salon, first.'

'Bloody cheek!' I seethed. 'Madam has just spent three hours up in the beauty salon, actually!'

'Ah, but not in the depilatory section, I'll warrant,' he purred.

'Oh!' I clenched my arms to my side. 'Yes, right. Well, I'll see.'

Flushing but fuming I paid and stalked away. Actually I was a teeny bit grateful, too. God, imagine hailing Sebastian in the Wigmore Hall, looking like a Romanian shot putter? Flowing freely? I shuddered and dashed to Boots for a packet of Gillette, decorated a lavatory pan in the ladies, and then totally plucked, shaved, coiffured and painted – and somewhat stressed now, too – I hailed a taxi to take me to the other end of the Kings Road, where I was pretty sure the latest Hugh Grant film was showing, and where I was also pretty sure I could hole up for a couple of hours and pick my nails in private.

The first time I watched it I laughed, the second time I slept through it, and then when I awoke, sometime later, it was five thirty. I looked at my watch and blinked. Perfect. I'd had a nice relaxing snooze, felt totally refreshed, and now I had precisely half an hour in which to go back to Harvey Nichols, monopolise the ladies, put on my dress, fiddle with my fringe, apply the make-up, and dump my clothes and shopping bags in the boot of the car.

I arrived at the concert early. For some reason I'd imagined the Wigmore Hall to be somewhere arty, somewhere on the South Bank perhaps, or even in the Barbican, so when I hailed a cab, it was with a good half an hour to spare. I felt slightly foolish when I realised the venue was literally five minutes away in, funnily enough . . . Wigmore Street. Once outside I loitered nervously on the steps for a bit. There was no one else going in and I didn't want to be the first, so I pretended I was studying the programme which was stuck up in a glass case, like a restaurant menu, and which meant absolutely nothing to me, save for the fact that Sebastian's name was writ large at the top.

'*Night of the Spirits* by Sebastian Faulkner; performed by the London Sinfonietta.'

I swallowed. Quite something, really, one way and another, to have one's work performed here by the likes of them, surely? I suddenly wondered if a little black dress and a floppy fringe were quite the thing? I also wished to God I'd thought to ring Imo at work. How stupid of me! We could have gone together, met at the gallery, had a couple of drinks first perhaps. Still, people appeared to be arriving in dribs and drabs now, and even going inside, so I crept in behind a hugely sartorial group, pulling my dress down a bit at the back.

I bought a programme on the basis that I could at least put it across my knees to hide some thigh, and then went into the hall, wondering nervously if Sebastian would already be in the auditorium or perhaps backstage? I realised, with a little leap of pleasure, how excited I was about seeing him. All the ghastly horrors of yesterday and the equally ghastly horrors that would no doubt befall me tomorrow, fell away like a melting drift of snow, as I thought of his kind, sensitive face, relaxing into a smile of welcome as he spotted me. I glanced around. He didn't appear to be about just yet, though, so I found my seat and perched on the edge, peering at the now gathering throng and looking for Imo.

It soon became clear that this was a very sophisticated London audience: there were no waving programmes, no excited shouts of 'Co-ee! Over here!' as there had been at the more provincial Abbey; merely hushed, excited murmurings about the importance – musically speaking, darling – of this supremely momentous occasion. Highbrow to a man – and a woman, too – they were all very much in the Ursula Mitchell mould, until I realised that one of them actually *was* Ursula Mitchell, and that a few paces behind her was her daughter, Imo.

She was coming down the aisle behind a group of her mother's friends looking absolutely stunning in an ankle-length, blue slip of a dress, arms bare and golden, the dress, loose and fluted around her ankles. I instinctively opened my programme on my knees and wished I'd listened to my friend in Donna Karan.

I stood up. 'Imo!' I hissed, waving wildly and blessing my friend for his other tip, but she didn't hear me, and sailed on down the aisle, talking animatedly. I kept my eyes trained on the group, watching closely as they made their way to the very front. Then, seeing them cluster around some seats, murmuring excitedly and fanning themselves with programmes, I left my chair and hastened down.

Ursula was looking very much at home and holding forth in hushed tones to anyone who cared to listen about what a marvellous season the London Sinfonietta were having and what a tremendous violinist Stenbusky was and how lucky we'd been – *we'd been*, mind – to pinch him from the Birmingham Philharmonic, when, mid-stream, she saw me appear.

'Olivia!' She turned in surprise.

Imo swung around. 'Good heavens – Livvy! What on earth are you doing here? How lovely!'

'Molly and Hugh gave me their tickets,' I said with a grin, kissing them both. 'And I was in London anyway, so I thought – why not?'

'Why not indeed?' agreed Ursula, generously. 'And what fun! Tell me, is Johnny with you or is he meeting you from work? You can't *imagine* how delighted I was when Imogen told me you were back together again. That is *such* good news, my dear! Oh, Simon! Lovely to see you!' She turned as someone approached.

'Well no, it's not good news, actually,' I grimaced to Imo. 'You see, we're apart again now.'

'No!' Imo clutched my arm in horror. 'Oh God, I don't believe it! Don't tell me the bastard did it to you again?'

'Noo,' I said slowly, 'actually, Imo, I did it to the bastard this time.' I smiled wryly. 'I just realised how appallingly badly I'd been treated by him, you see. Oh, Imo, you were so right, right back in the very beginning when he'd first left me and you said I'd be mad to have him back!'

'I said that?' Her eyes widened.

'Yes, you did, and that was so incisive of you, but I just couldn't see it at the time! It was almost as if I had to have him back to realise it. It was like – like some sort of warped rite of passage – and I had to be the one finishing it too. In the end I realised – well – I just realised I didn't love him enough to swallow it all, I suppose.'

'Really?' Imo looked startled. Bewildered even. 'Gosh. B-but, Livvy, surely now that it's on your terms, now that you've got the upper hand – well, you can call the shots for a change, can't you? Be in the driving seat for once?'

'No,' I shook my head firmly, 'still wouldn't work, because you see I was in love with a dream. A fantasy Johnny, who just didn't exist. The *real* Johnny McFarllen was a weak, selfish, vain, manipulative man who— Oh, but don't get me on all that now, Imo,' I grinned. 'I'll tell you another time. I promise, there's loads, and when you've got at least six hours and an extremely large gin I'll fill you in on all the details, but what's more important now,' I lowered my voice excitedly, 'and what's *so* thrilling, actually, Imo, is that for the first time in years, I find myself seriously attracted to someone else. Someone who I think is fond of me, but who up to now – well, I've just been so blind to! I was so consumed by Johnny, you see, I couldn't even see this guy, not even when he was right in front of my nose!'

She gazed into my bright, excited eyes. 'Who?' Quietly.

I grinned. 'Sebastian.'

'Sebastian?'

'Yes, Sebastian Faulkner, the composer, silly, our man of the moment tonight! Oh, Imo, I *knew* he liked me and I was so stupid, I simply couldn't do anything about it until I'd got Johnny out of my—'

'Imogen—' Ursula suddenly leant between us and put a hand on her daughter's arm.

'So sorry to interrupt, Livvy, my dear, but I'd just love Imo to meet Simon Allsop, the impresario, and this is absolutely her last chance. Hector!' She called loudly to her husband. 'Hector, darling, introduce Imo to—' She pointed wildly to a man in a flamboyant red coat, then turned her daughter round and gave her a little push in their direction. Hector obediently came to collect her.

'Now.' Ursula turned back to me, smiling broadly. 'Olivia, did you say Sebastian, my dear?'

'Sorry?'

'When you were talking, just now to Imo. About someone you were fond of?'

'Oh! Oh yes, that's right!'

'Well, good heavens, I must warn you, I really must.' Her eyes widened.

'What?'

'Well, Imogen is seeing Sebastian.'

I stared. 'Imogen's . . . what?'

'She's seeing Sebastian. Walking out with him, as we used to rather coyly put it, and they've been together for

494

some time now, quite some time, and terribly in love. They're off to Vienna tomorrow, in fact. Sebastian has a performance out there.' She looked anxious. 'I'm so sorry, Olivia. I'm really surprised you didn't know.'

'But . . . she was seeing Hugo!' I felt panic fly through every vein, strange flutterings besieged me. 'I-I thought it was Hugo she was so infatuated with, so besotted by and—'

'Oh, Hugo,' she interrupted impatiently. 'Heavens, for a bit, maybe, but he was far too puppydog-ish for her. Good Lord, he followed her everywhere, hung on her every word – much too needy for our Imo. No, no, Sebastian is altogether a different kettle of fish, very much his own man, far more cerebral and eminently more suitable for Imo.' She smiled, raised her eyebrows confidentially. 'D'you know, I think I can quite confidently say that This Is It, Olivia? Isn't that marvellous? Because I know that you and Molly – and, good heavens, even Hector and I at times – had almost given up on her, almost despaired of her ever finding the right man and settling down, but I honestly believe that this time, she's finally done it!'

I gazed into the confident, grey eyes beaming down at me. But what about me? I wanted to say. Surely I found him first?

'And you didn't really want him, did you, my dear?' she said softly, putting a hand on my arm as if reading my thoughts. 'You told him so, remember? Although actually, he was terribly embarrassed about that. Came round one afternoon and told us about it.'

'Wh-what d'you mean?'

'Well,' she gave a tinkly little laugh, 'between you and me, he wasn't really aware that there was anything to finish!'

I stared at her. It occurred to me that this was actually an incredibly bitchy remark. I straightened up.

'Well, Ursula, believe me, there was. We'd become very fond of each other. Maybe he was too upset to admit that.'

A spot of colour came into each of her high, pale cheeks. She glared at me.

'Olivia, I've known you for many years, since you were a little girl, in fact. I'd hate to see you make a fool of yourself.'

'I have no intention of doing that.'

'Good, because I feel I must warn you that this time you'd be out of your depth. This time you're in an entirely different league.'

'What d'you mean, *this time*?'

Her sharp grey eyes went cold. 'I mean this time, as opposed to last time. When you crept in and took Johnny right from under her nose.'

I stared at her, aghast. My mouth dropped. 'I did *not*!' I managed to gasp. 'God – how can you *say* that? Imogen finished with Johnny, she—'

'Oh, she cooled it with him, all right,' she said impatiently, 'but she hadn't actually *finished* with him, hadn't actually ended it, and that's the difference. No, no, she was testing him, Olivia. She wanted to marry Johnny, you see, and she was adamant about that – had been right from the very beginning – and we all knew that, the whole family knew, and frankly I'm surprised you didn't, or perhaps you chose not to, hmm?' She sighed. 'But she was so young, you see, still so very young.' She pursed her lips as I gazed, horrified at her. 'For a long time, too, I'd felt that Johnny had had the upper hand in the relationship, was a bit too . . . well, a bit too conceited, too big for his boots, so I concocted a little plan, a way to bring him down a peg or two. To test him out. Imogen was convinced he was the only one for her, but I wanted to see if Johnny was up to it, if he was up to marrying my precious daughter. I wanted to bring him to heel,' she breathed, 'to deserve her, to beg her to have him back!'

I stared at her, astounded. 'What – so you told her to cool it with him?' I gasped. 'To hardly even speak to him after Oliver's funeral, to never come home at weekends and – and to sleep with Paolo in Italy!'

Her face closed. 'Don't be so crude, Olivia. No, I merely suggested she play the fish a little, make him jealous, make him see that there were other men besides him who were attracted to her, desperate to take her out, see what his reaction would be. And he reacted pretty well, I must say. He even trekked all the way out to Italy to get her back, and I was impressed. I thought that with a little more of the same treatment she'd bring him quite conclusively to his knees, have him begging to marry her.' Her eyes hardened. 'But I hadn't reckoned on you, Olivia. Hadn't reckoned on your part in the tale. Because then you appeared on the scene, didn't you? You, with your green fingers and your broken home, wheedling your way into Angie's garden with your secateurs and that wide-eyed, little-girl-lost routine of yours, winding yourself like bindweed around a broken-hearted Johnny.'

'Mrs Mitchell!' I gasped. 'You're rewriting history! He was devastated about Imo, sure, but he was equally adamant he wouldn't have her back, not after what she'd done!'

She smiled. 'Oh no. *You* persuaded him he was adamant he wouldn't have her back. All those cosy little lunches in the City while you did some two-bit secretarial course and while my talented daughter studied Botticelli in Florence, waiting for him to come to her.' She tilted her chin up at me. 'You played on a vulnerable young man, Olivia, a man whose girlfriend was conveniently studying abroad and whose father had just died. It was insidious, calculated, and very, very shrewd, I'll give you that.'

I gazed at her, aghast. My God. All these years she'd thought this of me, all these years she'd harboured this bitterness, this resentment, considered me the fly in the ointment. And Imo too? I swung round to find her, but couldn't see her. My heart lurched in horror. I also felt shocked into wondering – was this so? Was she right? But I'd asked Imo, I'd cleared it with her when Johnny and I had first—

'I *asked* Imo, Mrs Mitchell. I wrote to her in Florence, got a letter back saying—'

'Oh yes, and that was jolly clever of you too, wasn't it?' she sneered. 'Let's get it in writing. And what did you expect her to reply? Keep your thieving hands off my boyfriend? Over my dead body, you conniving bitch? What – dear, sweet-natured Imo? No, no, you knew darned well she'd give you the all-clear. You're a sharp little thing, Olivia, you always have been. You sneaked in and—'

'I did *not* sneak in,' I trembled. 'I was fully aware of how delicate the situation was and—'

'Not aware enough,' she snapped sharply. 'And actually, for all your sharpness, not smart enough to see what was *really* going on, which was that Johnny took you on the rebound because he couldn't have my daughter!' Her voice trembled. 'Christ, she even came back from Italy to be your bridesmaid. You made her do that, and I'll never forgive you for that because, God help me, I had to pick up the pieces the following day. The poor child nearly had a breakdown.'

I caught my breath in horror. Her face was pale now, taut with pent-up loathing. 'My precious girl,' she breathed, 'you did that to her. And she never found anyone else, never found anyone like Johnny.' She raised her chin high. 'But she has now, you see. She's all right now. She can be whole again – Sebastian's seen to that. And we're all so relieved, so thankful. They're in love, Olivia, very much in love, and I'm not going to ask you not to interfere, not going to ask you not to meddle, because this time, you can't. No one could possibly come between them now. Even if you tried, believe me, you'd be pissing in the wind.'

Something in the vulgarity of this expression, totally out of character, and the flash of steel in her grey eyes made me realise what Molly and I had always suspected. That Mrs Mitchell was a very, very tough cookie. I stared at her jutting jaw and her hawklike nose which seemed to be almost quivering with rage, just as Imogen came rushing up.

'Mummy! Are you all right? What's happened? You . . . you look so upset!'

Ursula raised a brave chin. 'I'm fine,' she whispered. 'I was just explaining something very fundamental to Olivia here. Frankly, I'm surprised she didn't know before. Any of it.'

She held my eyes a moment longer, then turned and walked away.

The orchestra were ready on the stage now, tuning up, violinists brandishing their bows, anticipating the appearance of their conductor. Imo stared after Ursula, then shot me a confused, anxious glance, before hastening to her mother. I watched them go, transfixed, literally welded to the spot by the ferocity of her words. A moment later, I saw Sebastian materialise from a side door. His face wore a defended, public look as he glanced about at the audience. Then, seeing Imo at the front, quickly walked across to join her as she stood, comforting her mother. I watched as he lightly touched Imo's back and kissed her cheek.

Ursula's back was still to me, but I saw her delve into her bag for a hanky and pat her eyes, as Imo reached anxiously across to clutch her hand. What is it, what's wrong? I saw her ask. Ursula began to speak but the strings were growing louder and I couldn't hear what she was saying, could only watch Sebastian's face grow darker, more concerned, more – angry. Imo's eyes widened, her jaw dropped, then as Ursula dabbed with her hanky once more, they both turned and stared in my direction, turning shocked, horrified gazes on me. There was a brief moment when we all locked eyes. Then they turned away, back to Ursula. I saw Sebastian put a hand under her elbow for support, and as she gravely nodded to them both that she was fine, fine now, they helped her into her seat.

The orchestra had gone very quiet and the audience were hushed with anticipation, with only the odd muffled cough punctuating the silence. Imo sat down next to her mother with Sebastian beside her. Realising suddenly that I was the only person in the hall left standing, I turned and made my way shakily back to my place at the rear of the auditorium. A moment later, Hugo Simmonds took the podium to an enormous roar from the crowd. I sat, dazed and bewildered, watching blankly as he acknowledged the audience, then turning his back on them, he raised his arms, brought them down with a flourish, and with a blast of trumpets and horns, the music began. I looked down and realised my programme was shaking on my knees. I must have listened to three, maybe four bars of the piece, before getting up, gathering my bag and my programme, and leaving the hall.

Chapter Twenty-Eight

I don't remember hailing a taxi, sitting shocked and white-faced as I no doubt did in the back, gazing blankly at the thronging London streets as they swept by, or even arriving at the car park, and somehow, dazedly, finding my car, but I suppose I must have done that too. I do remember the drive home, though. I remember how dry my throat felt, how knotted my chest was, and how I had to keep a really firm grip on the wheel to stop my hands from shaking and the car from veering into another lane. But if my body was having problems reacting properly, my mind was compensating by going into overdrive. Imo and Sebastian – of course. God, what a fool I'd been! It was him she'd been angling for all along, not Hugo. Cosy dinner parties at her parents' house, all no doubt arranged by her Svengali, Ursula, and then yesterday – why, I even *saw* Imo, alone, going into his house. Why hadn't I clicked? Even Hugh had hinted at it now I came to think of it, and of course, she'd been so thrilled when Johnny and I got back together, coming round with flowers, hugging us, tears of relief in her eyes: 'Oh God, guys, this is what we've all been hoping for!' Well, of course it was, of course!

I buzzed down the window and gulped in some air. So – how long had it been going on? While he'd been seeing me?

If indeed he *had* been seeing me, I thought with a jolt, because actually, in *his* eyes he probably hadn't, which would explain his reluctance to comply when I offered him my body on a plate after Molly and Hugh's barbecue, and his bemused expression when I popped round later to inform him that our tempestuous affair was over. No wonder he'd looked surprised. No wonder he hadn't broken down in floods of tears. As far as he was concerned I was Mrs Friendly Neighbour with whom he had the occasional matey drink when he wasn't canoodling with his main squeeze, Imogen Mitchell! I thought of Imo's beautiful, shining face tilted up to his and a hot flush washed over me. 'Don't make a fool of yourself,' Ursula had said. Well, it was too late for that. I'd done that already. In fact, it occurred to me I'd been doing it for years. About thirteen, to be precise.

Yes, thirteen years ago, I thought with a wave of misery, when Imo had apparently decided she wanted to marry Johnny, but unlike me, had thought through the implications, had known intuitively what she was taking on. She knew full well she had to bring a man like Johnny to his knees, drag him out to Italy, shove Paolo in his face, humiliate him, have him storm off in high dudgeon, but all the while be waiting, waiting for his anger to cool, for his unquestionable passion to surface, for him to beg her, on bended knee, to come back, at which point she'd have tossed her blonde head, slipped on her Gucci mules and returned to have him right where she wanted him. Except that she hadn't reckoned on me, creeping stealthily in, like some fat, spotty teenager who'd never been allowed to join in the games, and who'd spotted a gap and gone for it. Oh yes, in I'd nipped, always on the sidelines, always marginal, but, boy, was I seizing my chance now – but only, mind, only because Johnny had no one else to play with.

I gritted my teeth and breathed hard. And I'd never been enough for him, never – I saw that now. He'd always wanted more, needed more, and so he'd turned to Nina. It wouldn't have happened if he'd married Imo – she was more than enough for any man – and now, because of me, because of my pathetic eagerness to have him at any cost, there was carnage all around. Broken marriages, mistresses, thwarted love affairs and at the heart of it all, a small, fatherless, disabled boy. My heart lurched. My fault. I shot my chin up and swallowed desperately, but it was no good, tears were falling relentlessly, sliding silently down my cheeks as chaos howled inside me. It was all of my making.

And all that time, I thought wretchedly, wiping my face with the back of my hand, all these years Imo must have secretly hated me. Must have swallowed it bravely, but how her guts must have twisted every time she looked at me, every time she saw Johnny and me together, came to our home, sat at our table. Always in her mind – that should have been me! And I never *knew*!

I pulled off the motorway with an astonishing lack of care, horns blaring in my wake, and sped blindly away into more traffic. The sky was darkening overhead and a rainstorm threatened. At length it broke, and I drove the rest of the way in a torrential downpour, concentrating hard on the frantic dance of the windscreen wipers, grateful for their distraction.

When I finally pulled up in my drive I turned off the engine and sat for a moment. The rain had abated to a dismal drizzle and I leant forward and rested my head on the wheel. My insides were twisting themselves into a fierce ball of anguish, but I knew too that monthly abdominal cramps were also to blame. How convenient of my reproductive system to make its presence felt at this particular moment. Thank you, God. I dragged my head wearily from the wheel, massaged my tummy and leant back, reliving for a ghastly moment Sebastian's face as he'd turned to look at me. Shook and disbelief seemed to be the overriding emotion in those dark eyes. So what exactly had Ursula said? That I was intent on the same, destructive course of action that I'd perfected thirteen years ago? That I was determined to muscle my way into his life and crowbar her precious daughter out, at all costs? I rested my head back wearily on the head-rest, and it was at the moment that I realised I wasn't alone.

Just round the corner of the house, in the little car port that no one ever used, was a car I didn't recognise. It was blue, an Escort, I think, and it occurred to me that I didn't know anyone who drove a car as middle-aged as that. Its position in the car port rather than dumped in the middle of the drive gave it an alarming gravitas too, as if it had been carefully positioned, and as if its owner knew they may have to wait some time. Why yes, of course, I realised with a start, it belonged to the protagonists in the *other* disastrous chapter in my life, the chapter which, despite my desperate efforts to keep it under wraps, had clearly been unfolding relentlessly in my absence. The jolly old police. Oh yes, the boys in blue, who no doubt had been told I was out, but armed with a search warrant and an unending ability to sit soft and drink copious cups of tea, had camped out patiently in my sitting room, awaiting my return. Oh good. More music to face, and why not? Might as well get it all over in one day; might as well face a symphony as a string quartet.

I got out and slammed the door hard, rehearsing, slightly defiantly in my head – why yes, officer, I'm well aware that one of my workforce recently knocked off his wife, but seeing as it was a complete and utter accident I decided to give him a day's grace to get away. You see I—

'*Ahhh!*'

I leapt inches in the air as someone stepped out of the shadow of the hedge and caught my arm from behind. Terrified, I swung round.

'Lance!'

'Shhhh!' He put his hand gently over my mouth, glancing quickly about to check I hadn't been heard.

Wide-eyed I stared at him, then nodded to let him know I wasn't going to shriek again. Slowly, he took his hand away.

'What's going on? I gasped, when I'd regained the use of my vocal cords. 'What's happened?'

'I'm waiting for Spiro,' he whispered. 'The police should be back with him any minute. I don't want them to know I'm still here.'

'Spiro?'

'Yes, poor bastard, he's down at the station. They took him there this morning. He's been there all day, being questioned.'

'Oh God! And you too?'

'Most of the day, but they let me out on bail a couple of hours ago.'

'On bail!' I stared. His face was very pale under his tan. 'But, Lance, you weren't even there when Vi died! You were here with me that weekend. You haven't done anything!'

'Quite, but in the absence of Dad or Alf, Spiro and I are all they've got to go on. You were right to go to London, Livvy.'

'Did they want to speak to me?' I whispered fearfully.

'Yes, but only as a matter of course. Just as a formality, so they said, and certainly not as desperately as they wanted to speak to us,' he added drily.

'But,' I glanced back at the house, confused, 'why is Spiro down there? I mean, if they're up here—'

'Who?'

I jerked my head. 'Isn't that their car?'

He stared, then clicked. 'Oh no, that's your mother-in-law. I let her in. She wanted to wait for you. She's inside.'

'My—'

'Livvy? Is that you, darling?'

The front door opened and Angie stood there framed, peering out into what was now just a light drizzle, shading her eyes in the gathering gloom.

'Good God, does *she* know anything about all this?' I hissed, appalled.

'Of course not,' he hissed back. 'What d'you take me for? No, by all accounts she just came round to discuss the state of your marriage.'

'Oh terrific,' I groaned.

'Livvy, is that you?' she called again.

'Go on.' Lance gave me a little shove. 'Go in and act naturally, for heaven's sake. I'll let you know when Spiro gets back.'

He slunk back to his position behind the hedge, pulling up the collar of his leather jacket and lighting a cigarette, shading the match with his hands and looking for all the world like Orson Welles in *The Third Man*. I raked a despairing hand through my wet hair. God, Angie. She was all I needed right now, but then again I reasoned wearily, she was, admittedly, somewhat preferable to the police. I trudged dismally up the path and kissed her damply on the doorstep.

'Angie, I didn't recognise your car.'

'It's a hire car, darling. Remember I pranged the last one? And the bloody door leaks like a sieve so I have to put it under some shelter when I park. Good gracious, you look all in! Come in and I'll make you a stiff gin and tonic. Are you feeling all right?'

'Period pains,' I said weakly, and not untruthfully. 'But I'll take you up on that gin,' I said following her in and collapsing into the nearest armchair. 'It's the best offer I've had all day.'

She bustled off to the kitchen and I rested my head back and gazed blankly at the ceiling. So, Spiro was, at this very moment, being grilled rotten in some cold grey interview room, was he? Poor boy. Heavens, he'd be terrified, and probably in floods too, wringing torrents out of his hat. I wondered when they'd be back for me. I shut my eyes and rubbed my forehead wearily. I could hear Angie rummaging about in the kitchen, no doubt looking for ice and lemon, which could be a very fruitless search in this house. How long had she been here, I wondered? And what was so important that she had to come over, rather than telephone? And then wait? I twisted uncomfortably in my chair, rubbing my aching tummy, as Angie reappeared with two large gins, predictably, *sans* ice. She handed me one and I took a large gulp as she settled herself opposite. She was looking lovely, as usual, in a pale suede jacket and biscuit skirt which went beautifully with her copper hair, but her face wore an anxious look. She went to take a sip of her drink, then thinking better of it, put it aside and leant forward urgently.

'Livvy, I've got to talk to you.'

'So I gather,' I murmured. I took another gulp. God, it was strong.

She leant back for a second and massaged the corners of

507

her mouth with thumb and forefinger, gazing at a spot somewhere above my head as if for inspiration. Then her eyes came back to me. They were wide and frank.

'Livvy darling, I know what you're up to.'

'Oh?' I blinked. Crikey, I wish I did.

'With Johnny. I know the game you're playing.'

'I'm not playing any game.'

'Yes you are, and you've played it brilliantly, quite brilliantly. But listen, darling – he's desperate. You've brought him comprehensively to heel now, brought him right back into line, so don't make him suffer any more, eh? He so badly needs to come home.'

'Needs?' I muttered.

'Wants,' she corrected quickly.

I frowned. 'So – he's with you?'

'Of course he's with me, where did you think he'd be? He's been with me since you threw him out!'

'Well, funnily enough, Angie,' I said slowly, 'I had a sneaking suspicion he might be with another woman. The woman who, actually, was the initial *cause* of my throwing him out.'

'Oh her,' she said dismissively. 'No, no, that's all finished. He's over her now, and that's all thanks to you, my dear. Golly, you've made him sit up. By showing him the door, just when he thought he'd got his feet under the table again and all was forgiven – oh, that was inspired, Livvy, and I told him so too. Told him he jolly well deserved all he got from you, and that it was up to him to win *you* back now. You've really brought him to his senses, my love, and it was absolutely what he needed – a good kick up the chauvinistic pants. But . . . I'm worried now.' Her well-preserved forehead puckered with anxiety and she clasped her hands tight. 'I'm worried that if you leave him in the wilderness any longer your plan might backfire, that he may get *used* to being out there on his own, find some other form of distraction. Now's the time, Livvy,' she said urgently. 'He's learnt his lesson, bring him in from the cold. He'd crawl back now if you said the word, and with everything out of his system! You've won hands down, darling, but – just be careful. A man like Johnny won't stay on hold for ever.'

I swirled my drink thoughtfully in my glass. Frowned into it. 'But . . . I just told you, Angie. It's not a game. I don't want him back. Ever.'

I looked up and met her hazel eyes. Saw a wave of hurt pass over them. I steeled myself.

'D'you have any idea what he's done?'

She nodded quickly, swept her hair back nervously. 'I – I know how long it went on for.'

'And?'

'And – I know about the child,' she admitted quickly.

'And *you'd* forgive him?'

'Yes,' she nodded, before her eyes darted out of the window. 'Yes, I know I'd find it in my heart.'

'Would you? Really? So – where d'you draw the line then, Angie? What is forgivable and what's unforgivable?'

She didn't answer. Glanced down at her hands. I put my drink aside.

'Come on, Angie,' I urged, 'let's see. What exactly would you forgive? How about – a quick snog on the dance floor with a girl at a party? Well, one would be furious, naturally, but it's hardly grounds for divorce, is it? Well, what about a quick one-night stand then? In a hotel? Or a brief affair? Ghastly, of course, humiliating in the extreme, terribly degrading and the marriage would never be quite the same, et cetera, et cetera, but still, yes, one probably *would* forgive, wouldn't one? Because frankly, what's the alternative? A bleak, single life and a solitary, uphill struggle to bring up one's child?' I shrugged. 'And so one staggers on, bravely, as I staggered on, and I forgave him all that, Angie. But what about a long, long, love affair? A year? Two years? And what if there's a child?'

Angie continued to inspect her nails. 'I still think,' she murmured levelly, 'the home, the breaking up of the family—'

'OK, so what about ten years of infidelity then? Twenty, no – thirty? And what about—' I cast about wildly – 'what about if you knew, for instance, that the moment your betrothed had shaken the confetti from his hair, the moment his honeymoon tan had begun to fade, he was off, dropping his trousers at every conceivable opportunity, and spreading himself about as thinly as possible? With – ooh, let's see now – half a dozen bastard children knocking about the place?' She stayed silent. 'Of course not!' I exclaimed. 'Of course one wouldn't forgive that, but don't you see, Angie, it's all subjective. It all comes down to what one's prepared to stomach, and call me old-fashioned, but knowing what I know now, I'd advise any woman to gag after that first snog at a party!' I angrily knocked back a swig of gin.

'No, not old-fashioned,' she said slowly, her hazel eyes coming up to meet mine. 'Very modern. You girls want everything now, don't you?'

'Well, if fidelity's having everything—' I exploded.

'Oh, for God's sake, Livvy, grow up!' she snapped. 'Women have put up with this for centuries! Johnny's not exactly the first oversexed man who went off to relieve himself elsewhere!'

There was a pause. I stared into her hazel eyes. Slowly it dawned. 'You mean . . .?'

'Oh yes.' She smiled thinly. 'Yes, for years. Scarcely had Oliver's feet hit the tarmac at Heathrow airport after our honeymoon in India – you see, I fit very neatly into that little analogy of yours – than the extracurricular activity started. Complete with bastard children too. Clearly in your book I shouldn't have stomached it.'

I stared, incredulous. 'But – you and Oliver. You were so happy!'

'Exactly.'

'But—'

'Happiness doesn't necessarily conform to the story-books, Olivia,' she said impatiently. 'We *were* happy, genuinely happy, but we'd ironed out our own *modus vivendi*, not one decreed to us, laid down by society.'

'But didn't you care? About the affairs?'

'Of course! Desperately, at first, of course I did. And he didn't know I knew, but privately I cried myself silly over them, particularly as a young bride. I thought it was the end of us.'

'So why didn't you confront him!'

'Because it would have been counterproductive,' she said patiently. 'I loved him, you see, and I didn't want to leave him. Telling him would have forced my hand, forced me to make an issue of it, make a decision. And in time, I also began to realise that actually, his affairs had no bearing on me, were no reflection on our marriage at all. He loved me, you see, adored me, probably even more so at the height of each adulterous liaison than at any other time. Physically, too, that side of our marriage never died. If anything it just got stronger.'

'So – then why did he need them? Why did he need those women!'

She shrugged. 'Different, I suppose, so therefore exciting.

511

Different women – different sort of sex too, if you know what I mean.' She eyed me beadily.

I blinked. 'No, I—'

'Well, I do,' she interrupted firmly. 'I know. And I tried it once, let me tell you, tried to be novel and imaginative and outrageous, tried to give him the sort of dirty sex he sought elsewhere, and he was appalled. I was his wife, you see, his shining madonna, mother of his children; he didn't expect that from me.' She passed her hand wearily through her hair. 'Oh, I don't know, Olivia. Why have men always gone to brothels?'

'But how could he face you? Wasn't he mortified? Ashamed?'

'Oh, totally, but that was his problem, not mine. I could rise above it all, look after the children, the house, the garden, and all the time he walked around tormented. He was riddled with guilt.'

'Jesus, I'm not surprised! But you're not saying you liked that? That you enjoyed occupying the high moral ground? You surely would have preferred it otherwise?'

'Of course I would, but that wasn't my particular marriage bed. Mine was the one I've just described, and I had to lie in it or go elsewhere. Every marriage is different, Livvy.'

'But it's outrageous that you should have been forced to compromise like that!'

She shook her head. 'I wasn't forced. I loved him, and he loved me. Really, like we'd never loved before. You saw how he was with me, he adored me, worshipped me, and that's why I stayed.'

'But . . . were there always other women?'

'Oh no, not necessarily, but I always knew when one was about, because he prayed incessantly. He was deeply religious, as you know, but the minute he was involved with someone else, there he'd be, kneeling at the foot of the bed, rosary beads winging frantically through his fingers, muttering endless Hail Marys, eyes shut, mouth taut with concentration, and then off he'd rush to confession the next day to absolve himself.' She smiled wryly. 'And maybe you're right. Maybe I did take some perverse kind of pleasure from it as I sat up in bed reading Barbara Pym, with half an eye on my husband kneeling at the foot of the bed trying to save his soul. I certainly felt in a stronger position than he was. He was in torment.'

She gazed up at the spot above my head again and I realised her eyes were filling up.

'And . . . is that why . . .?' I asked softly.

She swallowed. Shook her head. 'No. Well, yes. Yes and no, really. It wasn't *why* he did it, but shooting himself was a direct result of his infidelity. There was a baby, you see.'

'Oh!'

'Only one. Oliver prided himself on being so bloody careful, and that, to him, would be the ultimate sin, to bring an unwanted child, born out of holy wedlock, into the world. When I found out that this particular woman was pregnant, suddenly it all made sense. I realised why Oliver had only been sleeping for two hours a night recently, why he was walking endlessly round his paddocks in the early hours, why I'd find him weeping on the bathroom floor, why, on one occasion, he even tried to tell me, grabbing me round the knees as I found him sobbing, hunched by the bath.' Her face buckled briefly. 'Perhaps I should have let him. Perhaps that was cowardly of me, perhaps I could have saved him, but I didn't want to know. I shook him off. I couldn't, you see. Couldn't let him know I knew his secret. And I knew he wouldn't just tell me about this one woman, I knew the whole lot would come spewing out. And it would change the entire fabric of our marriage. From being a shining innocent, serene and above it all as he believed, I'd suddenly become a downtrodden doormat who knew the whole grimy truth and had to put up with her lot. Put up, or get out.' She took a large swig of gin; stared into space.

'So,' I cleared my throat, 'so when the child was born, is that what pushed him over the edge?'

'No. When the child was born,' she said carefully, 'Oliver was all right. Oh sure, for a day or two he was desperately distracted, but then, he began to calm down. It was as if the inevitable had finally happened and the pressure was off. He didn't know I knew, of course, but I watched him carefully as the days went by, very carefully, and I was relieved. It seemed to me that we could ride this storm, as we'd ridden all the others. But then the terrible news came. The news that all was not well. That the baby was severely disabled. Blind as well as crippled. That evening Oliver went out into the field and blew his brains out. He blamed himself, you see, thought that God's finger was pointing right at him, that his sins had been singled out for retribution, and been manifested in his son. My God, you've gone so pale, Livvy. I've shocked you.'

I was on my feet now. 'No, no...' I crossed to the window, my hand clutching the sill, trembling. Disabled. My God. Like Johnny's child. I swallowed.

'Have – have you seen Johnny's baby?' I whispered, staring at the wet lawn.

'Of course not, and neither shall I,' she said staunchly.

'And –' I cleared my throat – 'and, Angie, does Johnny know all this? About his father? About how the baby was?' I turned.

She shook her head. 'No one knows. I prided myself on that, although . . .' she hesitated, 'recently I've wondered if I

514

shouldn't tell Johnny. Let him know that his father wasn't all he was cracked up to be, all that Johnny thought he was. Part of Johnny's problem, I've always believed, was living up to Oliver. He idealised him and thought he himself never quite came up to the mark.'

I remembered how Johnny had stopped going to church when his own affair had been going on, wouldn't accompany me and Claudia, how he hadn't used religion to absolve himself, and how he had at least tried to look after the child when it was ill, and hadn't blown his brains out.

'Knowing what I now know about Oliver,' I said slowly, 'I don't think Johnny's got anything to worry about. He more than surpasses Oliver's mark.' Suddenly Oliver's words came back to me, that night, that last party at the McFarllens', Tara's birthday party, as he and I stood by the pool, watching Johnny and his sisters swim. 'Perfect, aren't they?' he'd said. I shivered. Just before he'd found out, no doubt. Before he'd discovered the condition of his illegitimate son. I cleared my throat. 'And I wouldn't tell Johnny about his father either, Angie, wouldn't disillusion him. To him, Oliver was a god. Let him at least hang on to that memory unscathed.'

If anything could completely destroy Johnny, I thought, this surely would. Like dysfunctional father, like dysfunctional son. And I didn't hate him enough to want him to know himself and his father for what they really were.

We were silent for a while, Angie and I. I thought of little Peter and his struggle through life. Perhaps Johnny would go back to them? How odd that I didn't care; quite wished he would.

'What happened to the child?' I asked suddenly, breaking the silence.

Angie was staring out of the window, blankly. 'Hmm?' She came back to me.

'Oliver's child, what became of him?'

'Oh, he lived, but other than that, I don't know. His mother was one of the few women I ever actually met though, although Oliver didn't know it.'

'She was a friend?'

'No no, not a friend.' She gave a wry smile. 'Oliver was not susceptible to our own class. Only the lower orders brought out the beast in him. No, her husband was a mechanic, he mended Oliver's cars. They had a vintage car place in Finchley, and I had to take one of Oliver's Lagondas in for him once. I saw her there.' She frowned. 'Livvy, what is it?'

I'd crossed to the French windows, shot back the bolts and flung them wide despite the rain. I stood there, letting the cool breeze gust into my face, blowing back my hair. 'Nothing.' I shook my head. 'Nothing, Angie.'

Oh God. Oh *God*. I remembered the faded blonde prettiness of Nina's mother. The kindly, no doubt unsuspecting father who'd believed he'd fathered the crippled, unseeing lad whose chair I'd seen. Nina's brother. Martin. Oliver's child. Tummy churning and feeling quite faint now, I gulped down great gusts of air. Angie was behind me, her hand on my shoulder.

'What is it, darling, what's wrong?'

'Nothing,' I murmured, 'nothing at all. It's all in the past.'

And if it remained Angie's intention to have nothing to do with Johnny's child, then that's where it would stay, I thought as I shut the doors again and bolted them. She'd never know, and let it remain that way. Let it all stay buried under a mountain of years; years of rich, privileged people playing carelessly with other, less privileged people's lives. Let the little family of the 'lower orders' beside the garage in Finchley, who now had two disabled children to their name, just get on with it, just cope, whilst those who'd created the carnage, those carefree, rich, amorous, glamorous men like Oliver and Johnny, who lay either dead and buried, unable to bear it, or at home with Mummy, unable to bear it, absconded themselves. Whilst Nina and her mother had no choice but to soldier on. Day after exhausting day, bearing the horror and the brunt of living with disability. Of coping with a sick child.

At length, I found my voice. 'Angie, does Johnny know you're here?'

She hesitated. 'Of course not, darling.'

I turned. 'He does. He sent you.'

'N-no, no really, I wanted to come,' she faltered. 'I—'

'It's all right, Angie,' I interrupted wearily. 'I have no intention of shooting the messenger, and actually, it makes more sense to talk through you, because the way I'm feeling at the moment, I'm not sure I could look at him anyway, let alone speak to him.' I folded my arms. 'Please tell him from me, Angie, that I'll be serving him with divorce papers just as soon as I've contacted my solicitor. Tell him that access to Claudia will of course be amicably and cordially arranged, and that I also intend to sell the house and move further away into the country. You can also tell him that—'

'Olivia, you don't mean this!' Angie was on her feet, agitated and pink, her drink spilling over her skirt. 'You're upset, I've upset you with all this talk of Oliver! Think it over, please. You'll regret acting hastily, I swear it! This is *Johnny* we're talking about, not some nobody you can cast aside like yesterday's paper! He's worth more than that, he's— Oh!'

To my everlasting relief – because I truly loved Angie and didn't want to tell her exactly how much her son was worth – at that moment there was a loud bang, as the front door flew open on its hinges. A great gust of wind billowed through the house, and then a moment later, two bodies lurched through, like a couple of desperate souls reaching their journey's end. Staggering down the hallway came Lance, looking wet and bedraggled, and supporting someone I almost didn't recognise. With his black hair mussed all over his face, eyes wild and staring, one arm slung around Lance's shoulder and dragging his feet like a dead man – was Spiro.

Chapter Twenty-Nine

'Spiro!' I ran to them. 'Oh God, Spiro, are you all right? Lance, what did they *do* to him!'

Lance, panting, dragged Spiro to the nearest chair and deposited him heavily, whereupon Spiro, with a great moan of misery, doubled up, put his head in his hands and wept. Angie was on her feet, beside herself with consternation.

'Good heavens, what on earth's happened to the poor boy? Livvy, what's wrong with him!' She wrung her hands.

'Nothing, he's fine,' said Lance shortly. 'He's just upset, that's all.'

'Lance is right,' I said quickly as Lance shot me a meaningful glance and jerked his head towards the door. I picked up Angie's handbag and took her by the arm, trying to propel her doorwards. 'He's absolutely fine, Angie,' I said firmly, 'really he is, but sadly – well, sadly he's had some bad news. From home.'

Angie wasn't going anywhere, though. She stood rooted to the spot at this, appalled. 'Oh Lord,' she clutched my arm. 'Has someone died?' she whispered.

Lance flinched at the mention of death. 'No,' he hissed roughly, 'no one's bloody died. Now listen, why don't you just mind your own bloody—'

'It's the goats,' I breathed quickly, realising as soon as I'd

519

said it I'd just picked the first Greek thing I could think of. It could have been yoghurt. Or dancing.

'Goats?'

'Yes, they've got some – terrible disease. Scurvy, or something ghastly. Wiped out the whole herd.'

'Oh heavens, how awful,' she breathed, 'and with it his livelihood, I suppose?'

'Exactly,' I agreed soberly as, to my alarm, Spiro looked up in horror.

'My . . . goats?' he croaked, red-eyed.

'Oh, you poor boy,' said Angie, touching his arm. 'But, Livvy, have they really *all* gone?'

'No, no, there's one or two left,' I said wildly, 'now come *on*, Angie.'

'Only . . . one or two?' Spiro gasped, horrified, getting slowly to his feet.

I groaned. Oh God, why hadn't I gone for yoghurt? 'Yes, but the best ones, Spiro,' I soothed, 'the absolute pick of the bunch. Now come on, Angie. You really don't want to get involved in—'

'Because, darling, if there *are* some left, there's the most marvellous vet in Athens,' she insisted. 'Theodore Popolopolus or somebody – Johnny will remember. Oliver flew him over when one of his horses had a rare blood disorder – said he can cure anything. Why don't I—'

'Angie, *please*,' I insisted, shoving her forcefully out of the front door now. 'Heavens, the poor boy's got enough on his plate without forking out for horrendous vet bills. Now come along!'

As I hustled her out and down the drive I had one ear on Lance behind me, listening as he placated a distraught Spiro, putting him straight on the goat front if nothing else.

Angie shook her head sadly, groping about in her bag for

her keys. 'That poor boy,' she sighed, shaking her head and suddenly looking very old, her forehead fretted with fine lines. 'There just seems to be so much sadness about at the moment, doesn't there?' She hesitated. Glanced up hopefully. 'Will I – will I say anything else to Johnny? Give him a few words?'

'Yes,' I said grimly, 'you can give him a few words. Give him—' I stopped, ashamed, as her eyes grew round and fearful. 'Just – give him my best.' I finished lamely.

She nodded, and I saw her eyes fill. 'And if you change your mind?'

'He'll be the first to know. But I won't, Angie, believe me, I won't.'

She swallowed. 'I know. And you know, Livvy, sad as I am about this whole wretched situation, about losing you, I admire you for what you've done. Truly I do. I couldn't have done it.' We regarded each other for a long moment.

'You haven't lost me,' I whispered.

She gave a grateful smile, nodded again, but tears were imminent now, so she didn't speak. Instead she patted my arm, turned, and got in the car. I watched as she reversed out of the car port, turned out of the gateway, and waved as she purred off slowly down the road. Then I stood for a moment, in the empty drive, remembering. Remembering happier times, long ago, when we'd gardened together; roared with laughter as we'd battled against elder and thistles, up to our knees in brambles and—

'LIVVY – GET IN HERE!' Lance's voice came roaring through my memories, and abruptly I came to. Oh Christ – Spiro!

My hand went to my mouth and I dashed back into the house. Slamming the door behind me, I hurtled to the sitting room where I found Spiro, hunched up in my yellow

Colefax armchair, leaning forward now, and being violently sick into a potted plant. Lance looked up grimly and handed it to me.

'Yours, I believe.'

'Oh, help – hang on. I'll get him some water.' I took the pot, hustled it to the loo, couldn't face chucking it in, so just shut the door on it, then, retching violently at the terrible smell, ran back via the kitchen to get a glass of water. As I flew back in, Spiro reached out and took it with a shaky hand. I dropped to my knees beside him and took his hand, appalled.

'Spiro, what on earth *happened* to you in there!' I gasped. 'Was it really as ghastly as all that? God, what did they *do* to you?'

'They didn't *do* anything to him,' said Lance drily, lighting a cigarette and perching on the arm of the chair. 'This isn't Occupied France, you know, Livvy; we're not living with the Gestapo. They didn't pull his fingernails out or anything beastly, they just questioned him, that's all, frightened the life out of him, I expect. I don't know what they said to him actually, he hasn't uttered a word yet.'

I squeezed Spiro's hand. 'Spiro, it's me, Livvy.' He was staring at the carpet between his feet, shaking his woolly head and moaning.

'Come on, Spiro, you can tell me, can't you? You can tell Livvy? What is it? What happened?'

Suddenly he sat up bolt upright, his dark eyes wide and strange. His head turned slowly – and his gaze fell on Lance.

'I so sorry!' he blurted out, staring at him.

Lance frowned, shook his head. 'Why, Spiro? Why are you sorry?'

'Because – because they go on and on, questions,

questions, and I know nothing of what they speak, but then – then I theenk of something, and—' He broke off, gave a strangled sob, hid his face in his hat.

'What?' Lance insisted. 'What, Spiro?'

Spiro lowered his hat. 'I theenk I let the rabbit out of the bag!'

'Cat.'

'*Ti?*'

'Never mind. What rabbit, Spiro, what did you say?'

He glanced about furtively, as if to check we were alone, then beckoned for us to lean in. Lance and I both bent our heads.

'They want the body!' he hissed.

I jumped back. 'The body!' I yelped.

'I know,' said Lance calmly, 'that's what they kept asking me. Where was she, where was she buried, what have they done with Vi? But we don't know that, do we, Spiro? I don't, so you certainly don't.'

'No, I don't, but they keep saying – theenk, Spiro, where could she be? Where you theenk they could have put her? What were Mac and Alf doing at the time, in those few days of her death?'

'Well, they were working here,' I said staunchly, 'that's what!'

A terrible silence fell.

'Exactly,' said Lance, at length, quietly. 'They were working here.'

Spiro turned to me and nodded, wide eyes full of portent.

I stared at him. 'Shit!' I squeaked suddenly, leaping to my feet.

'And the bald man, he keep saying – where you bury her, Spiro? Where you put her? And I say – I know nothing! And then he say – so if you know nothing, perhaps you were not there to see? And I say – what you mean? And he say – well, did they perhaps get you out of the way, while they got rid of her? And I say – no! No, I work there every day, like a dog, that not possible, I see everything, *everything* that go on, and she not there!'

'Quite right!' I squealed.

'But he so persistent, Meesis McFarllen, he go on and on, and he say *th-e-e-nk*, Spiro, *th-e-e-nk*, and he tap his bald head, like this, like an egg.' Spiro broke off to tap his temple. 'Was there not a day when you go out on an errand? When your services not required at the house? When you sent elsewheres? And I theenk, and slowly, *very* slowly, I say, yes, yes there *was* such a day, because I remember Lance, that day when we have so much to do, so very busy, and we both surprised, because Mac – he send us to builders' merchant for bricks, remember?'

'I remember.'

'Together, both of us, so unusual, both in truck. And when we get there they say – oh no, so sorry, we know nothing of brick order, and we ring Mac and he say – oh, so sorry I mean *timber* merchant. So we go there, and it take hours in traffic, and when we get there, *they* know nothing either. So we ring Mac again, and he say – oh, no order? Oh deary me, well, get us some bits of four-by-two then – and so we come back with these teeny tiny bits of wood, and it feel *so* much like a wild-boar chase – remember, Lance?'

Lance had gone very pale. 'I remember.'

'And I don't theenk anything about it at the time, I just theenk, oh bleeding heck, with all the work we got to do back there at the house, that *beeg*, heavy job, and Mac – he send us for pieces of wood! Remember, Lance? Remember what Mac and Alf have to do all alone here on that day?'

'I do.' Softly.

'And I hadn't theenk of it before, but the police, they griddle me, griddle me something rotten, and I *say* it – I say it without even theenking and—'

'What!' I gasped. 'What did you say? What job were Alf and Mac doing?'

Spiro went quiet. Glanced down at his hands.

'It's all right, Spiro,' said Lance softly. 'I thought of it too. Not before, but when they were questioning me, down at the station. It suddenly occurred to me, too. I could just as easily have said it.'

'WHAT!' I shrieked. 'What could you just as easily have said? Tell me, you bastards, or I'll— Christ!'

I broke off as a terrible banging came on the door. We all swung around – then stared back at each other. I froze. Only one man knocked on my front door like that. Only one, very small man, with one very bald head, who clearly made up for his lack of height and hair by announcing himself in a big way. My insides curdled as the banging came again.

'They're here,' I breathed. 'It's them.'

Spiro whimpered, got up from his chair and backed away into a corner. Lance had gone very pale.

'Open it, Livvy.'

I nodded and went to the door, holding my side now where the stomach cramps and the shock were searing through me, making me feel light-headed as my hand went up to the latch. I swung it back. Sure enough, the bald-headed man with the big fist and his blonde accomplice, in another shiny suit, were neatly ranged on my doorstep. But this time, they weren't alone. Behind them stood two, much larger men, wearing blue overalls and carrying tool bags, and behind them, stood a couple of uniformed policemen, too. Six, in all.

'Yes?' I breathed.

'Mithith McFarllen, may we come in?' Baldy lisped softly.

'Yes, yes, of course,' I stood aside. 'I see you've brought . . . reinforcements this time,' I managed weakly.

'Indeed we have. How very obthervant of you.' He gave me a thin little smile as he shuffled through with his hands in his mackintosh pockets, closely followed by the rest of the crew.

As I shut the door behind the last one, I went weak for a moment, leaning back on the door and shutting my eyes. It occurred to me that I was heaving around a stomach which under normal circumstances would have had me doubled up on the sofa with a fistful of paracetamol and a hot-water bottle, and I had a nasty feeling I might need Spiro's pot plant in a minute. As I opened my eyes, though, I realised – no time. No time to exercise that jolly little option. Baldy's pale brown eyes, the colour of a certain doggy detritus, were trained on me like searchlights. I jumped nervously. Me? Why me? I glanced behind, wondering perhaps if there was someone standing behind me, but no, just the empty kitchen. Realising I wouldn't be the one slinking off in there to make the tea, I crept forward nervously. Clearly I was expected to join the party. Still staring, his eyes, it seemed to me, full of hideous portent, he nodded his head almost imperceptibly, but out of the corner of my eye, I noticed one of the overalled men quietly unzip a tool bag in response.

'Mithith McFarllen,' he lisped, 'so thorry to bother you, but we have here a warrant to search your house and garden.' He quickly flashed a piece of plastic at me, eyes pale and watchful.

I held on tight to the back of the sofa. The garden? Christ Almighty, was she out there? Buried under my Bobby

Brown rambler perhaps, or – or under the phlox and the delphiniums? Beneath my beautiful clematis-covered pergola?

I felt both hot and faint. 'A-Any . . . particular reason?' I faltered.

'Oh yeth. For the very particular reason that we believe the body of Mrs Violet Turner to be buried here.' He kept his eyes on me.

'That's Alf Turner's late wife, I take it,' I muttered, edging along the sofa and playing for time, although what I was going to do with it Lord only knows.

'The very thame.'

'I see,' I gulped. 'And did you have any particular place,' I gripped the sofa hard, my legs feeling odd and my head woozy, 'any particular corner of my beloved, much-treasured home or garden in mind for excavation, officer? Or are you just going to dig away indiscriminately at the whole lot?' I managed to raise my chin defiantly.

He took my point, but his eyes slithered away. He wasn't interested in whether or not he was violating my precious home. He wasn't even interested, it seemed, in my garden. His eyes didn't slither that way, you see, to my herbaceous border, for instance, burgeoning over as it was with late lupins and asters, or to my rockery, thick with alpines and heather. Nor did he gaze beyond, down to the cedar tree, to the marshy banks of the river, nor even beyond that, to the caravan on the other side. No, no, Baldy's eyes were trained somewhere much more proximate. On the doorway, in fact, behind me. The doorway which led, via a small passage-way, through into the new kitchen, and more specifically, those eyes were trained on something at the far end of that room. I glanced around.

'Yeth,' he said softly, slowly making his way past me in

that direction, 'yeth, we do have a particular corner in mind.' He stopped, just beyond me, in the doorway. 'You thee we believe, Mrs McFarllen, that she's embedded in concrete.'

'Concrete!'

'Yes, or to be more precise, in a concrete plinth. A concrete plinth commonly built to support a heavy, free-standing, cast-iron, range.' He turned to face me in the doorway, his nose almost touching mine. 'In fact it's our belief, Mithith McFarllen, that Violet Turner is buried underneath your thtove.'

'I gaped. 'My . . . thtove?'

'Your Aga, Mrs McFarllen.'

I jumped – then stared incredulously past him to my new kitchen. To my shiny pride and joy at the far end of the room, surrounded at it was by Portuguese tiles, edged with dados and doo-dahs, with its pine shelf above brimming with pretty plates, antique jugs and Mary Berry cookbooks; where I stood every day, frying the bacon, prodding Claudia's fish fingers, turning occasionally to warm my bottom, content-edly cradling a mug of coffee, chatting on the phone . . . and all the time . . . yes, all the time, stretched out beneath it, face up perhaps, hands clasped across her bosom, or maybe in a black bin liner, curled up in a foetal position, eyes shut, or possibly even wide and staring . . .

As the dawn came up I gasped in horror, as simultane-ously a stab of pain seared straight through my abdomen. My hand clutched vainly at my stomach, but I had white lights flashing before my eyes now. My ears roared, my brain sizzled, my fingers slipped from the back of the sofa, as with a little gasp of 'Shit!' I collapsed, insensible, at Baldy's feet.

Chapter Thirty

'Best thing you could have done,' said Hugh, dunking a soldier into his son's boiled egg.

'What?' I raised my head feebly from their breakfast table.

'Faint like that, last night. Makes it so convincing, so much more obvious that you had nothing to do with it.'

'She didn't have anything to do with it,' snapped Molly, opening her dressing gown and clamping Flora firmly on to her left bosom. 'What – you think she might actually have assisted in some way, Hugh? Bundled the body under the Aga in a bin bag and arranged the feet neatly whilst Mac and Alf stood poised, ready to pour on the wet cement mix?'

'Oooh, *don't*,' I groaned, dropping my head like a stone again.

'No, all I'm saying is that when the police rang and asked us to come and get her, it looked pretty good,' said Hugh. 'You were still out for the count, Livvy, flat out on a sofa and completely away with the fairies, whereas poor old Lance and Spiro were shifting about pretty nervously, I can tell you.'

'I still don't quite understand how they came to ring you,' I said bleakly, opening an eye from the stripped pine table.

'Apparently Lance suggested us when the police said they wanted you out of there,' said Hugh. 'Presumably they couldn't cope with you doing the dying swan all over the place when they had a house to excavate and a body to exhume. I must say I was hugely intrigued. Those guys had bloody nearly shifted that stove when I got there. I reckon she was damn nearly out! I hovered about a bit and tried to play for time by pretending you weighed a ton and that I was having difficulty lugging you off the sofa, then stagger-ing e-ve-rso slo-wly to the door –' Hugh got up to demon-strate – 'then coming back for your handbag which happened to be, oops, in the kitchen, then – ooh yes, better pop upstairs and get your nightie, and then, damn it, just as I was popping back for your toothbrush, that bald chap sussed me and hustled me away. Shame. I reckon two more minutes and they'd have had the old bird out.'

'Hugh!' Molly slammed a milk bottle down.

'Well, it would have been fascinating, Moll. I've never seen a dead body before, and don't forget, I've been there in spirit. Would have been great for research.'

'Macabre,' shuddered Molly. 'And to think you'd been *cooking* there, Livvy, and all that time she was—'

'Oooh, stop it!' I moaned. I raised my head feebly. 'I really don't know how Alf and Mac could have *done* that to me!'

'Well, to be fair, Liv, they never meant for you to find out, and as long as you were none the wiser, so what?' said Hugh, reasonably. 'They had to put her *some*where, and actually I think it was a jolly good idea.' He frowned. 'Can't help feeling she might have got a bit hot, though. Maybe even gone a bit – you know – whiffy.'

'*Hugh!*' Molly was pink. 'God, you are *so* distasteful. Poor Livvy here is *distraught*, and so would I be if I found a dead woman under my cooker! Christ, it's gruesome!'

'All right, all right,' he muttered. 'God, you're so flaming genteel, Moll. I just think it's incredibly exciting, that's all, to be suddenly slap-bang in the middle of a murder like this. Talk about street theatre.'

'I told you,' I growled, 'it wasn't a murder.'

'Well, OK, whatever you call a pissed-off husband knocking off his shrewish wife with a swift hammer blow to the head and then squirrelling her away under some kitchen appliances. Rather an apt ending, I feel, for a harridan of a housewife? Back to her roots, as it were?' His eyes gleamed. 'And it gives a whole new dimension to the old Aga saga, eh?'

Molly gave an exasperated little cry and pointedly swivelled round in her chair, turning her back on her husband. 'Liv darling,' she said gently, leaning forward and taking my hand, 'd'you remember much about last night?'

'Not much,' I said miserably. 'Just coming round in the back of Hugh's car, that's all . . . shouting a bit, I think.'

'Shouting a *bit*!' spluttered Hugh, spraying egg everywhere. 'Jesus, you were screaming blue murder! There you were, flat out and comatose on the back seat, quiet as a mouse, when suddenly – "GET ME OUT OF HERE – DON'T LET THEM PUT ME IN THE BIN BAG – OH GOD NO NOT THE BIN BAG SOMEBODY HELP ME!!!" Then the next thing I knew you were crawling over into the front seat with these mad, staring eyes, like something out of a Hammer Horror movie, trying to get me in an arm lock and turn the wheel at the same time. You damn nearly drove us off the road! Christ, I had to stop the car. I was scared witless I can tell you!'

I groaned. 'Sorry,' I muttered, shaking my head. 'God, I'm so sorry, Hugh, I had no idea. I really wasn't with it.

When I woke up I just couldn't think where the hell I was!'

'Of course you couldn't,' agreed Molly staunchly, closing her dressing gown and putting Flora over her shoulder to wind her. 'Frankly, I'm surprised you're as *compos mentis* as you are now! If that had been me I'd be on that phone right now, booking myself into the Priory for the next couple of weeks I'd be so unhinged. And what about those two bastards who dropped you in all this? Why aren't they sharing the angst, Mac the knife and Alf the half-wit? Where are they while all this drama unfolds? On the Marrakesh Express or something?'

'I don't know,' I sighed, 'and, Molly, I know it sounds crazy, but they weren't really bastards. Just a couple of hard-working guys who got caught up in a horrific domestic drama and then – well, then did the wrong thing. Ran, instead of facing up to it.'

'All the best murders happen like that,' observed Hugh, sagely, wiping Henry's eggy mouth. 'Ninety per cent are committed within the family, which makes a copper's job something of a doddle really, doesn't it?' He scratched his head and affected a dim PC Plod. 'Er, so what d'you reckon, Sarge, shall I 'ave a word wiv the relatives?'

'So why do they still want to speak to me then?' I said, suddenly fearful. 'If it all hinges on the relatives, why ring me here, at the crack of dawn this morning, and ask me to present myself down at the station!'

'Just routine they said, remember?' soothed Molly. 'Nothing to worry about. What time did they say they wanted to see you?'

'Ten o'clock,' I said, glancing at the clock. My heart was hammering. 'In half an hour. I must go soon.'

'D'you want me to come with you?' She squeezed my hand.

I shook my head. Gulped. 'No, I'll – be fine. You've got Flora to see to and your mother's still asleep and—'

'Well, Hugh's not doing anything today. He could easily take you.'

'No, no really, I'm sure you're right,' I said quickly. 'I'm sure it's nothing to worry about.'

I wasn't entirely sure I could cope with Hugh wisecracking his way to the police station with yet more corpse jokes, because actually, suddenly, I felt very scared. I wished I could just hole up here in Molly and Hugh's tiny, warm, chaotic kitchen with its airer groaning with bibs and babygrows, and Flora sucking away contentedly at her mother's breast, and Henry eyeing me carefully from his high chair, thumb in mouth, not entirely sure if I was generally present at his breakfast table.

'So what happens next?' said Molly softly, as if reading my thoughts.

I grimaced. 'You mean, what am I going to do?'

She nodded.

'Well, sell the house, of course.'

'Of course,' she agreed quickly, shooting Hugh a look as he opened his mouth to protest.

'And move, I suppose, but God knows where. I'll have to decide soon, though, because Claudia's term starts in September. You know she's been offered a place at St Paul's?'

'No! In London? Blimey!'

'I know. I'd forgotten I'd even put her down for it, must have been ages ago, in an ambitious moment. Haven't had many of those recently.'

'But that's seriously hot stuff, Livvy. Places like that are *fought* over! God, about two hundred girls going for twenty places!'

I sighed. 'I know, can't think how she managed it, although apparently she did rather well at her interview. They asked if she had any hobbies and she said, rather disdainfully, "Certainly not" – you know Claudes. And then they said, "Well, do you collect anything, dear?" And she said, "Yes, money." '

Molly giggled. 'That's my girl. No shrinking violet, eh?'

'Hardly. But do we really want to live in London, Moll? And a day school too – not really what she'd had in mind.'

'A *brilliant* day school, though,' said Hugh through a mouthful of toast. 'Hell of an opportunity. She'd probably end up Prime Minister or something equally bloody frightening.'

'True,' I sighed again. 'Anyway, I'm going to have to think about it.' I hauled myself out of the cosy Windsor chair. 'Right now, though, I have to gird my loins for my chat with Shiny Suit and Baldy. Perhaps it'll be Pentonville for me, with Claudia on visiting rights.'

'Don't be silly. It's quite obvious you were just an innocent bystander,' Molly protested. Nevertheless, I noticed, rather nervously, that they both followed me to the door and that Molly still had her arm round my shoulders when we got there.

'You're welcome to stay here as long as you like, you know that, don't you?' She gave me a squeeze. 'A year if you want, whatever it takes.'

'Thanks.' I forced a smile. 'But it'll only be a few days. We wouldn't want to cramp your style.'

'We don't have a style,' announced Hugh loftily, sticking his chest out. 'Makes life so much simpler.'

'Speak for yourself,' muttered Molly, 'I wouldn't mind a bit of style.'

'Nonsense, my dear, you're totally à la mode as you

are, modelling for us this morning this season's must-have basic, the cheesy dressing gown with baby puke down one shoulder and— Oops! There she goes again!' He caught Flora's sickly projection and grabbed Molly's muslin to mop it up as the baby proceeded to do another mouthful.

'She keeps doing this,' said Molly anxiously. 'I'm getting terrible *déjà vu*. I keep waiting for her to actually take aim and get my mother in the face, like Henry used to.'

'Henry's grown out of that,' I soothed. 'Flora will too.'

'Ah, but you haven't seen Henry's latest trick,' said Hugh proudly. 'Irritated that he can no longer hit Molly's mother in the eye with a stream of puke, he's taken to dropping his trousers, presenting dear Millicent with his bare backside, then letting rip with the most almighty fart.' Hugh sighed, wistfully. 'Something I realise that I, too, have long wished to do myself.'

'Hugh!' Molly scolded.

'Well, I can't see this little angel doing anything as gross as that,' I said fondly, stroking his daughter's cheek.

'She's going to be a stunner,' he agreed.

'And talking of stunners,' Molly rearranged Flora and looked me in the eye, 'I heard about Imo.'

'Ah.' I scuffed my toe on the doormat. 'That.'

'Flaming cheek!' she said hotly. 'You were well in there first!'

Hugh cringed. 'Well In There? Is that how you speak of us gentle menfolk?'

I sighed. 'Yes, but while I was making up my mind, Moll, Imo saw a gap and went for it. And who can blame her?' I added ruefully.

'Saw a gap and . . .? Good heavens,' gasped Hugh faintly, clutching the doorframe for support. 'We're just a mere line of traffic now, are we? With gaps! Whatever happened to romance?'

'What indeed?' I agreed ruefully.

'And, anyway, I don't know why all this comes as such a big surprise to you girls,' he went on. 'If we're intent on using disgusting analogies, if you ask me, she wormed her way in long ago.'

'When?' demanded Molly.

'Oh, come on, Moll, ages ago, at that backstage party at the Abbey, for starters. And then when I saw her the other day, cosily ensconced at his house . . .'

They debated on, but suddenly I wasn't listening. Suddenly I felt like Flora: I wanted to be sick all over someone's shoulder. Cosily ensconced. Really? For how long? How long had it been going on? I wanted to ask.

'Livvy?' Molly was watching me anxiously. I forced a bright smile.

'Bye then. Wish me luck in the cells.' I made towards my car, which Molly had driven back last night when I'd been in Hugh's.

'Good luck!' they chorused. 'As if you're going to need it,' added Molly scornfully.

In the event, they were right, I didn't. Down at the city police station Baldy was conspicuous by his absence, and since I'd clocked him as being the more dynamic of the duo, I relaxed when I discovered that Shiny Suit was going to interview me alone. As I followed her into a little grey room, sat down and regurgitated all I knew, I could tell by her demeanour that although she was affecting high dudgeon, she was actually only going through the motions to scare me.

'So why on earth didn't you come straight in and report to us the moment you knew she was dead!' Her eyebrows shot into her overtreated fringe.

'I was scared,' I admitted, with more than an element of truth. 'I knew I should have done, but I'd never been involved in anything like this before. What Mac and Alf told me terrified me. I shot off to London like a bat out of hell, telling myself it was only what I'd normally do on a child-free day.'

'And what did you do in London?'

'Oh, just some shopping, went to a concert, that sort of thing.'

The eyebrows shot up some more. 'Very relaxed.'

'Yes but while I was there I realised I'd done completely the wrong thing,' I added quickly. 'And – and I decided I'd come in and see you the very next day. I really meant to.'

'Did you indeed?' she snorted doubtfully. 'Yes, well, I could mutter on a bit about the road to hell being paved with good intentions and all that,' she shuffled her papers sniffily. Glanced up. 'You know, of course, that I could throw the book at you for sheltering known criminals and withholding crucial evidence?'

I nodded dumbly.

'Staying silent is as much of a crime as actually aiding and abetting. It's calculated corroboration.'

I nodded again. 'Yes, I – I can see that now.'

She sighed wearily. Closed her file. 'But under the circumstances,' she said, pushing it to one side, 'I think it's fair to say you've probably been through the mill enough. It's not every day you find a corpse under your cooker.'

I gulped. Too true. I glanced up and met her eye. 'Thank you,' I whispered gratefully.

'We will, of course, get them, though,' she added, fixing me beadily. 'Your chums, Mac and Alf. There's no question of that.'

'Of course,' I agreed quickly, wishing she hadn't called them 'my chums'.

'Gone are the days of the Spanish being wet about extradition. We'll put a rocket up their backsides and they'll deliver them tout suite. This isn't the Ronnie Biggs era, you know, this isn't the slap-happy, swinging sixties where anything goes on the Costa Brava.'

'Oh no, I know,' I agreed fervently. 'And quite right too,' I added toadishly. Just let me go, please let me go.

'So.' She folded her arms and flashed me a thin, professional smile. 'I imagine you're free to go.'

I sprang to my feet. 'Thank you!'

'Provided,' she warned, 'that you don't wander too far afield. We will need you later on to give evidence and I don't want to find you've skipped the country or anything dramatic.' She got up and opened the door for me, propping it open so I had to go under her arm. 'Your house has been put back pretty much in apple-pie order, you'll be pleased to hear. Our boys worked fast last night and Forensics have been in and out already. You're not even cordoned off, either, because the press don't know and we didn't want to draw too much attention to the place, so you don't have to wait, you can move straight back in.' She frowned. 'I'm not sure the cooker is fully operational, though. Some people are apparently coming in next week to fix that, but other than that,' she flashed me another, wintry smile, 'you wouldn't even know we'd been there!'

I managed a tremulous smile in return and even muttered a thank you before scurrying away. Wouldn't even know they'd been there? I thought, bug-eyed with horror as I sped down that corridor in the direction of the free world. Excuse me, but I think I would. Oh, I'd know all right. I'd know every time I lifted the hob to put the kettle on, every time I bent down to take the roast chicken out of the oven. Know? Bloody hell – I'd *heave*! Christ, I wouldn't stay in that house now if you *paid* me, I thought, barging angrily through some swing doors, and she was right, I *had* suffered enough. So much so that I was having to – Well, I was having to sell up! I stopped still for a moment, shocked by that thought, blinking in horror, and conveniently forgetting, of course, that I'd actually been planning to sell up anyway. Yes, that's right, I thought, slowly walking on, outraged, I was the victim here. I should be offered compensation! God, I could sell my story to the tabloids, spill the beans for millions! I must talk to Hugh about it. He'd enjoy that.

Once in the car park, though, all thoughts of anything other than the fact that I was a free woman paled into insignificance as I threw myself with relief into my familiar old, boiling-hot sauna of a car. Free, I thought, resting my head back gratefully and shutting my eyes. Thank God. I gave myself a little shake and started the engine, then realised, with a start, that I didn't know where the hell I was going. I turned it off again. Frowned. Right. So, Livvy. Here you are on your own again. I bit my lip. And what now? Where to? Long term I had absolutely no idea, but more immediately . . . I narrowed my eyes, frowned into the middle distance, then started the engine again. Yes, yes, I *did* know, actually. Knew exactly where I was going. Before I could change my mind I reversed at speed – slowing dramatically when I remembered I was still in a police station – then once out of sight, roared off. The house. It had to be Orchard House. Let's face it, at some point I had to go back because Claudia and I had no clothes at all at Molly's – as it was I was wearing a skirt of Molly's to avoid climbing into the disastrous Donna Karan number – so I may as well go and get it over with. I was due to pick Claudes up from Lucy's this afternoon and if the poor child had neither a father, nor a home to come back to now, she should at least have a clean pair of knickers.

With a gathering sense of dread I drove slowly down the familiar roads, turning down into George Street, bumping over the cobbles, past the little antique shops, then left into the arched, Abbey gates with the Abbey tower looming over my shoulder. As I turned left into The Crescent I couldn't help driving very, very slowly and peering up at Sebastian's house. His car wasn't outside so I knew he wasn't in, and for some reason, all the shutters were closed. It looked strangely – well, shut up, as if he'd gone away for some length of time, too. Was he in London? I wondered. Living at Imogen's, maybe? I gritted my teeth and swung into my drive.

I sat for a moment, drumming my fingers on the wheel, steeling myself, and not relishing this little visit one iota. Finally, telling myself not to be stupid – it wasn't as if she was *there* any more, was it? – I got out and marched up to the front door. I propped it open with a plant pot – didn't want it slamming behind me or anything gross – then, studiously avoiding the kitchen from which I reasoned I needed precisely nothing, I nipped upstairs, humming maniacally to calm my nerves. Once there, I dragged a large suitcase out from under a bed and, working quickly, emptied all of Claudia's drawers into it, not forgetting a few books, her jewellery case, her schoolwork, and a much-loved blue rabbit. Then I ran across the landing into my own room, did exactly the same, lugged the almost exploding suitcase heavily back downstairs, dragged it across the gravel, and heaved it up into the boot of the car. I slammed it shut. There. I brushed off my hands and stared back at the house. Now. Anything else? Surely I'd got the bare essentials? And surely I could just get some professionals in to clear the rest? Store the furniture somewhere perhaps? Yes, exactly, except – hang on, the photos in the sitting room; I'd like them with me. Taking another deep breath, I dashed back inside, gathered up all the silver frames full of photos of Claudia, took the albums from the bottom drawer of the chest, and was just about to skedaddle again, when stupidly, I glanced out of the French windows. I paused. And as I did, a lump came to my throat. My garden. My precious, beloved, glorious garden. I could quite happily leave the house, but the garden – oh, that was a huge wrench. I simply had to say goodbye.

I dropped the photos on the sofa and, almost as a reflex action, my hand reached up and shot the bolt across at the top of the French windows. Flinging them wide I wandered sadly outside. Around the terrace, stone urns tumbled with white pelargoniums, hostas, and variegated ivy, and in the surrounding beds, day lilies and michaelmas daisies jostled for position while lamb's tongues crawled towards my feet over the mellow York stones. The lavender path ahead was humming with bees and above it, arches of heavy, tumbling climbers – Albertine, Madame Alfred Carrière and my lovely, lusty Rambling Rector – nodded invitingly to me in the breeze. Dredging up a great sigh from the soles of my feet, I ducked under it for the last time, reaching up to touch a blossom, which, being so overblown, fell to pieces in my hand. Scattering the petals regretfully on the parched grass I went on, on to take a last look at my herbaceous border, stunning now with its great clumps of delphinium, larkspurs and poppies, all finally out together and looking pleased as punch to be so thoroughly synchronised. It brought a lump to my throat to think there'd be no one out here with the hose at seven o'clock as usual tonight, seeing them through this dry spell, giving them just a few more days of precious growth.

Down the yellowing lawn I wandered, my skirt brushing the fragrant brooms and hebes, shading my eyes to the river, to the glorious cedar tree, spreading its branches to give a cool blanket of shade beneath. I gazed across the river to the caravan. Still there, of course, I thought wryly, obscuring the view of the cherry tree as usual, except that – blimey – hang on, no – it was off! The bloody thing was moving! Well, of course it was, because – I squinted hard into the sun's dazzling rays – there was a car attached to it. A car, attached and pulling. I ran down towards the water's edge to watch, but just then the car stopped. Somebody got out, slammed the door, and walked round to peer down at the caravan's wheels, checking to see if they were stuck. I stopped. Lance.

'Lance!' My hand shot up in delight. He turned, shaded his eyes, then waved.

'Livvy!'

I grinned and ran, picking my way across the rickety bridge, brushing against bull rushes, and then along the bank on the other side. By the time I got there, Lance, bare to the waist, bronzed and bleached blond as ever, was busy digging a stone out of the way of one of the caravan's wheels. He straightened up with a smile.

'Well, I didn't expect to see you back here after last night!' His blue eyes found mine, gently. 'Are you all right? I tried to ring you at Molly's but she said you'd gone.'

I nodded. 'I'm fine now, absolutely fine, it was just – well, it was just such a shock, Lance. I don't usually pass out like that, like some nineteenth-century drip having the vapours, but a large gin and tonic on top of a very gippy tummy, plus –' I rolled my eyes – 'well, plus everything else . . .'

'Well, quite. It's not every day you discover a dead body lurking in your kitchen. I tell you, Livvy, I quite felt like passing out myself.' He regarded me earnestly with clear blue eyes. 'And I really didn't know anything about it, Liv, you must believe that. I would never have sanctioned it, however desperate they were.'

I nodded. 'I do know that, of course I do.'

'And I can understand how – well, how you must hate them,' he said with difficulty. 'For what they did.'

'Well, as you said,' I said carefully, 'they were desperate. Desperate men.'

He nodded. Glanced down. Scuffed his toe miserably in the dirt.

I sighed. 'Look – don't feel you have to take responsibility, Lance. It's not your fault. I just wish – well, I just wish they'd driven back via the Thames and gone for the more conventional East End burial ground, that's all.'

He smiled ruefully. 'They shouldn't have done that either; should have gone straight to the police, right from the start.'

'Bit late now,' I said grimly.

Lance scratched his head. 'You'd think so, wouldn't you, but you know, perversely, apparently not. Who knows whether to believe them or not, but the police say there's a good chance they'll get off with manslaughter if they return to face the music. Apart from anything else their story is perfectly true, and since literally everybody will back them up – oh, and apparently there's some marvellous left-wing brief who's prepared to take Alf's case on, and all on legal aid too – he stands a really good chance of getting off. I just have to persuade them to come back, that's all, and that might be tricky.' He grinned. 'Spiro reckons the ouzo will agree with Dad and I can just see Alf—'

'Ouzo?' I interrupted.

'Oh,' he flushed suddenly. 'Oh, no, nothing.' He bent down quickly, attending to the wheel.

Ouzo, I thought, astonished, and Spiro knew about it, so – so not Spain at all. Greece, or to be more precise, I thought rapidly, a little island off the tip of Greece, a Greek-speaking community in the Balkans, a disputed territory just off Albania. Yes, a place where you could disappear, literally for ever, without a hope of anyone finding you. Particularly on a close-knit little island where everyone closed ranks. A little island called Mexatonia. An island where a certain Gullopidus family pretty much ruled the roost, ran the show, owned the boats, the goats, the bars, and where a couple of Englishmen – friends of Mr Gullopidus's son, don't you know, friends of young Spiro, who'd been looked after so magnificently during his stay in England – could quite easily be found shelter, houses, jobs. God, I could just see Alf, mending boats on the beach, patching up the fishing nets, whistling away, quiet, contented, happy in his work, and Mac – yes, Mac behind the bar in town, measuring out the Metaxa, turning his quick mind to the lingo – unlike Alf, who'd barely mastered English and certainly wouldn't be mastering Greek – ingratiating himself into local life, becoming part of the community. Yes, Mac, a colourful figure, bringing out his wife, Karen, the grown-up kids coming out for holidays, and running the place; drinking long into the night with all the old men, playing backgammon in the village square, chewing the cud with Spiro and Atalanta up the road . . . I smiled. Well actually, in spite of myself, I grinned, really quite widely. My God, what a life! They'd never come back. And, of course, Mac had very cleverly told me Spain, had let that slip quite deliberately to put me off the scent, and perhaps even hoped I'd tell the police. Which come to think of it . . . I frowned. Had I? Well, I certainly hadn't disagreed when Shiny Suit had mentioned the Costa Brava as the spot she'd be dragging them back from. Well good, I thought suddenly. I probably shouldn't think that, but I did. Good.

'Forget I said that,' muttered Lance, straightening up for a moment.

I smiled. 'Forget you said what?'

He grinned, but I glanced away, point made, but not wanting to prolong that conversation, thank you very much. I gazed back to the house, to the new kitchen, its windows flashing knowingly at me in the sunshine. When I'd turned back, Lance had bent down again and was tightening up a bolt on the wheel. His broad back was smooth and brown. I remembered it well, felt I knew it intimately, in fact, from our suntanning session, together with that blond hair that curled rather seductively on the nape of his neck. I watched him working for a moment. Swallowed.

'Um, Lance, I don't suppose you fancy a drink, do you?'

He straightened up. 'Oh, Livvy, I'd love one, it's just that . . .' He hesitated, glanced down at his oily hands.

'What?'

'Well, it's just that, I sort of said I'd—'

'Lance!'

We both turned as a shrill voice rang out behind us.

'Hey! You said twelve o'clock. It's way past that. Come on!' Nanette was hanging out of her upstairs window, dressed in some sort of scanty, Caribbean sarong affair, complete with a flower in her hair. She waved an armful of jangling bracelets when she saw me. 'Co-ee, Olivia! I say,

545

all sorts of action been going on at your place, eh? Can't wait to grill Lance!'

I turned and raised amused, quizzical eyebrows at Lance. He had the grace to blush.

'Ah, I see,' I murmured. 'Off for a grilling.'

'Well, you know,' he said sheepishly, scuffing his toe in the dirt. 'Seeing as how I'm going today, I thought – well. I thought just for old times' sake I'd pop round and have a drink with Nanette. But you're welcome to join us,' he added quickly. 'I'm sure she won't mind.'

'Oh, I'm quite sure she *will* mind,' I laughed. 'I'm not convinced that's entirely what our Nanette had in mind, are you?'

He looked at me a moment, then grinned. 'Perhaps not. Well, bye then, Livvy. Best of luck.' He leant forward and kissed my cheek.

We regarded each other fondly for a moment, and perhaps even a touch regretfully.

'Bye, Lance,' I said with a smile, then I turned to go, making my way back up the parched lawn. A few steps on, though, his voice halted me.

'Oh, by the way, that musician chappie called round.'

I swung back.

'Oh?'

'Yes, he's gone to Vienna.'

'Oh. Right.' My heart thudded on again. Of course. Ursula had said. With Imo. Hence the shuttered house.

'But he popped in to say goodbye. Left a note, I think.'

'Really? Where?'

He shrugged. 'Kitchen table?'

Kitchen. Bloody kitchen. I hurried on up the garden, heart racing again, through the French windows, then steeled myself to— Yes, yes I could . . . I went in. I avoided looking at the Aga and glanced quickly at the table. Nothing. Totally bare apart from the fruit bowl. In the fruit bowl perhaps? No. Notice board? No. Counters, surfaces, pinned to the larder door? No, no note, nothing. I glanced all about now, even casting a desperate eye at the Aga. All was neat and tidy, and there wasn't a fluttering piece of paper to be seen. He must have changed his mind. Dejected, I turned to go, but just as I was leaving, noticed that the rubbish bin was practically overflowing. Damn, I'd have to empty that or it would stink to high heaven in this weather. Irritated, I pulled out the plastic sack, but as I did, realised there were some balls of screwed-up paper on the top. They were from my telephone pad. I opened one.

Dear Livvy,
    I popped round to say goodbye, but I also wanted to say

I opened another.

Dear Livvy,
    I'm off to Vienna today, but I just wanted to write to

And another.

Dear Livvy,

I dropped them back in. One by one, slowly. Stared at the wall. What? What had he wanted to say? Deep in thought I lugged the bag outside and dumped it in the bin. I locked up the house, then, realising I'd left the photographs on the sitting-room sofa, went back in again, but I was totally distracted now. What? What had he wanted to say, for God's sake? And why start a letter three times? I carried the photos back in my arms towards the front door, just as the telephone rang. I stared at it for a moment on the hall table. For some reason, I felt full of foreboding. Almost didn't answer it. Then slowly, I put my bundle of photos down, and my hand went to the receiver. I picked it up.

'Hello?'

'Livvy, it's Imo.'

I gazed into the hall mirror, saw my eyes widen. 'Imo, hi.'

'Darling, I'm so sorry.'

'What about?'

'My bitch of a mother.' Her voice wobbled.

I lowered myself very slowly on to the hall chair. 'How did you know?' I whispered. 'I mean – did she tell you what she'd—'

'No, no, of course not,' she sniffed. 'When she came across to us in tears at the concert she just said you'd insulted her, called her some terrible names, accused her of being a culture vulture or something, but Daddy overheard the whole thing, he was just too terrified to interfere. We're all too terrified. Have been for years.' Her voice sounded small and sad. Very far away.

'So you know—'

'Not quite everything, but I'm keen to learn because, believe me, it'll all be bollocks,' she rallied defiantly. 'It always is with Mum, and there's no way she's coming between you and me, Livvy, no way on earth. So go on, darling, spill the beans. What's the old cow been up to now?'

I licked my lips. 'Well, she said . . . well, first of all she told me about Johnny. Imo, I had no idea. I never knew you were so besotted back then. If I'd thought for one moment you were still in love with him—'

'You'd never have married him?'

There was a silence. I swallowed hard.

'Don't be silly, Livvy,' she went on quietly, 'you'd have followed your heart, and quite right too.'

'So – you were in love with him then?'

'Oh, back then, yes, I was, but the balls-up on that front was nothing to do with you, it was my own private tragedy, and my own stupid fault, too. You weren't to know what was going on, but yes, there was a plan afoot, instigated by Mum, of course.'

'So that was true? She did intervene?'

'Of course! You know Mum. She knew that I was deadly serious about Johnny and was adamant that if he was going to take me to the altar so young he had to deserve me, or some such crap. Not coming back for weeks on end after Oliver died was her idea. It was all her idea.'

'And Paolo?'

'The son of a gallery owner she knew. He just arrived at my apartment one evening, asking if I'd like to have supper. Oh, I didn't *have* to sleep with him, of course, but in those days I did most things Mum suggested . . . "a delightful little dalliance" was her euphemism for it, a brief romance, she said, before settling down as a wife and a mother for good. And I complied. Thought she was right. Thought I needed my last fling. Staggering really; I didn't seem to have a mind of my own. She's a control freak, you see, Liv, totally manipulative, and look where it's got her. One of my brothers is dead from drugs, another one can't stand her and married a hairdresser to thwart her, and the other one lives in New Zealand, so far away she can't get at him. I always wanted to please her – we all did – but I can't do it any longer.' She sucked in her breath. At first I thought she was crying, then I realised—

'Imo – you're smoking!'

'I've smoked for years. Secretly, of course. Mummy would be horrified. And I've never, ever gone against her,' she said vehemently, her words tumbling out in a rush now. 'Oxford, Florence, an art gallery where I'd meet nice, cultured young men – everything was her idea, and I so envied you with your sweet, unpushy mother who never—'

'*My* mother? Jesus, Imo, my mother was a nightmare!'

'Only in your eyes. Molly and I were as jealous as hell. She was so discreet and elegant and unambitious, whilst I had the She-Devil Incarnate to deal with and poor Moll had the ghastly Millicent. But I envied you for defying her, too,' she said softly. 'She was strong, your Mum, no pushover, but you signed up for that Cirencester course against her wishes and married without her blessing. I could never have done that.'

I remembered the rows Mum and I had had when I'd told her I was marrying Johnny.

'Well no,' I said slowly, 'I'd certainly never let her run my life.'

'You see? And I did. And look where it got me. I've gone from man to man to please her. Oh, she thought Hugo was absolutely marvellous in the beginning, but then Sebastian came along and he was even *more* marvellous. It's been the story of my life. I don't even know what I think any more,' she said unhappily.

I licked my lips. 'She said – Ursula said – that you were in love with him. With Sebastian.'

'Ah. Yes. That much, at least, is true. But then again, it's not the whole story. You see sadly, he's not in love with me. And no point forcing a square peg into a round hole, eh?'

She gave a hollow laugh and I heard her drag hard on her cigarette.

'But I thought you were going to Vienna with him! Your mother said—'

'Well, of course she bloody did. That's her oh-so-subtle way of angling for an invitation for me, and warning you off. Christ, I'm surprised she didn't book the bloody ticket, drive me to the airport, shove me on the plane and strap me into the seat next to him, taking absolutely no notice of his horrified face!'

There was a silence.

'It's you he wants, Livvy,' she said softly. 'You must know that.'

'Wh-why should I know that?'

'Because . . .' she struggled. 'Oh, I don't know, don't know for sure, but – listen, darling, I spoke to him this morning, before he left for Vienna. I wanted to set the record straight – *my* record straight, at least. Christ, I've made such a bloody fool of myself one way and another and I wanted to explain things, things that— Oh, but that doesn't matter right now, the important thing is that he was asking about you. I think he might try and get in touch with you, Liv, write to you perhaps, or even—'

'Oh!' I nearly dropped the phone.

'What?'

I couldn't speak for a moment. I went hot, then finally pulled myself together and dragged my eyes away from the window by the door. In the mirror I could see the colour rising rapidly up my neck.

'Imo, it's – it's all right,' I breathed. 'He's here.'

Chapter Thirty-One

'You're kidding!' Imo's voice was still in my ear even though I wasn't with her. I was glued back to Sebastian's eyes again as he looked at me through the hall window. 'Gosh, I thought he'd gone!'

'What?' I whispered.

'I thought he'd gone to Vienna!'

I swallowed. 'Obviously not.'

'Ah. Right.' Her voice went quiet. 'Good luck then, Livvy. You deserve it.'

Her subdued tone made me glance into the receiver. 'Imo?'

'Hmm?' She sounded distant.

'Lots of love.'

She paused. 'You too, darling. You too.'

I slowly put the receiver down and stood up to open the door, my heart hammering around somewhere up by my oesophagus. Sebastian was there on my doorstep, leaning against the doorframe with his hands in his pockets. He was in khaki trousers and a pale blue shirt – quite smart for him, not his usual battered composing kit – but his eyes were the same as ever, dark and glittering, and he was wearing that devastating smile, the one that transformed his face, creasing it up into angles and slanting his eyes. It seemed to me it lit up the whole street.

'Hi.'

'Hi.'

With these modest monosyllables, I found myself to be suddenly wide awake. Alive again. I felt my whole body begin to glow and every nerve tingled.

'Can I come in?'

'Hmm?' I gazed, wantonly.

'Inside?'

I jumped. 'Inside? Oh – no!' Hurriedly I hastened distinctly *out*side, and joined him on the step, slamming the front door firmly behind me. He looked surprised.

'Ah. I see. A doorstep conversation then.'

'Well, it's just that – I'm rather off my house at the moment,' I explained hastily. 'It's – the wallpaper.'

'The wallpaper?'

'So depressing.' Or did that sound neurotic? 'Er – no, OK, it's not the wallpaper, but it's a long story, Sebastian, and a rather tortuous one at that, so I won't go into it right now, but . . .' I glanced about desperately, no, not out the back because Lance might still be there so, 'tell you what, let's go and sit over there.'

I hastened down the drive to the front wall, excitement mounting. It was a bit high and covered in creeper, but somehow, with a superhuman spring, I managed to jump up, and then contrived to look comfortable even though I had ivy up my bottom. He glanced at the filthy wall and in his smart clothes, clearly decided to stand. Suddenly it occurred to me he was spruced up for travelling.

'Oh yes, Imo said you were off to Vienna.'

'Imo?'

I flushed. God, why did I have to mention Imo? Right at this moment? 'Yes, that was her on the phone just now.'

'Oh, right.' He coloured too, then recovered. 'Yes, well,

she's right, I am, but the plane's been delayed. I'm leaving any minute actually.' He glanced at his watch. 'The taxi will be here soon. I just came round to say goodbye.'

'Oh! Right.' For some reason the excitement began to drain out of me. Seeped right down into my shoes. This didn't seem to have the makings of an embryonic romantic conversation, more – well, more a matter-of-fact, bon voyage conversation, actually. I wondered if Imo had got the wrong end of the stick. I felt slightly foolish too, sitting up here like a little gnome, with him standing before me, his shoulders level with my knees.

'The symphony's going to be played in the Musikverein tomorrow evening,' he explained, 'so I'm flying out tonight to listen to the rehearsal. I'm leaving the house, too, hence all the frenetic activity.' He jerked his head down the street. I looked, and realised that his front door was wide open and that two men were busy heaving a heavy desk down the steps to a lorry. 'My desk and my piano are the only things I actually brought with me to the house, so they're going down to the country. The rest stays.' He grinned. 'I thought you might think it a bit odd if I disappeared from the neighbourhood overnight without saying goodbye! I must pop in and see Nanette, too.'

My throat felt curiously dry all of a sudden. 'Oh . . . right. Yes, I'd forgotten you . . . only rent it.'

'Oh yes, I'd never buy it. Renting was ideal. I needed to be here to write the music for the Abbey, because, somehow, being close to the old building got the inspiration going, but now that it's finished, I don't need to be here any more. I'm keen to get away, actually.' He smiled, his eyes creasing up at the corners.

For some reason his words chilled me. 'Of course,' I

heard myself saying. 'That part of your life is over. Time to move on.'

'Quite. And my parents have been dying to move out of their house to a cottage in a village nearby. It's far too big for them now, so I'm taking it over. It's an old rectory with a lovely garden, and I'm not really a city person. It'll be good to work in the country again.'

'I see,' I said quietly. I met his gaze. 'You're all set up then, aren't you? I'm moving on too, you know.'

'So I gather.' He grinned.

'Who told you?'

'Your builder, the chap round the back.'

'Ah. Yes, well, I'm sure he didn't tell you exactly why, but believe me, it's out of necessity. I don't have your luxury of choice.' I met his eye, somewhat defiantly perhaps for someone who I'd been keen to share a special harmony with.

'To Dorset?' He grinned again.

'Sorry?' Why was he grinning at me like that.

'Aren't you going to Dorset?'

'No no, to Chiswick, that's where Claudia's school is.'

'Chiswick!' He looked appalled.

'Yes, she's got into St Paul's Girls' School. It's a hell of an opportunity and it would be crazy of us not to take it up, so I'm pretty sure we're going to be moving up there, although I have to say,' I grimaced, 'I haven't squared it with Claudes yet. Might go down rather badly.'

He stared at me. 'Livvy, is this because . . . is it because of Imogen?'

I frowned. 'What?'

He licked his lips. 'You know, we were never an item.' He ran his hands through his short dark hair. 'I mean I know it *looked* as if we were, and if I'm honest, that's the way I *wanted* it to look. I wanted you to think that I was going out with her, I was so bloody furious.'

I gazed at him, completely lost. What did Imo have to do with me moving to London?

'And I didn't seek her out deliberately, either, didn't make a beeline for her at all, but when she kept asking me to supper at her parents' house, practically zooming into position beside me at the dinner table – with her mother doing most of the shoving incidentally – well, I was so bloody cross, I thought – why not? Why not escort a stunningly beautiful girl for a while? Why not let her arrange a pre-concert party at my house, if that's what turns her on? Why not let her be seen on the composer's arm at the premiere of the concert too, even if I do have to stick her ghastly mother as well!'

'But – why?'

'Why?' he spluttered. 'Because I was feeling very firmly rejected and pissed off, since you ask!'

'Rejected?'

'Yes, Livvy,' he said patiently. 'By you.'

'*Me!*' I gaped. Eventually I found my voice. 'God – how can you say such a thing? Good grief, that – that is so not true!' I slipped into Claudia speak in my outrage. 'I mean, that night after dinner at Hugh and Molly's I practically *threw* myself at you in the car! Asked you in for coffee, fluttered the old eyelashes seductively, the whole damn bit, and you sat there beside me like a frigging ice man, before politely showing me the car door! Oh, no, no,' I said vehemently, 'I think you'll find that if there was any rejecting going on it was instigated by *you*, Sebastian! God – and what about that day I came round to see you, to explain about Johnny coming back, just in *case* there'd been a smidgen of feeling on your part, just in *case* you thought

557

we'd built up something of a relationship those past few weeks – picnics in the park, suppers together, concerts – but you couldn't have cared less! In fact, if I remember rightly, you sat down next to me with a big cheesy grin on your face and said how *pleased* you were for me, yes – gosh, how *nice*, Livvy, your husband's back – and then you couldn't hustle me away quick enough, so desperate were you to see the back of me and get back to your composing! Oh no, I think you'll find the cold-shouldering was all yours!'

He lifted his chin and folded his arms, regarding me, pink and indignant as I was, perched up on the wall.

'Fine, Livvy,' he said quietly. 'OK. Let's take this step by step, shall we? The night you "threw yourself at me," as you put it, after Molly and Hugh's, you were drunk.'

'Oh excuse me,' I blustered, 'I most certainly was *not* dru—'

'Oh yes you were, and you'd intentionally got plastered too. I watched you knocking it back, glug after glug of Pimm's. I watched the way your mind was going too, you were so bloody desperate to forget Johnny and get back into the land of the living, and you kept glancing at me in that garden with "he'll do" written all over your forehead. He'll do, you thought, he's got a pulse, he doesn't smell, he hasn't got dandruff, he's probably got all his own teeth, and, Christ, I've got to do it with *some*one, at *some*time, haven't I, so why not him? Oh, your body might have been with me that night, had I taken you up on your oh-so-generous offer, but your heart most certainly wouldn't have been. It was with that bastard Johnny, as you so neatly proved by opening your arms and your bed to him again that very evening.'

I gazed at him in horror for a moment. Then my mouth shut. 'I had to do that,' I muttered defiantly. 'Couldn't help myself. I had to have him back in order to exorcise him. It was like a rite of passage; I had to get him out of my system.'

'The other occasion you refer to,' he swept on, ignoring me, 'was when you so sweetly popped round a few days later to inform me of Johnny's return. And believe me, that was equally galling. Livvy, I do have eyes in my head. I do live in your street. I do stand at the window every day waving my arms like a lunatic, composing my stupid tunes. I did *see* him, believe it or not, in his *car*, going in and out of the *house*, playing with Claudia in the back garden, helping you pull up your radishes, helping you in with your shopping, and how d'you think that made me feel? Bloody wretched, actually, and very smartly kicked in the teeth, but I damn well wasn't going to show it! Oh, I'm absolutely de*light*ed you found me so cool and distant when you tripped merrily into my study that day, because believe me, I'd had a few days to think about it, and that's precisely how I'd planned it. That's how I fully intended to be!'

'But—'

'And now,' he went on, with a sort of clenched fury, 'you have the gall to sit up there, grinning like a pixie, swinging your little feet around and telling me you're *not* moving to the country after all, you're going up to London! Jesus Christ, what is it with you, Livvy? Can't you make up your bloody mind just once!'

My jaw dropped as I stared uncomprehending at him. Finally I shook my head. 'Sorry,' I said at last. 'Sebastian, I'm really sorry, but you've completely lost me now. I have absolutely no idea what you're talking about. What on earth has us moving to Chiswick got to do with anything?'

'I thought Claudia wanted to board,' he said patiently.

'She does.'

'At a school near Frampton.'

I blinked. 'Well, yes, that was her first choice, why?'

'My parents live near Frampton. Or should I say –' he thumped his chest – '*I* now live near Frampton.'

I gaped. 'You do? Good heavens, what a coincidence!'

'Not really.'

'Why not?'

'Because I suggested the school to Claudia.'

'You . . . ?' I boggled. 'When!'

'Oh, ages ago, when she was chatting about where to go. My niece went there and loved it. It's got an excellent reputation, and I showed her a prospectus. Ponies, swimming, all that sort of thing.'

Suddenly I remembered the much-treasured prospectus under her bed, well thumbed and scrawled over. I also remembered that I couldn't recall where it had come from. He'd given it to her. My head swam. 'But – why?'

'Because I wanted you close by.'

A huge wave crashed over my head. I gazed at him, but actually, didn't seem to see him. My world was starting to spin. Those sweet, precious words: 'I wanted you close by.' He gazed back at me and suddenly the spinning abated, and everything fell into place. Everything went very still. Very quiet. And it seemed to me that, in that silence, his eyes gazed into my very soul.

'Mr Faulkner?' A cab drew up beside us, its familiar purr breaking the exquisite quiet.

'Yes,' muttered Sebastian, not turning.

'I called at the 'ouse, like, but they said you were over 'ere. 'Op in, mate, if you're coming, 'cos we're gonna have to shift if you're gonna catch that plane. The traffic's diabolical.'

'Your taxi,' I muttered, not taking my gaze from those dark, shining eyes.

'I know.'

The sound of running feet didn't distract us either, when towards us, down the street, came Maureen, dragging a case on wheels.

'Well, thank heavens for that,' she gasped, panting. 'I had a feeling you'd be here but you might have said! You'll catch it if you hurry, and they've been ringing from Austria in a right old state asking how long you were going to be delayed. Come on, Sebastian.' She grabbed his arm and hustled him round, out of my garden to the waiting taxi. I watched as Maureen thrust some tickets in his hand. 'Get in or you'll miss it!'

She bundled him in, together with his case, then slammed the door shut behind him and passed his passport through the window. I swung my legs round to the other side of the wall. Jumped down. Despite all that activity, we'd hardly taken our eyes off each other. I'd followed him all the way round. The driver shifted into gear.

'Hang on,' I heard Sebastian say. He leaned out of the window, past Maureen.

'I wanted to give you time, Livvy,' he called, 'that's what you need. I didn't want to rush things. I did that before and it didn't work out, that's why it's good that I'm going away. You *need* that time, Livvy, to recover, to get over Johnny.'

I nodded, greedy with longing. Johnny, bloody Johnny.

'I'll ring you from Vienna and we'll meet when I get back, take it from there.'

I nodded again, tears of joy and relief and all sorts of other scrambled emotions making my eyes swim.

'And while I'm gone, go to Frampton,' he called. 'Go to the school, see if Claudia likes it. She may not!' He grinned.

I opened my mouth to find my voice but the taxi had slowly moved off. All I could do was wave, eyes flooding now, and with a bemused Maureen beside me. I waved until he was out of sight.

'Well then, dear,' said Maureen eventually, when we were left alone in silence. 'What a to-do, eh? Still, must get on.' She gave me a sly, secret smile, squeezed my arm, and then bustled off down the road, leaving me there on that hot, empty pavement.

I stood for a while, then moved on myself. Away from my house, and away from Sebastian's house. I needed to go somewhere quiet and green, like the park. Yes, the park would do, to think, to hug my joy. My feet tripped lightly along the hot pavements. Yes, I'd wait, I thought, dizzy with longing. I mustn't be greedy, mustn't be impulsive. He was right: we both needed time. And then when he got back, we'd see. We'd take it from there, reassess the situation. It might not be right, I might not be right . . . And meanwhile – I stopped at the park entrance. Yes, meanwhile, I'd be sensible. I bit my lip. And actually, being sensible meant not going to the park and dreaming and longing and hugging myself, because my dreams had a habit of not coming true. Instead – I turned – instead I'd walk to Lucy's and get Claudia. It wasn't that far, and we could walk back together, discuss Dorset, rationally, but I wouldn't mention Sebastian, just in case. Excitement threatened to bubble up again at the thought of him, the thought of those precious words 'I wanted you close by', but I bit it down. No, I mustn't be disappointed again, mustn't be let down, and heavens, I hadn't even kissed him yet. Nothing was certain. But I could ring the school, plan a visit. I could even find a cottage, maybe, go and see some estate agents. There was a lot to do and—

'Livvy!' I stopped. Didn't turn. I must have imagined it. Then: 'LIVVY!' again, only louder. His voice – no doubt about it – and running footsteps too. I swung about. Down the old cobblestones of George Street, worn smooth with the traffic of time, and under the gaze of the ancient towering nave of the Abbey, came Sebastian. At the double. I stood still, could hardly breathe, and waited, until he arrived in front of me, panting hard.

'Come to Vienna,' he gasped. 'Bugger restraint, bugger giving you time – come to Vienna!'

My head swam. 'Wh-what now? I can't, I—'

'Tomorrow, we'll both go tomorrow.' His voice was taut with emotion. 'I can miss the first rehearsal tonight. It always sounds lousy with an unfamiliar orchestra and I wonder how I ever wrote the wretched thing. Come tomorrow!'

I stared. 'Sebastian, I can't, Claudia—'

'Oh, God, kiss me first, and then say you can't.' He took me in his arms and kissed me very thoroughly on the mouth. I could hear his heart pounding against mine, could smell the sweet fresh cotton of his shirt, and when I came up for air, his eyes were glittering intently into mine, searching my face.

'God, you're lovely, Livvy,' he breathed, 'and what really flips my heart over is that you don't know that. No one's ever told you, have they? That bastard Johnny never breathed a word, did he, kept it to himself, and you've lived most of your life thinking that people like Imogen Mitchell are better than you.' He traced my mouth with his fingertip. 'It's criminal, actually. You're special, Livvy. When I saw you I confess I simply lusted after you, but when lust turned to love I was lost. Come with me, Livvy. Come and love me in Vienna.'

I gazed up at him. 'Yes,' I breathed, 'I'll come. I love you too, I know that now. I've known it for ages, actually, and couldn't believe I'd been so stupid. Mum can have Claudia and—'

'Bring her,' he commanded. 'Don't leave her behind. Bring her, we'll all go.'

My head swam. Lovers together in Vienna, holding hands over café tables, walking arm in arm down boulevards, drowning in each other's eyes . . . with a small, agog, ten-year-old girl in tow. Grey eyes huge behind her specs, fascinated beyond belief. Mum and a *man*! Blimey, she'd be taking notes!

'No,' I said firmly, 'no, she can stay with my mother, she'll be fine there and – *oh*!' Suddenly my hand shot to my mouth. 'Oh God, no, I *can't* go!'

The taxi, with a bemused driver behind the wheel, still full of luggage, had trailed Sebastian back and was trundling up behind us.

'Why not?' demanded Sebastian.

'Because I can't leave the country! I'm sort of on bail!'

'Bail!' He stepped back in horror.

'Yes, well, I was this morning, anyway. You see there was this murder and—'

'Good God!'

'No – no, manslaughter, actually,' I added hastily, 'but the body ended up in my home—'

'Jesus!' He tore at his hair.

'I know, dreadful, under my cooker of all places, and the thing is, I promised the police I'd stay around, but – well, Vienna isn't far away and they won't need me for ages yet. There won't be a trial for some time, I'm sure, so – so maybe if I asked – they're terribly obliging down there at the station – maybe I could come next week!'

He stared at me in astonishment. 'Right,' he said eventually, looking totally bewildered.

'You coming, mate, or what?' from behind us.

'He's coming!' I called. 'Go,' I insisted softly, pushing him gently. 'Go. It's enough for me to know you *wanted* me to come, that you came back for me. I don't *need* to go to Vienna now, but I'll join you when I can, I promise.'

He gazed at me, still with a degree of astonishment, then stepped forward, and gently took my hands.

'Livvy, it seems to me you lead a very unusual and complicated life. You see nutters and weirdos at every corner, you rant and rave and wave rakes in defence of your child, you consort with murderers, you stow dead bodies in your house and you're on intimate terms with the local police. Heaven only knows what I've been doing with my life apart from writing the odd symphony, but I want you to know that I'm keen to be a part of this rich and varied tapestry of yours. If being with you means sitting in damp cellars forging passports, laundering money and stowing spare bodies away, then I'm your man. I'll follow your lead blindly, be Clyde to your Bonnie, if that's what you want.'

I giggled. 'Idiot. I'm not in any sort of real trouble, it's just – well, strange things have happened recently.'

He smiled. 'You're telling me.'

'There's twenty quid on the meter, mate!'

'Go.' I bundled him in, and this time he went. I shut the door, and he held my hand through the window until the taxi started up and trundled away.

I watched Sebastian's face in the back window, and as the cab turned into the main road, I raised my hand in salute, as he did too. I stood on that hot pavement, and knew I had yet more tears in my eyes. But this time, I knew why. I never thought I'd say that to a living soul again, not after

Johnny. Those three little words. Not a living soul. Never believed I'd have that sort of luck. But I had. I'd said it, and what's more – I sailed joyfully off along the hot pavements, my shoes feeling as if they'd got wings on – what's more, I meant it.

Going Too Far

Catherine Alliott

*From the bestselling author of The Old Girl Network;
'[An] addictive cocktail of wit, frivolity and madcap
romance' Time Out*

*'You've gone all fat and complacent because you've got
your man, haven't you?'*

There are some things only your best friend can
tell you but this outrageous suggestion is met with
indignation from Polly Penhalligan, who is recently
married, trying for a baby and blissfully happy in her
beautiful manor farmhouse in Cornwall. At least, she
was, until Pippa's unfortunate remark forces her to
realise that her idyllic life of gorging on chocolate
biscuits, counting her seemingly endless blessings
and not getting dressed until lunchtime could be
having a few unwelcome side-effects.

So Polly decides to razz things up a bit – and agrees
to allow her home to be used as a location for a com-
mercial. Having a glamorous film crew around
should certainly put something of a bomb under rural
life, shouldn't it? But even before the cameras are set
up and the stars released from their kennels, Polly's
life and marriage have been turned upside down.
This time, it seems, she's gone too far . . .

0 7472 4607 6

headline

A Married Man

Catherine Alliott

When Lucy Fellowes is offered a dream house in the country she leaps at the chance. It's hard enough living in London on an uncertain income, but when you're widowed with two small boys it's even harder. And anyway, a rural retreat will bring her closer to Charlie. Charlie? The only man in four years to make her heart beat faster. Perfect. Or it would be. If only he didn't belong to someone else . . .

A wickedly witty new novel about how complicated relationships get when you grow up, from the best-selling author of *Rosie Meadows regrets* . . . and *Olivia's Luck*.

'Alliott's skilled handling of such delicate, difficult and deep material marvellously counterpoints the Cotswolds comic archetypes and provides psychological depth and shadow to the sparky surface action. Sensitive, funny and wonderfully well-written.' Wendy Holden, *Daily Express*

0 7472 6722 7

headline

Now you can buy any of these other bestselling books by **Catherine Alliott** from your bookshop or *direct from her publisher*.

FREE P&P AND UK DELIVERY
(Overseas and Ireland £3.50 per book)

A Married Man	£7.99
Olivia's Luck	£7.99
Rosie Meadows regrets . . .	£7.99
The Real Thing	£7.99
Going Too Far	£7.99
The Old-Girl Network	£7.99

TO ORDER SIMPLY CALL THIS NUMBER

01235 400 414

or visit our website: www.madaboutbooks.com

Prices and availability subject to change without notice.